M000194635

A FLAME THROUGH ETERNITY

Also by Anna Belfrage:

The Graham Saga
A Rip in the Veil
Like Chaff in the Wind
The Prodigal Son
A Newfound Land
Serpents in the Garden
Revenge and Retribution
Whither Thou Goest
To Catch a Falling Star
There is Always a Tomorrow

The King's Greatest Enemy
In the Shadow of the Storm
Days of Sun and Glory
Under the Approaching Dark
The Cold Light of Dawn (coming 2018)

The Wanderer
A Torch in his Heart
Smoke in Her Eyes

Praise for *The Graham Saga*

"A brilliantly enjoyable read"
HNS Reviews

"This is a series that will take both your heart and your head
to places both light and dark, disheartening and uplifting,
fantastic and frightening, but all utterly unforgettable"
WTF are you reading

"Anna writes deep, emotional historical novels, adding the
fantastical element of the time slip and a "what if?" scenario,
and creates for us a world in which to be lost in on rainy days
and weekend reading fests."
Oh for the Hook of a Book

"It seems Belfrage cannot put a foot wrong. Long may she
continue to give us installments in this truly wonderful series."
Kincavel's Korner

"An admirably ambitious series"
The Bookseller

Further to excellent reviews, The Graham Saga has been
awarded multiple B.R.A.G. Medallions, won a bronze and
a silver medallion in the annual Reader's Favorite Awards,
has five HNS Editor's Choice, has been shortlisted for the
HNS Indie Book of the Year in 2014, and the sixth book
in the series won the HNS Indie Book of the Year in 2015.

Praise for *The King's Greatest Enemy*

"The writing itself is a huge success from every angle – great and memorable characters, marvellous descriptions, lively dialogue, a complex and intriguing plot, and large-scale conflict."
Readers' Favorite

"There is something rather wonderful about this exciting historical series which, with every successive story, grows in depth and complexity, and which offers a fascinating glimpse into life at one of the most controversial royal courts."
Jaffareadstoo

"Anna Belfrage is a born storyteller, and she obviously has done exceptional research, adding to the credibility of the facts (…) this is commendable, highly recommended historical fiction."
Historical Novel Society

"You need this book. You won't regret it. If you're an historical fiction lover, you will fall into this book like no other. If you're not an historical fiction lover? You're about to be."
Pursuing Stacie

Further to lovely reviews, The King's Greatest Enemy has been awarded four B.R.A.G. Medallions, an IPPY award, been nominated as a Reader's Favourite Finalist and Runner Up in Historical Fiction. Two of the books have also been named HNS Editor's Choice.

Praise for *The Wanderer* series

"Time stood still when I lost myself in this
masterpiece of a story"
CoffeePot Book Club

"To say I was captivated by the words, love story, plot etc
would not be enough. This book devoured me"
Evie's blogspot.

"A poignant, gripping, and beautifully written story of love,
passion, revenge, obsession, forgiveness, and hope"
Sincerely KarenJo

"A compelling and suspenseful story, and a brilliant foray into
new territory by Anna Belfrage"
Sayara St Clair

"The writing is beautiful, insightful, and atmospheric"
Reader's Favorite

Other than great reviews, The Wanderer has also been awarded
two Brag Medallions and a Reader's Favorite Bronze Medal.

ANNA
BELFRAGE

A FLAME THROUGH ETERNITY

Copyright © 2019 Anna Belfrage

The moral right of the author has been asserted.

Apart from any fair dealing for the purposes of research or private study,
or criticism or review, as permitted under the Copyright, Designs and Patents
Act 1988, this publication may only be reproduced, stored or transmitted, in
any form or by any means, with the prior permission in writing of the
publishers, or in the case of reprographic reproduction in accordance with
the terms of licences issued by the Copyright Licensing Agency. Enquiries
concerning reproduction outside those terms should be sent to the publishers.

Matador
9 Priory Business Park,
Wistow Road, Kibworth Beauchamp,
Leicestershire. LE8 0RX
Tel: 0116 279 2299
Email: books@troubador.co.uk
Web: www.troubador.co.uk/matador
Twitter: @matadorbooks

ISBN 978 1838593 759

British Library Cataloguing in Publication Data.
A catalogue record for this book is available from the British Library.

Typeset in 11pt Bembo by Troubador Publishing Ltd, Leicester, UK

Matador is an imprint of Troubador Publishing Ltd

In the long lost ancient past, two men fought over the girl with the golden hair and eyes like the Bosporus under a summer sky. It ended badly. She died. They died.

Some souls do not die easily. The golden-haired girl tumbled through time, reborn over and over again. She forgot her past, she forgot her lover and her nemesis. They, however, never forgot her. Where one searched the world for her wanting only to find her and love her, the other was as determined to find her—and punish her.

After thirty centuries of this existence, Helle is finally back with the man she loved more than life itself. After an endless sequence of lives, Jason is at last reunited with the girl he first met so long ago. Unfortunately, where Helle and Jason go, there goes Samion. This time, he intends to destroy them both, ending this vicious circle of love, hate, rebirth and death.

Twice in this life, Sam has tried to destroy them and failed. If anything, this makes him even more determined to do whatever it takes to extinguish them permanently. But he is in for a surprise: the girl he once crushed so easily will not go down without a fight. And beside her stands Jason, who will never back down. Never.

Chapter 1

Her son died by degrees. Jason's eyes were shuttered and cold, his face pale and haggard. Nefirie could not reach him, could not help him. All she could do was watch as her beloved son sank into a mire of self-disgust and guilt, becoming a dark shadow of who he'd been.

She heard him call out for Helle at night and would go to him, shushing him as she had done when he was a small boy. But the man could not be comforted as the child: he'd stare at her with haunted eyes before turning away to glare at the wall.

She listened in stunned silence as he told her of how he had exacted revenge. Her son, her beautiful golden-eyed boy, had sullied his hands with blood, had taken life where she and their tribe of healers were devoted to saving it. He laughed at her disgust, twisting her heart.

When he came to her, despair in his eyes, and asked that final question she had known: he would go, he would hurtle after Helle, flee this life in the hope of finding her in another. His heart tugged him onwards, his lost love called to him, and there was nothing she could do or say to dissuade him. So instead she'd cradled his cooling body in her arms, her soul howling in anguish.

She refused to lay him to rest beside Helle.

"But he would like that," Kantor said. "And so would she."

Nefirie turned away to look at the sea. Kantor's daughter had stolen her son from her in life. She would not get him in death.

Helle Morris tightened her grip on the pitcher and took another step towards her husband. Sprawled on his back, Jason was fast asleep in the shade of the apple tree, his Kindle discarded beside him.

She still had moments when she had to pinch herself to ensure she was truly awake and that the man before her was, in fact, real, not just a ghost visiting her dreams. After all, theirs was an incredible story, spanning far more years than Helle cared to think about, and she still wasn't entirely sure she believed their tale of endless lives, of intertwined fates, of love and loss.

No more loss, she reminded herself. After eight excessively exciting months since they had rediscovered one another, their lives had settled into a regular pattern of work and play, of long days at the office in the City and extended weekends here, in Tor Cottage, just at the foot of Glastonbury Tor.

For the past two months, everything had been perfect in their lives. Their nemesis Sam Woolf was dead—or presumed dead, at any rate—and they were free to live their lives without the constant fear that any moment he would swoop down and kill them, or worse.

The pitcher slipped in her hands. Thinking of Sam Woolf made her jittery, and even here, in the bright sunlit garden, she felt the shadow of evil graze her. Gone, she reminded herself. Drop-dead gorgeous, warped Sam Woolf had been feeding the fishes since late May. She would never again look into his black eyes, watch that beautiful but cruel mouth quirk into a little sneer—not in real life.

When she hung in that intermediate stage between being properly awake and properly asleep, she was often afflicted by fragmented images of Woolf, long legs striding purposefully towards her, his dark presence swirling like black smoke around him. Brief moments of choking panic, snatches that made her gasp awake, expecting to see Sam Woolf looming over her.

There was a cough from under the tree, recalling Helle to the here and now and her sleeping husband. Husband. She tasted the word, could not stop herself from grinning goofily. That gorgeous creature in the shade was hers, all the way from the thick glossy mahogany hair to his long, muscled legs, at present encased in a pair of old ripped jeans.

After several days of sun, his skin was a burnished copper, a rash of darker freckles adorning the bridge of his nose. His face was all planes and straight lines: dark eyebrows over eyes that shifted from the deepest copper to a glowing gold depending on the light, a straight nose, a strong chin—a harsh face, had it not been for the mouth, soft and relaxed in sleep. She was almost tempted to desist from her little plan and kiss him instead.

Long, dark eyelashes fluttered against his high cheekbones and there was a tell-tale twitch to his lips.

"Enjoying the view?" he asked without opening his eyes.

"You have no idea." She upended the pitcher and he leaped to his feet with a yelp when the ice-cold water drenched his t-shirt. Helle exploded with laughter and darted away, with him in hot pursuit.

"You bad, bad little girl," he snarled playfully, pulling off his wet t-shirt. Well, that was a nice side-effect. He threw himself at her. She shrieked and fled limping towards the next stand of trees, ignoring just how much her toes protested when she ran. Once, she'd have run rings round him, but since their last encounter with Woolf, her left foot was a mess of healing bones, that damned Woolf having stomped down with all his might on her poor toes.

Jason came bounding after. "I will get you for this," he promised, trying to grab her.

"You wish." She stuck her tongue out, he pounced and she backed away. Too late, she saw his satisfied smile and tried to take off to his right, but he had it covered, forcing her further in under the lilacs.

"I fear you lose, lioness," he said, extending one arm towards her. She slapped it away and tried to sidestep him. An arm snaked round her and pulled her tight to his cold chest

"Naughty," he said. He tried to glower, a smile tugging at his mouth. Helle stood on tiptoe and kissed him, running her tongue over that luscious lower lip.

"Not good enough," he growled, the smile breaking through. "Try harder."

She kissed him again, her mouth as soft as she could make it. And he kissed her back, his hands around her waist as he lifted her off her feet for a slow twirl.

She was carried back to her lounger, his lips welded to hers. Some bickering as to who should be on top ended with him simply lifting her onto his lap and lying back.

"Does it still hurt as much?" he asked.

"No," she lied, carefully flexing the toes in her damaged foot.

"You're lying." His hand tightened in her hair. "It will get better."

"Sure it will," she replied, infusing her voice with as much conviction as she could. She had days when she seriously doubted that. But right now, she didn't want to think about her foot, so instead she nuzzled his neck and he hummed in response, a deep sound resonating in his chest.

They made out in the sun, a leisurely session of kissing and exploring, his jeans-clad erection pressing against her sex. He gripped her head and covered her lips with his own, his tongue fucking her mouth while she rode the hard ridge of his penis. Jason laughed into her mouth.

"Wanton," he said, his hands sliding over her back to cup her buttocks. "But for now let's just stick with the kissing."

She pouted. She wanted more. Heck, she needed more. He tapped her on the nose. "My call. You know that, lioness."

A constant game of theirs—or maybe it wasn't a game, because Jason rarely relinquished control in bed, no matter how generous a lover he was. He gave a lot, he took a lot, but one of the things he never compromised on was that it was he who decided when she came, he who controlled just how intense her pleasure was. It mostly was very intense.

His fingers brushed her cheek. "Kiss my breath away, my lioness."

So she did, except that at some point he took over, and she was left gasping for breath and hot all over.

"Nice," he murmured, licking his lips. Eyes the colour of sunlit amber burnt into hers.

"Very," she said, pillowing her head on his shoulder. She nestled closer, made drowsy by the sun, by his warmth. He combed his fingers through her curls in long soothing movements.

"Love you," she said through a yawn.

"And I love you, wife." His voice caressed the last word. He didn't miss out on any opportunity to use it. 'My wife', he would say, his face glowing with pride.

"Lucky me," she said.

In response, he tightened his hold on her. "Lucky us."

The best thing about Tor Cottage was its seclusion, Jason reflected, lying with his arms round his wife and staring up at the July sky, dotted with picture-perfect fluffy clouds. For now, it was a sun-drenched, peaceful place, but in a couple of years he hoped to hear the sounds of children as they barged about the garden. The thought made him smile: his wife, his children—completion he had always yearned for, never found.

He teased at her hair, winding a golden curl around his finger. Today, it was exactly two months since the day he'd thought he'd lost her, watching with horror as she and Sam Woolf—accursed be his name—fell off the cliff to what seemed a certain watery grave, forty feet below. But she had lived, he had saved her, while Woolf had disappeared without a trace. Drowned, they said. Of course he'd drowned, he told himself, but the fact that there'd been no body, no trace of him, made Woolf's death a supposition, not a certainty. He didn't like that. It made his skin itch.

"What are you thinking about?" Helle sounded sleepy.

"Nothing much."

Helle rose on her elbow. "You're thinking about Woolf, aren't you?"

No point in denying it. "I am. It's—"

"Two months ago." She gave him a crooked smile. "We could have been dead, you shot through the head, me crushed on the cliffs."

Except that they both knew that had Jason died, Woolf would have dragged her off to spend the rest of her life at his mercy.

"Didn't happen, lioness." He cupped her cheek. "This time, we won." Just in case, though, Jason had contacted DCI John Stapleton in Winchester to ensure Woolf's crimes had not been forgotten. Stapleton had snorted and told Jason to eff off as he was fully capable of doing his job without oblique hints, and yes, the compiled stuff on Sam Woolf was stored in a safe place—both physically and electronically.

"Thanks to Duncan," Helle said. "He saved us." Jason rolled his eyes. Duncan Wilson had been a lowlife, a soldier in Woolf's army, but somehow Helle had upgraded him to hero status. Admittedly, Jason didn't remember too much of the events on the clifftop—beyond the shock of seeing Helle topple over the edge—but he wasn't about to credit Duncan with any heroism, no matter how dead he was.

"Do you think he's out there somewhere?" Helle waved at the sky.

"Who? Duncan or Woolf?"

"Duncan." She sounded grim. "Woolf, as we both know, will come back in some form or other."

Unfortunately. Hopefully, by the time he did, Jason and Helle would be too old to care.

Despite the warmth of the sun, Jason shivered. Theirs was an improbable story, spanning more than three thousand years. He stroked her head. An endless sequence of lives he'd spent searching for Helle, the girl he had loved and lost all those years ago, thanks to that accursed bastard Samion, Prince of Kolchis. This time round, the prince had gone by the name of Sam Woolf, as evil now as he'd been back then, and as determined to destroy them. A businessman with impressive mental skills, Woolf could bend most people to his will, use those hypnotic powers of his to enslave all but the strongest of souls.

"He's gone for now." Helle's voice recalled him to the present, her eyes so close he could count the green streaks that adorned her blue irises. He nodded, wondering why he didn't feel more relieved, why there were days when he woke to the oppressive sensation that Woolf was still here.

Helle shifted, grimacing slightly. "Your hand," she said, reminding him that he too had gifts.

"Sorry." He brought the heat back under control, clenched and unclenched his hand a couple of times to cool it off.

"So, do you think he is?" she asked. It took him some time to realise they were back to the issue of Duncan. Jason craned his head to look at the sky above them.

"Maybe." He couldn't give her more than that.

She sighed. "Duncan wasn't a bad person. He just lost his way."

"He helped abduct you." He clenched his jaws. "Bastard." He could feel her inhale, knew she was about to burst out in defence of Duncan, mentally enslaved by Woolf. Instead, her phone rang, the distinctive signal announcing it was her mother Miriam calling. Saved by the bell: he left her to it and went to check on his slow-cooked chilli.

"Mum? You okay?" Helle pressed the phone to her ear. For the past four weeks, Mum—always 'Mum', never 'Mom', courtesy of Mum being British, no matter how American Helle was— and Phil had been engaged on some sort of financial project in Saudi Arabia. Well, to be accurate, Phil was on a project, while Mum was there in her capacity as wife, no more, no less.

"Bored stiff." Mum lowered her voice. "There's only so much sunbathing a person can do before going crazy."

"Poor you." Helle laughed. "Isn't there a pool boy to gawk at?"

"Nope. So, how's life in paradise?"

"Great." Helle studied the rings that adorned her hand. His rings, and whenever Jason took her hands, his fingers would trace them, his face illuminated from within. Mum groaned when Helle shared this with her.

"Borderline nauseating," she said, but Helle could hear the smile in her voice. Seeing as Phil had a tendency to look at Mum as if he would willingly kiss the ground she walked on, Mum was not in a position to do much teasing.

"Romantic, not nauseating," Helle corrected.

"Yeah. He loves you to bits, doesn't he?"

"And I love him." Inadequate word, love: what she felt for Jason was a complex dependency, a sensation of walking about half-flayed when he wasn't close by, of being made whole in his arms, of needing his breath in her lungs. A love that was neither pink nor fluffy, rather a deep vibrating red with claws that could tear you asunder.

Mum laughed. "You do? I wouldn't have guessed. Not in a million years." She sighed. "The difference, darling, is that he just fell into your lap. Like winning the lottery without even having bothered to buy a ticket. But he had to work his arse off for that to happen. He did the looking, he did the finding."

Very single-minded, her Jason: more than sixty lives spent looking for his one lost love. One of a kind, probably. Helle hugged herself. He loved her. That much.

They ate outside, summer dusk staining the skies above them a deep violet. Jason lit a couple of candles, cleared the dishes and returned with pie and ice-cream—home-made the both of them.

"I'll get fat if you keep on feeding me like this." Helle licked her spoon clean.

"I'll help you burn things off." He settled himself beside her. She leaned against his chest and traced a heart on it. He cupped her head, one finger rubbing up and down her nape until she was almost purring with contentment.

"Will you do your fire thing for me tonight?" she asked, lifting her gaze to his.

He smiled. "Later," he promised.

She nodded. Later was good. It sort of helped if it grew totally dark first.

It was almost midnight when he took her hand, leading her barefoot through the damp grass. It was quiet, the occasional chirp from a bird breaking the silence. The night was fragrant with the scent of roses, and before them the distinctive silhouette of the Tor rose towards the sky, like a protective sentinel keeping them safe in this little corner of the world.

Jason released her hand and stepped away. He spread his arms, fingers splayed wide. Slowly, he brought his hands together, and electricity crackled between his palms, leapt from hand to hand. Little flames danced over his fingertips, a ball of fire spun into being between his hands, a glowing globe he shaped into a beating heart of fire.

He set the skies ablaze with trails of frothy flame, he drew a circle round them and raised a wall of red hot heat, suspended in mid-air. Helle was entranced by the fires and the flames, but mostly by him, her tall and magical torchbearer, the man who had followed her through time—the man she called her own.

Chapter 2

Nigel arrived early next morning, his car-horn blaring, probably to make sure he didn't catch them in a compromising situation. Ever since they'd got married, this was his standard joke, with Nigel ending every Skype session with a little speech about the need for abstinence, telling Jason in a serious tone how dangerous it was for men not to control themselves.

"It's not as if we didn't have sex before we got married," Helle had told him some weeks before, laughing when Nigel had groaned in pretend horror, asking loudly what the world was coming to.

"Besides, it weakens you," he'd said, ignoring Jason's exasperated snort. "There won't be any brain-matter left between your ears if you're not careful."

Jason had tapped the webcam. "Just for your information Nigel, it isn't brain-matter that leaks out. But maybe you wouldn't know."

Nigel grinned. "First-hand experience. For me, it is definitely brain-matter."

"Poor you," Helle had teased. "So what do you have in your head now? Air?"

Huh. Nigel Hawkins had anything but air in that strange brain of his. Dark eyes regarded the world with piercing intelligence, his Sex Pistols fanboy look more of a façade than anything else.

Jason leapt down the stairs at the sound of the car, with Helle hot on his heels. It was ages since they'd seen Nigel in the flesh and she knew for a fact Jason had missed his friend more than he'd let on, despite the regular Skyping sessions.

By the time they made it outside, Nigel was unfolding his long body from his car. In jeans that rode too low on his slim hips, one of his customary t-shirts, this one a bright thing proclaiming the rainbow revolution, and an assortment of necklaces and bracelets, he looked just as he'd done last they saw him—bar the very short hair. The piercings were back in place, that odd saffron thing he'd worn during his recent weeks at some sort of Buddhist community in Thailand was gone, and he was just as thin as he'd always been—the man could hide behind a doorpost for a week without anyone noticing him.

Nigel's narrow face broke out in a wide grin. "Lion-tamer!" he yelled, pumping his hand in the air. Helle bit back on a pleased smile at her nickname, a reference to the ancient life in which she'd had lions for pets, however utterly incredible that sounded. "Jason," he said in a more normal voice, and then he was hugging Jason, slapping him on the back, and hugging him some more. "We did it," he said as they disengaged. "Or rather, you did it." Nigel nodded at Helle.

"Most involuntarily." After all, she hadn't planned on falling off a cliff with Sam Woolf. She tilted her head to the side. "So, no more Buddhism?"

"Nah." Nigel gestured at his various necklaces. "I'm more of an ecumenical bloke."

"Really?" She gestured at the silver pentagram that adorned his chest. "Not very Christian, is it?"

Nigel grinned and rifled through the symbols that hung from his neck: crosses, skulls, amethyst moons, lapis lazuli eyes, a serpent biting its tail, a copper sun—even a huge yellowing tooth.

"Who cares?" he said, shaking his bangles at her.

"Not me." She gave him a long hug. "I've missed you."

"You have?" He sounded pleased, even if he fidgeted in her arms. "Not all that surprising, I suppose. Spending all your time with Jason here must be mind-numbing."

"Twat." Jason bumped him on the shoulder with his fist. Nigel punched him back, and one of those strange male rituals followed in which they shoved and slapped playfully at each other.

Once they'd calmed down, Nigel slouched over to his car and popped open the boot. "I brought some food and stuff." He unloaded several carrier bags, handing them to Jason.

"It's only us, Nigel," Jason protested, staggering exaggeratedly towards the door.

"Nope." Nigel smiled, his arms full of wine bottles.

"No?" Helle raised an eyebrow. It would be nice if he had told them before he brought a house guest. Besides, they'd been looking forward to catching up with him, bringing him up to date on everything that had happened.

Nigel scraped his foot on the gravel, looking like a gangly, anorexic version of Homer Simpson.

"I asked Miranda to come as well."

Ah, the elusive Miranda. Helle threw Jason a look and winked. He leered back, grinning.

"I hope that's okay," Nigel went on, his gaze darting between them. "She was in the area anyway, some sort of tattoo artist convention."

"Of course it is," Jason assured him, "she can sleep on the couch."

Nigel frowned, causing the piercing in his brow to bob up and down. "She sleeps with me." He didn't wait for an answer, making for the open kitchen door.

"Suit yourself," Jason laughed, "but it's a narrow bed."

"All the better," Nigel replied over his shoulder.

"Beware of brain damage," Helle said.

He stuck his tongue out, flashing yet another piercing, and ducked into the cottage—16th century doors had not been built for men as tall as Jason and Nigel.

Some hours later, Jason hooted in triumph as Nigel shoved the Scrabble board to the side.

"I almost had you," Nigel said, making Jason laugh out loud.

"You've never beaten me."

"Not at this, no," Nigel muttered. He stretched for his beer and leaned back in his chair, face to the sun. "So, how's your new company doing?"

Jason grinned. His most recent acquisition was going from strength to strength, the three former owners having just delivered a beautiful cyber security software programme that was the virtual equivalent of a six feet high-voltage perimeter fence.

"Wow," Nigel said, cracking his knuckles. "Want me to test it for you?" Seeing as Nigel was one of the best hackers around, what he didn't know about circumventing protective software was probably not worth knowing. They spent a couple of minutes discussing the commercial possibilities offered by the new product. Some more beers, and they were more into squinting at the sun than doing any serious thinking, passing the occasional comment, no more.

Further down the garden, Helle was on her stomach reading, one foot lifted to swing back and forth in time to whatever she was listening to through her headphones. Nigel studied the foot for some time before turning to look at Jason.

"What have they done with all the documents?"

It took Jason a couple of seconds to catch on, and when he did, he frowned. It was thanks to Nigel's hacking expertise that they'd been able to compile that huge file on Woolf, complete with incriminating e-mails and photos—all of them lifted from Woolf's own network, or those of his partners', through creative access procedures that had bypassed both the law and whatever security had been in place.

"Does it matter?" Jason said. Woolf was gone, damn it, so the file would no longer be of any use.

"Hopefully not." Nigel met his eyes. "But I get the feeling you're not a hundred per cent convinced he's gone, and so…" He lifted his shoulders. Jason threw a cautious look in the direction of Helle, still oblivious to them, still marking the rhythm of her music with her foot.

"Not totally, no," he admitted, before going on to explain Stapleton was holding onto the file.

"Good." Nigel lifted his beer bottle. "Never hurts to be prepared." A smile flashed across his face. "Which brings us neatly back to the subject of cyber security doesn't it?"

They'd moved on to the relative merits of IPA and microbrewery in general, when a small car nosed its way down the lane, music blaring through its open windows. Nigel leapt to his feet.

"Miranda," he said, setting off at a run in the direction of the cattle grid, waving wildly.

"What? He doesn't think she's seen a cattle grid before?" Helle sounded amused, tugging her sundress down over her bikini. Short and bright blue, it enhanced her long legs, straining somewhat over her round breasts.

"City girl. The country is a novel and exotic concept."

"I can see that." Helle jabbed him with her elbow. "No self-respecting country dweller would drive around in that."

No, probably not. The little Golf had survived the cattle grid and came to a standstill between his Tesla and Nigel's old Toyota. Painted a bright green, the entire car was decorated with tattoo motifs, depictions of elegant panthers and airborne dragons vying for space with a crimson and black serpent. He rather liked that last one, could see it decorating his right arm—except that he didn't hold with tattoos.

Nigel opened the door to the driver's seat, his tall frame doubled over, and there was a lot of intense kissing going on, at least to judge from the sounds. Then he stepped back, allowing Miranda to get out.

Jason's initial reaction was one of utter surprise. He smothered a laugh, looking from tall, gangly Nigel to this curvy creature, dressed in something that resembled a vintage wedding dress, slightly yellow with age. Beside him, Helle snorted softly.

"Doesn't go with the ink, does it?" she said.

It most definitely did not. The closer Miranda got, the more difficult it was not to stare at her bare arms, decorated with the same serpent motif that adorned her car. Dark hair hung in multiple braids down to her waist, and Jason couldn't quite stop himself from calculating just how long that silky black hair would be if unbound, how it would feel to slide his fingers through it, as he'd done repeatedly with Helle's hair in that long gone past when she had hair that fell in a golden cloud all the way to her buttocks.

"Hi." Miranda extended her hand, first to Helle, then to him. A surprisingly firm handshake, given her looks. Two dark slanted eyes met his, her rosebud mouth softening into a smile. "What, you didn't expect an Asian chick?"

"Or an American one," Helle put in drily, making Miranda laugh.

"As British as they come, actually," she said, reverting to a Midland accent.

"It's nice to meet you at last." Jason glanced at Nigel. "I was starting to believe he'd just made you up—you know, like an imaginary girlfriend."

Miranda threw a coy look at Nigel. "He's been talking about us?" Her voice had a smokiness to it, an attractive hoarseness that had Jason thinking of whisky and log fires.

"Incessantly," Jason said, smiling down at her. No wonder Nigel was over the moon about her, he thought. His admiration must have shown, at least to judge from the way Helle folded her arms over her chest. It made him want to smirk, this possessive streak in her, but at the same time it made him glow inside, which was why he took hold of her and pulled her close enough to kiss her head. All of her softened.

"I've barely mentioned her," Nigel muttered, shoving his hands into his pockets.

"No," Helle teased, "only like twenty times in each conversation."

"Well, I suppose he would," Miranda said. "After all, how a bloke like him could find a girl like me is something of a mystery."

Nigel laughed. "No it isn't. You saw my naked arse when you did that ink-work, and that just undid you. I have that effect on women. It's all that sex appeal." He waggled his brows, gripped Miranda's bag in one hand, her hand in the other, and led her off, saying something about a proper welcome. Jason couldn't stop himself from glancing at Nigel's skinny arse. A tattoo, there?

Nigel and Miranda reappeared a while later, walking hand in hand towards where Jason and Helle were sitting. She'd changed out of that awful old dress, and in Helle's opinion, Miranda looked much better in shorts and a minimal tank top that clung to her generous boobs, even if this meant exposing numerous tattoos, from a Celtic cross between her shoulder blades to the little butterfly just above her hip bone.

Miranda stopped halfway across the lawn and did a slow turn. She extended her arms, looking as if she would at any moment break out into a spontaneous sun dance. Helle threw Jason an amused look. He winked.

"Very peaceful," Miranda said, lowering her arms, "peaceful and safe." She threw Helle an oblique glance, her eyes suddenly very penetrating. "Don't you agree?"

Helle moved closer to Jason. Yes, Tor Cottage was safe. It should be. First of all, it was probably benignly haunted by Jason's white witch great-grandmother, zooming in invisible circles round the garden she had once planted. Then, of course, there was the perimeter fence, a man-high metal mesh construction that came with the added benefit of being electrified if required. Finally, the whole cottage was suffused with the warm presence of Anne, who had been Jason's most recent mother. Plus, as icing on the cake, there was the Tor itself, buzzing with powers that were very much older and far more dangerous than people really knew.

"It's the Tor," Helle explained, pointing at the hill. Miranda turned to look, shielding her eyes with her hand.

"It is?"

"According to what Jason's mum said, the King of the Fairies lives there," Nigel put in with a grin. "Everyone knows one should not underestimate them."

"Fairies are dangerous creatures." Miranda looked serious. She extended her arms again. "Right now, though, things are okay. There's no evil around at present."

"What's that supposed to mean?" Jason asked, glaring at Nigel. Too right: Helle glared as well. By necessity, Nigel knew the entire Helle and Jason story, complete with reincarnated lives and an ancient nemesis, but he had no right to share it— nor, to judge from his responding scowl, had Nigel done so.

"Mean?" Miranda dropped down onto a chair. "Nothing. I was merely making a statement of fact."

"Ah." Jason sat back, an inscrutable look on his face. Whatever initial admiration he'd felt at seeing this petite sloe-eyed sex-bomb was now replaced by wariness. Not, in Helle's book, a bad thing.

"Where did you find her?" Helle asked Nigel later, standing in the kitchen. He was staring out the window at Miranda with a look Helle recognized from seeing herself in the mirror. Pure drooling.

"Isn't she absolutely marvellous?" Nigel said, ignoring Helle's question.

She shrugged. Not her type. Duh. Nigel flashed her a smile.

"She has a small tattoo parlour near Paddington—and she does readings."

Figures, Helle thought as she watched Miranda dance and twirl. There was something decidedly otherworldly about her. As if she could feel them looking at her, Miranda turned, fixing her gaze on Nigel. And then she smiled, sweeping him a deep curtsey. He was out of the door in a second.

"Great. I guess that leaves me to do all the hard work," Helle muttered, but with no real heat.

Being alone in the kitchen was no hardship, rather the reverse, as the ancient space was imbued with so much peace she always felt a desire to just sit for a while. In pride of place stood a cream-coloured Aga, but it was the heavy beams and the dark bricks of the floor that gave the room character, as did the old cracked Delft tiles that adorned the walls. Generations of women scrubbing the floor with soft soap before polishing it with beeswax had left behind a permanent scent of evergreens, and despite the small windows, set in deep window recesses, the overall impression was one of light, at present helped along by the wide open door, through which the sound of birds spilled into the room.

"There you are." Jason grabbed her from behind. "Wasn't Nigel supposed to help you?"

"He got distracted," Helle said, handing him the salad bowl.

The evening was chilly but far too beautiful for them to retire indoors, so they ate outside, with candles burning in lanterns placed on the ground and all the blankets the house could muster to wrap themselves in. The sky was almost purple, edging towards turquoise to the west.

"This is a wonderful place," Miranda said, eyes on the distant heavens.

"It is." Jason sounded pleased. "Our own slice of paradise."

Helle pushed him. "Not when the toilet clogs. Or when the drainpipe comes loose. And definitely not when we have to chase mice through the kitchen."

Miranda laughed. "More of a city girl, are you?"

"Not really," Helle replied. "I just think paradise may be a bit of an exaggeration." She stood to stack the plates, stumbling on her left foot. Pain shot up her calf. Jason's hand flew out to steady her, a quick glance checking that she was okay. Helle gave him a little nod in reply.

"What happened?" Miranda sounded concerned.

"My foot." Helle tried to smile. "I had an accident a couple of months ago."

"Accident?"

"Some guy crushed her toes," Nigel clarified, ignoring Jason's frown. He spat to the side. "May he rot in hell, bastard that he is."

"Ah, yes. Sam Woolf," Miranda said, as calmly as if she were discussing the weather. "I've heard about him, but as I understand it, he's history now, isn't he?"

"History," Helle agreed, and limped off towards the kitchen. She didn't want to talk about it; not about her foot, not about the horrible free fall from the cliff to the sea. Definitely not about her growing premonition that Woolf might not be dead.

The child was a godsend.

When they brought the girl, Nefirie had at first refused to see her. She did not need a new child. She had her son. He was no longer here, but he was still her son. But they had insisted. They had found the child alone by the sea and she needed a home. She needed someone to care for her and help her grow into her talents, already so formidable.

She was not yet three, they pleaded, and she was too young to carry her gifts on her own. It was so unusual, they said. A fire child.

Like her son. A child that was wise beyond her years, who never cried.

"She does not speak," they told her, and her heart opened. She no longer spoke much either.

Nefirie thought she would die when they led the girl into the room. She stared down into eyes the colour of polished amber—like her son's eyes, like her own eyes. Merciful Mother! The child that was stolen, Helle's child, Jason's daughter.

The little girl did not say a word. She just held out her hand, fingertips touching Nefirie's arm. That was all it took. Nefirie welcomed the child into her aching heart.

Chapter 3

Helle woke with a start. Light flooded the bedroom from the huge uncurtained windows facing the east and the returning sun, at present hiding shyly behind a thin screen of morning mist. A fairy morning, Helle thought, one of those days when it took little imagination to convert the wisps of condensation lifting from the ground towards the brightening sky to dancing see-through creatures.

They should probably order curtains, she reflected, as she'd done so often these last few weeks. But she knew she wouldn't—Jason's mum, Anne, had refused to cover up the light. Other than the windows, the room held little of Anne's presence. The large sleigh bed was something Jason had invested in some years ago, as was the circular blue and green rug that decorated the floor below the window. There was a chair and a little table. Only in the carefully framed dried plants, twelve little squares arranged in a three by four pattern above the antique chest of drawers, was Anne's influence visible.

Jason had told her Anne had pressed each plant herself, picking it when it was at its most potent. Rosemary, sage, St John's wort, angelica and betony—each plant had been chosen for its protective properties, and by now Helle knew them by heart, all the way from the delicate mugwort leaf to the flattened bells of the foxglove.

Most of the plants grew somewhere in the garden as well, and every year new wreaths of blackberry, rowan and ivy would be made to hang on the front door—a tradition started by that witch great-mother of Jason's, and since then never broken. A year ago, Helle would have grinned condescendingly at such nonsense. These days, she was more than happy to help Jason pick what he needed to make that wreath.

Jason slept heavily, flipped on his front. His face was buried under his pillow, and he had kicked his covers into an untidy pile at the foot of the bed. Helle drew up his sheet, her hand lingering on his warm, broad back. Jason grunted and slept on.

Helle sat up. No point in trying to go back to sleep, not now. She snatched at the vaguely remembered images of the dream that had woken her, but like most dreams, what had been singularly vivid seconds after she started awake had now faded to nothing but a residual feeling—in this case one of fear.

There was a burst of birdsong from outside, and Helle decided to go for a run, cleanse her mind and body of her lingering unease. She slipped out of bed and tiptoed down the stairs, wincing when some of the treads squeaked loudly. Once outside, she stood for a moment in the stillness of the garden and inhaled. It was cool outside and the grass was silvered with dew, little swirls of fog rising upwards from the ditch. To the west, dark clouds promised rain, but for now the sunlight filtered through the screen of clouds, gilding the misty air.

Helle bounced carefully up and down on her feet. Since Woolf had crushed her toes, running was a painful if necessary exercise, leaving her with a limp for several hours afterwards.

"No pain, no gain," she told herself, gritting her teeth when she set off at a slow jog. According to Janine, Dad's second wife and therefore by definition Helle's stepmother—a thought that mostly filled her with horrified amusement, seeing as Janine was only ten years or so older—the foot would never heal completely, but to refrain from movement was to risk losing all flexibility in it.

"You have to walk and run, flex that foot of yours, y'hear?" she'd said, sounding like an enthusiastic cheerleader. Helle was tempted to scoff—as far as she knew, Janine was great at graphic design, not physiotherapy—but she didn't, given that her doctor said the same.

By the time she reached the top of the Tor, she was covered in sweat and her foot was reduced to a howling mess of nerves. Enough for one day, she decided, sliding down to sit by the tower that was all that remained of St Michael's Church. Before her, the Somerset levels extended every which way. To the west she could see Glastonbury proper, more due south was the little town of Street, but other than that and the odd car or two, she supposed the landscape looked pretty much as it had done two thousand years ago. Helle rested her elbows on her knees, wondering as she always did if Arthur and Guinevere had sat on this same exact spot.

A hand on her nape recalled her to the present and she turned to squint at Jason.

"Hi," she said, and he dropped down to sit behind her, one leg on either side of her.

"You couldn't sleep?"

"No. Not that it matters, on a morning as beautiful as this one." She gestured at the view, at the thinning mist that hung in sheer veils over the countryside. "People must have climbed up here since time immemorial just to enjoy the view."

"Probably. Aesthetic pleasure is not exactly a modern invention." Jason pulled her closer and wrapped his arms around her. "How did your run go?"

"If you ask me, okay. If you ask my foot, it was pretty bad."

"So we'll have to pamper it later." He tickled her nape. "Or we pamper all of you right now."

"Now? Here?" The beautiful morning had clouded, a fine drizzle starting to coat her skin with a glistening layer of wet.

"Definitely not here." He rose gracefully to his feet and helped her up. "But how about in the shower? Still wet, but warm wet."

"We have house guests," she reminded him, trying to sound stern. He swooped like a hawk, cupped her face and covered her mouth with his. He'd brushed his teeth, and the faint taste of mint lingered. His tongue flitted over hers, his hands slid into her hair, holding her very still as he kissed her breathless. The drizzle became rain, she shivered in the sudden chill, and still he didn't let her go, his longer frame pressed so close to her she could feel every ridge of muscle, every bulge. One bulge in particular, she amended dizzily, grinding her crotch against it.

"Let's get you inside." His voice was hoarse, his eyes smouldering, as he released her to take her hand instead. At her obvious limp, he frowned, and moments later she was in his arms, being carried in haste down the hill.

"I can walk," she protested. In response, she got a wheeze. "Hey, I can, okay?"

Jason snorted and increased his pace.

"I'm too heavy," she said.

"Tell me about it," he gasped, and she whacked him over the head until he set her down. They stood in the downpour and laughed, by now soaked to their skins. A slow, shuffling walk had them back at Tor Cottage some ten minutes later, a trail of wet following them all the way to their ensuite bathroom.

Helle loved this space—her Jason had a thing about baths in general, and here he'd gone a bit wild and crazy, the walls covered in glass mosaics of every shade of blue imaginable, the floor in white Italian tiles. A large bathtub right below the skylight, and in a corner an equally large shower, sporting one of those gigantic showerheads. Frosted glass walls separated the shower from the rest of the room, and it was to the shower Jason led her once he'd helped her out of her wet clothes.

"No time for a bath," he said, and Helle just smiled. Baths with Jason were long sessions in which they talked about anything and everything, enveloped in steam and each other.

Hot water, a bodywash that smelled faintly of honey and roses, and soon enough she was covered in lather, his large hands painting the contours of her body with soap suds. One moment, he was brisk about it, the next his movements slowed, travelling slowly over her wet, warm skin. She leaned back against him, he kissed the side of her neck, hands sliding over her belly to cover her pubic mound. His erection pressed against her bum, she reached back to touch his thighs. Water cascaded over them, the soap stung her eyes, and she could have remained like this, held tight in his arms, forever.

No urgency, just a fusing together, him shifting on his feet to press himself that much closer, his hands urging her back, towards him. His hands slid lower, one long digit stroking her. He was moving back and forth, small, sensuous movements that had his erection sliding up and down between her butt cheeks. He was big, he was hard, and when his finger circled her clit, her knees dipped.

Too much weight on her sore foot made her bite back a muffled groan. He stilled his hands, making her moan out loud, even more when he crouched to study her foot. Yes, it hurt, but so what? She didn't want his warm, warm hands tenderly caressing her foot, she wanted them somewhere else entirely, and she was just about to say so when he gripped her by the butt and slowly licked his way up her thigh. Jesus!

She braced herself against the wall. The bathroom was enveloped in steam, his wet hair glistened under the overhead spotlights, and she nearly fell when two fingers slid inside her, his mouth tight around her bud. Teeth, lips, tongue—she came suddenly, explosively, and he just wouldn't stop, he kept on doing those magical things to her, and it was borderline unbearable and so, so wonderful and here she came again, this time so powerfully she had problems remaining on her feet.

Helle sagged against the wall. He was leaning over her, kissing her mouth with as much passion as he'd just expended on her pussy. Hard and demanding, his erection prodded at her. Helle knelt before him and ran a gentle finger over his glans, dark red and sticky. His penis twitched, she closed her hand around it and squeezed. He uttered a gratifying, hoarse sound. One hand cupping his balls, the other moving up and down his rigid penis, she took him in her mouth. From somewhere above came a whispered 'Helle'. His hands sank into her hair, his hips jerked, and she twirled her tongue around the glans. He sighed, his thighs trembling. She sucked and tightened her hold, and with a series of grunts he came, filling her mouth with the taste of his semen.

Unsteadily, she got to her feet, swaying against him. He turned off the water, wrapped her in a towel, and kissed her nose. She reciprocated by kissing the hollow of his throat.

"I'm starving," she told him, gnawing gently at his jaw.

"Luckily, we have a full fridge." Jason wiped the towel over the mirror and peered at his reflection, still blurred at the edges by condensation. "Do I look like a man whose wife has just gone down on him?"

"I have no idea." She pinched his butt. "How am I supposed to know that? You're the only man I ever go down on."

23

"I bloody well hope so." He drew a loopy heart on the mirror, making her smile.

"That was a long shower," Nigel said when they entered the kitchen. "For a moment there, I thought you might have drowned."

"I had to help Helle with her foot," Jason said smoothly, pouring himself a glass of juice. "She'd been out running and overdid it, so it needed some TLC." He smiled to himself.

"Her foot?" Nigel's gaze raked Helle up and down, lingering for an instant on her bandaged foot. "It needed that kind of TLC? You are one kinky bastard, Jason Morris." He grinned, gesturing at the spread on the table. "You probably need to get your strength back."

"It was a long jog," Helle said, helping herself to some granola. When she met Jason's eyes, a faint pink coloured her cheeks. As if by accident, he brushed his arm against hers, and the blush deepened.

"I bet it was." Nigel reached for the bacon.

"And Miranda?" Jason studied the scrambled eggs with something between disgust and amusement. Nigel was more enthusiastic than capable in the kitchen, and this effort looked like yellow glue.

"Asleep." Nigel stretched, his far too short t-shirt riding up to expose a very white belly with a new tattoo around the navel. "I didn't only do her foot, you see, so she needs her beauty sleep."

"No I don't." Miranda entered the kitchen, light as a feather on her feet, despite the clunky Doc Martens that clashed with her outfit, yet another white dress consisting mostly of lace and not much else.

"Sleep well?" Helle asked politely, eyes shaded as she studied this miniature *femme fatale*. In response, Miranda tossed her head, her black hair swirling through the air before it settled back to lie like rippling black silk down her back. Beautiful hair, Jason thought.

"Very," she said, eyeing Nigel who went quite pink.

Jason busied himself preparing coffees, listening with half an ear to the conversation at the table. Miranda was back to asking about the Tor. Helle told her what little she knew, before Nigel changed the subject to Glastonbury Abbey and the Chalice Well.

"Ancient, isn't it?" Nigel asked.

"Very," Jason replied without turning round.

"Nigel says it is a source of power." Miranda nodded her thanks when Jason set down a large latte in front of her.

Helle laughed. "Or water, at any rate. Thanks, honey," she added, smiling up at Jason before pulling the mug close.

"It's been a holy site for thousands of years," Jason said. "But as to what powers it has, who knows?" He didn't quite like this turn of conversation, disconcerted by the gleam in Miranda's dark eyes. She fingered her necklace, a long affair of brightly coloured beads and miniature bronze medallions decorated with ancient swastika symbols and pentagrams. New Age people were eager to explore the boundaries of their spirituality without fully understanding the dangers in doing so. Evil was just as prone as good to lie in wait for these innocent souls thirsting for knowledge of the unknown.

"Can we go there?" Miranda asked.

"Of course we can," Nigel said.

"Will you come too?" Miranda looked at Helle, at Jason.

Jason shifted closer to Helle. "Been there a hundred times. So no, you go on your own—it's not far."

"You have to come, Jason," Nigel said. "You're the local guide, remember?"

Helle placed her hand on his thigh. "We can stop by the bakery afterwards."

He could hear the smile in her voice. She knew just how irritated he was by the infestation of New Age people—an exaggeration, according to Helle—that plagued Glastonbury: air-headed fools who danced at solstices and equinoxes, who called themselves wiccans and practised home-made rituals. Bah! At best the fools dabbled in things they didn't understand. At worst, they might wake powers they would have no notion how to control.

The bakery was run by one of these seekers, a self-professed witch of ample proportions with hennaed hair and tattoos running every which way up her arms. But she did bake excellent sourdough bread, and her *pains au chocolat* were to die for.

They wandered through the various gardens of the Chalice Well, entered through the wrought iron gate that led to the well-head, and strolled towards the main attraction, Nigel reading aloud from Google. Miranda looked disappointed.

"I was expecting something more pagan, more…genuine," she said, studying the stonework that surrounded the well. "You know, a pool in which people have thrown coins for centuries while making a wish."

"You can still make a wish," Nigel said, handing her a couple of pound coins. Miranda laughed, sent a coin spinning through the air. It disappeared with a little splash.

"You're not making a wish?" she asked, turning to Jason and Helle.

Jason shook his head.

"Oh, come on!" Miranda grinned. "There must be something you wish for! What harm would it do?"

Jason shared a look with Helle, saw in her eyes the same flicker of darkness he suspected she saw in his. She tightened her hold on his hand.

"One wish," she murmured, and he nodded. Yes, one wish: that Sam Woolf be well and truly dead. He rummaged in his pocket for a coin and came up empty-handed.

"Here." Miranda grabbed hold of his hand and pressed a coin into it, small, strong fingers closing round his. She gasped, reclaimed her hand and backed away, staring at him.

"What?" he demanded, giving her a puzzled look.

"Nothing." She smiled blandly. "Go on." But for the rest of their little excursion, Miranda kept well away from Jason, even though he felt her eyes drilling holes through him whenever he turned his back on her.

"Seriously?" Helle handed him the sliced mushrooms. "You're overreacting, or maybe it's me that's under-reacting, maybe she just has the hots for you."

Jason snorted "Good luck to her with that." He stirred the pancetta frying in the cast-iron pot, added onions, garlic and a knob of butter. "Something got to her," he continued. "She took my hand, blinked, dropped it, and…"

"Were you unusually hot?" She added the cubed beef to the pot. She glanced at him. "You know, fire-spouting hot?"

"No." He gave her a tender smile. Helle rarely talked about his gift, but if she did, it was always with admiration, never with fear.

"Strange. She's a bit weird. Next thing you know, she'll tell us she wants to read our future or something." Helle laughed. "Maybe it's all part of building up tension, you know, *I felt it the moment I touched you that you've got dark, dark secrets.*" She leaned against him, slipping an arm round his waist. "You do, of course, but she doesn't know that."

"Dark?" He rested his cheek against her head. "Makes me sound very sinister."

She elbowed him. "You know what I mean."

Their private moment was interrupted by Nigel, with Miranda trailing him like a curious puppy.

"Smells great," Nigel said.

"Will taste great as well," Jason said, throwing in his *bouquet garni* before adding wine. "In about two hours." He opened the fridge. "Beer, anyone?"

They sat in the garden enjoying drinks and olives. The sun was agreeably warm, Helle's weight a comforting presence against his right side. He toyed with her hair, watching Miranda perch herself on Nigel's knee. Her dress rode up, a slender green vine that snaked up her thigh clearly visible.

"So, is it good business, being a tattoo artist?" Jason was only mildly interested.

Miranda shrugged. "I earn enough." She smoothed down her dress, giving Jason an impish smile. "My clients like my ability to combine the exotic with the sensual."

"Ah." He pointed at her arms. "Like those snakes?"

"Serpents," she corrected, studying the one on her left arm with evident pride. "One of my better designs."

"What, you tattoo yourself?" Helle asked.

"No." Miranda laughed. "I have a tattoo buddy."

Jason raised his brows. "A buddy?"

"We share our designs, we help each other out, we have a common website. He's more into Celtic stuff, I do a lot of designs inspired by William Blake and those Pre-Raphaelite blokes—you know, water lilies, red-haired beauties and burning tigers."

"And drowned Ophelias," Helle added *sotto voce*, making Jason chuckle.

"But I make most of my money from my readings," Miranda continued, throwing Jason a challenging look.

"Like palmistry?" he asked.

"Tea-leaves, tarot cards—but yes, mostly palms." She clasped her hands together. "I'm very good."

"I can imagine: I guess the important thing is always to promise a handsome stranger, right?" Helle laughed. Miranda bristled.

"You're making it sound very silly."

"And it isn't?" Jason didn't even try to keep the derision out of his voice.

"No," she replied curtly. "It isn't. It's a real talent."

Jason extended a leg sufficiently to kick Nigel on the ankle.

"Perfect fit, Nigel. A New Age mate with whom you can share your theories of predestination. I hope you've done a thorough analysis of your horoscopes, to ensure you're compatible—in all aspects, not only in bed."

Nigel flushed. "Why are you being so rude to her?"

"Why?" Jason leaned forward. "Because I have no respect for charlatans who pretend to 'see' and 'feel' things, thereby screwing with other peoples' heads."

Like a cobra, Miranda struck, launching herself over the table to grab hold of Jason's left hand.

"Let me show you," she said, setting one finger on his wedding band. He wanted to shake free of her hold, was aware of a surge of defensive heat in his fingers. Her eyes, widened, no more, but she held on. "What, you don't dare to?"

Jason shrugged and forced himself to relax, all too aware of Helle's tense presence beside him. Miranda ran a finger over his palm, sending a jolt up his arm. He sat up straight. Miranda's brow furrowed in concentration, his hand held in both of hers. She raised her face and looked Jason straight in the eyes.

"So many lives."

Jason stiffened.

"So many fruitless existences, wandering the world time and time again."

Jason pulled his hand free, clenching it to disguise its trembling. "What are you on about?" Helle's fingers were digging into his thigh, and Miranda had gone a chalky white, eyes like dark pools in her small face. Nigel cleared his throat.

"I told you she was good," he said.

Jason was tempted to spit in Nigel's face. He'd primed her, of course he had!

"It's true, isn't it?" Miranda said, her previously pasty face now aglow with excitement.

"I have no idea," Jason replied coolly. "You tell me. Or maybe Nigel could tell us all exactly what he's told you."

"Me?" Nigel glowered. "I've never told a soul—never!" He inhaled. "How can you think—"

"Well, excuse me for being a tad sensitive about some things," Jason snapped.

"Stop it!" Helle got to her feet. "Let's just calm down and forget all this, okay?"

"Forget?" Miranda leaned towards her. "Forget what, exactly?"

"All this hand-reading nonsense to begin with," Helle said briskly. "Anyone want more beer?" She collected the empties, reached for Nigel's bottle, and Miranda grabbed hold of her wrist.

"Nonsense? I don't do nonsense."

"Let her go," Jason warned, leaping up.

"Don't touch her," Nigel said, intercepting him. Helle was yanking at her hand. Miranda swayed. Her eyes rolled back in her head.

"It isn't over yet," she intoned. "He's not gone. He's back. And this time he intends to win."

With a little whimper, Helle tugged herself free, dropping bottles everywhere. She fled; Jason caught up with her and pulled her into his arms, holding her tight while eye-fencing with Nigel over her head. To be fair, Nigel looked as stricken as Jason felt.

"What the fuck do you think you're doing?" Jason demanded.

"I—" Miranda began.

"She's telling it as she sees it." Nigel jumped in, giving Jason a defiant look. "Not her fault, is it?"

"She's scaring the hell out of my wife!" Jason snarled.

"I'm sorry, I..." Miranda stuttered.

"What? Didn't think? Were too eager to see how we'd react to your little act?"

"Act?" Miranda sounded offended.

"What has Nigel told you?" Jason asked.

"I already said! I've told her nothing—nothing—and it pisses me off no end that you think I'd do something like that!"

"So how does she know?" Jason demanded.

"Know what?" Miranda gave him a confused look. An excellent actress, the little minx. Her mouth wobbled. "I don't know anything. I just felt it: an oppressive presence, a dark shroud of fear. And there was this man, stepping out of the night..." She fell silent. "I didn't mean to scare Helle," she added after some seconds.

"Of course you didn't." Nigel ignored Jason's scowl and came over to pat Helle on the back. "Hey," he said, "it might just be her picking up on your fears, Lion-tamer."

"What fears?" Miranda asked.

Jason ignored her. "It'll be fine, love."

"'Course it will," Nigel agreed.

"Will someone please tell me what's going on?" Miranda's pretty little mouth set in an irritated pout. "Nigel?"

Nigel exhaled. "Not my call, pumpkin."

"You don't trust me?" Miranda demanded, looking from Nigel to Jason.

"I do," Nigel replied just as Jason said, "Not really."

"Thanks a lot." Miranda crossed her arms over her chest.

"We don't know you," Helle said from within the circle of Jason's arms. She sounded tired, was leaning heavily against his chest.

"So this is some major, major secret?" Miranda's voice lightened, eyes bright with curiosity. "You can tell me—I bet it has to do with those multiple lives of yours." She nodded at Jason.

"My what?" He laughed lightly. "You're delusional."

"And you're a very bad liar." She turned to Nigel. "You know I can keep confidences."

"But this is not my story to tell." Nigel gave Jason a level look. "And I don't share my friends' secrets."

"Good for you." Miranda stalked off.

Jason flushed, meeting Nigel's eyes. "Sorry."

"Whatever." Nigel hurried after Miranda, moving at speed down the garden.

"We're going to have to tell her," Helle told him, her voice muffled.

"Absolutely not!"

"We have to, for Nigel's sake." Helle extricated herself from his arms. "But let's keep it very brief, okay? No previous lives, no magically gifted you, just bad guy chasing after us, a couple of nasty incidents ending with him falling off that cliff." She shivered. "He should be dead."

"He is dead."

Helle leaned back in his arms, searching his face. "Do you truly believe that?"

He couldn't lie to her. "Sometimes. Not always."

Helle nodded. "Me neither."

Chapter 4

They salvaged the rest of the weekend by feeding Miranda an abbreviated and censored version of the truth. Nigel filled in when he could, taking his cues from what Helle and Jason were willing to share, causing Miranda to gape when he explained how he'd hacked into Woolf's networks to find evidence of his illegal activities.

"A trafficker?" Miranda pulled a face.

"Among other things," Helle said.

"Hmm." Miranda looked from one to the other. "It's not the whole truth is it?"

"No." Helle saw no reason to lie. "But it's what we're comfortable sharing with you—for now."

Miranda twirled a long strand of hair round her finger. "For now. I can live with that." Jason snorted and Helle felt him tighten his hold on her, his hand suddenly uncomfortably hot.

"That's fortunate," he said. "After all, we decide when and what we want to share."

Helle gave his fingers an admonishing squeeze. Nigel draped an arm round Miranda's shoulders and asked if there was any hope of food before he died of starvation.

"And wine," he added hopefully. "You've got some nice Nebbiolo just begging to be appreciated by a true wine lover."

"Nebbiolo? With my boeuf bourguignon? Not likely."

Nigel winked at Helle. "You're such a snob at times, Morris."

"I know my wines, Hawkins. Not my fault if you don't."

By the time Miranda and Nigel drove off next morning, it was as if the entire palm-reading incident had never happened. Except that Helle couldn't stop thinking about it. She turned her hand this way and that, trying to convince herself all this stuff was bullshit anyway. Jason's hand closed on hers.

"Forget it," he said, bending down to kiss her on the nose. "Until we have far more tangible proof than the say-so of a self-professed seer, we assume Woolf is dead. Very dead."

Helle nodded. Rationally, he had to be. Rationally, no one survived hours in the cold waters of the Channel. Rationally, there'd been no sign of life from Sam Woolf in two months. Unfortunately, Woolf was not bound by the laws of logic. Jason shook her.

"Helle!" His copper-coloured eyes flashed. "Don't overthink this."

"I just wish…" She broke off. If only there had been a body.

"I know. So do I. But logically, he is dead." He dragged his free hand through his hair, making it stand every which way.

"Logically, yes. But does logic apply here?"

"We cross that bridge when we get to it, lioness. And at present there is no bridge to cross, is there?"

She gave him a half-smile. "Not as such."

"Good." He pulled her close and planted a soft kiss on her forehead. "Hold on to that thought."

Monday and they were back at work, a haven of exacting Excel sheets and analyses that kept Helle happily occupied. Morris & Son had its premises on the top floor of an older red-brick building on Queen Street—perhaps not the most obvious of premises for a company specialising in alternative technologies, except that behind the traditional exterior was a very modern interior, with a lot of glass and polished hardwood floors. Over the last few years Jason had acquired several leading-edge high-tech companies, turning visionary ideas into commercially viable products. What had been a pure investment company when he inherited it from his father, was now a small group, with companies in various countries. This in itself was something of a headache, and after much thought, Jason had decided to bring a financial manager on board.

"Angela won't like it," Helle had said when Jason broached the idea with her. Angela was Jason's everything rolled into one, a capable assistant who handled most of the accounting as well as molly-coddling Jason whenever the opportunity arose to do so. Recently, Angela had been as irascible as a hungry bear, this because her office love-interest was interested elsewhere. Very messy, seeing as Steve was Jason's Mergers & Acquisitions manager, and the girl he made sheep's-eyes at was their new M & A intern—well, had been their new intern, until Jason decided either she or Steve had to go.

So now Steve was in a foul mood because his Charlotte was no longer around, Angela was all stormy weather because pretty boy Steve no longer seemed to notice she existed, and on top of that to bring in a financial manager? Dynamite…

"She can't cope," Jason said. "You've said so yourself."

"I know that, you know that. Angela most certainly doesn't." Helle pulled a recent balance sheet her way. "I had to redo most of this, but according to Angela that was because I was being anal." She chuckled. "She didn't like it when I pointed out the equity has to reconcile from year to year."

There and then, Jason had lifted the phone and initiated a search.

On this Monday morning they were meeting two of the candidates, and Angela was all icy politeness when she showed the first of them into the office. She'd actually taken the whole thing better than expected—probably due to the long chat she and Helle had had in the ladies—but today her previous equanimity was gone with the wind, her eyes shooting darts at Jason.

"But surely you understand?" Helle asked her during a quick tea break. Angela swept her long hair into place and adjusted her blouse.

"I do. Doesn't mean I like it." She lowered her voice. "And could we please hire someone who doesn't resemble Will?"

"Hey, I heard that!" Will protested, standing up behind his desk. Their resident IT expert was a red-headed individual with a fondness for jeans that hung a tad too low on the hips.

Helle suppressed a little laugh: neither candidate had much in common with Will, but one of them did have ginger hair.

It was relaxing to escape into a world of mundane matters such as these. While concentrating on Morris & Son, Helle kept all thoughts of Woolf at bay. But once she was sitting on her own, in crept Sam Woolf, planting himself as a menacing presence in her brain.

Her mother listened in silence when Helle finally found the nerve to call her and tell her about her fears.

"Jason's right," Miriam said. "Until there is any reason to believe he's not dead, we keep on assuming he is a collection of bones littering the bottom of the sea."

"But—"

"No buts, darling. And this new friend of yours strikes me as something of a drama queen. Palm-readings… Pshaw!"

"She's not a friend. At most she's an acquaintance."

"And a tattoo artist." Mum sounded vaguely disapproving. "Next thing you know, she'll suggest you tattoo 'Jason' on your bum or something."

"Mum! Besides, I wouldn't." She studied the patch of shiny skin on her forearm, a tangible reminder of the humiliating experience of being tattoed by Woolf.

"Huh. When it comes to Jason, I'm not so sure." Mum made a gagging sound. "Anyway, stop this nonsense, okay? Unless the man has webbed feet and gills, he's gone."

Nigel said the same thing. "I've spent the last twelve hours trawling through the internet, searching for anything that would indicate he's still around. So far, nothing."

"You have?" Helle smiled and adjusted her earpiece.

"I had to." Nigel sighed. "Miranda scared you. Not intentionally, but still. So it's up to me to reassure you."

"Wow." Helle blinked a couple of times. "Thanks."

"Anything for you, Lion-tamer."

At night, she couldn't shut her fears out. She'd lie awake after Jason had fallen asleep, staring into the night while her brain was populated with images of Woolf. When she finally fell asleep, chances were she'd dream of him, a powerful man striding across the centuries to seize her and carry her off. She would wake to a rushing heart and a constriction in her lungs, and it would take her ages to dare sleep again. As a consequence, she became tired and grumpy—and damned resentful of Jason's undisturbed nights.

"You're not sleeping well," Jason stated one morning, peering at her face. He set down a mug of tea in front of her before joining her at the breakfast table

"Not really, no." These last few nights hadn't only been about Woolf, they'd been about that little red-haired girl she believed to be her long-lost daughter. Those dreams woke a hunger deep inside of her, a yearning for a baby, their baby. Discreetly, she slid a hand down her front. Not discreetly enough, and Jason's gaze followed her hand, brows puckering into a slight frown.

"The child?" he asked.

Helle nodded, wanting to add that it wasn't about the daughter they'd lost so long ago, it was also about making a child, a new start, somehow. But she was afraid she'd sound totally ridiculous saying this out loud, and so far Jason had never raised the subject of actively making babies, beyond assuring her that there would be time for them.

He was probably right: a couple of years without the complication of children was a good thing. Or not. A loud tick-tocking filled her head, a not-so-subtle reminder that sometimes time ran out before you expected it to, and instead of Happily Ever After and children playing in the dappled shade of the apple trees, there could be death and separation— just as in their first life.

Jason swept her hair off her face. "Why don't you wake me?"

Helle shrugged. What would it help, to have him lying sleepless beside her? Besides, of late some of her Woolf dreams had taken a turn towards something that bordered on forbidden fruit, so she woke feeling not only scared but soiled. But she didn't tell Jason that. Instead she mumbled something about there being very little he could do.

"I can hold you. That helps, doesn't it?"

She gave him a tentative smile. "Mostly it does, yes."

Jason's dark brows rose. "Not always?"

Helle sighed. "Almost always."

Jason was frowning down at his latest PowerPoint presentation when his phone rang. He'd delegated the task of showing the new financial manager the ropes to Helle, calmly pointing out that it was she, not he, who'd been doing most of the finances lately. She'd thrown him a black look, making him blow her a kiss.

"You just don't want to handle the Angela thing," she'd muttered.

He picked up the phone, eyes on his wife and Angela, at present looking very enthusiastic as she described something to their newest employee. It probably helped that Jim Taylor was good-looking in an unobtrusive way, if somewhat too conservative in how he dressed. Well, give it a week or two and the man would conform to the office standard—less of the boring black suits and white shirts, more of trousers and shirts with rolled up sleeves.

"Why is Hawkins trawling through the internet, searching for anything connected to drownings or sea incidents?" John Stapleton's voice on the line was as precise as ever.

"Good morning to you too," Jason said.

"Is it?" John snorted. "I hadn't noticed. Pissing down over here. So why?"

"How do you know he's searching the internet?" Jason found a paperclip and amused himself by straightening it out.

"Hawkins does little without setting off our alarms these days," Stapleton replied. Jason smiled. If Nigel wanted to disappear into the virtual world without leaving a trace, he would. In this case, he probably felt it didn't serve any purpose.

"Ah," he replied, trying to sound impressed. "Does he know Winchester's finest have him under surveillance?"

"No."

Jason's smile broadened into a grin as he began reconstructing the deformed clip. According to Nigel, he was keeping the plods happy by pretending not to notice them.

"So why?" Stapleton repeated. "And why only anything after mid-May?"

Jason sighed. "You know the answer to that as well as I do. He's hoping to find some confirmation—either way." He stared at the glass wall again, but this time, instead of seeing Helle, he saw Sam Woolf, his large frame quivering with rage as he lunged for Helle. "She isn't sleeping all that much," he added. "Instead of becoming more reassured he's dead, she seems to become more convinced he isn't, saying that something should have turned up."

"Really? Why?"

Jason threw the clip on the desk. "Someone read her palm and told her it wasn't over." He gritted his teeth. Every night Helle tossed and turned, Miranda sank deeper and deeper into his black books.

"Bloody dilettantes," John muttered. He fell silent for a while, and Jason was considering hanging up when John spoke. "She's right, you know. Something should have floated ashore. With the tides and the wind that night…" He didn't finish.

"I'd prefer it if you kept that to yourself," Jason said, rubbing at his temple. Not again. Please God, no more Woolf. "Helle doesn't need to be more apprehensive than she already is."

"What Helle needs is the truth—however bad."

"I think I'm in a better position to determine what she needs. She's my wife, not yours."

"Too bad you had such problems with the possessive pronoun last time we met," Stapleton retorted, his voice crackling with frost. "Oh, right: that time it was my wife—not yours—and as I recall you were doing a hell lot more to her than expressing concern, weren't you?"

Ancient shame heated Jason's face. "How much longer do you plan to milk that?" Hell, it was close to four centuries in the past now.

"As long as I feel like it," came the clipped reply. Jason hung up. Seconds later, the phone rang again.

"What?"

"I didn't just call out of idle curiosity," John snapped. He cleared his throat. "Look, there's something you should know. A week ago, a report was filed with the police in Honfleur."

Something pitched inside of Jason. "And?"

"An empty boat was found drifting just outside the harbour."

"And this is important because…"

"Because there was blood all over the deck." There was a rustling sound as if John was flipping through pages. "The owner, a certain Pascal Ides, has gone missing."

"So maybe he slipped and fell." Jason clutched at this comforting thought.

"Maybe." John exhaled. "Or maybe he was kind enough to help someone aboard and was attacked for his kindness."

"You said a week ago. Did Woolf float about like a happy walrus until then? More than two months?" Jason attempted a dismissive snort, clenching his overheated fists.

"Ides went missing in May—he's from just north of Bordeaux. A loner, he was going to spend the summer sailing round the British Isles, so no one missed him until last week—but no one has seen him since May."

"Shit."

"It may be nothing," Stapleton said.

"Yes. A mere coincidence." Jason took a deep breath. "I'm not sure I should tell her," he said. "If I do—"

"And if you don't?" Stapleton asked. "What if she finds out from someone else?"

"Shit," Jason repeated. Stapleton was right. He closed his eyes, opened them, only to find Helle standing in the doorway, looking at him. "I have to go." He ended the call and held out his hand to her. She walked slowly towards him, the fabric of her dark trousers swishing softly with each stride. "That was Stapleton," he said, responding to the unspoken question on her face. He shoved his chair back from the desk, made room for her to sit on his knees. "He had some news, well, speculation really, and—"

"About Woolf?" She cut him off, her voice strained.

"Potentially." He tightened his hold on her. "It's probably nothing." Yes, of course it was. Nothing. The missing Frenchman had met an unfortunate accident, no more. Briefly, he told her what Stapleton had shared with him, and felt her go absolutely still, as if frozen mid-breath.

"Oh God." She hid her face against him. Jason ran his hand up and down her back, eyes lost in space. If Woolf was alive, it was only a matter of time before he made his move. Jason swallowed in an attempt to lubricate a throat gone very dry. Dearest Mother, he thought, invoking that oldest of deities, please don't do this to us.

"Mrs Morris? About that tax issue…" Taylor came to a confused halt. "Sorry, I—"

"I'm fine," Helle straightened up, rising elegantly to her feet. Jason gripped her hand, caught her eyes. Dark shadows lurked in the depths of her turquoise gaze. "I'm fine," she repeated in an undertone. She squeezed his hand. "We will be, right?"

He just nodded, managing a smile.

The moment she was out of the door, he did two things. First, he called Tim Burns, his former bodyguard, and explained the situation in a few terse sentences. Tim listened, uttered five syllables or so, thereby confirming he'd be back on duty as of the next day. Then he called Nigel.

"Honfleur," he said, "a week ago. Find out everything you can. Everything."

And once he'd done that, he swept out of his office, found his wife and took her home. He needed her. Now.

She studied the child for any traces of him, her son. She saw him in the girl's eyes and in the wideness of her smile. She could see him in her demeanour, so serious in one so young. Nefirie smiled, remembering her boy: how he would crouch for hours by the shore, muttering to himself as he piled pebbles into intricate constructions of surprising height and grace: how he would hold her hand when they walked at night, his eyes glued to the firmament above. And how he would swirl his fires, making them dance for her.

Korine was her mother's child too; the dimple that flashed in her cheek when she grinned, the wild curly mass of hair that had to be tamed by force into a braid, the sudden outburst of temper—all from Helle.

But when the little one slept, sprawled on her back with her hands thrown high, she was all him, her beautiful dead boy.

Chapter 5

Nothing had changed. Helle kept telling herself this, a silent mantra that echoed uselessly round and round her head. First Miranda's hand thing, now the abandoned boat in France, and it was as if she'd split open, jagged edges of fear making it difficult to function properly. So she escaped on long walks or long limping runs in Kensington Gardens, always with the patient Tim some steps behind her. He never intruded, he never spoke unless she spoke first, but he was always there, a protective hulk of a man with ears like deformed cauliflowers courtesy of his background as a professional wrestler.

Very often, these walks of hers ended up with her sitting on a bench, eyes glued on children who might be visiting the gardens at the time. Her preferred place was a bench just by the Round Pond. While Tim leaned against a nearby tree, she just sat there, watching little girls and boys play and laugh, and it was as if a fist tightened round her lungs. A child—his child. She clutched at herself in a self-hug, wanting, wanting so desperately, and now it seemed time was running out—again.

One day, she felt tears slide down her cheeks. No matter how she tried, she couldn't stop the flow, a silent weeping that made her rock back and forth.

"Mrs Morris? You all right?" Tim's concerned voice came from somewhere to her right, but Helle waved him away, incapable of saying anything. Her behaviour must have worried him, because some time later, Jason's hand squeezed down gently on her shoulder, startling her.

"Are you looking at the dogs or the children?" He slid down on the bench beside her, cupped her face and wiped at her eyes with his thumbs.

"Both." She smiled through her tears at a little boy, all sticky fingers and a mop of unruly hair. "But mostly at the children."

"Imagine when we have half a dozen like him," Jason said, his voice loaded with tenderness.

"If," Helle corrected, shoulders slumping.

His hold on her tightened. "No," he said firmly. "Don't you dare sound that despondent."

"But—"

"No." He sank his gaze into hers. "First of all, we don't know if that damned boat has anything to do with Woolf. Secondly, even if it does, I will not—not, you hear—allow him to win this time round. Never."

He sounded so certain, so strong. His fingers were so warm on her face, his eyes blazed with determination, more amber than copper in the sun. Helle slumped against him, he wound his arms around her.

"We will have children," he said, kissing the top of her head. "But I do hope they look a bit cleaner than that one does." He nodded discreetly at the boy with the wild hair. "What is that on his leg? Duck poo?"

Helle laughed, sat back and dragged her sleeve over her swollen face. "Probably—he's been chasing those poor birds all over." A couple of deep inhalations, and she rested her cheek against his reassuringly broad chest. "You truly think we'll get to the happily ever after?"

Jason brushed the back of his fingers over her cheek. "As far as I'm concerned, we already have, lioness." His voice softened. "We're here, aren't we? Together."

But for how much longer, she thought, pressing her face closer to his beating heart. His hand came up to stroke her hair, she closed her eyes and inhaled his scent, that comforting and familiar mix of salty sea and firewood, tinged with the distinctive fragrance of sun-warmed cedars.

"It'll be all right," he said.

"All right," she echoed, and nodded. Yes, she had to believe that—she needed to believe that.

Next time she spoke to Mum, she carefully brought her up to date with recent events, relieved to hear her mother scoff and query whether she wasn't making a mountain out of a molehill.

"If that tattoo-vamp of yours hadn't spouted all that nonsense when she grabbed your hand, would you have been so worried about an abandoned boat? And anyway, he's been gone for three months—wouldn't he have made himself known by now if he was still alive?"

All very rational, very Mum; within ten minutes, Helle was almost convinced her misgivings were nothing but figments of the imagination, her brain playing up as it processed the unusual events of the last year or so.

"Unusual?" her mother laughed. "Tell me about it. It can't be considered normal to be like you—or Jason—an ancient reincarnated soul, no less. I kowtow to you, oh spiritual being so close to nirvana."

"Shut up," Helle said, giggling all the same.

"Seriously, though," Miriam said once they'd stopped laughing, "didn't you tell me you'd had previous encounters with Woolf? In other lives?"

"Yes—but not so I remember. Jason told me." Helle fiddled with her phone. According to Jason, last time Helle had encountered Woolf, she'd ended up dead at a very young age—sort of a repetitive pattern.

"So maybe what you're experiencing isn't so much about what's happening now, but rather about what happened then. Maybe that's what the tattoo girl picked up on, a repressed memory, if you like."

Helle was silent.

"You there?" Mum asked.

"Yeah. And sort of shocked to hear you talk so casually about stuff that, if we're going to be honest, is so inconceivable it can't be true."

"But it is true." Mum's voice dropped an octave. "We both know that. All those dreams when you were a child, and now Jason…" She cleared her throat. "I don't question it, Helle—not anymore."

That was nice to know, Helle thought, recalling an uncomfortable dinner where Miriam had gone after Jason as if he were a freak.

Jason had just drawn the Friday afternoon office meeting to a close when Nigel called. Helle and Will were locked in a heated argument about the benefits of outsourcing servers versus having your own, with Jim's gaze leaping from one to the other, for all the world as if he were watching a tennis game.

Jason squeezed past Steve's chair, smiled at Angela who beamed back before transferring those bright eyes of hers to Jim instead, and retreated to his office.

"Still on for padel tennis tomorrow?" Nigel asked, making a swooshing sound. "I've worked on my serve, so I'm planning on murdering you."

"What a nice choice of words. Besides, we both know it's me that will win."

"You wish." Yet another swooshing sound. "I've got a new racquet as well."

"Only those athletically inept rely on their equipment."

"Huh." Nigel laughed. "Let's see what you say after the game." He sobered up. "There's something else."

"Yes?" Jason strode over to the window, standing on the old Turkish carpet he'd inherited—together with the business and a sizeable fortune—from his father.

"That boat in Honfleur," Nigel began, and Jason closed his eyes. "There's nothing—nothing at all—that points to Woolf being on board."

"But?"

Nigel exhaled. "According to the police reports, someone was killed. Arterial spray all over the deck."

"So maybe the owner managed to hurt himself somehow."

"Maybe. But their experts are saying everything points to someone having his throat cut—from behind."

"Fantastic," Jason muttered, pinching the bridge of his nose.

"It could be anyone," Nigel said.

"It could." Jason studied the street, many floors below. A taxi pulled up; two people stepped out, hurrying through the rain in the general direction of the office building's main entrance. "Or it could be him."

"If it was, he's been lying low for ages. Based on the deterioration of the blood, they reckon the murder took place in late May." May. Jason dragged his hands through his hair.

"You still there?" Nigel asked after some moments of silence.

"Yes."

There was a tapping sound—Nigel's fingers flying over his keyboard, Jason assumed. "In itself, this proves nothing."

"You're right." Jason straightened up, just as two people entered the reception area, visible through the glass walls.

"No need to tell Helle," Nigel said.

"Of course I have to tell her." Jason watched Angela hasten over to greet the two visitors. He squinted at the woman, a familiar combination of buxom curves. Did he know her? She turned to face his window, and his jaw set. Alison? Here? "But not right now," he added, before hanging up.

"Fetch Helle," he told Angela when she showed Alison and Mr Unknown into his office. Eyes an intense green met his, did a quick up-and-down of his body, before returning to meet his gaze. He inclined his head in greeting.

"Alison, what a surprise," he said.

"Yeah, one you really, really like, right?" she said.

Jason shrugged. "About as much as you like me."

Alison blushed. "I—"

"Blamed me. For everything, including your own stupidity."

Something flared in those cat's eyes of hers. "It was your fault! If you'd—"

"Alison," the man beside her interrupted. "Don't let your feelings run away with you, honey." He extended his hand to Jason. "Paul Davies. I'm Alison's fiancé." He gave Jason a bland smile. "And her therapist."

"Isn't that a tad unprofessional?"

"In this case, it's convenient." Davies laughed, placing an arm round Alison's shoulder. "We met during Alison's therapy sessions, but these days the only relationship we have is a personal one." His arm tightened somewhat round Alison. "She needs security," he went on, "but I assume you'd know that, being present when…err…"

"Yes," Jason said. He'd most certainly been present that day last December when Helle had found Alison injured, a collection of welts, blood and bruises after Sam Woolf had taken out his anger on her. Helle's and Alison's flat had been in shambles, Woolf's destructive rage wreaked on everything within reach.

"I give her that, don't I, honey?" Davies' hand sliding possessively down her back.

Alison merely nodded.

"Structure and stability," Davies added directing himself to Jason. "I find it always helps with fragile creatures such as Alison."

Fragile? If anything, Alison looked robust, but appearances could deceive.

"Structure," Davies repeated. "Rules, scheduled activities—it all helps." He leaned forward and kissed Alison's cheek. "And love, of course."

Alison blushed, a wave of vivid red flying up her face. Jason threw Davies a thoughtful look. If he was a day under forty, Jason would eat his hat. Slim, with a receding hairline and vivid blue eyes, he was a commanding presence, further accentuated by the bespoke three-piece suit, the starched white shirt and the heavy gold cufflinks. A man who'd done well for himself, adding one last accessory in the shape of a pretty, much younger wife-to-be.

"You didn't tell Helle you were coming," Jason said.

"Well, she didn't know," Davies replied in her stead. "I made the arrangements. We flew in from Chicago yesterday."

"Ah. Vacation?"

"Vacation? Here?" Davies gestured at the rain-spattered window. "No, no. I'm here for a series of lectures and I decided Alison should come with me."

Once again, Alison blushed, but she remained still and silent beside the pompous git.

"How fortunate it didn't collide with anything on her schedule, then," Jason said.

"Oh, Alison's schedule is always flexible, isn't it, honey?" Davies turned a toothy grin Alison's way. To Jason's surprise, the formerly fiery Alison ducked her head and acquiesced. What had happened to her? Woolf, he reminded himself, flooded with pity for the woman in front of him.

"Alison?" At the sound of Helle's voice Alison swivelled on her toes. Helle took a couple of long strides towards her, but her steps faltered as she approached, until she came to a halt a foot or so away. "What happened to your hair?"

"It never grew back," Alison said harshly, self-consciously lifting a hand to her gamine haircut. Jason thought that this severe style served to accentuate her eyes and beautiful brows, but from Alison's expression, she didn't agree with him.

"Oh." Helle took yet another step towards her, a tentative smile on her face.

"Paul Davies." The man extended his hand, placing himself slightly in front of Alison. "Alison's fiancé."

"You're getting married?" Helle asked, eyes on Alison while shaking Davies' hand.

"In October," Davies replied. "No major ceremony, just the two of us and the priest." He smiled again. "That's the way we want it, isn't it honey?" He lowered his voice to a croon. "Just you and I. No one else."

"You and me," Alison said with a nod.

"We're hoping to start a family," Davies confided. "I think it would do Alison good, and she'd make an excellent stay-at-home mother."

"I'm sure she would. After all, she's an excellent psychiatrist," Helle said and Davies' mouth curled into a little sneer, while Alison gave Helle a grateful look.

"She is, but once we marry, I think she'll prefer to help me out at my office, won't you, honey?" Davies said.

As an unpaid assistant, Jason thought, meeting Helle's eyes.

Jason invited their guests to sit in the leather armchairs closest to the window. He fetched a chair for Helle, listening with half an ear as Alison described Paul's house just south of Chicago.

"Lakefront property", Paul put in proudly. "Huge pile of a place with acres of land." He chuckled. "Alison here will be marrying a very successful and wealthy man." He leaned back in his chair, giving Helle an avid look that had warning bells going off in Jason's head. "I'm considered something of a trailblazer in my field."

"Oh?" Helle said.

"Paul," Alison murmured, covering his hand with hers. "Maybe we shouldn't…"

Davies ignored her and gave first Helle, then Jason, an unctuous smile. "That's why I hope there will be an opportunity for you and me to talk."

"About what?" Jason asked.

Paul Davies raised a brow. "Why, about your supposed reincarnations."

Helle turned to stare at Alison. Jason moved closer, placing a hand on Helle's shoulder.

"I have no idea what you're talking about," Helle managed.

Davies wagged a finger at her. "Alison has told me everything." He bounced on his seat. "I would like to start with some hypnosis sessions, and then—"

Jason cut him off. "You heard my wife. She has no idea what you're referring to." He scowled at Alison, any compassion he might have felt for her wiped away by this betrayal. "Trying to make yourself interesting again?" Alison opened her mouth, but before she could say anything, Davies jumped in.

"Interesting? Understatement of the year." He licked his lips. "If we can prove previous lives, then—"

"Good luck with that." Yet again, Jason interrupted. "I've never met a reincarnated soul."

"According to Alison—" Davies began.

"Alison recently suffered severe trauma. I don't think we can consider her statements to be fully reliable," Helle put in. She held out her hand to Alison. "Want a tour of the office?" Her turquoise eyes flashed in Jason's direction. He nodded infinitesimally: he'd entertain the obnoxious Davies for a while.

"So you're saying Alison lied during therapy," Davies said, once the women had left the room.

"I have no idea. But I can assure you Helle is as normal as they come."

"And you?"

"Me?" Jason managed a loud guffaw. "Well, I definitely do not suffer under any delusions of having been reborn repeatedly."

"Hmm." Davies looked in the direction of the door. "I don't like it, when people lie to me."

"I thought that's what therapy is about: peeling away the lies we all hide behind to cope with the tragedies that mar our lives. And as for Alison, she was in a bad way. God knows what nonsense Woolf might have filled her head with."

Davies made a guttural sound Jason chose to interpret as agreement—but he didn't like the glint in the older man's eyes as he studied Alison, still visible through the glass wall.

"How could you?" Helle rounded on Alison the moment they were alone.

"How could I do what?"

"Tell him," Helle hissed.

"Heck, he's my therapist! Of course I told him—I told him everything." Alison gave Helle a defiant look, her tongue darting out to lick her lips.

"Our past had nothing to do with what happened to you."

"Sure it did." Alison's dark brows pulled together in a formidable scowl. "If it hadn't been for that ancient mess with you and Woolf, he wouldn't have—"

"If you hadn't played with fire, it wouldn't have happened. I warned you, remember?"

"It was his fault. His!" Alison stabbed a finger in the direction of Jason's office. "If he'd not meddled, you would have stayed with Woolf, and—"

"Never." Helle sank her nails into her palms, so badly did she want to hit Alison.

With a loud sigh, Alison slumped against the wall. "No, probably not."

"Too right," Helle said, leaning against the opposite wall, arms crossed over her chest.

They stood like that for some time, assessing each other in silence. Helle found Alison somehow diminished: the prim little suit she was wearing didn't do much for her, other than making her ass look three sizes too big for the skirt.

"So this Paul dude is the one and only?" she finally asked.

Alison gave her a tired look. "What do you think? He's safe. He's predictable, I know what he likes. If I do as he likes he's a happy camper, and I don't get hurt."

Beyond living in a stunted and controlling relationship, Helle thought, but she didn't say that, too aware of the look in Alison's eyes, more or less begging her to confirm she'd made the right decision. So she opted for a neutral sound, no more.

"What about your new job?" she asked. Alison had e-mailed her some time ago, sounding very pleased with her new job in a small medical clinic.

"Don't have time for it. Paul is a high maintenance kind of guy." Alison gave her a crooked smile. "And I feel safer at home." She looked away. "I can't handle big guys anymore—especially not if they have dark hair."

Helle took her hand. "I'm so sorry for you."

Alison disengaged herself. "Yeah. Whatever." She straightened up. "At least the bastard is dead, right?"

"Mmm." Helle stuck her hands in her pockets.

"You okay?" Alison looked at Helle's feet, encased in new suede boots.

"Almost." She wiggled her toes. They twinged, no more.

"That's good."

They were silent again. The chasm that had opened between them because of the whole sordid mess with Woolf, was too deep and too wide to bridge with words—at least when they were face to face. On the phone, or by e-mail, it was easier, distance and invisibility making it possible to pretend nothing had changed, that they were still the same girls who had grown up together, gone to Michigan State together. But here, standing within touching distance from an Alison fundamentally different from the confident woman she'd been...Helle sighed softly.

"Seriously, Alison, you can't marry him."

Alison snorted. "You don't know me anymore. You have no idea what I need, okay?"

"No, but still..."

"Paul takes care of me. I'm happy to pay the required price."

"Which is?"

"Jesus, woman, use your imagination! He's not exactly Adonis, is he?"

Helle tittered nervously. "So what, you close your eyes?"

"All the time." Alison grinned and for a nanosecond the old Alison peeked through the groomed façade. "He likes blindfolds—and cuffs."

"Alison!"

Alison snickered. "Still a prude, hey?"

Helle raised her brows, no more.

"Oh, fantastic: your red-headed Reincarnation Boy remains as hot as ever," Alison said.

"Don't call him that!"

"Why not?" Alison hissed back. "That's what he is, isn't it? Some ancient soul who's been carrying a torch for you over three millennia." She sounded jealous. Helle's chest flooded with warmth, as it always did when she considered just how tenacious and determined Jason had been to find her again. So many lives...would she have been capable of the same devotion?

"Some people would call him obsessive," Alison continued.

"Some people would call you a bitch," Helle retorted. Alison cringed. Helle felt ashamed, but met Alison's eyes. "What exactly does your fiancé want with me?"

Alison looked taken aback by the abrupt change in subject. "Paul? He's hoping to sell a book or two—speculative science if you will. A couple of chapters on time-travelling souls would be the icing on the cake." Her tone was bitterly amused.

"He's not getting any icing from me," Helle said. "Or Jason."

"Which I've told him—repeatedly." Alison looked away. "He won't like it, though."

"Tough."

"Yeah." Alison straightened up, her hands shaking as she smoothed her skirt into place. "I guess he'll just write it anyway, based on what I've told him."

"What?"

"Relax. He can't use your real names, can he?" Alison leaned forward, close enough for her fingers to brush Helle's sleeve. "It's good to see you."

"That was weird," Helle said once Alison and Davies had left.

"And uncomfortable." Jason swiped through his contacts. Once Curtis Crew's smiling dark face filled the screen he clicked 'dial', fingers drumming impatiently while he waited for Curtis to pick up.

"'lo? You're not calling to cancel tomorrow, are you? I've spent two weeks training."

"Since I last beat you, you mean," Jason said.

"Luck," Curtis said with a loud snort.

"Skill. Listen, Curtis, I need your advice."

His solicitor friend's voice changed immediately, all traces of banter wiped away. "Has anything happened? Is the bastard back?"

"No, no, it's not about that." Jason interrupted, wishing he hadn't used the loudspeaker function. "I just had a disconcerting little quack come visiting."

Curtis listened in silence. Once Jason was done, he muttered something about unsavoury arseholes, before assuring Jason this would not be a problem—at all.

"Just in case, I'll throw the book at him right now, ensuring he is well aware you will prosecute should he decide to print any of that rubbish." He fell silent. "Why would this Alison person have made something like that up?"

"No idea." Jason met Helle's eyes. "I think she had it from Woolf, and you'll have to ask him as to why—once you meet him in the afterlife."

"Fat chance. I'm aiming to end up as a bluebell or two in some peaceful country graveyard."

Jason smiled. "Sounds like a plan." He hung up, took a deep breath, and turned to face Helle. "About Honfleur," he began, and she froze.

Kantor sighed, looking at Korine. "I miss her," he said, "every day I miss her. And him."

Nefirie nodded in agreement. She missed Jason every day too. Not Helle, though: it was Helle's fault that he was gone.

"He would have made a good ruler," Kantor went on, "somewhat more level-headed than my firebrand of a daughter."

She smiled crookedly at the unintended pun. Jason had been the fire child, not Helle.

"She wasn't meant for him. And he wasn't meant to be a king." Nefirie sighed. "You should have forced her to honour the marriage contract with Samion, then they would still have been alive." As it was meant to be. She'd tried to make it happen, she reminded herself. Hot, black guilt flooded her.

"How can you say that?" he barked. "How can you ignore the fact that they loved each other?"

"Love has nothing to do with duty, Kantor. Over time she would have made Samion a good wife, and Jason would have found other women with whom to forget her."

Kantor shook his head. "You don't know, do you?" he said bitterly. "You have no idea what it would be like to live without the other. You cannot comprehend the pain that comes from having your heart torn out of your chest." He looked away. "I do. Not one single day since Anayae left have I not woken to the hope that maybe today she would be back. It would have been the same for them. But you wouldn't know. You have never loved like that."

Oh, yes I have, she though. Twice. I still love like that. I have loved you since I first saw you, and I loved my son from the moment I felt him flutter in my womb. She had lost both and still she lived. So would they have done—in pain, but still alive. My boy, she moaned silently, my beautiful son.

Chapter 6

The bed was canopied, the sheets were cool silk, and her wrists were fettered to the exquisitely carved headboard. Windows stood open to the balmy night, a breeze playing over her sweaty skin. She was naked, a large hand cupping her breast, another sliding in between her legs. Such skilful fingers: she writhed on the sheets. Something—a feather?—caressed her breasts, her belly. Fingers. Feather. More fingers. A heavy weight settling between her legs. That feather. The restraints tightening round her wrists; it hurt, but it didn't. Strong hands parting her thighs. She gasped when he rammed into her, his penis pushing itself inside tissues as yet unprepared to receive him. Again, and she wanted to cry out in protest, but knew better than to do so. Someone laughed in her ear.

"*Pain and pleasure, little Helle,*" a dark voice purred. "*Pain and pleasure.*"

Helle sat up in bed, gasping for breath. Her wrists were burning, as if those dreamed bindings were still in place, and there was an ache between her legs, causing her to press her thighs closed. Not again: these nightly visitations were becoming increasingly more explicit, more difficult to ignore. She slipped out of bed and padded over to the bathroom where she sat down on the toilet.

Her sex throbbed. She touched herself, mortified to find herself wet. Shit. There had to be something wrong with her—how could a dream so intimidating be a turn-on? With a little headshake, she stood, washed her hands and drank some water. In the mirror, she met her eyes, a wave of guilt rushing like wildfire up her face.

When she slid into bed she rolled over to lie very close to Jason. He stirred, muttered her name, and drew her close, warm lips finding her nape. The demanding ache between her legs flared into life, but she was damned if she was going

55

to succumb to it, soiling their love-life with her sick dreams. Helle stared out into the dark, reluctant to fall asleep again.

Come morning, the dream had faded. Besides, Helle had other things to think about, like her planned afternoon rendezvous with Alison, a tentative attempt on both sides to find their way back to the friendly familiarity they'd had B.W.—Before Woolf. That Alison was permanently damaged was apparent, it sufficed to look at the puffed-up man she was about to marry. What was also beyond any doubt was that the friendship they'd once had was forever gone, destroyed by what Woolf had done to Alison, but just as much by what Alison had said about Jason.

At least it seemed Paul Davies had given up on discussing the potential of multiple lives with Helle or Jason. Not that he hadn't tried, persistent as an annoying wasp, but seeing as both Helle and Jason maintained they'd never heard anything that ridiculous before, he had finally backed off.

"I have no reason to doubt Alison's version of events," he'd sniffed as a parting shot.

"Up to you if you want to come across as a nutter," Jason had retorted, looking uncomfortable at having been cornered, once again, by Davies, this time as they were returning to the office from a very nice lunch.

Davies' mouth had shrunk to something the size of a desiccated plum. "Nutter? Me?" He'd leaned forward, balancing on his toes. "It's not me claiming to have led multiple lives."

"Me neither," Jason replied, steering Helle in the direction of the lifts. "Oh, and just so you know, I've informed my staff not to allow you entry again."

Alison, predictably, was incensed by Jason's snubbing of her man. "As if he's some sort of scruffy mongrel!" she exclaimed when Helle and she met for tea.

"He's harassing us," Helle told her.

"Huh." Alison seemed on the point of saying something, but to Helle's surprise she deflated. "He's a fucking pest when he gets something in his head," she muttered, massaging her forehead.

"Tell me about it."

"At least he's normal," Alison flashed back.

"What, so Jason isn't?"

In response, two well-plucked brows travelled so far up Alison's forehead Helle worried they might never come down again. "Normal? Him?"

"Careful," Helle warned, already half out of her chair.

Alison gripped her forearm. "Sorry. He just rubs me up the wrong way. I've never liked him."

"I would never have guessed. What I don't understand is why—Jason has never done anything to you."

Alison rolled her eyes. "You don't get it, do you? They're part and parcel of the same package—that's what Woolf told me. He finds you, Jason turns up. Jason finds you, Woolf shows." She made a disgusted face. "As if you were some sort of queen bee."

Helle attempted a snort, but deep inside, she knew Alison was right, and that made her stomach turn.

"Woolf's dead," she said harshly. "I guess just because both turn up, it doesn't mean both survive."

"No." Alison's breathing became shallow, her hands clasped so tightly round her cup the knuckles stood in stark relief against her skin. "I'm not sure I believe he's truly gone." Her voice dropped to an agonised whisper. "I wake up too often to dreams of his face."

Helle stirred her tea, watching the spoon go round and round.

"You're not a hundred per cent convinced either, are you?" Alison said.

"Did you have a good time with Alison?" Jason's voice broke through Helle's silence. She sat back in the car seat and made a so-so movement with her hand.

"It was good to see her, but she's still too angry—with you, of all people."

"Mmm." He adjusted his shades, frowning at the sunlit road ahead of them. In typical fickle fashion, days of English rain had converted into blazing heat, an early Indian summer, so they were on their way to Tor Cottage.

"She says you and Woolf are yoked together—one can't have one without the other." Helle closed her eyes. "Is it true?"

Jason was silent. On the radio someone was singing about love and loss—sort of a recurring theme in popular music.

"Is it?" she repeated.

"I don't know."

When she looked at him, he was dragging his hand through his hair.

"It might be," he said at long last. "The only time I've come close to finding you before, he was already there." He cleared his throat. "There was nothing I could do. You'd jumped to your watery grave before I could save you."

"The time in Paris?" Close to two centuries ago, just after the Napoleonic wars—or so Jason had told her.

His hands tightened on the steering wheel. "Yes."

"Are you back to being friends, then?" he asked a few seconds later. She smiled slightly at his clumsy attempt to change the subject.

"Me and Alison? I'm not sure. It's easier to talk with her on the phone than face to face—it gets to me, to see her so changed. Sometimes I catch her looking at me in a way that makes my skin crawl."

"You do?" Jason's shades turned her way for an instant. "Why, do you think?"

"Jealousy." She leaned back. "Methinks she protests too much and all that. Alison resents me for emerging from all this relatively unscathed and she thinks you're hot."

Jason burst into laughter. "Me?" he said once he'd calmed down. "She can't stand me!"

"Because you've never as much as looked her over."

"Ah." He shrugged. "What can I say? Not my type."

"I sincerely hope so." She placed a hand on his thigh and squeezed before going back to looking at the speeding landscape.

"I don't have many friends, do I?" she blurted some minutes later.

"What do you mean?"

58

"You have all your guy friends, but I just had Alison, and now she's sort of gone." By this time tomorrow, Alison would be on her way back home to the States, and Helle didn't think she'd see her again any time soon.

"There's Miranda," he said. "You've been out with her a couple of times."

"Hmm." Helle had gone along out of obligation. Miranda had asked so many times that to keep on turning her down felt rude. To give Miranda her due, she'd been chirpily normal the few times they'd met—no mention of palmistry, no spurious questions about Helle's past. "I'm not sure she qualifies as a friend, more like a potential friend. Besides, you don't like her much."

"Not much, no," he agreed. "But she's been all right the last few times we've met up." Jason chuckled. "And then there's Nigel—he's your friend."

Helle smiled. Yes, Nigel was definitely her friend.

"And Stapleton," Jason added in a darker voice.

"John? He's not my friend."

"He isn't? He sounds like one—a bloody overprotective one at that."

"Oh." Helle was pleased. "Still, they're guys." She turned to face him. "Did I have any friends back then, in our first life?"

"You had me."

"But you're a boy. Why didn't I have any girl friends?"

"You didn't want any. You only wanted me." Said with a very self-satisfied smirk. Helle huffed. There were moments when it was decidedly weird to be married to the guy you grew up with three thousand years ago. He knew her better than she knew herself, because he remembered all of that first life in detail; she just saw it in flashes.

"Aren't I enough this time round?" he asked quietly. Of course he was, she assured him. In response, he grabbed hold of her hand and lifted it to his mouth, placing a soft kiss on it.

They arrived just as the sun dropped out of sight behind the nearby copse, the hitherto bright afternoon morphing into purple dusk. This late in the season, the foliage was no longer vivid, but rather a collection of various hues of darker green, here and there with a tinge of yellow and red that announced the coming of autumn.

Jason deactivated the perimeter alarm, drove his precious Tesla carefully over the cattle grid, and parked by the front door. As always, it sufficed for Helle to step out of the car and take a couple of deep breaths for her to relax, all those gnawing thoughts about Woolf scurrying away to hide.

She helped Jason carry their bags inside, made as if to start their dinner, but Jason shook his head, taking her by the hand and leading her into the downstairs living room, a space dominated by a comfortable if hideously purple sofa.

He pulled off his long-sleeved t-shirt and gestured for her to sit before falling to his knees in front of her. His eyes radiated that soft copper glow that always sent her heart into erratic rushes.

"Slow?" he asked, smiling as she nodded. He liked taking his time about it, teasing her with his hands and his mouth until she more or less begged for him to come inside. And now he opened her shirt, one button at the time, his fingers exploring the revealed skin with unhurried strokes.

"I love you," she whispered in his hair as he kissed his way along her jawline, lips like butterflies on her sensitive skin. "God, I love you," she added, when he continued down the side of her neck, one warm hand cupped around her right breast, the other working its way up under her skirt.

"I know," he said, and his mouth widened into a grin when he found her naked beneath the skirt. "All day at the office like this?"

"Yup." She reclined against the back of the sofa.

"And you didn't tell me?"

"Shouldn't you be finding out some things on your own?" she teased, parting her legs to his hand.

"That way, is it?" He drew back to look at her, releasing her breast to tuck a strand of hair back behind her ear, Slowly, he leaned forward, lips brushing insinuatingly over hers. His breath tickled her cheek. She could hear the floorboards squeak when he shifted his weight, but most of all she was aware of that mouth; warm and moist it nibbled its way over her lips, his tongue flitting out to trace the contour of her mouth.

A long kissing session followed. No words, no hurry, just his mouth taking hers, his tongue exploring her mouth, tasting her, teasing her, until she felt about to pass out for lack of oxygen. His hands held her still, one sliding in between her legs to cup her sex, the other in her hair, exerting enough pressure that she arched her back, lifting breasts and hips his way.

When he released her mouth, his eyes had darkened, his breathing loud and ragged. She rocked back and forth, trying to entice him to do more than cup her sex, but all he did was smile and increase the pressure, the heel of his hand offering a point of friction she rubbed herself against.

He tugged at her bra. Her breasts popped free. With a soft laugh he stood, looking down at her as he undid his belt. She made as if to take off her few remaining clothes, but he shook his head.

"No. I like how you look, your skirt rucked up around your waist, your breasts still—well, almost—in their bra." He bent, kissed her. "It makes you look wanton—even more so when you're not wearing knickers."

He undid the buttons on his fly, tugged at jeans and briefs, releasing his erect penis. Still looking at her, he cupped himself, stroking his hand up and down his erection.

"Touch yourself," he commanded.

Helle slid two finger through her wet folds, gyrating her hips in time with her fingers.

"Open your legs so that I can see you." His voice was hoarse and breathless. "But don't make yourself come."

Helle groaned and closed her eyes.

"Look at me," he hissed, and she did, taking in his naked torso, the dark line of hair that ran from his navel and downwards, his hard cock, his thrusting hips. "You want this?"

In response, she lifted her butt off the sofa in invitation.

"Do you?" he repeated, his voice tight.

"I do," she said, "yes, I do, I do." Her fingers churned, her hips jerked, and she was so close, so very, very close.

"Turn around," he said, and she almost fell off the sofa in her haste, kneeling on the floor with her ass bared to him. He kneeled behind her, warm thighs pressing against hers. He sat back and pulled her on top of him. One swift move and he was so deep inside of her she could feel his balls pressing against her.

"Move," he said, hands on her hips as he lifted her up and down, up and down. Like a piston, she reflected fuzzily, moving in time with his hands, feeling his mouth on her nape. Oh, God!

He shifted, taking her with him. She was suddenly tilted forward, her cheek on the carpet, her ass lifted upwards.

"Helle," he grunted, and he came and went, deep thrusts that made her sink her fingers into the plush carpet. Her insides tightened. His fingers found her clit, circling, pressing, and her legs began to shake. The buttons on his jeans scraped against the back of her thighs, but she didn't care, all she could concentrate on were his fingers and his cock, in and out, in and out, filling her, stretching her, possessing her.

He came with a hoarse shout. She followed, calling his name. A strong arm holding her safe, hot breath tickling her ear. With a little grunt, Helle collapsed.

Afterwards, they lay on the carpet, still joined. He braided his fingers with hers, she pressed her ass back towards him, wanting to keep him there, inside of her. His breath slowed, his hold loosened, and with a little chuckle he swept her hair aside and bit her nape, hard enough for her to shiver.

"So, am I enough?" he growled in her ear.

"Totally," she replied, patting him on his thigh, "but you already know that, don't you?"

It took them some time to pull themselves together, which was why it was gone nine before they finally made it to the kitchen. Jason whistled softly under his breath as he chopped up the ingredients for the pasta sauce. Helle sat and drank him in with her eyes. These last few weeks had woken the fear again, the fear that this would end far too soon and that they would never have the time to do the things they hoped for.

Her gut tugged in yearning. She wanted his child. No, her body wanted his child. Her heart wanted it, making her blush at the total mushiness of that sentiment—seriously, 'I want your babies' was an utterly pathetic statement—while her brain insisted there'd be plenty of time later for kids. Blah, blah, blah, went the voice of reason. There was never enough time, remember what happened last time, her gut protested, with her heart thumping in agreement. Helle pressed a hand to her belly, longing for a child with amber-coloured eyes, his eyes. Like the child they'd lost so long ago. She pinched herself. No baby. Not now. Later.

Jason had turned and was watching her intently. "What are you thinking?"

"That I want it all. But that I might not get it." It sounded very blunt. He knew exactly what she meant. His face hardened and his eyes narrowed slightly.

"Of course you will."

"Maybe, maybe not." She fiddled with the cutlery, not wanting him to see how scared she was. They'd been lucky back in May. If Woolf had survived…she exhaled. Jason put his hand under her chin, lifting her face to his. His eyes were only inches from hers.

"We'll handle it, Helle. Whatever Woolf throws at us, we'll handle it."

She quickly put her hand on the wooden table. Knock on wood. One shouldn't challenge fate, even if one didn't believe in it. But she smiled at him, trying to lighten her mood, and nodded.

"Of course we will. Wonder Woman and Boy Wonder. Impossible to beat."

"Man Wonder," he growled, making her laugh.

Much later, Jason was watching Helle sleep. She'd fallen asleep with her head pillowed on his chest, his thumb in a firm grip, but now she was on her side, facing him. Her lips were slightly parted, a tumble of blonde hair obscuring part of her face. Jason moved closer, listening to her breathing. Closer still, and he placed his lips on hers.

"Jason?" she mumbled, stirring slightly. One eye opened, her mouth softened into a smile, and she groped for his hand, sighing when she found his thumb.

Jason used his free hand to brush her hair off her face. His fingers lingered on the contour of her face, traced the elegance of her ear. Almost a year since he'd found her again, a year of miraculous moments such as these when she was lying beside him. His Helle... Jason ran a finger down her bare arm. For so many years, she'd been nothing but an impossible dream, a fading image he had no choice but to try and find again. Truth be told, there'd been times when he no longer wanted to try, exhausted by endless lives, by repeated disappointments. But the love for her burned too strong, and so he'd died, been reborn, searched and searched for her, died...

He nuzzled her, inhaling her scent, and she squirmed and frowned, too deeply asleep to rouse. She smelled of sun, of rose petals littering the ground, of lime and lavender. Her skin was soft beneath his cheek, and when she rolled over on her back he followed, carefully resting his head on her breast, just above her heart. Helle muttered something, her arms came round him, and he relaxed against her, listening to the reassuring thudding of her pulse.

A year ago, he had almost given up on her. Then he'd found her, and all those futile miserable lives were vindicated by her smile, by the way her turquoise eyes glittered when she saw him. Now here they were, married and happy. Jason pressed his ear closer to her chest. Happy for now, he amended, because if Sam Woolf was back...Shit!

Once he'd allowed Woolf entry, there was no banishing him from his head. Jason extricated himself from Helle's arms and rolled over on his back, pillowing his head on his arms. Moonlight spilled in from the uncovered windows, dancing across the ceiling in a swaying pattern of leaves and light. But what Jason saw was Woolf—Prince Samion of Kolchis as he'd been—his hands streaked with blood, one sandal-shod foot planted firmly on Jason's chest. Moonlight caught on a raised blade. Woolf yelled in triumph and brought it down. Jason sighed and rolled out of bed. He needed a drink.

In that ancient life, Samion had killed Helle, not Jason. It had been Helle's chest he'd sunk his blade into, it had been Helle's blood staining Samion's robes and hands. It had been Helle who died, while Jason was left incapable of any emotions but that of all-consuming anger.

The whisky splashed into the tumbler and Jason retreated to sit on the sofa where so recently he'd made love to Helle. He sipped, a rush of comforting heat travelled down his throat. This time, Woolf had no intention of killing Helle. No, if Sam Woolf was back, it was Jason he'd come after, and should he succeed, Helle would be dragged off to God alone knew what hellish existence.

That, Jason decided, could not be allowed to happen. He snapped his fingers and sparks of fire flew upwards. Again, and several miniature flames burnt merrily before he closed his hand around them, extinguishing them. If he had to, he'd incinerate Woolf. Or die trying.

"Come child," Nefirie held out her hand but Korine stayed where she was, crouched by the riverbed. Her hair had come undone, escaping in long corkscrew curls, and she dug her stick time and time again into the sand. She was staring intently at something in the water.

"Korine!" Nefirie's voice was sharp, and the child started, looking up at her in surprise. Then she looked back at the water and smiled.

"Helle," she said, before skipping over to take Nefirie's hand.

Chapter 7

"It's as if summer has hopped forward," Helle said, stretching in bed. First last weekend in Tor Cottage, then a whole sunny week and now today, yet another warm September day. "June was cold and wet, so now we get a glorious September instead."

"Mmm?" Jason didn't seem too interested in the weather.

"Fiend," she muttered with little heat when he pulled her close.

"Complaints?" he asked.

Helle rolled them over so that she was on top. "Nope." She caressed his face, the dark red stubble that adorned his cheeks. His eyes, his mouth, those beautiful dark brows—she traced them all with a light finger.

"You have the longest eyelashes I've ever seen," she said, and obligingly he batted them at her, making her smile. Dark and thick, they fringed eyes that at present were a golden colour, the pupil expanded with desire. She could feel him, hard and throbbing against her belly. Helle kissed him, bit down ever so gently on his lower lip, and slid downwards.

She liked doing this to him. With previous lovers, it had been something she did to seduce and please, but with Jason there was a thrill of her own, a pooling of heat in her sex that left her short of breath. She stuck her nose in his groin and inhaled, drawing in the salty scent that was uniquely his. When she exhaled, his pelvis shifted, even more so when she cupped his sac, giving it a little squeeze.

Jason's thighs widened. She ran a finger along the seam that led all the way from his balls to his anus, and his buttocks clenched when she rimmed the puckered entrance. She kissed his balls, fingers dancing over the smooth skin of his penis. She nibbled her way up his erection, feeling it throb and twitch in response. Her insides tightened when he gasped her name, and she met his eyes before taking him in her mouth.

"Aahh!" His hips shifted, she sucked harder, one hand round his cock, the other exploring further beyond his balls. He quivered when she put a finger to his anus and pushed. He groaned her name when her finger slid inside, trapped in a hot softness that closed round her digit. Finger, mouth. Mouth, tongue—even teeth, and Jason's thighs went rock-hard below her.

She just had to look at him; eyes closed, head thrown back in abandon, his muscles taut with tension. He jerked in her mouth, a hand came down to rest on her head, holding her to him, asking her for more. More. She could do more. She wiggled her finger deeper, and his ass lifted off the bed, a guttural sound escaping him.

The sheets rustled, his legs twisted, and she tasted him now, a drop no more of saltiness she carefully licked off his glans. She released him, had to take a couple of deep breaths before going back to what she was doing. He uttered a sibilant 'yes' when her mouth yet again closed round his pulsing penis. Moments later, her mouth was flooded with several bursts of semen she swallowed down. She'd never swallowed anyone else's cum. She'd never wanted to.

"Good?" she asked, reclaiming her finger. In response, he gave her a slow smile, eyes narrowed to golden shards. Helle rolled out of bed and made for the bathroom, returning a few minutes later. He was still sprawled in bed, a collection of tanned limbs draped in white Egyptian cotton sheets.

The bedroom in their Kensington home was huge, a former attic Jason had converted into a tasteful combination of dark hardwood floors, exposed beams and white walls. Other than the large bed and the closets, the room was dominated by a modern bathtub, deep enough and wide enough to comfortably seat two. It stood in front of the window that gave onto the little garden, surrounded by candlesticks of various heights and thickness.

"Come here," he said, holding out his hand.

"Later." She patted him on the leg and made for her chest of drawers.

"But you didn't come," he protested.

"So?" She turned to smile at him. "I enjoyed myself anyway. It doesn't always have to be quid pro quo, does it?"

"I like it when you come for me." Gracefully, he leaped off the bed and enfolded her in a hug. "Thank you."

"My pleasure." She stood on her toes to kiss his nose. "And now I'm running late—I'm supposed to meet Miranda at eleven." She couldn't help it; her nose wrinkled of its own accord. Nigel and Jason were off to do their padel tennis thing again, and somehow it had been decided Helle was to meet up with Miranda.

"If you don't want to see her, just tell her so," Jason said.

"She's pretty persistent. Besides, Nigel lights up whenever he sees me with her." And it wasn't as if it was unbearable to spend time with Miranda—rather the reverse in fact, even if the petite tattoo artist could be very weird, starting with her penchant for always dressing in white.

"Hmm." Jason slid her a look. "She hasn't tried to do any more readings, has she?"

"Nope." The moment she did, Helle would be off like a shot.

"Good." Jason rummaged about for a pair of clean boxers. "Scrambled eggs for breakfast?"

"Sounds good. Do we have any smoked salmon?"

"I think we do." He ruffled her hair as he passed. "Curtis will be by any moment."

"It's not me walking about in my underwear," she said, adjusting her shirt.

"Me neither." He hopped into his jeans, winked, and disappeared down the stairs.

"Oh, come on!" Miranda tugged at Helle's arm. "It's not that far away."

"But why would I want to go there?" She threw an apologetic look at Tim, patiently trailing them.

"I just want to show you where I work." Miranda made a face at Tim. "Your babysitter can come too."

"One tattoo parlour must look pretty much like any other tattoo parlour," Helle teased, deciding to ignore the snide comment about Tim.

"Which just goes to show you've not seen mine. I cater to the discerning clients."

"Discerning?" Helle laughed. "Is anyone getting a tattoo discerning?"

"You'd be surprised," Miranda said, sounding miffed. "Members of royalty like ink too, you know."

"They do?" Despite herself, Helle was curious. Did Prince William sport a heart with a big C in it?

"Discretion, Helle," Miranda said. "Comes with the high-end establishment."

"Ah."

Because it was a nice warm day, they walked through Kensington Gardens, evading tourists, dog-walkers and an innumerable progression of parents with prams—or maybe that was her subconscious speaking, because when she commented to Miranda about the surprising high incidence of babies, her friend looked bemused.

"No more than normal," Miranda said, after having studied the people nearest to them. Her dark eyes glittered. "Feeling the biological urge to procreate, are we?"

You have no idea, Helle thought. But out loud she laughed and shook her head, telling Miranda not to be an idiot.

"Hmm," was all Miranda said. She placed a hand on Helle's arm. "You'll have kids," she said lightly, before moving away.

"Most of us do," Helle replied, folding her arms over her chest to avoid any further contact.

"Yes, but in your case I can see them." Miranda smiled. "Red-haired, like their father."

"Sure," Helle scoffed, trying to ignore the rush of hope and joy that flew through her. Miranda didn't know, she reminded herself: this was all theatrical, her pandering to Helle's obvious yearning.

"I can." Miranda's chin rose. "As I've said before, I have gifts." Her expression softened. "I understand if it freaks you out, but there's nothing I can do about it. Ever since I was a kid, I've been able to see things—just like my grandmother could."

"A genetic handicap?" Helle said.

"Putting it mildly. Every time I touch someone, I see glimpses of their future. Imagine what that does to your sexlife."

They walked in silence for a while. "Seriously, you sleep with someone and you see their future?" Helle asked.

"Not all the time. After all, there are moments when I'm pleasurably distracted."

"And with Nigel?"

Miranda's face wreathed into a huge smile. "He doesn't channel anything."

"What, he doesn't have a future?"

"Of course, he does. But in his case, I can't see it." She sucked in her lip. "My grandma always said that was the sign of your true mate—they won't burden you with visions."

"Ah." Helle glanced at Miranda, all black hair and white clothes. Nigel, on the other hand, was mostly black clothes and rainbow coloured hair. His latest dyeing efforts had left Jason laughing so hard Nigel had finally kicked him—that's what you got when you went for purple and ended up with a bright green fuzz. "And you think Nigel is this true mate of yours?"

"I know," Miranda replied with a grimace. "We don't really match, do we?"

"Not on the outside, no." Leaving aside their clothes preferences, Miranda was an astoundingly attractive woman while Nigel...well, Nigel was Nigel. Helle tilted her head. "But maybe you have more in common on the inside."

Miranda laughed, a dark rich sound that made Helle think of rumpled beds and odalisques.

"You bet we do."

They arrived at the shop, tucked into a small alley just off Praed Street. "Not exactly on the beaten path, is it?" Helle commented, studying the drowsy former mews. An elegant sign in red and black proclaimed this to be *Miranda's World*.

"Word of mouth." Miranda unlocked a sober grey door and shoved it open.

"I'll go first, Mrs Morris," Tim said, moving Miranda aside.

"Sorry," Helle muttered, but Miranda waved Tim on with a little smile. A minute or two later, Tim was back at the door, gesturing that it was safe to go in.

The room they entered was a gallery, every wall crammed with printed versions of Miranda's motifs. In red, green or black ink, dragons and serpents, stylised flowers and prowling cats clambered the walls, the heavy texture of the paper they'd been printed on highlighted by the narrow frames and the deep red walls.

To one side of the room stood a couple of armchairs, on the opposite side one of those reclining seats high-end salons used. Inks were neatly lined up on a shelf nearby, an ancient Chinese cupboard standing half-open to reveal various other implements.

"Nice," Helle said.

"Thank you." Miranda sounded pleased. She beckoned for Helle to follow her towards the back of the room and a massive wooden door. It creaked when Miranda shoved it open, standing aside to allow Tim to check it our before gesturing for Helle to enter first.

Same blood-red walls as in the front room, but here the window was covered in matching curtains, and everywhere were cushions and tasselled throws. Four armchairs clustered round a massive wooden table, its feet carved to resemble lions' paws. A thick Persian carpet dulled the sound of their feet and there were lanterns everywhere, ancient, most of them, the brass permanently stained by generations of sooty candles. On the shelf running the full length of the room stood a number of books, thick tomes with titles such as *The Mysteries of the Tarot*. At one end was one of those glass dome arrangements the Victorians had been so fond of, this one with a stuffed squirrel as its centrepiece.

"Wow," Helle said. "Like stepping back in time."

"It is, isn't it?" Miranda went over to the tall wardrobe and opened it to reveal a full-length dress. In creamy white, with a high collar, long sleeves and multiple pleats and ruffles, it looked like some old-fashioned wedding dress.

"Vintage," Miranda said. "The real thing. It used to belong to my great-great something." She closed the wardrobe. "I aspire to create an atmosphere conducive to spiritual matters."

"Like a séance?" Helle spied a deck of Tarot cards on the table. "They were very much in the vogue in the nineteenth century, weren't they?"

"They were. People didn't dismiss the occult back then." Miranda disappeared behind a curtain, there was the sound of water running, and presently she came back, this time with two teacups in her hands. "I thought we could have some tea here," she said breezily.

Helle gave her a wary look. "Here? Why?"

"Why not?" Miranda smiled. "Nothing to be afraid of here."

"I'm not afraid." Helle sat down in one of the high-backed chairs. "But neither do I intend to let you do any of your readings."

"I know." Miranda tilted her head. "I don't need to read you to sense there is something very different about you—just like with Jason."

"I don't want to talk about it," Helle bit out.

Miranda held up her hands and busied herself in the little pantry before returning with a heavy silver teapot.

"This Woolf character, is he an old soul too?" she asked, eyes on the tea she was pouring.

"I said—"

"You didn't want to talk about it. And yet you're tiptoeing about, constantly scanning your surroundings. You're scared—badly scared—and in my experience it sometimes helps to talk." Miranda offered Helle sugar and milk before helping herself. "Maybe I can help."

She'd be about as effective as a pug confronting a Rottweiler. This miniature woman was no match for Woolf or any of his goons.

"You'd be surprised," Miranda said, sitting back in her chair with her cup. "Men generally commit the mistake of underestimating me." She grinned. "And no, I wasn't reading your mind, I was reading your facial expression." She stirred her tea and waited.

"Why do you want to know?"

"Well, I'd be lying if I didn't admit to a huge dose of curiosity. When I took Jason's hand, back at Chalice Well…" Miranda shuddered. "Like a kaleidoscope of images, all of them with him, none of them with you, and I could sense such pain, such grief." Her dark eyes met Helle's. "He's lived through endless lives, hasn't he? Existences devoted to finding you, and now that he has…" She frowned. "I sense darkness and more pain."

Helle blanched, the teacup slipping through her fingers to land with a clatter on the saucer.

Miranda shook herself and threw her a concerned look. "I'm sorry, I didn't mean to scare you."

Helle cleared her throat. "What you see, does it always come true?" And what kind of question was that, seeing as she didn't really believe in all this occult nonsense.

"Not always." Miranda leaned forward and took Helle's hand. "And I didn't say I saw permanent darkness, did I?" Her fingers gripped Helle's wrist. "Whoever this Woolf guy really is, he's strong—damned strong."

"Shit." Helle snatched her hand back. "You said is."

"Eh?"

"You said whoever this Woolf guy *is*, not *was*." Helle inhaled, did it again, forcing air into uncooperative lungs.

"But that's not news to you, is it?" Miranda said. "You've been aware of his presence for several weeks."

The dreams, the odd sensation of hearing his voice, the way her skin prickled all of a sudden…Helle nodded, no more.

"So who is he?" Miranda asked. Helle looked away, gnawing at her lip.

"Originally, his name was Samion," she began, before coming to a stop. Was she really going to tell Miranda? No, she couldn't. She sat back, shaking her head.

Miranda studied her with such intensity it made Helle's cheeks burn. "A powerful man," Miranda said softly. "A man unaccustomed to being denied what he wanted." She looked Helle full in the eyes. "And he wanted you." She found a pen and did a little doodle on a crumpled napkin.

"He did. But I didn't want him." She only wanted Jason—she still did, making her pathetically single-minded. An impossible match, back then—she a royal princess, he the son of an itinerant healer. And Samion had insisted: either Helle was given to him as his wife, or he'd eradicate the miniature kingdom she called her home. Not exactly an empty threat, seeing as Samion ruled the neighbouring country of Kolchis. Helle shivered. She stirred her tea, keeping her eyes on the table.

"And then what?" Miranda asked.

"I don't like talking about this," Helle said. "It's too..."

"Unbelievable?" Miranda filled in.

"No." Helle gave her a cool look. "It's too personal."

"Oh." Miranda pursed her lips. "And probably painful as well. I get the feeling things didn't exactly end with a happily ever after."

"Nope." Helle traced a large, loopy J on the tablecloth. Her father had acquiesced to Samion's demands—he really couldn't do otherwise—but when Samion had tried to bed Helle by force, she'd fled, running all the way back home to Jason. Her father had relented, and for some years she'd been blissfully happy, looking forward to a long life with Jason.

Helle fiddled with her rings—Jason's rings, the heavy betrothal ring he'd bought her in Istanbul, the matching platinum wedding band, adorned with diamonds. In that first life, they'd never got to pledging their vows. Things, as they said, happened.

She slid Miranda a look. "He abducted us." On a hot day in that secluded glade they called their own, out of nowhere came Samion and his men. Helle pursed her mouth. How had he known where to find them? She shrugged. Eons ago, who cared?

"Did he kill you?" Miranda didn't look up from her drawing, the pen moving back and forth. Helle frowned, not sure she should share much more than she already had. Miranda chose that moment to lift her gaze from her doodling, two dark eyes brimming with tears. "He did, din't he?"

"Not then. He probably wanted to kill Jason, but he didn't." No, because Jason came with his own protection. To kill a

Wanderer was to risk scourges and pestilence, and in Jason's case he also had Nefirie, his impressive if intimidating mother to support him. Red-haired and golden-eyed, Nefirie had always remained aloof, those piercing eyes of hers regarding Helle with little warmth. But she'd adored her son, and God help whoever hurt him—not for nothing did people bow and scrape in the presence of this, the most powerful Wanderer alive.

"So what happened?" Miranda asked. Nope: not going there. She had no desire to relive these ancient memories, months of humiliation and abject terror. Months in which a very young and frightened Helle tried so hard to be defiant and brave when all she wanted was to beg and grovel. In the end she had begged, she had grovelled, and it had served her for naught, Samion ramming home repeatedly just who was the master and who was the slave in their relationship.

Miranda's fingers slid over Helle's forearm. She sat back. "He abused you," she stated. "Repeatedly."

Helle squirmed. How did she do that? "He did. But he would say we made a deal. He promised not to harm Jason and in return I would be an obedient and willing bedmate." Never willing, but definitely very obedient. Not that it had helped, because Samion had found other ways to crush Jason, visiting him every day to regale him with detailed descriptions of Helle in his bed—a happy, welcoming Helle. It still hurt, that Jason had believed him. He should have known her better, Helle thought, feeling a flash of that old anger.

"Jason was pretty young as well." Miranda said, adding yet another doodle. "Don't be too hard on him. Imagine months in the dark, with only one voice speaking to you, filling your mind with unwelcome images of the person you love."

Helle gave her a surprised look. Miranda made a vague sound.

"I saw his memories. When I held his hand. And it's still an open wound that he failed you back then."

But for that he has paid, Helle thought, living life after life looking only for her. Stunted, incomplete lives that he cut short to be reborn again, always searching for her.

"Go on," Miranda urged, folding the napkin and setting it aside.

"It was eight months in hell." Eight months which ended the night Samion saw her newborn daughter—Jason's child, not his. She closed her eyes, and she could feel the weight of the child in her arms, recall the warm scent of blood and iron. And then the baby was gone, torn out of her embrace by Samion.

Miranda stroked her arm. Helle drank some tea in an attempt to regain some composure. "He destroyed us. I was left without a shred of self-esteem, and Jason hated me for being faithless. He wouldn't even talk to me, he just avoided me." She felt that little flare of anger again. "He should at least have asked."

"He couldn't," Miranda said. "He was convinced that anything you might say would be a lie."

"He only had to use his eyes to see what Samion had done to me." Helle hugged herself. "Anyway, the long and short of it was that he killed me."

Miranda sat back. "Jason?"

Helle looked ashook her head. "Indirectly, maybe. But the man who wielded the blade was Samion." A knife in her chest: Helle had drowned in her own blood. Unfortunately, one of the memories she *did* have from that first life of hers... "My death destroyed Jason. And one day he found Samion and exacted a gruesome revenge."

Mirande nodded, her eyes blank. "Horrible. He died in agony."

"He deserved to."

"He would probably disagree." Miranda stared at the opposite wall for some moments. "In fact, he'd feel entitled to revenge."

"Yeah. Which is why he promised Jason he would come after us—well, me—in one life after another and make me pay."

"A singleminded man," Miranda said softly. Singleminded? Try obsessive.

"Since then we've been tumbling through time; me in headlong flight, Samion in grim pursuit and Jason trying to find me and save me. And he did, this time." Helle traced a pattern on the table. "We actually thought we had Woolf whipped, but now it seems the bastard is back, and I have no idea how to defeat him." She cradled her head in her arms. "So yeah, I'm scared. Shit–scared, actually."

Miranda reached across the table as if to grip her hand. Helle avoided contact by lifting her teacup to her mouth. The discarded napkin fluttered to the floor and Helle bent to pick it up. She froze. A wolf's head leered up at her from the paper, lips pulled into a snarl. "What…"

"It just popped into my head," Miranda said, snatching the napkin out of Helle's hand and scrunching it up. Helle stood, already regretting this whole conversation. What on earth had made her confide in Miranda? She swallowed back a rush of bile. That wolf's head looked just like the emblem on Sam Woolf's ring.

And that was when her phone rang.

Chapter 8

Jason high-fived Nigel and did a little dance on the spot before turning to grin at Curtis.

"Luck," his solicitor said, bracing himself against his knees.

"Luck?" Nigel crowed. "You and Reggie here were so out of your league."

Jason slapped Curtis on the back. "It's the added weight. All that sitting about on your arse has made you go soft and doughy."

"I'll show you soft and doughy," Curtis growled, flexing an impressive biceps. He wiped his face and held out his hand to Reggie. "Next time, mate. Thanks."

"In your dreams." Nigel stroked the rim of his racquet. "Me and this baby are undefeatable."

"It was mostly Jason doing the running," Reggie pointed out. "You just stood there, looking decorative."

Nigel huffed. "Decorative, my arse."

"You're right," Curtis said. "You're too ugly to be decorative."

Jason smiled, listening with half an ear to their continued bantering. Two hours of padel tennis had left him agreeably tired, and what he wanted now was a pint of lager and something to eat.

"Want to do something tonight?" Nigel asked as they were showering.

"Hmm?" Jason could see Nigel only as a vague shape through the frosted glass partition.

"The four of us," Nigel clarified.

"Oh." Jason turned off the water and stretched for his towel. "Don't know—I'll have to ask Helle first."

"Women, hey?" Nigel sounded happy. "They take over our lives, don't they?"

Jason smiled, thinking back to the morning. He could never get enough of her, craved her touch as much now as when they first had met. To wake and find her beside him in bed, to see her all sleepy-eyed and tousled, that hair of hers a glorious mess of curls, to feel her feet caress his shins, her hands travel over his body—a dream come true. At last.

They dawdled over their pints, discussing everything from the future of the EU to the financial implications of a digitalised society. At some point Reggie left, and Curtis was regaling them with a story about one of his more colourful clients when a man walked into the pub. Just like that, Jason's good mood evaporated.

"Shit," Nigel said, "not him."

Curtis swivelled on his seat. "Who?"

"Your Mr Smith." Jason shared a look with Nigel: Smith was something very high up in the shadier areas of law enforcement, at present in charge of the investigation into Woolf's criminal empire. Just because Sam Woolf was presumed dead, this didn't mean his complex trading network involving everything from recreational drugs to trafficking young women was a thing of the past—rather the reverse, from what Jason had understood, even if the gathering of rock-solid evidence remained something of a challenge.

Nigel's skills had been commandeered by Smith, which explained the sour look Nigel directed at Smith. Nigel, according to himself, was a free spirit, and to be shackled to a law enforcement operation—on pain of otherwise facing prosecution for his more daring hacker exploits—was not something Nigel found amusing.

"Morris," Smith said in lieu of greeting before plonking himself down at the table. "Just the man I want to see." As always, he looked dapper, his beard neatly trimmed, his suit as crisp as if it had just come from the cleaners. An enigmatic man, was Mr Smith—and Jason would bet a minor fortune on his real name being something entirely different. Smith crossed his legs, adjusting the crease on his trousers. He'd chosen to do without the tie today, his pale blue shirt sufficiently unbuttoned to reveal a short gold chain round his neck.

"It's Saturday." Jason popped a piece of cheese in his mouth. "Make an appointment."

"That annoying prick Hans von Posse is back." Smith pulled a face. Woolf's German solicitor had somehow twisted the arm of one of Smith's superiors some months ago, obliging Smith to close down the investigation into Woolf's sordier business dealings. Hadn't helped them much, seeing as Smith was as tenacious as a terrier.

"How 'back'?" Von Posse had been conspicuously silent since May.

"Long document in which he denies all charges, insisting his client has never engaged in anything but bona fide business transactions. Plus he demands we give him access to all the material we presently have."

"Well, he would say that, wouldn't he?" Curtis put in.

"Won't help him much," Nigel muttered. "Not with the evidence we have in place." Jason lifted a brow. Not that long ago, they'd had even more, until someone in Smith's team had chosen to erase substantial amounts before scarpering to somewhere in Italy.

"That's not the point," Smith said. "He also goes on to demand bail be set so as to allow his client to return to England without being automatically thrown in jail."

Jason carefully set his glass down, noting with detachment that his hand was shaking—badly. He fisted it, unclenching it immediately due to the surge of heat. Woolf was back. Jason bowed his head, studying the scarred wood of the table, the condensation on the beer glasses, the stalks of celery still on Curtis' plate. Dearest God, he was back!

"Woolf is dead," Curtis said.

"Is he?" Smith shook his head. "If so, why this posturing?" He shifted his shoulders. "Although I must admit it's all very strange. No one has seen hide nor hair of him in what? Four months?"

"Do we know he isn't dead?" Nigel asked.

"Do we know he is dead?" Smith replied, making Jason smile mirthlessly. No proof, and now this…His fingers were tingling with heat, and he placed them palms up against the underside of the table in an effort to control the fires that seemed about to burst forth. There was a faint smell of burning wood, and Jason snatched his hands back.

"He must be." Curtis said. "The man fell off a cliff in May, and since then, nothing."

"Yes," Smith agreed, stroking his neat beard. "Except for that boat in Honfleur."

"Damn!" Curtis shoved his unfinished pint aside. "So what happens now?"

"I have no idea," Smith said. "First of all, we don't know, do we? If Woolf is still alive, that is. This might be the solicitor playing us, an attempt at buying time. Anyway, I've told him to sod off, I will not recommend bail be set."

"Assuming Woolf is alive, will the case hold?" Nigel asked. Curtis and Smith shared a look.

"It would put him away for some years," Curtis said. "But unless we can pin actual murders on him, he'd be out in ten— at most."

"Great." Jason stood. "Helle," he said, pulling out his phone. No, he couldn't call her and tell her this.

"She's with Miranda," Nigel told him. "And Tim."

"I…" Jason made for the door. He had to go to Helle. Now.

Jason hurried into the dim interior of the parking garage, with Nigel trotting at his side, while Curtis and Smith were several feet behind. The garage was half-full at most, their footsteps echoing in its dark space.

"If he were alive, we would have found some trace by now," Nigel said, sounding breathless. "I've scanned CCTV, looked through hospital records, trawled police reports both sides of the Channel—nothing."

"So why the demand for bail?"

"No idea. Smith may be right, the solicitor could be playing for time. After all, if this goes to trial our German friend is one of the accused. Besides, insinuating Woolf is still alive is a good intimidation tactic."

That made some sort of sense. Jason's shoulders dropped a fraction.

"I'll redo all that once I get home," Nigel added. "And this time, I'll include the CCTV footage for the last three months."

"You can't go through all that on your own!"

Nigel rolled his eyes. "Face recognition software, you moron. Somewhat enhanced by yours truly."

"Ah. And if he disguises himself?"

"He's big. He sticks out anyway. I review anyone over six foot two." Nigel sounded confident. Jason squeezed his shoulder.

"Thanks."

"Anytime, Jason." Nigel ducked his head, causing his collection of necklaces to jangle.

There was a scuffling sound from somewhere to their right. Jason wheeled, peering into the shadows.

Nothing.

Smith and Curtis caught up. "What?" Curtis said.

"Nothing." Jason shrugged.

"Afraid of things that go bump in the dark, Morris?" Smith said. "I wouldn't have taken you for…" Whatever he'd been intending to say was drowned by the roar of an engine. Headlights blinded them at the same time as four shapes detached themselves from the surrounding dark.

"Run!" Jason shoved Nigel in front of him. Two men jumped him, the others tackled Smith, who went down with a loud "Oomph". Someone punched Jason in the face. There was a yelp when he responded in kind. He blocked another blow, was clapped hard over the ear. His head rang. Another punch, and his lip burst open. Shit! Jason swung wildly, half-blind with pain. An arm round his throat, throttling him, and Jason kicked and punched, desperately trying to break loose. Someone kicked him in the stomach. Once, twice, and he wheezed and slumped.

Blood in his mouth, a burning pain in his belly, and he was being hauled over the uneven floor, towards the waiting car.

"Hey!" Curtis yelled, throwing himself at one of the men. They went down in a flurry of arms and legs. The guy still holding Jason cursed. Still woozy, Jason set his hands to the thighs of the man holding him and turned up the heat. The arsehole shrieked. Careful, he reminded himself, don't let Smith see your fires, because if he does…If he does? Smith was wrestling with two men and was in no position to notice anything much.

The man's hold on his throat tightened, with a hissed promise that he'd make him pay. Jason gargled, kicked out, and when that didn't help, lifted his hands to the man's head. This time, he allowed the fires to escape unchecked. The man howled and let him go, batting frantically at his burning ski-mask.

Jason landed on his back, rolled over, and hauled air in through his aching throat. Curtis yelled for help. Jason staggered to his feet. The car. The engine revved, and here it came, a black SUV making straight for them. Curtis. He had to get Curtis out of the way. Jason tried to run, broke into a shuffle.

"Curtis!" he called, but it came out like a hoarse croak, no more. Run, damn it! His legs stumbled into a jog. Time seemed suspended. His pulse echoed through his head. The car. Out of the corner of his eye, he saw Smith, still locked in a clinch with his attackers. Curtis. Jason threw himself forward in a tackle. They tumbled to the floor, all three of them, Curtis, the goon, and Jason.

From behind them came the sound of something hitting the floor, followed by a sickening crunch and the sound of screeching brakes. Lights flashed. The man with the burnt ski-mask hurried towards the car, half-dragging one of his mates along. The goon Jason had felled attempted to stand but failed, crawling feebly on the ground. On the concrete floor nearby lay something that looked like a heap of clothing, a hand protruding from the bottom.

Curtis tried to get to his feet, screaming at them to stop, in the name of the law to stop. Jason didn't even try, his eyes fixed on what had once been Smith's head. The car accelerated— backwards, over Smith. Wheels squealed, the engine roared, and the car disappeared down the ramp.

Silence.

"Jason?" Curtis' voice bore little resemblance to his normal self-confident booming. "Can you...effing hell!" He turned away and vomited.

Wearily, Jason got to his feet. Where was Nigel? There, shaking like a drenched cat.

"He's dead," Curtis said. "Smith is dead."

Someone groaned: the bloke Jason had tackled, trying to drag himself away. Curtis made as if to go to him, but his eyes were wild, his teeth visible in a snarl.

"Don't." Jason wrenched his friend to a stop. "Just don't."

"I've called 999," Nigel said, coming over to join them. He kept his eyes on anything but the oozing heap that had been Smith. Jason, on the other hand, could not tear his gaze away. The car, the impact...the sounds echoed in his head.

"How?" he asked. Smith had been nowhere close to the car's trajectory.

"He..." Nigel wiped at his face and cleared his throat. "They just threw him in front of the car." He coughed.

"You saved me," Curtis said, gripping Jason's hand. Too hard, and Jason winced. His hands hurt—they always did when his heat spiralled out of control—his face felt numb, his shoulder and right arm hung useless. He used his left hand to inspect his face, swollen and sore all over. The adrenaline rush receded as suddenly as it had come, and Jason slid to the floor, incapable of standing, even less of talking—or thinking.

"Hey," Nigel said, crouching in front of him. "You did good."

Jason nodded and closed his eyes. They'd come to grab him, not kill him. The thought made icicles form in his guts, shards of ice-cold fear that left him trembling all over.

"Why?" Curtis asked. "And who?" He growled a warning when the injured man attempted to rise to his knees, causing the bastard to sag back down.

Nigel gave him an incredulous look. "Who? Well that's obvious, don't you think? Just because Woolf is gone doesn't mean the rest of his organisation is going to roll over and play dead, is it? Plenty of bad apples in that barrel, and they all have a vested interest in closing Smith's investigation down."

"Seems they've managed that," Curtis said with a sigh. "Poor man, to die like that."

At least it was quick, Jason thought.

Nigel pursed his mouth. "They were dragging you towards the car."

"I noticed." Jason managed a crooked smile. "Didn't work out so well for them, did it?"

"No." Nigel straightened up and cocked his head. "Sirens."

"Fantastic." Jason dug for his phone. "I have to call Helle." His hand shook, fingers too numb to scroll through the contacts.

"I'll do it." Nigel lifted the phone out of Jason's hands. He helped Jason stand. "You need to see one of the paramedics. Your face looks as if you've played basketball with it."

"Thanks," Jason mumbled through his rapidly swelling lips.

Helle almost fell through the front door, shadowed by Tim and Miranda.

"He's fine," Nigel said, hurrying to meet her. "Just a couple of bruises, nothing that won't heal."

Helle pushed past him, half-running towards the living room. Beethoven's Third Symphony was on at low volume, Nigel had lit the gas fire in the circular suspended fireplace, and on the large Howard sofa Jason was half-lying, holding an ice-pack to his face. When Helle stormed into the room, he made as if to sit up.

September sun patterned the polished wooden floor with squares of golden light, the door to the garden stood open, and a faint breeze, tinged with the smell of ripe apples, ruffled the ceiling-to-floor curtains. Helle scarcely registered all this. Her entire attention was focused on Jason, his face a collection of purples and blacks, here and there highlighted by a dash of red.

"Who?" was all she said, dropping to her knees beside him. She lifted her fingers to his face, carefully tracing the swollen eye, the burst lip.

"Four blokes," Nigel replied in Jason's stead. "They attacked us in the garage carpark."

"Us?"

"Mostly Smith," Jason said. His gaze darted this way and that, and Helle took hold of his hand and squeezed. He sighed.

"Mostly me," he amended. "And Smith."

"Woolf?"

"Who else?" Jason said bitterly.

"Who?" Nigel's voice was sharp. "How about any of the other lowlifes he used to work with? That sleazeball of a solicitor?"

"Why would he go after Jason?" Helle could understand if they'd gone after Smith, hoping to kill the investigation by eliminating its head. She swallowed a couple of times. Poor Smith—not that she'd ever warmed to the man, but still.

Nigel ignored her question. "Bastards," he said, hugging Miranda to him.

"Shouldn't you go to the hospital?" Helle lifted Jason's shirt, studying the dark bruises on the left side of his torso.

"I'm fine." He took her hand. "Truly." He lowered his voice. "I self-heal quickly." Courtesy of his Wanderer blood, Helle supposed, but all the same those bruises looked damned painful.

"They were dragging Jason with them," Curtis interrupted, limping over to join them. He had a couple of beer bottles in his hand, handed them to Nigel and Jason. "First, that letter from von Posse, then this: it's starting to look likelier and likelier that Woolf is still alive." Jason's hand tightened on Helle's, an uncomfortable wave of warmth scalding her skin.

"Sorry," he whispered when she winced, but he refused to let go. She didn't want him to.

"We don't know that." Nigel glared at Curtis. "There's nothing proving he's alive."

"Or dead." Curtis drank deeply.

"No one can survive four months without leaving some sort of trace. Not in this world," Nigel insisted.

Jason met Helle's eyes and shrugged. If anyone could, it would be Sam Woolf. The damned man could hypnotise whoever he needed to help him, lurking in the shadows while food and clothes were bought, doctors were found. Helle leaned her head on Jason's thigh and closed her eyes. His fingers combed through her hair.

"Lion-tamer!" Nigel barked, and Helle jerked upright. "We don't know." He waved a hand at the sideboard. Three laptops were presently processing a myriad of pictures, a constant streaming of images that resembled a blurry stream of black and white. "If I can't find him—somewhere—he's not around."

"Or you're looking in the wrong place," Miranda said. "Woolf seems to be a resourceful man." Nigel gave her a look that should have reduced her to a puddle of goo. "Wishful thinking never helps," Miranda continued calmly.

"So what do you propose we do?" Helle asked.

"Prepare." Miranda stretched gracefully before bending over and planting her palms on the floor. "What else can you do?"

Jason shared a look with Helle. She made a face: sometimes, Miranda was a pain in the ass.

Korine stood by the sea, the long red curls billowing behind her. Nefirie watched her from a distance as the little girl raised and dropped her arms, time and time again. The sea grew. Waves rose and crashed at her feet, covering her in spray. Korine laughed, a tinkling sound that carried in the wind. She raised her arms and jumped. The wave towered over her head, immobilized by her lifted arms. Nefirie felt her heart stutter in panic. She ran towards the sea. It would be too late.

Korine brought her arms down and Nefirie watched the wave crash down on her, enveloping her in water. Not her too. She could not bear another loss. The sea drew back and Korine still stood, drenched but on her feet. She turned to face Nefirie, her eyes as calm as ever.

"I will never die in water" she said and smiled that rare and dazzling smile. Her little face became pinched. "Helle will." She sighed. "Helle has. But I won't let her drown again."

"Helle?" Nefirie asked, trying to will away the spiders that crawled up her spine at the child's utterance. "Your mother is dead, child."

Korine shook her head. "Not forever, Nana. You know that." She tilted her head to her side. "There will be no peace for her—or him—until he finds her."

Nefirie stared out at the sea. Her son, condemned to live and die, live and die. And all because of her, because of Helle. She clasped her hands together. She had tried. Where Kantor was swayed by words of love, Nefirie had tried to bring things into balance again. She had done what she had to do, it wasn't her fault things had ended up the way they did. Or was it? No. Nefirie shook her head firmly. She had listened to the Mother.

"Nana?" Korine's clear eyes met hers and Nefirie flinched, quickly shielding her thoughts.

"Let's go home." She took Korine by the hand. "You can help me tend the goats."

Chapter 9

There were no repeat incidents. Jason's bruises faded over the coming week, leaving nothing but a slight soreness behind. Nigel spent close to four days searching footage for anything resembling Woolf and came up with nothing. Stapleton did something similar and came up with about as much.

"Assuming he made it to Honfleur, it's a mystery how he made it out of there," Stapleton said over their Skype connection.

"He could have kept to the alleys and skulked," Helle suggested. "He strikes me as a man who is good at skulking."

"But he should have been captured somewhere." Stapleton rifled through the papers on his desk. "Not that I want to know just how Hawkins has been able to download the images stored on various surveillance cameras, but he's done a thorough job, and nowhere is there as much as a glimpse of a man who could be Woolf."

"So he stole another boat," Jason said. "Took off somewhere else."

"And whoever he stole it from didn't report it?" Stapleton scoffed.

"Maybe he borrowed it." Helle massaged her temples. Over the last few days, she'd been afflicted by headaches, each one more severe than the last, and as to her nights... She shivered. Her most recent dreams had been so detailed, so disturbing, she delayed going to bed as long as possible. If Jason noticed, he didn't say, but she'd caught him looking at her with a furrow between his brows, and recently he'd taken to suggesting they work out in the evenings, long hard sessions that left her physically dead while her mind remained as wired as ever.

The moment she closed her eyes, she saw Sam Woolf. And every time she did, she knew he was still around.

Stapleton scribbled something on his papers and promised to come back with any news. He made as if to close down the connection, but Helle stopped him.

"John? You have to be careful, okay? I'd hate it if you ended up like Smith—I like you too much."

Even through the screen, she could see the deep blush that crawled up Stapleton's face, obliterating his freckles. He smiled, clearly pleased, and promised he'd take care. Helle closed the Skype window, turned to look at Jason and was met by a humongous scowl.

"What?" she said.

"Nothing." He rose abruptly and made for the ancient Chinese cabinet that housed his bottles of whisky. He sloshed a generous measure into a tumbler, a somewhat smaller quantity in another, and handed her the latter. "You don't have to be so friendly with him."

Helle suppressed a little smile. "He is a friend."

"He's a policeman. And he's not exactly my friend, is he?" He downed his whisky. "Bed?"

"Already?" It was only around ten or so.

Jason smiled. "There are things one can do in bed other than sleep, Mrs Morris."

"There are?" She batted her lashes at him. "I had no idea."

That made him smile, his hands on his desk as he leaned forward to touch his lips to hers. "Such a little innocent," he murmured against her lips. "What am I to do with you?"

"Take me to bed and teach me." She slipped her arms round his neck and deepened the kiss.

"What an excellent idea."

It was after midnight. Jason was fast asleep, his naked body a comforting warmth behind her. She pressed her butt against him, he grunted but accommodated her, his larger body spooning itself around her. She felt safe like that, enveloped by him. Safe enough to allow herself to drift off into sleep.

The dream sneaked in. Sometimes, if she wasn't too deeply asleep, she could wake herself in time, but this time it slithered its way into her head, taking advantage of the fact that after several wakeful nights she was too tired to fight it.

It started pleasantly enough. A scent of citrus tickling her nostrils, cool tiles under her bare feet. A room lit by flickering lanterns, a bed heaped with pillows and rumpled sheets. No glass in the window, an oblong square open to a night alive with the sound of cicadas, the distant sky decorated by a sickle moon. In her sleep, Helle frowned and turned on her back.

A man entered the room. Or maybe he'd been there all along, she didn't know. But her insides knotted at the sound of his voice, even more when his hand tightened on her heavy braid, pulling her close. She recognised those coal black eyes. Her throat closed. A snapped command and she disrobed herself. Another, and she was on her back, the braid undone to spill her hair over the pillows.

The man's hands, his mouth; she lifted her hips towards him. Heat collected in her loins, her blood ignited by his touch, and just as she was about to fall apart there was a sharp burst of pain, causing her to twist and whimper. On her knees, and there was more pain, so much pain. She tried to crawl away. His fingers touched and teased, and she quivered and moaned, pleasured by one hand while punished by the other.

In her sleep, Helle parted her legs. Her hips rocked back and forth, she was no longer quite as deeply asleep, was all too aware that it was Woolf she was dreaming about, Woolf who knotted his hand in her hair and reined her back as he took her from behind. Woolf's laughter, Woolf's voice, Woolf's hard, hard hands, and any moment now she would come, despite the pain, despite it being Woolf, not Jason.

Helle woke with a yelp, shoving Jason aside.

"What?" he asked, returning his hand to her pubic mound, his thumb brushing over her skin.

"A dream." She couldn't quite look at him, was glad of the dark that hid her face. Shit!

"A dream about me?" He nuzzled her.

"A nightmare."

His hand stilled. "A nightmare?" He stretched, and the bedside light came on. "You were moaning in your sleep, touching yourself. What sort of nightmare does that to you?" There was an edge to his voice that made her want to roll over and press her face into the pillows, but his hand on her shoulder arrested her, forcing her to meet his eyes. "Answer me."

Helle shook her head, overwhelmed by shame and disgust.

His voice dropped to Arctic temperatures. "You were dreaming about him." Not a question, but a statement. "Fuck, Helle, you're having erotic dreams of Samion in our bed?"

"You think I want to?" She flew out of bed. "You think I want these dreams?" She was shaking all over. In her dreams, he hurt her—repeatedly. In her dreams, he still made her come. And now Jason was looking at her as if this was her fault. Her fault? Goddamn him!

She stumbled down the stairs, still stark naked. Jason called her name, and before she reached the basement kitchen, she heard him coming after her. Helle filled the kettle. A cup of tea would help—Mum's mantra, even if Helle had never seen it work, least of all on Mum.

The lights came on. Helle squished her eyes shut against the surprising glare. There was enough ambient light in the kitchen as it was, what with the windows facing the light well just below the street lamp.

"It's not the first time, it is?" Jason asked, coming to stand opposite her, arms folded.

"No." She rubbed at her face. "But they're becoming more explicit."

"And whatever he is doing you're clearly enjoying it."

"Fuck you!" She threw the tea-mug at him, he ducked, and there was a shattering sound as the blue and white china exploded into fragments.

"Hey!" Jason scowled. "That was my mother's favourite mug."

"Seeing as she's dead, she won't be needing it, will she?" Helle crossed her arms in imitation of Jason's pose and glowered at him.

How long they stood like that, she didn't know. And then the phone rang. They both jumped, staring at the red phone on the wall. Jason took four strides across the floor to pick up, cursing when he trod on one of the fragments.

"Yes?" he barked, balancing on one foot while pulling out the shard from the underside of the other. His features tightened. "What, now?" A shadow flitted over his face. "Yes, yes, of course. I'll be there in two hours."

"What was that?" Helle asked once he'd hung up only to stare vacantly into space.

"Everett," he said, "he's dying." He dragged his hands through his hair, and the gesture pushed back the thick mass of mahogany coloured hair sufficiently for Helle to see the diamond ear-stud he always wore—a gift from dear Juliet, no less. Just the thought of Juliet had Helle drowning in a complex cocktail of jealousy and guilt: jealousy because Juliet had been Jason's lover in repeated lives, guilt because she was glad Juliet was dead.

"He's dying now?" Helle tore her attention away from Juliet. She loved Everett, Jason's great-uncle. For the last six months or so, he'd been hovering in Death's waiting room, surprisingly reconciled to the notion of dying as long as his partner George was around to keep him company.

"They give him six hours at the most." Jason made for the door. "Coming?"

Fifteen minutes later, they were making for the M25. At three in the morning traffic was not much of an issue, and they made good time towards Warwickshire. The silence in the car was oppressive, so Helle kept her eyes on the dark outside.

Finally, Jason exhaled. "Look, Helle—"

She held up her hand. "Just shut up, okay? But for the record I've never asked for these dreams. I don't want them and they scare the shit out of me."

More silence, this time for so long Helle nodded off to sleep.

"How long have you had them?" Jason's voice made her open her eyes.

"Dreams of Sam? Or erotic dreams of Sam?"

In response, Jason scowled. "Answer my question."

"For a couple of weeks." More or less since that evening in Tor Cottage when Miranda had gone all gypsy seer on them.

"And you haven't told me?"

"About the dreams where he drowns me? Hurts me? The ones where I see him chasing me? The ones where he whips me and fucks me? No. I've been trying to ignore them."

Jason's hands tightened on the wheel. "Shit."

"Yeah." Helle looked out of the window. "He's back, isn't he?"

"Well, he isn't sending you dreams from the other side of the grave. Not even he can do that."

"So you think it's him sending them?" For some odd reason that made her relieved: far better to have someone plant these strange dreams in her head than have her subconscious invent them.

Jason nodded, his jaws clenched.

"How?" She twisted in her seat to look at him.

"No idea." Jason sounded tired. "Like a bloody cockroach," he muttered. "Indestructible."

Everett was a shadow of his former self, reduced to a caricature of a face from which his large nose protruded like a miniature craggy mountain. But when he saw them, he smiled, extending a sticklike arm in their direction.

Jason allowed Helle to greet him first, taking the time to shake George's hand while composing his features. He had no experience of dying of old age—his deaths had been self-induced at a far earlier age—and from what he'd seen of Everett's slow march towards death, it wasn't an experience to look forward to.

His gaze drifted over to Helle, leaning over Everett's bed to kiss the old man on the cheek. He had reacted badly to her dream, to waking to her soft moans, her flushed skin, only to realise she was masturbating to a dream starring that accursed Samion. He clenched his hands. She was his, damn it, and any sexual fantasies she had should be focused on him!

"You all right?" George asked in a hushed voice, making Jason start.

"Not really."

George clasped his arm. "He doesn't fear it. All we have to do is help him over the great divide."

Jason gave him a slight smile, no more. It wasn't Everett's impending death that had his insides in a twist, it was the hurt look in his wife's face, the way she'd stayed well out of reach on their short walk from the car park, ignoring his offered hand.

He approached the bed, coming to stand beside Helle. Immediately, she retreated to the other side of the bed. He tried to catch her eyes, but she pretended to concentrate on Everett. Shit. Jason bent over to kiss Everett on the forehead.

"Jason," the old man said, his face wrinkling into a smile. "I'm so glad you came."

"Of course I came." He took Everett's hand. The closest thing he had to a grandfather, was Everett, and besides, he owed him his life—or so Helle insisted, even if Jason himself had no memory of Everett dislodging the buried bone fragment from his brain that threatened to leave him a permanent vegetable a few months before when Woolf had shot him. A Wanderer, just like Jason was—or more correctly, like Jason's formidable first mother had been—Everett was yet another ancient soul who retained amazing healing gifts. At present, he didn't look at all formidable: he was just a shrunken old man breathing his last.

"So," Everett said, turning his head to look at Helle. "How is everything?"

Jason tried to signal to Helle they should not burden him with their concerns, but she pointedly ignored him.

"Sort of bad," she said, and then it all spilled out, a garbled summary of how one thing after the other pointed to Sam Woolf not being dead but very much alive.

Everett lifted a shaking hand and placed it on Helle's head. "He is no more dangerous now than he was before."

"Not much of a comfort," Jason put in.

"No," Everett swivelled his head in Jason's direction, slowly. The movement reminded Jason of a giant tortoise, the resemblance further underlined by the wrinkled skin that hung off Everett's scrawny throat. His free hand groped for Jason's, found it and squeezed down—hard. "But you've bested him before." Ha! This frail old man was not entirely without powers: a surge of energy travelled up Jason's arm and settled like a warm glow in the pit of his stomach.

"We have." Jason smiled at his great-uncle. "We will again."

"Good." Everett released Jason's hand and closed his eyes. "A child would help."

"What?" Jason's gaze flew to Helle.

"You heard me." Everett inhaled noisily.

"A baby?" Helle leaned forward, eyes alight, and Jason could hear the yearning in her voice.

"Not now," he said. "How can we risk bringing a child into the world before…" His voice trailed off.

Everett's eyes opened. "A child comes with its own protection. In your case, chances are it will be a gifted babe."

"How 'its own protection'?" Helle asked.

Everett sighed. "An innocent child is a powerful shield against evil—all untarnished souls are."

"Sam Woolf would crush any child of mine without a second's hesitation," Jason said bitterly.

"He would try," Everett agreed. "But he might not succeed." His mouth drooped. "Tired," he mumbled. "George?"

Jason stepped aside to allow George to perch on Everett's bed. He gestured for Helle to leave the two old men alone, and placing a hand at her back, guided her out of the room. There was a promising smell of coffee coming from somewhere to his right, and Jason led the way towards it.

Once they were settled in a corner of the small coffee-shop, he took her hand. She let him.

"I'm sorry," he said. "I was out of line before. It's just that it kills me, that he…"

"I know." She put a finger to his lips. "But in the future, please remember it kills me too."

He nodded, studying the muffin on his plate. "How often do you have these dreams?"

"Dreams of Sam? Almost every night. Dreams like that? Very rarely." She gave him a tired look. "Sometimes, I try not to sleep."

"Why didn't you tell me?"

"I don't know." She bit her lower lip and studied her milky coffee. "Maybe because I feel soiled somehow. There must be something wrong with me, to dream of a man hurting me, and wake up aroused."

He sat back. She'd pulled her hair into a messy ponytail, but small curls had escaped at her hairline.

"Look at me," he said softly. She shook her head. "Helle, look at me." She squirmed, but finally raised her head to meet his eyes. "It has nothing to do with you, this is just him playing with your mind." He took her hand. "And later, I'll show you just who your man is—and what he wants from you." His fingers closed round her wrist. "Mine," he said possessively, allowing a burst of heat to escape his fingers. She flinched, but made no effort to retrieve her hand.

"Yours," she replied, lips softening into a little smile. "Forever."

The day dragged on. Everett fell into periods of deep sleep, rallied for some minutes, drifted off again. George refused to leave the room and had appropriated the chair closest to the bed, his pudgy fingers firmly braided with Everett's. Helle and Jason hovered on the other side, taking turns to hold Everett's other hand. Now and then, the nurse popped by, but mostly they were left alone.

Just outside the window was a maple tree, its foliage an explosion of autumnal colours. Whenever Everett woke, his gaze fastened on the maple, drifted over to rest on George, before passing to Jason and Helle. He didn't speak—his eyes did that for him, and George wept openly but silently.

The autumn day was slipping into evening when Everett woke for one last time. This time, he looked first at Jason, an agitated expression on his face.

"Nefirie," he said. "She's…"

And just like that Everett died, taking whatever he intended to say with him to the other side.

Jason leaned forward and closed Everett's eyes. "Go in peace," he said in the language of his first life. "May the great Mother receive you and hold you, may your journey onwards be safe." He pointed at the window. "Open it," he said to Helle. "His soul must be allowed free passage."

She raised her brows but did as he asked.

George produced a bottle of whisky and poured them each a measure in a small paper cup.

"To Everett," he said in a hoarse voice. "With him goes my heart."

Helle edged over and slipped her hand into Jason's. "What was that about Nefirie?"

"I have no idea." Jason gave her a perplexed look. "Maybe he saw her, in the hinterland between the dead and the living."

"Why did my father die?" Korine stood so close Nefirie almost jumped. The child kept her large eyes on her.

"He died because he had to." He died because he could no longer stand the pain of living.

Korine nodded, as if this only confirmed what she already knew. She chewed her cheek and frowned in concentration.

"He went after her," Korine stated.

"Yes." Her son chasing after his one love, in penance and guilt. Nefirie's hands tightened on the pestle. If only she had never brought him to Kantor's court! He might still have been alive if he had never met Helle. She pounded the dried mint into powder. Fate, she thought darkly, and fate was not to be meddled with—as she had learnt so painfully. Her son, gone, but his daughter stood beside her. Nefirie smiled at her grandchild. The child did not smile back.

"It will be very long before they meet." Korine said. "It will not end well, Nana. Not unless you help them."

Nefirie stroked the copper head. She already knew. She had seen it as her son lay dying. Those endless years, those stunted lives, and all would end so badly unless she found it in her to help them. Nefirie's guts twisted. Dearest Mother, give her strength.

Chapter 10

Jason threw the hotel key onto the small coffee table, before taking Helle by the hand and pulling her into his arms. He buried his nose in her hair, inhaled her scent and just stood like that. Although he'd spent it doing absolutely nothing, this had been an exhausting day, and only now could he relax sufficiently to acknowledge the dull weight in his chest: Everett was gone. Jason had no family left beyond his wife.

Helle's arms lay tight around his waist, her cheek pressing against his shirt. She turned her face slightly, and he felt the soft pressure of her lips against his bare skin just below the open collar.

"It was a good death."

Jason made a vague sound. A good death? He supposed so—as deaths went this had been undramatic. But dying was always painful, the soul tearing at the edges as it was expelled from its bodily home, and he couldn't resist throwing a look out of the window, hoping for a view of star-streaked skies but getting the bland façade of the building opposite instead.

Helle disengaged herself and made for the kettle. Complimentary tea and biscuits seemed to be the norm these days, and right now Jason considered this an excellent idea. They'd bolted some food at a nearby pub, him with a pint, she with a glass of wine, but neither of them had been in a mood to hang around for more.

"I have to check my e-mails," he said, kicking off his shoes. His phone had been buzzing madly ever since he'd turned it back on, and a quick peek in the pub had indicated an overflowing mailbox but nothing that seemed too urgent.

"Me too." Helle dunked teabags into mugs, added boiling water, and carried them over to the bedside table. She toed off her trainers and joined him on the bed.

Ten minutes later, Jason was done. There was nothing that wouldn't keep. A couple of mails forwarded to Steve and Jim respectively, and he set his phone aside, snatched Helle's phone out of her hands, and eased her down on her back. She lifted her hands and fiddled with her hair, shaking it free of the ponytail. Jason twirled a curl round his finger. In the lamplight, her hair shimmered in hues of gold. He ran his fingers through her curls, tightened his hold, and kissed her.

She reciprocated, grabbing enough of his hair to make him wince when she lifted herself off the bed to kiss him hungrily. He pressed her down, cupped his hands around her face to hold her still, and covered her mouth with his. His tongue invaded her mouth, tasting her. His lips moved against hers, setting the pace. She lifted her hands to caress his face. He stroked a finger down her cheek and neck and felt her shiver.

Her hand crept down to his waist, explored its way in under his shirt. When she pinched his nipple, he grunted, moved swiftly, and suddenly she was pinned below him, her arms over her head, both wrists in one of his hands.

"Behave," he said, nuzzling her neck. "You don't, and I'll tie you to the bed."

Helle gazed up at him from eyes gone dark with desire. He kissed her again, nibbling at her lower lip. She pushed her hips up, grinding her crotch against his erection. Jason kissed the corner of her mouth, her neck. He undid the buttons on her shirt, slid his hands in under her back to undo her bra, and soon enough she was naked from the waist up.

He fondled her breasts, she hummed deep in her throat. Her jeans came off, as did her cotton knickers, and there she was, lying naked on the bed, her legs spread in invitation. Jason made her wait for it. First his shirt, which he peeled off with infinite slowness, then his jeans and boxers, tugged down one millimetre at the time, until his cock sprang free. Helle reached for it, fingers sliding gently up and down his length.

Jason urged her back down and buried his head between her thighs. He shot his tongue into her pussy, did it again and she tilted her pelvis to meet him. She tasted salty, she tasted

Helle, and when he rubbed his nose in her pubic curls, she groaned his name.

Two fingers inside of her, his mouth on her clit, and her hips swayed back and forth, rocking to the rhythm he set. Helle's thighs bunched, her breathing grew rapid, and he kept her there, hanging on the edge, by the simple expedient of now and then stopping what he was doing, long enough for her muscles to soften, her hips to sink back onto the bed.

The fourth time he did that, she uttered a guttural sound, hands clawing at him.

"What, you want more?" he asked, moving so that he could kiss her on the mouth. In response, she sucked on his tongue, hooking her legs round his thighs. "You want this?" He nudged at her entrance with his cock.

"Yes! Yes, yes, yes!" Nails in his buttocks urged him on, and he pushed into her. "Jason!" she gasped, and he eased out, waited until she opened her eyes, and then slammed back in, all the way. Hard enough to rock the bed, to have the headboard thumping against the wall, but he didn't care, not now, not when he was pumping into her, when his balls contracted and his cock thudded with heat.

Beneath him, she tensed, inhaled, and her insides tightened around him, her thighs quivering. A couple of more thrusts and he came, buried so deep he could feel her pressed to his balls.

They'd fallen asleep, waking some time later to the chill of lying naked on top of the bed.

"Shower?" Jason suggested, and Helle happily agreed, standing for a long time under the hot water with him.

He'd forgotten his toiletries at home, so he rummaged through her little plastic bag in search of toothbrush and toothpaste.

"Oil?" he asked, holding up a small golden bottle.

"Yeah—argan oil. For my hair, mostly."

"Can be used on your body as well," he said, peering at the label.

"I guess. It's too expensive to use as body lotion." She grabbed the toothbrush. "Me first."

Once in bed, she couldn't sleep. Neither, it seemed, could Jason, who was lying on his elbow looking at her.

"What?"

"I thought I'd give you a massage." He pecked her on the cheek. "And then you can give me one." In his hand, he held the bottle of oil.

He began with her front. Long fingers on her breasts and belly, smoothing their way down her arms. Helle relaxed under his warm hands.

"Turn around," he said.

Jason started with her shoulders. In between kissing her nape and spine, he massaged his way down her back, slow circles of pressure that had her moaning into the pillow, so good did it feel.

He skipped her ass and went for her legs. Slow hands up and down her thighs, diving in to touch her sex, and she wanted more of that. Much more.

Jason laughed softly. "Lie still." When she didn't, he slapped both butt cheeks, hard enough to make it sting. "I said, lie still."

His oiled hands settled on her backside, rubbing the heated patches of skin he'd just slapped. More oil, and she lifted her butt up, drunk on the caressing touch sliding so sensuously up and down her ass. His finger, there, rimming her anus, and her hips gyrated in time with his oiled digit. She was hot, she was cold—she trembled and wanted, she quivered and feared. Would it hurt? No, not with Jason—never with Jason. With Woolf, however…She hid her face in the pillow.

Soft, soft fingers dancing over her butt, warm, moist lips kissing her neck, her ear, recalled her to the here and now, to this bed, to Jason.

"Do you want this?" he murmured, one finger sliding inside of her. Oh God! Helle couldn't quite breathe—or she could, loudly and wetly. His finger moved deeper and she felt so full, so sinful, so…agh! Two fingers, and she moaned, surprised by how good it felt.

"Do you?" he asked again, nipping her nape.

"I…" Could he please stop talking and leave her to concentrate on sensations at once forbidden and delicious?

"You do, don't you?" He chuckled and retracted his fingers. "My lioness, offering herself to me, wanting me to take her, possess her." His teeth again, this time biting down hard enough on her nape to make her wince—but she didn't care, not when his fingers were back to exploring, thrusting gently into her oiled backside while his other hand slid in beneath her to cup her sex.

"I want…" she croaked.

"To submit," he filled in. More oil, more of those skilful fingers, sliding round and round, in and out.

She just nodded, lifting her ass to invite him in.

Jason laughed softly. "A submissive lioness."

"Not like that." She turned her head and captured his eyes, at present blazing like embers. "I want you to take me, own me—all of me."

"Oh, sweetheart, I already do, don't I?" He shoved a pillow in under her hips, hands resting for an instant on her buttocks. "Just like you own me," he said, and she could feel the tip of his penis touching her anus.

Her skin prickled, her thighs tensed. He lifted her to meet him, and slowly he slid inside, an inch at most. Helle gritted her teeth.

"Relax," he said, his warm fingers stroking her, circling her anus. She exhaled and did her best to comply. He pushed, sliding in another inch or so. Jesus, he was big! Huge, more like it, and there was a moment of intense discomfort as he breached the sphincter.

"Okay?" he asked.

She nodded. "Wait," she said through her teeth. "Give me a moment to…"

"We don't have to do this." His hands caressed her hips.

"I want to." God, she did, she wanted him everywhere.

Jason rocked gently back and forth, and with every little thrust he slid that much more inside of her. It was like being impaled on something warm and hard, her tissues stretching to accommodate him. He whispered her name, his hands tightening on her hips as he pushed himself all the way in. Some moments of stillness, her muscles relaxing somewhat round the size of him. He moved, and she couldn't suppress the groan of sheer pleasure that escaped her. Their recent love-making, coupled with his sensuous massage, had left her nerves on fire, so sensitive to the touch, and when his fingers found her clit, she was sure she would die of sensory overload.

A bubble of laughter escaped her. Yes! Oh, yes, this was just what she needed, to have him claiming every inch of her as his. Jason's strong body, his scent, his touch—it all served to dispel those dark erotic dreams so tinged with fear and pain that had been plaguing her at night. This was her Jason, doing to her what she wanted him to do. This was her submitting freely, safe in the knowledge that he loved her and would never, ever hurt her. This was how it was supposed to be. This. With Jason. Only with Jason.

Afterwards, Helle couldn't so much as move a finger. From under half-closed eyes she watched Jason disappear into the bathroom, heard water running, and then he was back in bed, smelling of soap and carrying a washcloth. Gently, he cleaned her before pulling her close.

"You okay?" he asked.

"Never better." She made an effort and rolled over to see his face.

"A good first?" he asked, brushing at her hair.

"You know it was."

He looked very pleased. "My Helle," was all he said, and she just nodded. His in every sense of the word.

A whole night without a single dream. Helle stretched like a cat, one limb at the time, before kissing Jason good morning. He opened one eye, smiled sleepily and puckered his lips, a silent demand for more kisses. Helle laughed and complied.

Jason pummelled the pillows into shape and settled down on his back, patting for her to snuggle up close, her head on his shoulder. His hand stroked her back, she tugged at his chest hair, toyed with his nipple.

"What did Everett mean, about the baby?"

Beneath her, Jason stiffened. "Where did that come from?"

Not exactly a major leap, from lying naked in bed with her man to babies, she thought, but humoured him with a reply. "He said a baby could protect us."

"No. He said a baby comes with its own protection." Jason sat up against the headboard. "How can you possibly think a baby could protect us against Samion?" He sounded angry. Helle followed suit, sitting up beside him.

"I just…" She swallowed. "I want…"

"Damn it, Helle, don't you think I do too?" He draped an arm round her shoulders and pulled her close. "But I won't risk leaving a child of mine to cope on its own. Never."

Helle shivered despite his arm, despite the bedclothes.

"Lioness," he murmured. "It'll be all right. Somehow, it'll be all right."

She just nodded, hiding her face against his chest. Jason toyed with her hair.

"I won't let him ruin our lives," he said.

Helle didn't reply. As far as she could see, he was doing a great job of doing that already. That damned Sam Woolf tainted their lives with fear, and until they knew for sure he was dead, this was what it would be like. Was he dead? She still hoped he was, but something deep inside told her he wasn't. As if in reply, she heard a dark velvety voice chuckling, a whispered '*little Helle*' echoing through her brain.

Helle swallowed her fear and closed her eyes in an effort to will away that dark seductive voice. Loud laughter filled her head, increasing in volume until her entire head throbbed, a dull ache starting somewhere behind her temples, causing her to cradle her head with her hands. She couldn't see, she couldn't hear, she couldn't think. There was only that loud, loud laughter, that invasive presence that smothered her brain in blackness and despair.

"Helle?"

Someone was shaking her.

"Helle!" Hot hands burnt into her shoulders. Pain. It tore the black cobweb apart, cleared her mind of laughter. She blinked, licked her lips.

"Lioness, talk to me."

Helle opened her mouth a couple of times, but she couldn't quite produce the words she wanted to say. She managed to lift her hand to his face, caress his stubbly jaw. Jason groaned and somehow rose out of bed with her in his arms. Water. Scalding water that helped her regain her senses. Helle wept in the steaming shower while Jason crooned her name, promising her that somehow things would work out. Somehow.

Korine was almost eight when she had her first uncontrollable tantrum. They sent for Nefirie in panic. The fire that leaked out of her could not be quelled, and she stood and roared with rage and fear, lifting the fires higher and higher until Nefirie clamped her arms around her, holding her close. Heat surged through Korine's little body, spluttering flames stood around her hands and head. She hid her face against Nefirie's skirts.

"He scares her. He will hurt them so many times. He will kill my father time and time again. And I cannot help. I can only see."

Nefirie ran her cool hands over the child, gentling the heat down. "We'll find a way," she promised, shushing the child. "Somehow we'll find a way."

Chapter 11

Four days after Everett's funeral, Jason stood by his office window, deep in thought. Ever since that incident in the hotel, he'd kept a close watch on Helle, but there'd been no further such episodes. Neither had there been any sign of Sam Woolf, and as the man they'd arrested when Smith died refused to divulge anything about his employers, they were no closer to clearing up those events either.

"Sometimes I wish it was all right to extract a fingernail or two," Stapleton had confided earlier that same day. "The bastard just sits there, arms crossed over his chest, and smirks."

"Hmm," Jason replied, even if in this particular case he'd be more than willing to bend the law if it would produce results.

Tim had been designated Helle's constant shadow, with Jason ignoring Helle's protests at being followed around everywhere—even to the beauty parlour.

"You expect him to be in the same room when I get my legs waxed?" she'd demanded. "My bikini line?"

"He can wait just outside the door."

"He refused to do so last time." Helle scowled.

"Because there was a window in that particular room." Jason sighed. "In the future, make sure you book a windowless room."

"Hmph!" She'd stalked out of his room, rigid with anger—most of it directed at the elusive Sam Woolf, to judge from her commentary.

As for Jason himself, he was accompanied by Tim's colleague. Daniel Jones was a hulk of a man who looked capable of crushing a human skull with one hand. He was also something of a ladies' man, and these days Angela divided her attention between Jim and handsome Daniel, picture-perfect in black jeans and white Oxford shirts.

Jason sighed: their life was being derailed—by an effing ghost!

There was a soft knock at his door. "Jason?" Angela waited until he beckoned for her to enter. "I've booked a table for two at Wiltons." She smiled. "Champagne and oysters ordered."

"Good." He shook off his dark mood. Today marked exactly one year ago since he'd seen Helle for the first time since their ancient past, ironically while Helle had been working as an analyst at Woolf & Partner. A mop of bright curls, an elegant turn of the head, and he'd recognised her immediately, stunned to finally set eyes on the woman he'd spent endless lives seeking. Woolf & Partner…Jason's hand closed of its own accord. Shit! He was back to thinking about Woolf, and he didn't want to. Not today, when his intention was to present his wife with diamond earrings to celebrate that first glimpse of her, three thousand years after they were first parted.

"Diamonds are forever," he murmured to himself. Apt, he thought; an eternal stone for an eternal love.

"Excuse me?" Angela said.

"Never mind." He gave her a smile. "Thank you. And let me know when the flowers arrive."

An hour or so later, Jason strolled through the office, holding an arrangement of roses and ridiculously expensive orange blossom—apparently they weren't in season. Their scent, however, was worth every penny, even more so when he placed the armload of fragrant blossom and roses in every shade of pink imaginable in Helle's arms.

Her eyes brimmed. "Thank you."

"You're welcome." He wiped at her cheek, catching an escaped tear. "No crying," he said sternly. "We're going out later, and I want you to look your best."

"You could have told me." She smoothed at her navyblue trousers.

"I've done better than that." Jason grinned. "I've come prepared." He retrieved a bag he'd placed behind Helle's door. "That wrap-around dress I like, some lacy stuff and thigh-high stockings. I was thinking no knickers," he added in an undertone

"Incorrigible," Helle said, rolling her eyes. But she was smiling, already rummaging through the bag.

"What are you looking for?"

"Shoes."

"Ah, yes." He produced another bag. "These, I think."

Helle raised her brows. The shoes he'd chosen were strappy things with four-inch heels. Perfect for what he planned after dinner, with Helle in nothing but those kick-ass shoes and her stockings. And maybe the bustier—he rather liked it.

Wiltons was as it always was: sober and understated, the waiter whisking them off to their table, decorated with more roses. The same table as always, Jason reflected, recalling a sequence of dinners here, first with his grandfather and his parents, and once the rather intimidating old major died, just with his parents. It had been a family tradition started by his grandfather, a widower who doted on his only daughter, Jason's mother. In all other matters Anne Morris had been a free spirit, but when it came to dining at Wiltons with her military father, she was formality personified, Jason's shirt, school tie and jacket adjusted over and over again. He smiled faintly at the memory.

"What?"

"Just thinking of my mum—Anne. We celebrated all her birthdays here."

"You did?" She leaned back to allow the waiter to place the napkin in her lap. "You've really gone wild and crazy, haven't you?" She waited until the waiter disappeared. "This must cost a mint."

"It's a day worth celebrating." He reached for her hand. "Better get used to it, lioness. Many more such days coming up."

"You're crazy—or too rich," she replied with a shake of her head just as the waiter uncorked the Cristal. He smiled: she still had a problem with the pronouns, finding it difficult to accept that *they* were rich—very, very rich.

"One can never be too rich, trust me," he said. "Being poor has nothing going for it."

"Have you been poor?"

"Me?" Jason sat back to allow the waiter access to his glass. "Oh, yes." There was a discreet snort from the waiter. Jason waited until he was out of hearing range. "I was more or less a pauper in our first life."

And there'd been far too many existences following that one where he'd been at the bottom of the dung heap, slowly working himself up through society. It struck him that maybe this had been some sort of penance, akin to the teachings of Hinduism: the acts in one life defined where you ended up in the next, and if so it had been his gruesome killing of Samion which had resulted in several flea-bitten, impoverished lives. However, applying that logic, Samion should have been wandering the streets of New Delhi with a begging bowl, so maybe the Hindus had it all wrong.

"You were?" Helle scrunched up her brows. "I never seem to be able to remember more than the odd fragment—most of them with you." She ducked her head, a faint blush staining her cheeks. "And in those fragments, it doesn't exactly matter if you're rich or poor."

He laughed, leaning forward to tweak at her hair. "I'm glad you remember the relevant bits."

Oysters, Dover sole and for Helle something warm and chocolatey for dessert, Jason watching fondly as she closed her eyes, making a series of appreciative sounds. He sipped at his white Burgundy, dug into his pocket and produced the little red velvet box he'd been carrying all day.

"For you."

"For me?" She stroked the box with her index finger. "But I haven't got a gift for you."

"You can thank me in kind," he said, winking at her.

"Ugh. A totally disgusting comment, Mr Morris. Makes you sound quite lewd." Her rebuke was ruined by her twitching mouth.

"But you like me lewd, don't you?" He covered her hand with his own. "Open it."

110

He knew immediately he'd chosen the right thing. His Helle was not much for flaunting herself, and these little heart-shaped diamonds set in platinum might have cost a small fortune but were elegantly discreet. Her fingers shook as she took out her everyday earrings and replaced them with his hearts. He smiled to himself: on her hands, his rings, on her wrist his platinum and diamond bracelet—a two-edged gift, seeing as it came with a tracking device—and now her ears were equally adorned. All that was missing was a diamond necklace but that would have to wait until their first child was born.

He threw her a cautious look: babies were a subject best avoided, even more so after that last visit with Everett. She had a way of looking at the children they passed that tore his heart out, but he remained adamant—no babies until things had settled down. He picked up his glass of wine and toasted her, she returned the gesture, eyes sparkling.

"Thank you."

"My pleasure."

Daniel was waiting outside the restaurant with the Bentley SUV, and they sat holding hands in the back seat as he drove them home. Traffic was slow. A squall of rain meant the streets were wet and crowded with black taxis, the pavements teeming with pedestrians in rain ponchos and carrying umbrellas. Jason usually avoided the area round Piccadilly, and at present he wished he'd done so tonight as well.

His phone buzzed. Jason frowned down at the screen. Mails from unknown senders he generally deleted unread, but the headline caught his attention. *Resurrection*, it said. Before he had opened it, Daniel's phone rang, loud and shrill.

"What?" Daniel barked.

"Company." Tim's voice boomed from the sound system. "On bikes."

Jason threw himself across Helle, pressing her flat to the seat. Something crashed into the windowpane, but the reinforced glass held, a spider web of cracks spreading outward from the point of impact.

"Shit!" Daniel stood on the brakes. Two bikers surged past, one on either side. Two more appeared. Jason glimpsed black leathers, black helmets. Yet again, something blunt and hard crashed against the tinted glass. Yet again it held, raining fragments of pulverised glass onto the seat. Daniel cursed, threw himself forward on the horn, and bumped the car up onto the pavement, scattering screaming people right, left, and centre. "Hold on," Daniel cried, and proceeded to drive up the way they'd come, horn blaring in warning.

"I'm right behind you," Tim's disembodied voice said. Jason threw a look out the back window. A biker, this time in a red helmet. "Turn left here," Tim added, and Daniel spun the car, hurtling down a flight of steps. Helle was flung forward, cried out as she banged her head against the car door.

The bikers were back, two on each side. One of them placed his hand on the shattered window and pushed. The window collapsed. Something landed on the floor with a "thunk". Jason didn't think. He scrambled for the object.

"Get the partition up!" he yelled to Daniel. "Now!" There was a hissing sound, followed by a muted explosion. The car filled with fumes. Jason gagged, groped for the canister, and lobbed it out of the window. Daniel was driving full speed up a one-way street, the bikers following like flies round a corpse. Only three bikers, Jason noted, and nowhere Tim's distinctive red helmet.

Here they came again. This time, Jason was ready. The moment the biker was alongside, he reached out. Flames burst from his fingers, danced up his hand. "Watch out!" Helle yelled when he leaned out of the shattered window and grabbed hold of the biker's arm. The bike swerved, almost dragging Jason out of the car. Helle screamed, arms coming down like a clamp round his midriff. Jason channelled as much heat as he could, and the leather sleeve caught fire. He closed his eyes in concentration. A woosh, an inhuman howl and the biker was a human torch on wheels, crash-landing in a huge ball of fire.

Daniel cheered, veered abruptly to the right, and one more of the bikers was disposed of, skidding down the street. The abrupt movement almost had Jason falling out of the speeding car. Helle shrieked his name, holding on so hard to his belt he could feel the leather digging into his skin. Only one more to go. Anchored to the car by his screaming wife, Jason hung out of the window, glowing hands aloft. The biker did a 180 degree turn and sped away.

Jason collapsed on the seat. His eyes stung, his lungs burned, and as for his hands, they were bright red. Daniel brought the Rover to a halt and lowered the privacy screen.

"Everything okay, sir?" he asked.

"Just take us home," Jason said, before turning his attention to his wife. Helle's face was streaked with tears.

"Gas." She drew in a shuddering breath. "Tim?"

"He's fine, ma'am," Daniel said. "Forced one of those bastards off the steps."

"Oh." She clung to Jason, and he could feel the tremors. "What..." She broke off.

"I have no idea. But whatever their intention, they failed." He gathered her close and held her all the way back home.

Tim was there when they arrived. He'd already done a general check of the premises, but followed them inside just in case. Daniel came loping after, and together their bodyguards swept the entire house, while Jason and Helle stood in the hall.

"All clear, sir." Daniel handed Jason his briefcase, Helle her laptop bag. An incongruously normal gesture, given the circumstances.

"Thanks." Jason gave him a nod. "You did good tonight."

"As did you, sir." Daniel gave him a curious look. "How did you set him on fire?"

"Luck—and a lighter," Jason replied lightly.

"Ah." Daniel pursed his mouth. "Didn't take you for a smoker, sir."

"I'm not. But I used to be a Boy Scout."

"Well, that explains everything," Daniel said with a laugh. Jason gave him a bland smile, saw him to the door, and went in search of Helle and a whisky—not necessarily in that order.

She had curled up on the sofa, her high heels kicked to the side.

"Whisky?" he asked, making for the liquor cabinet.

"No thanks." She hugged herself. "Did they want to kill us?"

"I don't think so." No, because if they had, they'd have gone about it differently. That canister with tear-gas spoke of other intentions, no less sinister. Helle's eyes were huge and almost violet in the dim light.

"Was it him?"

Jason shrugged and downed his whisky. Of course it was. His phone buzzed again, just as Helle's phone chirped. She dug it out, frowning down at the screen.

"Resurrection?" she said, already tapping on the icon to open it.

"Don't," Jason began, filled with a sudden premonition, but it was too late. Helle's hand tightened round her phone, her eyes snapped up to meet his.

"Shit," was all she said, and then she was sprinting for the downstairs bathroom, a hand clapped over her mouth.

Jason picked up her phone.

And on the third day he rose from the dead – not necessarily something only Jesus could do. I'm coming to get you little Helle…

Damn! He glanced at his own phone. Exactly the same message—well almost. It ended with *You're dead, Wanderer.* Jason threw both phones onto the sofa. Not yet, he wasn't. With a muttered vow to make Samion pay, he made for the bathroom and his wife.

Chapter 12

Nigel popped up on their doorstep just before dawn the next day.

"Nothing," he said when Jason let him in, making for the kitchen.

"Nothing?" Helle felt a spurt of hope. Maybe someone else was toying with them. As if.

"Unless the man is walking about with an invisibility cloak, he's no longer around." Nigel poured himself some coffee, helped himself to some of Jason's bacon and perched on one of the high stools. "No one can evade notice in this world of ours. No one."

"Unless one has an invisibility cloak," Jason said drily.

"Oh come off it," Nigel said.

"Samion is a gifted magician. There's no knowing what he can do."

"I'd guess becoming invisible would be stretching it," Nigel retorted.

"So do I." Jason sipped his coffee. "But changing his appearance not so much." His voice was huskier than normal, his face a collection of sharp angles and bruised skin—a consequence of not having slept much last night. Helle grazed his hand with her fingertips, was rewarded with the slightest of smiles.

"So what do we do?" Helle asked. She needed a plan. Preferably a fail-safe plan, one which went from A to D and ended up with Sam Woolf permanently disposed of.

"We assume he's back," Jason said. "These last few incidents have the hallmarks of that fucking bastard."

The doorbell rang. Helle got to her feet, gesturing for Jason to sit. She made it to the hall, only to see Tim hovering at the door. "Who is it?"

"It's me," Miranda said, jumping up and down in an effort to see beyond Tim's shoulders. "I brought us all some croissants."

Helle made a face but nodded for Tim to let her through and seconds later Miranda was hugging her. To her surprise, Helle felt her face crumpling. She stepped out of reach and cleared her throat.

Miranda gave her an assessing look. "Were you hurt?"

"Yesterday?" Helle shook her head. Not physically, at least. Mentally, she was a wreck, and things hadn't been helped by the far too vivid dream in which Woolf cornered her and dragged her off to God knows where.

More coffee, more pointless discussions about how impossible it was that Woolf was still alive, and Helle shoved her plate to the side. The croissant had been demolished, not eaten, and her eggs remained untouched. There was a pressure just behind her eyes, a building ache that made her squint in the bright light of the kitchen.

Jason's phone rang, the ringtone making Helle wince.

"Stapleton," Jason explained, standing up to take it.

There was a sudden burst of pain behind Helle's left eye. She pressed the heels of her hand to her head, counted to twenty, and opened her eyes. Didn't help. The Aga was too red, the stainless steel countertops too shiny. She blundered over to the French porcelain sink and splashed her face with cold water.

"Helle?" Jason's concerned voice was at her back, his arms supporting her as she braced herself against the French tiles that decorated the splashback.

"I'm okay." She gave him a false smile. "Just tired." Helle straightened up. "What did Stapleton say?"

"He'll be here in ten minutes. He just got off the train."

She nodded weakly. John must have been up and about well before dawn to make it here at this hour—Winchester wasn't exactly on the other side of the block.

"Nice of him to come so promptly," she said.

"Hmph!" Jason's brows pulled together. "It's his job. Should have made it here last night, if you ask me."

"Too right." Nigel patted Helle on the back. "You okay, Lion-tamer?"

"Sort of. I need an aspirin."

When Stapleton arrived some time later, Helle was feeling better, although she suspected that was more due to sitting on the sofa with Jason's arms round her than the aspirin. John Stapleton stood for a moment in the doorway, studying the room. Helle followed his gaze, taking in the large space, the polished hardwood floors, the farther wall decorated with non-figurative art in various shades of blue and green. A room that breathed wealth, in everything from the B&O sound system to the aluminium and leather armchairs, contrasting with the old Howard sofa, a huge thing recently upholstered in some modern grey fabric.

"Done well for yourself, haven't you?" Stapleton said.

"Good morning to you too," Jason responded. He released Helle and stood. "Coffee?"

"Black, no sugar," Stapleton said. "But Kim here wants a dash of milk in it." Helle shared a quick smile with her. She liked the female officer, a quiet and efficient woman who looked disarmingly young.

"The kitchen is that way," Jason said frostily, gesturing to the stairs leading to the basement.

"Oh, no butler?" Stapleton said, and behind him his assistant, DS Kim Spencer, rolled her eyes.

"Guv," she said in a soft voice, and the understated reprimand stung, to judge from Stapleton's reddening cheeks. He cleared his throat.

"Sorry. Woke up on the wrong side this morning."

"We all do that at times," Helle said, smiling at him. "Want some digestives with your coffee?"

"I'll get it," Nigel said, heaving himself up from his lotus position on the floor. Miranda rose with him, as fluid as he was.

"Stay." Helle waved them down. She touched Jason's hand. "I suppose the DCI will want your statement."

"I need yours as well." Stapleton grimaced. "No matter how much of a potential lowlife he was, I need to investigate the dead biker." He eyed Jason. "The one who inexplicably burst into flames."

"Start with Jason." Helle made her escape.

An hour or so later, Stapleton sat back, closing the cover of his iPad.

"Well," was all he said. He pursed his lips, fixing penetrating light-blue eyes on Jason. "You think he's back, don't you?" His bristling auburn brows dipped into a 'v'.

Jason exhaled. "I do. I don't understand how, but I do."

Stapleton ran a finger round the rim of his cup. Most of the coffee was still in it, the chocolate digestive only half-eaten.

"And you agree?" Stapleton's eyes softened as he studied Helle.

"Unfortunately." She nibbled at one of her nails.

Tim appeared in the doorway. "It's Daniel," he said to Jason. "He's at the garage."

With a muttered excuse, Jason followed Tim out of the room. Helle leaned back against the Howard. God, she was tired! The headache was back, a dull thudding that reverberated through her brain. Something chirped. It chirped again, and Miranda was on her feet, sliding a hand into the pocket of jeans so tight one might think they'd been painted on her.

"Hello?" She turned her back on them. "Who?" She threw Helle a look over her shoulder, listening intently. "Yes," she said, nodding like a broken puppet. "Yes, yes, of course." She winced, a hand fluttering up to massage her temple. "Now?" She extended the phone to Helle. "For you." She looked dazed somehow, her tongue flitting out to moisten her lips.

"For me?" Who would call her on Miranda's phone? Helle clasped her hands behind her back.

"I'll take it," Stapleton said, but Miranda retreated a step or two. "It's not for you. It's for her." She held out the phone to Helle. "Go on! It won't bite you." She smiled, eyes wide and bright as they met Helle's.

Helle took the phone as warily as she would take hold of a snake. "Yes?"

"I knew you'd want to hear it from me personally, little Helle," Sam Woolf said, and Helle cringed at the sound of his voice. "I'm not dead, not at all."

118

The phone slipped in her hold. *Disconnect, now!* her brain yelled. Yes, disconnect. She fumbled and Woolf laughed, the sound trickling in through her ear to invade her mind.

"You don't disconnect until I tell you to," he said. "We have unfinished business you and I, don't we?"

"No," she croaked.

He laughed again. "Of course, we do. A matter of disobedience, of choosing another when you belong with me."

"No," she managed again. "I belong with Jason. I'm his wife."

The silence that met this remark was even worse than his laughter. Like liquid nitrogen, it slipped into her head, freezing her brain into numbness. Helle staggered, fell against Stapleton, who tried to wrest the phone from her cramping hand.

"Bitch," Woolf said. "You'll pay for that—and so will he."

The phone was out of her hold. "Hello?" Stapleton said. "Hello?" Helle sagged against his chest.

Her brain was on fire, it was deep frozen, it was on fire, it was dipped in stinking pitch, it exploded with fireworks. And all the time, she heard him laughing, heard him whisper that she'd pay—over and over she'd pay for being an adulterous slut.

"Helle?" Stapleton tried to keep her upright. She slipped out of his hold, collapsing on the floor. Vaguely, she was aware of Nigel calling her name. Then Helle was somewhere else, running as fast as her sandalled feet could carry her, leaping from rock to rock, climbing boulders and sliding down slopes. From behind, came the sound of determined pursuit. A jeering voice called her name, and still she ran, the red earth rising like dust around her.

A sheer drop. She came to a halt, not quite daring to leap into the unknown. He was upon her, his black eyes boring into hers, his hands closing on her arm. No! She backed away, and her heels slipped on the edge. His hand closed on her hair; she was dragged forward, thrown to her knees before him.

He raised his foot as if to kick her, which was when the child danced out of the sky, a little girl with copper curls and matching eyes, a miniature guardian angel who took Helle by the hand. And when she did, the man disappeared, the blackness receded, and Helle was back in her head, back to half-sitting in Stapleton's arms. In Stapleton's arms? She struggled weakly.

"Don't move," Stapleton commanded. "I think you had a seizure."

Helle almost wanted to laugh. A seizure? No, this was Sam Woolf demonstrating his powers. The child…Helle blinked. Her child, she amended. Their daughter—Jason's daughter, stolen from them all those centuries ago. Shit: she was going crazy.

"What exactly do you think you're doing?" Jason's icy voice startled Helle out of her half-doze. She tried to lift her head from Stapleton's chest, but it weighed a ton. Jason's hands had her by the arms, and she was lifted, as uncoordinated as a ragdoll, from Stapleton's hold to Jason's embrace.

"She collapsed," Stapleton sounded defensive.

"Jason," Helle said, "he—"

"Shush." Jason sat down, cradling her. "What happened?"

"No idea," Stapleton said. "Someone called for her on Miranda's phone, and—"

"Miranda?" Jason shifted his hold. "Who?"

"Err…" Miranda's voice was muted. "Well, he just…" She cleared her throat. "He said he had to talk to Helle and that it was a matter of life and death."

"It was Woolf," Helle mumbled.

"Shit." Jason stroked Helle's face; it was such a soft warm touch. "What did he say?"

"Dunno." She tried to concentrate, but all she could properly recall was the dread his voice inspired.

"She crumpled," Stapleton said. "Curled up into a ball, shaking all over."

"Why didn't any of you morons fetch me?" Jason demanded.

"'s all right," Helle slurred.

"No, it's not." Jason's arms tightened round her.

"Does this happen a lot?" Stapleton asked, lowering his voice to a whisper.

120

Jason brushed at Helle's hair. "He gets in her head," he replied after some seconds of silence, just as low. "She says she can hear his voice."

"And you believe her?" Stapleton's voice was carefully neutral.

"Yes." Jason exhaled. "You know what Woolf can do."

"What are you whispering about?" Miranda asked. Miranda: Helle grimaced. She'd still not told Jason about her little heart-to-heart with Mirande. He'd go ballistic—especially after the whole phone thing.

"I was speaking to the DCI." Jason shifted Helle to sit beside him. "And why would Woolf call you?" Good question. With an effort, Helle opened her eyes. Miranda was standing some feet away, being scrutinised by both Jason and John.

"Umm…" Miranda said. Helle's hackles rose along her back.

"Umm?" Nigel took Miranda's hand. "What do you mean, umm?"

Miranda shrugged. "I've called him a couple of times."

"You've done what?" Nigel gave her an incredulous look.

"I was just checking. If he was dead, the number should have been disconnected. Turns out it wasn't, but sometimes relatives like to keep the phones open for a while, you know, call in and listen to the voicemail, and—"

"Oh, so you did it just to hear his voice, did you?" Jason's tone dripped with condemnation.

"Of course not!" She broke off, looking from Nigel to Jason. "I didn't do anything, all I got was his voicemail. Besides, how was I to know it was such a big deal? No one told me she'd have a fit when she heard his voice."

"Enough." Stapleton rose to his feet. "Curiosity killed the cat, Miss Stephens. Best remember that."

Miranda's eyes narrowed. "I don't need a copper to teach me anything—especially not about the occult. I'm the expert, not you."

"The expert?" Jason snorted loudly before directing himself to Helle. "How are you feeling?"

"Thirsty." And dead tired. She rubbed at her head, at present blissfully free of any headache.

"Does it hurt?" Stapleton asked.

"Not anymore. But it always does before—" She cut off.

"Before what?" Miranda gave her an avid look. "Before he gets in touch? Like a premonition?"

"Miranda," Nigel warned, "don't."

"No, don't," Jason echoed. He jerked his head in the direction of the door. "Why don't you get Helle some water instead?"

If Miranda was less than pleased at being sent off, she hid it well. Nigel accompanied her, and from the look on his face he intended to have serious words with his girlfriend.

Stapleton crouched. For a bulky man, he was surprisingly graceful. "You need help."

"What, like a psychiatric ward?" Helle asked.

"No." Stapleton gnawed at his lip. "I know someone who—"

"No," Jason interrupted. "I'm not involving more people in this circus."

"But…" Stapleton said.

"No. Read my lips: N. O." Jason's brows formed one dark line of anger over his eyes.

"Shouldn't we at least listen?" Helle asked, mostly because she felt sorry for John.

"No." Jason kissed her temple. "I don't want you paraded before some bloody stranger."

"She's not a—" Stapleton began.

"This is a futile conversation!" Jason snapped.

"…stranger. Not to me," Stapleton finished, giving Jason a mulish look.

"I don't care if it's the Holy Virgin herself." Jason folded his arms over his chest. "How about you concentrate on doing some proper police work instead, DCI Stapleton?"

"Jason!" Helle couldn't believe he'd be so rude. "He's only trying to help."

"Well, the best help he can give us is by building a watertight case against Woolf, preferably so watertight the bastard spends the rest of his life behind bars." Jason's chin rose, a belligerent set to his mouth as he met Stapleton's eyes.

"Fine, have it your way." Stapleton said, making for the door. No sooner was he gone, but Helle's phone beeped. A text, from John. *Call me if you need to*, it said.

Nefirie found her by the sea, a small huddled shape staring out across the water. A northerly wind drove every vestige of warmth from the air, and Korine was shivering, eyes lost in the heaving waves.

"Here." Nefirie wrapped the narrow shoulders in the mantle she'd brought, rubbing gently to bring some warmth into the chilled skin.

"He hurts her, even when she sleeps," Korine said, lifting her tear-streaked face to her. "He talks to her, he fills her head with horrible pictures, just to hurt her."

"But you help her, don't you?"

Korine nodded, biting distractedly at her thumb nail.

"When I can. I walk into her head. I can feel how frightened she is. But when I take her hand he goes away." She smiled and shook her head, sending her curls flying around her face. "She sees me and she knows who I am. And she loves me."

"She's dead," Nefirie said harshly. "How can she love you from the other side of the grave when she never knew you?"

Korine looked at her, golden eyes shimmering in the setting sun. "She loves me. Just as she loves Jason—has always loved him."

It was disconcerting to hear her say his name, even more to meet that calm and penetrating gaze. With a little sigh, Korine returned to staring at the sea. "And he loves her," she said softly. "Will love her until the skies collapse and the seas go dry."

Chapter 13

It was a week since the car incident, a week plagued by far too many restless nights, Helle complaining of dreams and headaches. These dreams had no erotic overtones; they left her shivering and wide-eyed, sitting up in bed so as to avoid falling asleep again. She reminded Jason of a hare in the glare of headlights, shocked out of her wits but incapable of fleeing the approaching danger.

He tried everything: cocoa before going to bed—but that had her wrinkling her nose, saying she hated hot milk—long baths in the evening, slow extended lovemaking sessions that left them both relaxed and sated—or so he thought, until he realised that when he drifted off to sleep, she remained determinedly awake.

Helle's suggestion was that they should talk to John and meet this unknown friend of his, but Jason refused, insisting he didn't want to share their unorthodox past with yet another person. He'd not been able to keep the censure out of his voice: he detested that she'd told Miranda about them, even if Helle insisted she'd shared very little. But Helle kept on pestering him and only yesterday they'd had a heated argument about it, Helle accusing him of refusing to countenance the offer because it came from John Stapleton. She was right; it stuck in his craw to be beholden to John. Yesterday: Jason pinched the bridge of his nose.

Yesterday, before that damned TV appearance.

It was Nigel who'd called and told them to turn the TV on, and there he was, the accursed Sam Woolf, sitting at ease in a studio, replying to detailed questions concerning his survival— for all the world as a returning hero. To hear it, he'd survived thanks to floating debris, clambering on top of a door. Days of floating, of being so cold he was convinced he'd turned into a snowman.

"Any idea how long?" the TV presenter asked.

Woolf studied his hands. "Not really. Ten days? Twelve?"

"You can't be serious! That's impossible!"

"What can I say? I'm a medical miracle." Dark eyes flashed. "Maybe there were other powers at work."

The TV presenter coughed. Woolf laughed, holding up his hands.

"Look, I'm not sure. And no matter how many days, I'd be dead if it hadn't been for the gentleman who found me."

"And who is this saviour of yours?" the TV presenter asked.

"I have no idea." Woolf scratched at his head. "I must admit to things being very fuzzy. Next I remember, I was in a hospital—in northern Spain."

"Spain? Seems a long way from the Channel."

"I told you: very many days clinging to that door." Woolf sprawled in the sofa, legs wide, arms extended along the backrest. He looked sickeningly healthy, but he'd lost weight and the four parallel scars down his cheek left him looking like a matinée pirate. Much more dangerous than bloody Errol Flynn, Jason reflected, watching Woolf charm the presenter, while his opaque black eyes stared into the camera. Dead eyes, soulless eyes—Jason suppressed a shiver.

With a curse, Helle turned off the TV, midway through Woolf's speech about the unsubstantiated accusations levied against him and his determination to return home from France soon. Just as she did, her phone rang, a hysterical Miriam on the other end of the line. Jason relieved Helle of the phone.

"Miriam, calm down."

"Calm down?" His mother-in-law sounded as if she wanted to throttle him. "How do you expect me to do that?"

"Breathe." Jason watched Helle pace the room, shoulders shoved forward, hands clenched.

"Huh." Miriam inhaled noisily a couple of times. "And now what?" she asked in a more normal voice.

"I have no idea." He held out his hand to Helle, she took it and he pulled her down to sit beside him, wrapping an arm round her shoulders to keep her still. "It's not as if he can waltz into the UK, is it? Not with all those criminal charges hanging over his head."

"He did once before." Miriam sounded on the verge of tears. "That time, Helle almost died." There was an accusatory edge to her voice.

"But she didn't. She won't this time either."

"Promise?" Miriam whispered.

Jason cleared his throat. "Cross my heart." At that point, Helle reclaimed her phone.

In the middle of the night, he woke to a crash. Helle was lying on the floor beside the bed, the nightstand lamp beside her.

"Helle?" He scrambled off the bed. She was moaning, clutching at her head.

"Helle?" He tried to shake her awake, but she was trapped in her nightmare, screaming out loud as she tried to crawl away from whatever it was she was seeing. And then she vomited, on hands and knees as she emptied her guts out. That woke her, and she cried and cursed, apologised and cried some more, staring at the vomit on the floor, at her splattered hands. He just swept her up and put her in the shower, leaving her in the warm spray while he cleaned up the mess on the floor.

He washed her hair, wrapped her in a towel and carried her, a limp weight in his arms, back to bed.

"He's driving me crazy," she managed to say once she was under the covers. "I don't want you to see me like this."

"It's not your fault." Jason swept her still damp hair off her face.

"Still." She shrugged. "I need help, Jason."

"We'll fix it," he'd said. "I'll fix it, lioness."

They hadn't spoken much this morning, Helle encapsulated in a bubble of silence. The moment they got to the office, she'd disappeared into a meeting with Steve, waving off Jason's concerned comments by saying work helped. But he could sense she was disappointed in him, and it gnawed at him. Maybe he should reconsider regarding John's offer. Maybe. He studied his hands, noting that they trembled. Shit! Woolf was back.

Jason's musings were disrupted by Curtis, who bounded into his office, in a discreet black suit offset by his fuchsia-coloured shirt. It suited him, this bright pink, contrasting with his dark skin. For the first time since the events in the garage car park, Curtis seemed back to his normal self, buzzing with energy and purpose.

"I thought you'd like to see this," Curtis grinned. "I'm not sure Woolf will like it, though."

He handed Jason a document. *HMS Revenue & Customs*, the letterhead said, and the three-page document was covered in writing—too much for Jason to assimilate in his present state. He went back to thinking about Woolf, making vague responses as Curtis went on and on.

"You're not listening, are you?" Curtis slammed his hand down on the desk, making Jason jump. He gave his friend a sheepish smile.

"Not really."

"The TV thing?" Curtis asked. "Must have spooked Helle."

"Both of us," Jason corrected. "She's in a bad way." Understatement, really. It was as if the reality of Woolf sitting there, in a well-lit studio surrounded by flowers and admiring viewers, had flipped a switch inside her. Before Jason's concerned eyes, she'd crumpled, eyes dulling as they shrank into their hollows. Even talking to Miriam had not helped, the cheerful and calm façade she'd put on while talking to her mother cracking apart the moment she'd hung up.

"He's not here," Curtis said. "Not about to come here for quite some time." He grinned again. "And this won't make it easier for him to post bail, will it?" He pointed at the document. "In their infinite wisdom, the tax authorities have decided to freeze Sam Woolf's assets in the UK while they conclude their investigation into unpaid taxes." He tapped at the papers. "All his assets."

A weight lifted from Jason's chest. Without those assets, Woolf would be hard put to raise bail.

"And I just spoke to Stapleton—he's liaising with the police in Honfleur. They're going to go through that bloodied boat with a fine toothcomb. Plus, of course, there's still that open file on your shooting." Ah yes; Stapleton had done an excellent job there, a fuzzy videotape placing Sam Woolf very much in England that January day Jason was shot—not in France as Woolf alleged, substantiated by CCTV footage Stapleton could prove had been doctored.

"Good." Jason nodded, distracted by Helle passing the door to his office. She was wearing her coat, clunky boots loud on the hardwood floor. Where was she going?

"Helle?" he called. She came to a halt, popped her head in and gave Curtis a wan smile.

"Hi Curtis. I'll be right back, I'm just going down to Boots and get something for my headache."

"Take Tim with you." Tim was a godsend these days, a reassuring presence who was rarely more than ten feet from Helle, except in the office and at home. He was also under strict instructions to inform Jason if Helle requested they go see Stapleton, something that had caused Helle to yell at Jason for close to ten minutes when she found out.

"Sure." She raised her hand in a little wave.

"Lunch?" Curtis looked at his watch. "I have to be back in chambers before two."

"Two? What time is it?" Jason pushed the stack of agreements to the side. The Turkish company he'd bought a year ago was taking off, and after some consideration Jason had agreed to sell a stake to Samsung—at a price that ensured he recouped the entire original investment.

"Half past twelve." Curtis carefully closed the file in front of him, capped his expensive pen and stuffed it all into his battered briefcase. "I'll review your proposed changes and come back with a new contract tomorrow."

"Good." Jason stood. "Let's find Helle and ask her if she wants to tag along."

No Helle. Not in the conference room, not in Steve's office, not in Jim's. Jason flew through the rooms, inspected the toilets. No Helle. Jason fished out his phone. He called her and ended up in voice mail. His stomach heaved. He called Tim instead.

"Tim? Where's Helle?"

"Sir?" Tim sounded bewildered. "She's in the office."

"No she's not. She went to Boots." Jason glanced at his watch. She'd been gone almost an hour. An hour? Where was she?

"But…" A deep sigh followed. "Damn!"

"What?"

"She told me she'd changed her mind," Tim mumbled.

"And you didn't think to check she was still here?" Jason snapped.

"No, sir." Tim's voice hardened. "I wasn't aware I had a client who would purposely avoid me."

"Find her," Jason barked and disconnected. "Stupid woman!" He made as if to throw the phone at the wall, but was stopped by Curtis' firm grip on his arm. "She's…" He swallowed. Gone? Abducted? Jason flung out an arm, steadying himself against the nearby doorjamb.

"Maybe she just needed some alone time." Curtis tapped at Jason's phone. "Call her."

Once again, the call went to voice mail. Jason tried again, same thing. He wiped his sweating hand on his trousers and tried again. And again. Again.

"Text her," Curtis suggested, a worried crease between his brows. So he did. He counted to ten, to twenty, to thirty, his eyes glued to the little screen. At last, a response.

Can't talk right now. Busy.

What? *BUSY? WTF, HELLE!* he texted back.

Half a second later, he had a reply. *Relax, I'm fine.*

RELAX? WHERE ARE U?

With John.

Jason sent the phone sailing through the air. Only Curtis' quick reflexes saved it from smashing into the windows, his large black fist snatching it out of the air and handing it back to Jason. The phone beeped a couple of times.

She's ok. With me. I'll ensure she returns home. From Stapleton. Well, it didn't take a genius to guess what they were discussing. Jason dragged his hand through his hair and frowned at the new text.

129

Don't be mad, Helle wrote. His hand shook when he deleted it. No reply—she didn't deserve one.

Helle felt guilty as hell giving Tim the slip. But when she'd called John and he'd suggested they meet—he was in London for the day—she hadn't stopped to think, she'd just grabbed her coat and made for the door, stuffing her phone into her pocket as she went. Stapleton had promised help and unless she got some, she feared her head would implode under the weight of her nightmares.

Jason had refused to discuss taking John up on his offer. He had fussed like a mother hen these last few days, offering warm drinks, hot baths and his warm embrace to help keep the darkness out. Didn't work. Nothing worked—except self-induced pain. Difficult to administer when one was asleep…

It irked her that she felt insecure on her own. Every man she met, every sound at her back, had her doing a double-take, hand clenched painfully round her keys in case she should need to defend herself. Woolf's legacy, she thought bitterly, turning her into a frightened shadow of her former self. No, this would not do at all. Helle lengthened her stride and straightened her back. But she still clutched the keys.

She took the tube to Bank, changed to the District Line and rode in a half-empty car to Westminster. She kept on throwing looks over her shoulder, but by the time she'd exited opposite Big Ben, she had relaxed somewhat. She cut through the crowds of tourists on Parliament Square and set off up Victoria Street, frowning at a group of Italian schoolkids sprawling across the pavement. 'Pavement', not 'sidewalk': she smiled slightly. A year in England, endless hours with Jason, and his Englishness was beginning to rub off on her. It helped that Mum was English to begin with, she supposed.

True to his word, John was waiting outside the imposing building that housed the Metropolitan Police.

"Starbucks or Snax?" he asked.

"Whatever."

"Starbucks it is. I love their muffins."

It showed, Helle thought uncharitably. DCI Stapleton had something of a paunch.

She opted for a large latte, shook her head at the offered goodies.

"Does Jason know you're here?" John sipped at his coffee.

"No." Yet another twinge of guilt. He'd go ballistic, worried out of his mind when he found out she'd taken off. She dug out the phone and swiped the screen, swallowing at the six missed calls, all from Jason. She unmuted it, and as if on cue, it chirped.

WHERE R U? Nice, shouty capitals all the way. She responded, he texted again, she replied, he texted—all the while in capitals.

John snorted softly, pulled out his iPhone and sent Jason a text. "There. Now he knows you're safe—with me."

Helle nodded, busy tapping out one more text. This time, there was no immediate reply. In fact, there was no reply at all. She placed her phone where she could see it, but it remained dark and silent while she and John drank their coffees.

"You've had a rough week," John said once he'd finished his muffin.

"I have." Helle twirled her mug, causing what little remained of her latte to slosh about. "Don't sleep much."

"Because of your headaches?" He gave her a commiserating look. "It seemed pretty awful."

"It is." The dreams were worse, but admitting to them would make her come across as half-demented, so she chose not to say anything. "Do you think this person you mentioned could help?"

"Yes." He frowned slightly, folding and unfolding his napkin. "But I'm not so sure I should involve her. She's old, uses a wheelchair."

"Sounds just like the ally we need," Helle said sarcastically. She'd made it all the way here for nothing?

"Oh, don't underestimate her." John chuckled. "She scared the living daylights out of us when we were young."

"Us?"

"Me and my siblings, our cousins. We used to spend our summers with one of my aunts, and this lady is her paternal aunt, my grandfather's youngest sister."

"Sheesh! She must be pushing a hundred."

"I'm not that old," he told her in a dry tone. "Anyway, one year we amused ourselves by sneaking out at night and going skinny-dipping in the nearby lake. Until the night Chloe got her foot stuck in something and was pulled under." He shook his head at the recollection. "We didn't know what to do," he admitted, "and Chloe—we couldn't see her. Which was when Katherine suddenly came flying out of the house, pushed me aside and waded out into the water where she simply raised her arms. Moments later, Chloe was coughing and wheezing, on her knees on the muddy shore."

"Wow." She wasn't that impressed. It had been dark, they'd been scared, and this Katherine had probably seen poor Chloe and grabbed hold of her. Her scepticism must have shone through. John laughed softly. "She lifted the waters. That still lake rose into a huge wave that deposited Chloe on the shore."

"Oh." Now it all sounded incredible instead.

John tapped at her mug.

"Refill?"

"No thanks." She fiddled with her oh-so-quiet phone. "Will she be willing to help us?"

"I'll ask—if you want me to." John twisted his napkin. "She may say no. One never knows with her." He laughed darkly. "She's a bit...I don't know, aloof? Self-sufficient? A bit like Jason, if you know what I mean."

"No." Helle gave him a cool look. "I don't."

John rolled his eyes. "Fine, have it your way." His chair scraped as he stood. "Time to take you home, I think." He winked slyly. "That bodyguard of yours won't be pleased, will he?"

"Probably not." And neither would Jason. Helle followed John out of the café.

Nefirie was angry. She looked down at the girl. "Never do that again. When you enter someone else's mind, unbidden, you cause pain. A lot of pain."

132

The child stared at her.

"Remember when Kantor punished you the other week?"

Korine nodded, a wary look in her eyes.

"He did it to try to make you understand how dangerous it is to do what you did. Two boys ended up badly hurt."

Korine glowered. It wasn't her fault, she hadn't meant for them to fall off the roof.

"Don't lie, child. You stole into their heads and you willed them to jump."

Korine hung her head.

"I thought you had understood, and then you do it again. And this time, you tried to enter my head." Nefirie shuddered. The Mother alone knew what the girl might see, should she go exploring through the darker recesses of Nefirie's soul. "It hurt."

"I didn't know," the girl said, "I don't want to hurt you, Nana."

Nefirie studied her in silence. "Never again, Korine. Not once. If you do, I will send you away." And it would kill her to do so, she thought.

The girl backed away from her. "But I cannot help myself."

Nefirie shook her head. "Of course you can. Do not lie to me."

The girl blushed and dug her bare toe into the dirt.

"Your father would have been most displeased. He would have been even angrier than I am."

"Why?" Korine asked.

"For months on end he had his mind invaded. It destroyed him." Nefirie looked out across the sea. Her son, so damaged at the end. Because of Helle. Something deep inside snickered at this blatant lie. Dear Mother—Nefirie inhaled—because of her and what she'd brought down on her son. Small fingers curled themselves around hers.

"I promise, Nana," Korine said. "I will not do it again."

Chapter 14

Tim didn't even respond to her greeting. Shit, she was so in the doghouse. The living room was dark, as was Jason's study. Light spilled down the stairwell, and she walked slowly up the stairs, making for their attic bedroom.

Jason was half-naked when she entered, his suit jacket thrown on the bed, his shirt tossed in a heap on the floor. Uncharacteristic behaviour from Mr Morris, as was the fact that he didn't turn when she entered, presenting her with his stiff back as he tugged off his pants.

"Hi," she said.

No reply. Jason yanked open a drawer, produced a pair of running shorts and pulled them on.

"You going running?" Stupid question met with icy silence.

With jerky movements he retrieved his Asics, sat down on the bed to tie them in place.

"I'm sorry," she said, "I just…" The words dried up at the look he gave her. Helle sat down beside him, placed a hesitant hand on his shoulder. Jason shrugged it off, leapt to his feet, and disappeared down the stairs. Helle followed, tagging along like a little dog all the way to the basement gym, tucked into what used to be the cook's bedroom.

Without as much as a glance in her direction, Jason started the treadmill at a punishing pace from the start. His feet pounded on the rubber belt. Helle crossed her arms. She'd wait him out.

Fifteen minutes later, she was beginning to fidget. Her every attempt to apologise had been ignored. Fine, mister, have it your way. She pushed herself away from the wall, shrugged her leather jacket off, stepped out of her RM Williams' suede boots and undid her jeans. She caught him looking at her, but when she met his eyes, he averted his face.

Once in her underwear and top, she moved over to the rowing machine. If he intended to work out in absolute silence, so could she.

Thirty minutes later, her arms were aching, her heart thundering against her ribs. When he upped his pace, so did she, damned if was going to give up. Jason's breathing came in loud gulps, long, strong legs striding powerfully. He threw her a look, stumbled, crashed into one of the sidebars, and almost fell before he leapt off the band to stand with one foot on either side.

"Fuck," he said.

"You okay?" She freed her feet and rushed over.

"Don't touch me," he snarled.

"Oh, for God's sake, Jason! I've been trying to apologise for over an hour."

"You took off, Helle. Damn it, how could you?" He was so angry his voice shook.

"I sent you a text."

"Why, thank you very much! After I'd called you six times. Six times! Have you any idea what sort of hell I went through during that half-hour? Besides anyone can send a text! Anyone!" He towered over her, all sweaty male. "How could you be so reckless? So inconsiderate?"

"You knew where I was. John sent you a text to verify that."

"And why the hell did you go and see him?" He scowled. "I told you not to."

"Because he thinks he knows someone who can help!"

"Help?" He smashed his fist into the wall. "And you believe him? No one can help us with this—it's us against that bastard Woolf."

"How do you know?" She willed herself to speak calmly. "What harm is there in trying?" Once again, she reached for him. Once again, he brushed her off.

"I'm taking a shower," he muttered.

"I can join you."

"No thanks."

"Well, fuck you too," she snapped and stalked out of the room.

She found Tim in the hallway, fiddling with one of the monitors. Helle waited patiently. After some more fiddling, Tim straightened up and faced her.

"I'm sorry for giving you the slip," she said. "I just had to do something."

No reply. Sheesh, what was with these men, all of them suddenly gone mute.

Tim studied his hands. "Mr Morris was right upset."

"Yeah, I got that." She wiped a strand of sweaty hair off her brow. "He's like a thundercloud on legs at present."

Tim's lips twitched.

"I'm really sorry, okay?" she said, pressing her advantage.

"I heard you the first time, ma'am." With a nod, he excused himself.

Jason was out of the shower by the time she made it upstairs. He threw the damp towel in the laundry hamper and went about stark naked as he searched for his sweatpants.

"Behind the door," she said. He grunted something like a 'thanks', but kept his distance. Like that, huh? Helle drew her sweaty top over her head, undid her bra and stepped out of her panties. Without a word, she marched past him, making for the bathroom.

A promising smell of food met her when she finally came out of the shower. Some quick sweeps of body lotion over arms and legs, a brush to her wet and tangled curls, and she was ready to go, throwing on an oversized t-shirt as she walked down the stairs.

Jason stood by the state-of-the-art gas cooker, surrounded by heaps of chopped ingredients. Chillies, garlic and parsley, finely sliced fillet steak and ginger—Helle sniffed greedily, recalling she'd not eaten anything all day.

Her man was naked from the waist up, his black sweatpants sliding down to reveal the upper slope of his buttocks and his hip bones. A faint tan still clung to his skin, his dark red hair combed back to fall heavily to his nape.

Very much on purpose, she leaned across the kitchen counter, knowing full well her t-shirt rode up to expose her bare butt.

"Into distraction, are we?" Jason sounded sarcastic. "Think it will work?"

Helle shrugged. "Or maybe I'm out of underwear."

"Really?" He moved close enough to pinch at the hem of the t-shirt. "This is mine."

"So am I, remember?"

Jason snorted. "For my sins." His voice thawed. "How are your shoulders?"

"Fine." She wasn't about to admit they were burning like hell after her extended rowing session.

He went back to his sizzling pans, she set the table. At some point, a glass of chilled white wine appeared in front of her, and just as suddenly, the various candles in the kitchen had been lit, courtesy of her fire-boy, who gave her a self-conscious smile as he closed his hand, thus extinguishing the little flame on his index finger.

"So what did he say?" Jason asked, setting down a heaped plate of noodles, topped with the sliced steak and an assortment of mushrooms—fried a golden brown and smelling of ginger and garlic.

"Who?"

"Don't be obtuse." He wagged a finger at her. "I'm still mad as hell."

"He thinks he knows someone." Helle twirled her fork. "But he wanted to talk to her first."

"Her?" Jason chuckled drily. "Sounds promising."

"According to John, she's one impressive lady—but that's all I know." Other than what little information he'd offered initially, John had been less than forthcoming, answering all Helle's questions with a slight shake of his head. "Some sort of relative of his."

"Fantastic." Jason speared a slice of meat. "We all know how much John likes me."

"He's doing it for me," Helle said.

"Fantastic," Jason repeated, face darkening. "I don't like it that you run to him for help," he muttered. "He likes you too much and me too little." Helle rolled her eyes: because of Juliet—that frequently reincarnated *femme fatale* with a fixation

137

on Jason—and an adulterous matter back in the seventeenth century when Jason and Juliet had ended up in bed, despite gorgeous Juliet being married to John at the time.

"He's the obvious choice," Helle told him, pushing aside any thoughts of Juliet, her erstwhile rival. "Investigating officer and a man with similar experiences to yours, plus he has this potential hidden weapon in this distant relative of his."

"Similar?" Jason made a deprecating sound. "I don't think so. John may be an old soul, but he isn't ancient."

"Somehow, that word doesn't exactly work in your favour," she teased, and there was a responding little tug at the corner of his mouth.

"How fortunate I've just spent over an hour in the gym ensuring I keep nice and fit," he retorted.

"Yeah," she said, going back to her food—and murky thoughts about Juliet. "Do you miss her?" she asked.

"Who?"

"Her. Juliet." She shouldn't ask. As a topic, Juliet was a minefield.

He looked at her warily. "Why do you ask?"

"I don't know—maybe it was seeing John. It made me think about her, about how she was one of the few people you felt comfortable talking to about everything." Helle pretended great interest in a mushroom, trying to sound relaxed. Last spring, he had talked more to Juliet than to Helle—much, much more.

"Yes, I miss her," he said, busying himself with clearing the table. "She knew everything about me. Well, almost," he qualified, "I never told her about my fire thing. But other than that, I never had to pretend with her. And it was nice to have someone with whom I could share some memories."

The green-eyed monster in the Helle's gut crowed evilly. *I told you so*, it hissed, shaking its glistening gold green coils, *he loves her and misses her.*

"And I will always be sorry for what happened to her, because of us," he added, throwing her a belligerent look.

Yeah, damaged beyond recognition after that awful accident. Well: to be correct, it hadn't been an accident. Woolf had set fire to Juliet's car when she'd tried to take him on. Jason had crumpled with guilt, spending all his time at Juliet's bedside, shutting Helle out. The memory of those weeks when he wouldn't touch her, wouldn't kiss her, barely spoke to her, still hurt. Juliet had known, and she had been glad of the estrangement between them.

"I will never forget what almost happened to us, because of her," Helle finally said, catching his eyes.

"Yes, that was pretty close." End of discussion, his voice told her.

After dinner, he surprised her by putting on music and taking her hand. "I need to hold you," he explained gruffly.

Well, she wasn't about to object, and she needed his proximity too. She smiled when she recognised the music.

"Seriously?" she murmured, slipping into his embrace. "This is indeed ancient."

"My father always said that nothing beats *How Deep is Your Love* if you're into a slow dance." His hands were on her lower back, pressing her close. "Ample time to fondle and explore."

"Is that what you want to do? Fondle me?"

"To start with."

"And then what?"

"We'll have to play it by ear, won't we?" They turned slowly, her arms wound around his neck, his hands cupping her butt. His breath caressed her cheek, the skin of her neck. Warm lips on that sensitive point just below her ear; she shivered and squirmed at the same time. Her hands slid in under the waistband of his sweatpants, his buttocks tightened in response.

Helle sighed softly, rubbing her cheek against his chest. "Why can't it be like this always? Just you and me being normal."

"Normal?" His hands squeezed her bare butt.

"You know what I mean: no age-old nemesis at our heels, no strange stuff..."

"None at all?" He snapped his fingers and a little glowing ball of fire hovered over his hand. Despite herself, Helle smiled.

"Well, some of it is pretty awesome." She closed her fingers over his and the flame disappeared. She kissed his palm. "But the rest…" She traced the outline of his mouth. "We're not normal, are we?"

Jason shook his head. "Not entirely. Thank heavens for that. Who wants to be boring normal?"

She hid her head against his chest and laughed, could feel him laugh as well. His hands slid up her back, slid down her back, slow movements in time with the music.

"It will be all right," he whispered once the song had finished.

"Truly?" She stood on her toes, kissed him softly on the lips. His fingers sank into her hair, holding her still as he took over the kissing.

"I will keep us safe," he promised, his voice so low as to be almost inaudible. "But right now, I don't want to think about all that."

"Me neither." Her hands tightened on his arms, his biceps bunching under her hold.

The music changed. Jason lifted Helle into his arms and carried her up the stairs.

She was naked when they reached the bedroom, the t-shirt lying on the treads somewhere. Jason placed her on the bed, took off his sweatpants and settled himself between her legs.

"Come dance with me," he whispered, tracing a finger down her chest towards her sex. He shifted to the side and propped himself up on an elbow.

She just nodded. All night long, she'd dance this particular dance with him. He tugged at her pubic hair. "A rumba," he murmured, and his hips flexed languorously, his cock nudging at her. "Or would you prefer a samba?"

"Whatever," she said breathlessly, relishing the way his erection pressed against her, promising more, so much more.

"Or maybe a paso doble." His teeth tugged gently at her nipple.

"Since when did you become a dancing master?" Helle rolled towards him, trapping his stiff penis between their bellies. It made him exhale and close his eyes.

"A tango." His finger traced her mouth, she bit down. "A rose in your mouth, nothing but a garter belt, stockings and high-heeled shoes."

"No music?" She allowed him to push her down on her back.

"Carlos Gardel." He rested his cheek against her breasts. "Or maybe just the sound of your heartbeat." Down he went, his nose sinking into her belly, her pubic curls, her sex. "Or the sounds you make when I pleasure you."

Helle smiled at his old-fashioned expression, stroking his head. "I like it when you pleasure me."

"I know." He sucked gently on her clit, and she groaned. He did it again, and she was no longer quite as gentle with his hair, her fingers sinking into that shaggy mass, hard enough to make him protest.

Whatever rhythm he had in his head, it was driving her crazy, his mouth, his touch, playing her like an instrument as he followed a score only he could hear. There were pauses, moments in which his hands slid gently down her legs, up her torso. Warm, warm hands, wonderful hands…That tongue: following the outline of her ear, tracing its way down her throat, up to her mouth. Whispered endearments, his breath warming her skin, his mouth kissing hers, leaving a lingering salty taste behind—her taste.

He rolled them over, and she was astride him, his penis thrusting upwards, inwards. Helle swayed and rocked, following the lead of his hands on her hips. She leaned backwards, hands on his thighs to steady herself. It made him groan out loud, her name escaping his lips.

Her insides contracted. Abruptly, Jason sat up, wrapping his arms around her and widening his legs so that she was trapped in his lap, impaled on his member. His nose brushed against hers, his eyes so close she couldn't quite meet the intense heat in them. His hips bucked, driving him even further inside. Helle bit back a hoarse cry, all of her filled with her man, possessed by him.

"Dance with me, lioness," he said, and she did—tried to—pushing downward in time with his thrusts. Her blood roared, her pulse thundered. Jason. On her back again, legs lifted to rest on his shoulders. Copper-coloured eyes burning into hers, that heavy mahogany hair flopping over his forehead. A sheen of sweat on his chest, his mouth forming her name as he slammed into her, eyes squeezing shut as he came. But he didn't stop, he kept up his pace until she was twisting beneath him, helpless to do anything but feel. And feel. And feel.

Jason flopped over on his back. "Some dance, hey?" He gathered her close, tugged the duvet free from beneath her and covered them both.

Helle was beyond speaking. But she managed to raise her head and give him a smile. She was sticky with him, but she didn't care, had no intention of getting up to do anything about it. Besides, she liked it when she smelled of him.

"Left you speechless, did I?" He sounded pleased.

"Mmhmm." Helle snuggled up to him, found his hand and curled her fingers round his thumb.

"I love you," he whispered. Helle nodded and tightened her hold on his thumb.

"Love you too," she mumbled, and drifted off into sleep.

Chapter 15

"One more circuit." Helle jogged on the spot, gesturing in the direction of the Albert Memorial. Ever since her foot had been pronounced good to go, she couldn't get enough of running, challenging herself to run further and faster each time. Tim looked as if he was about to puke but nodded all the same, dropping back to run some paces behind her. Kensington Gardens in the afternoon was full of joggers, people who like her had taken some time off work to run in the autumn sun. Helle lengthened her stride and smiled at a young man coming the opposite way. She'd seen him twice already—apparently he had as much excess energy as she did today. The oaf didn't smile back, just ducked his head and ploughed past her.

She threw a glance at Tim. "We keep this up and you'll be able to do the marathon next April," she said.

"Not bloody likely, Mrs Morris." His breath came in loud huffs, his face a florid red, beaded with sweat.

Helle laughed. She was in a great mood, the result of several nights of undisturbed sleep and the fact that John had called, confirming his secret weapon was willing to meet them that night.

Jason had looked less than pleased but had promised to come along, probably more out of curiosity than any real hope this person could help. Her Mum hadn't sounded too impressed when Helle told her about John's elderly relative. In fact, she'd sounded pissed at Helle for hoping a little old lady in a wheelchair could help her.

"I'm not," Helle protested.

"No? Sure sounds so." Miriam had said. "Jason tells me you're pursuing the legal angles to ensure Woolf isn't allowed to make bail."

"We're trying." Curtis wasn't all that optimistic on that front but hoped for a very high amount, too high for Woolf to post. As if. Woolf probably had money and gold stowed away all over Europe.

"Hmm." Miriam sounded sceptical. "I can hear you're not holding your breath on that one."

"Woolf is too wily, too powerful." Helle swallowed. "But Jason says we'll fix things somehow."

"Hmm," her mother repeated. "Maybe you should take out a contract on him."

"Mum!" The thought had crossed her mind but Jason said Woolf was too well protected for an assassin to get close enough to eliminate him.

Once again, Mum had suggested Helle come for a visit. Even if Helle tried to tell her she was no safer in the wilds of the Arabian Peninsula than in London—perhaps even less so—Mum kept on insisting that the best thing would be for Helle to make herself scarce, leave Jason to sort things out on his own.

"Not happening," Helle had told her sharply just that morning. "How many times do I have to tell you?"

A small dog burst out of a nearby stand of shrubs, barking excitedly as it chased a squirrel along the path. Helle slowed down, made sure Tim was still following, and pointed up the path.

"I'll just run there and back," she said before taking off. Her toes protested loudly, but she loved running at full speed, the muscles in her thighs contracting with the effort. Sounds fell away, and she was nothing but a collection of blood and sinews, flying forward.

She rounded the old stone fountain, whooped and slowed to a more normal pace. Her right foot throbbed angrily, making her limp for a couple of paces.

Tim was plodding towards her. Helle waved, he lifted a hand in response. An old woman was sitting on a bench a couple of feet away, eyes obscured by sunglasses, hands crossed on an ancient wooden cane, black wood adorned with silver inlays shaped like serpents. A large hat covered her head, and as Helle came closer she had the distinct impression she was being scrutinised.

She lengthened her stride. When she set her foot down she bit back on a gasp. Her sole was on fire. Shit! She'd overdone it. Helle came to a halt, tried to walk instead. Both her feet shrieked in protest. In her head, she had an image of herself, that so much younger ancient self, screaming as her feet were whipped to pulp. Woolf. He was here, forcing these memories on her, making her body remember the pain.

"There's nothing wrong with my feet," she told herself, taking another step. The agony brought her to her knees.

"Mrs Morris?" Tim upped his speed.

Helle tried to smile. "A cramp or something." She managed to hobble over to a nearby bench and tore off her shoes. On the opposite side of the path, the old lady was leaning forward over her black cane. "My feet," Helle said when Tim sat down beside her. "There's something wrong with them."

"Your injury?" Tim asked.

Helle shook her head. It wasn't her toes, it was her soles— both of them. She took off her socks, and it all looked as it should, but the pain surged, her feet a collection of shrieking nerves begging her not to touch.

"Maybe you just need to rest," Tim suggested.

"Yeah." Helle lifted her head, and the old lady was gone. In her stead was the jogger she'd smiled at, standing far too close. There was something in his hand. A cosh?

"Tim," she warned, just as two other men broke out of the surrounding bushes.

"Run!" Tim yelled, and Helle did just that, ignoring the sensation of running on broken glass. Barefoot, she streaked off, and with every step she took, the pain in her feet receded, ancient memories wiped clean by this very imminent threat.

Helle risked a look over her shoulder. Her pursuer was fast, shrinking the distance between them. He increased his pace. The cosh whistled through the air, a hair's breadth from her shoulder. Helle threw herself to the left. He cursed and followed under the sweeping branches of a beech. A sharp twist to the right, and his fingers tangled with her ponytail. No. She tore free, jumped a dog that had ambled onto the path, and the moment her toes touched ground, she took off, legs moving like pistons. It had happened to her before, these impossible bursts of speed when her body took over, carrying her away from danger. Her vision narrowed to a tube, and she ran like the wind, people jumping out of her way.

A scream. Tim? Helle veered, turning back the way she'd come. Her pursuer came charging towards her, cutting across the lawn, but she sidestepped him easily and shoved, sending him sprawling. More screaming. A loud, high-pitched sound; it hurt her ears. Tim, oh my God, they'd knifed him or something, causing him to squeal like a pig!

There: Tim, standing but bloody, hanging onto one of the assailants, while the other kicked at him. People converged on them, there were loud calls for the police, and still that screaming went on and on. Helle didn't think. She ducked her head and barrelled straight into the man pummelling Tim. He went down like a sack of potatoes. Helle kicked. She kicked again. Could someone stop that damned high-pitched yowling?

Someone took hold of her shoulders, shook her. Tim? Tim. He was saying something, but she couldn't hear him, not over that infernal screaming. He slapped her—hard. Helle gulped, inhaled. No more screaming. Her legs folded.

"It's all right, Mrs Morris," Tim said, lowering her to the ground. "Look, the police are here."

Their would-be attackers had been cuffed, plastic restraints pulled tight. "Where's the third?" Helle asked. Her head was beginning to pound, sending waves of numbing blackness through her brain. She squinted in an effort to see Tim.

"Got away." Tim looked grim. He touched his bruised face. "I have to call Mr Morris."

Helle tried to nod. What felt like jagged glass sliced through her head. His voice, that distinctive velvet sound calling her name.

"*Little Helle,*" it mocked. "*Little Helle, trying to flee.*" The voice chuckled. "*You can't flee your destiny,*" the velvety voice said. "*You're mine, the Mother has said so, and the Mother always delivers.*" More laughter, more pain; Helle groaned, cradling a head that threatened to explode.

"Mrs Morris?" Tim's voice came from a distance. "Mrs Morris?"

In response, Helle fell forward.

Jason sat back and high-fived Curtis.

"Well done. David just sent Goliath flying." Not, perhaps, the best of similes, seeing as Curtis stood close to six feet six and had shoulders broad enough to balance an entire cheerleading team on.

Curtis adjusted his tie. "I wouldn't go that far. But at least we've achieved a Share Purchase Agreement I can allow you to sign."

Jason grinned. "An excellent little investment, don't you think?" He held up the small portable charger his Turkish company had developed.

"Well, Samsung seems to think so." Curtis made a money-rubbing gesture with his fingers. He stacked the various versions of the agreement in front of him. "Have you informed the Turks yet?"

"Yes." Jason replaced the charger on his desk. "They're thrilled."

"Ah. Good earn-out clause?"

"You would know, wouldn't you? You and Arthur drafted it." Jason shrugged. "I don't mind. They deserve it." He sipped at his coffee. "Any news about that bail?"

"No." Curtis made a face. "But that bloody von Posse is most eloquent. To read his latest missive, Sam Woolf is an innocent, led astray by darker forces."

"And will the court buy it?"

"Not in its entirety. But enough not to deny him bail." Curtis fidgeted. "Well, it won't happen any time soon. Stapleton is fighting it tooth and nail."

"Good for him," Jason muttered.

"You don't like him much, do you?" Curtis asked.

"He's the DCI. Whether I like him or not is immaterial as long as he does his job."

"Which he does." Curtis tapped a well-manicured nail on the desktop. "To judge from his latest correspondence, von Posse is rattled. Very rattled, even."

"Oh? He's worried he'll end up in jail?"

"With Woolf. I think that scares him more than jail as such."

"It should. Woolf will make him pay for his incompetence."

"Nigel has found some more stuff," Curtis continued, throwing Jason a cautious look. "Worth his weight in gold, he is."

Jason nodded, no more. He hadn't spoken properly with Nigel since the incident involving Miranda's phone.

"It's not Nigel's fault," Curtis said.

"No," Jason agreed grudgingly. It wasn't even Miranda's fault—she'd just meddled in things way beyond her. He sighed. "I'll call him later."

"You do that." Curtis stood. "Friends like Nigel don't grow on trees."

Jason gave him a crooked smile: Helle had been saying the same thing this last week or so.

At first it was a difficult conversation, but some minutes in things were just like before, Nigel chattering nineteen to the dozen.

"How's Helle?" he asked suddenly.

"So-so." Jason adjusted the photo of Helle on his desk. She was laughing, turquoise eyes startling in her tanned face.

"Miranda's so sorry," Nigel said. "She didn't mean to—"

"Helle should never have trusted her with our story. People like Miranda become far too curious when confronted with stuff like that. And as for Miranda calling Woolf, what was she thinking?"

"She wasn't. Silly girl thought she was helping."

"Woolf eats people like Miranda for breakfast."

"I know." Nigel sounded tired. He cleared his throat and moved them on to other subjects.

There was a knock on the door. Angela stood there, holding a phone. "Tim," she mouthed.

"I have to go," Jason said, cutting Nigel off midstream. He hung up, beckoned for Angela to hand him her phone. "Yes?" He listened in silence, his heart lurching to a painful stop before it started up again. "You're home now?"

"Us and the police," Tim replied. "DCI Stapleton just arrived."

"I'll be right there."

"She's fine," Stapleton said when Jason came rushing through the door.

"I prefer to see that for myself." Jason hastened towards the living room. Someone had lit a couple of candles, the coffee table held an assortment of teacups and his mother's old Wedgwood teapot. Helle was sitting on the sofa, wearing one of his sweatshirts. She'd pulled her legs up, and despite being surrounded by people she looked utterly alone, eyes huge in her unusually pale face.

When he entered the room, she held out her arms, the forlorn gesture of a frightened child, and he lifted her onto his lap, ignoring the others. To his credit, Stapleton made a shooing gesture, giving them space.

"Are you all right?"

"I guess." She rested her forehead against his. "I just hate it when he sneaks into my head," she murmured. "Makes me feel violated."

"I wish there was something I could do." He cradled her face, kissed her eyes.

"So do I." She knotted her hands in his shirt. "He said there was no point in running. Apparently, it's my destiny to be with him."

"And you believed him?"

"No." She hid her face against the crook of his neck. "But he does. He even said something about the Mother promising him I'd be his." She laughed softly. "Imagine that: Sam Woolf placing his trust in a female deity."

"The Mother is more powerful than you think," Jason said, keeping his voice low so that only she could hear him. "Mother, God—two names for the same power, the Creator who made us all."

"God is a she?" She raised her head. "Now that will come as a nasty surprise to some of the Church fathers, won't it?"

"God is everything." He swiped his thumb over her mouth. "God is everywhere. And God does not believe in destiny, but allows us all to carve our own fate." He could feel her relax at that, her weight that much heavier in his arms.

"You think?"

"I do." He kissed the top of her head. "You're mine, Helle. Woe betide the man who tries to steal you from me."

"Or you from me." She straightened up. "We'd best talk to Stapleton and rescue Tim from DS Spencer."

They found Tim in the kitchen. Despite his bandaged hand, the plasters on his forehead and his bruised and swollen face, he seemed to be enjoying DS Spencer's proximity and the large mug of milky tea she'd just handed him. At the sight of Jason, he leapt up, knocking over his chair.

"You look awful," Jason said, clasping Tim's shoulder. "Have you seen a doctor?"

"Mr Knucklehead here does not think he needs one." DS Spencer said.

"Nothing they can do," Tim retorted with a shrug. "Bruises take their own good time."

Stapleton suggested they talk in Jason's study. The arrested ruffians had gone into silent mode the moment the police had laid hands on them. Stapleton held little hope they'd reveal anything.

"But we know who sent them, don't we?" Jason said, studying Stapleton over the expanse of his huge antique desk.

"We think we do. Unless we have proof, we don't know— not in terms of the law, anyway." Stapleton fiddled with his iPad. "We do, however, have some rather interesting new developments."

"You do?" Helle lit up. "Good enough to put Woolf away for good?"

"One step at the time, Helle," Stapleton replied. Jason felt a flare of irritation. When had Stapleton and Helle dispensed with titles?

Stapleton tapped at his tablet and turned it so that Jason could see the photo.

"That's von Posse," Jason said. The formerly so aristocratic German lawyer looked a nervous wreck, face lined and haggard, sparse hair standing up messily.

"It is. Came waltzing into my office earlier today." Stapleton retrieved his iPad. "Officially, he was here to protest the sequestration of his client's assets."

"He came here?" Jason shook his head. "He's one of the defendants." Nigel had found a number of photos and documents placing the German very much in the midst of things, an active partner in Woolf's shadier dealings.

"The man's a basket case. Never seen anyone look happier at being arrested. Says Woolf is blaming him for everything, has even threatened to make him disappear if Posse doesn't squash our case." Stapleton smiled grimly. "Which is not about to happen. He may wiggle out of a lot of it, but some things will stick like tar." He tapped at his iPad. "I offered him a deal—a reduced sentence if he tells us everything we know. I've never seen a man go pale so fast in my life. Hasn't said a word since." Stapleton studied Helle, then Jason. "He did say Woolf has returned a changed man. Obsessed to the point of insanity." He fiddled with his tie. "With the both of you."

"Not exactly news, that, is it?" Jason said.

"Von Posse says it's different. He reckons those days at sea drove Woolf round the bend, says the man was out of his head for five full weeks in that Spanish hospital, prattling in a language none of them could understand."

"He was born warped," Helle muttered. Jason reached across the table and took hold of one of her hands.

"Nothing has changed," he said. "It's still us against him."

"And me," Stapleton put in. "Men like Woolf deserve to be buried alive." He grimaced. "Have you seen some of the footage Hawkins has found?"

"No." Jason glared at Stapleton. As if he would ever subject Helle to seeing pictures in which women were abused, treated like slaves. Woolf had made a killing smuggling young girls from obscure countries into the UK, promising them a life of luxury but delivering years of servitude.

"Wise," Stapleton said. "Unfortunately, I don't have the luxury of not having to."

At this point, Helle's phone rang. "Alison," she said, standing up. "I have to take it."

Jason rolled his eyes. Alison had been ringing her every other day lately, so shaken by the news Woolf was alive that she didn't seem to realise how it all affected Helle. He watched his wife go and turned to face Stapleton.

"Whisky?" he asked. "I think I need one."

"I'm on duty," Stapleton reminded him.

Jason nodded at the old grandfather clock. "It's after five." He produced tumblers and a bottle of Oban from the bookcase behind his desk.

"And I'm still on duty." Stapleton stood. "I told Katherine we'd be there by seven."

"Can't wait," Jason said sarcastically. "Will she wave a wand around and *pouf*, Woolf is gone?"

John Stapleton's mouth curled. "Had it been only you, I'd never have offered."

"And you don't think I know that?" Jason poured himself a stiff measure. "It takes two to tango, John. Maybe you should remember that." He tossed down his drink. Without a word, Stapleton left the room.

Korine smiled triumphantly at Nefirie and held up her straw doll.

"I made her run," she lisped through her tooth gap. Nefirie nodded distractedly and went back to pounding the cloves and dried ginger into the finest powder.

"You're not listening, Nana."

"You made your doll run."

Korine shook her head and threw the doll to the ground "Not her," she said disdainfully, kicking at the little toy with her foot. "I made Helle run. He didn't catch her, Nana." She grinned so widely her face seemed about to split in two and twirled to dance out into the sun.

Chapter 16

They walked, short-cutting through Kensington Gardens. Jason had objected, suggesting they take the car but John had insisted he needed the exercise, making a snide comment about not everyone having the luxury of incorporating gym-sessions into their lives. Helle was tempted to say something about eating too many giant muffins, but desisted.

After the stroll through the park, they crossed Bayswater Road and were now a couple of blocks from the park, where street after street of similar terraces extended every which way. Stapleton took a left, guiding them into Cleveland Square, a street which sported one of those enclosed gardens so typical of London. He gestured at the further end of the garden and a white stuccoed house, identical to the others in its row. Built as a single-family residence, it had been converted into flats, a series of doorbells by the door. The house was well-cared for, the iron railings a shiny black, its door sporting a recent coat of paint.

"First floor," John said, punching in a code.

The formerly generous staircase had been fitted with a stairlift—a must, Helle supposed, given that John's great-aunt was confined to a wheelchair.

Helle followed John up the stairs, Jason at her back. The house was silent—almost eerily so, the impression reinforced by the thick carpet that covered the stairs, muffling their footsteps.

"Who is it we're meeting again?" Jason asked once they'd reached the landing.

"My great-aunt," John replied. It made Helle want to giggle. These two were really keeping it in the family: last time round they'd been cousins, this time round an ancient relative might offer some sort of protection.

"I meant her name," Jason said.

"Katherine. Or Miss Healey, if you prefer." John knocked twice before opening with his own keys. "Katherine?" he called. "It's me, John." He let them through, closed the door and wiped his shoes carefully on the doormat. Helle stepped out of hers instead, somewhat intimidated by the expanse of pristine white carpeting that covered the floor.

Everything was white: the floors, the walls, the ceiling, the doors, the skirting boards. They passed a small kitchen— white—a guestroom—white—and entered the main room, just as white. White sofas, white armchairs, even white bookcases— IKEA, Helle noted. The curtains were white, the lampshades were white, and the white walls were bare. Somehow it didn't matter. The whole room should have felt antiseptic, but instead it felt warm and safe, helped by the many lit candles.

Only three things offered some sort of contrast to this sea of white: on the desk was a black laptop, there was an assortment of green plants on a low bench, and sitting in a wheelchair with her back to them was a woman, presently occupied watering the plants.

She had a bright blue shawl over her shoulders. Her white hair was cut short, hugging the shape of her head. There were streaks of a darker colour, but in the dim light Helle could not make out any more than that.

John greeted her with a soft hug. "Katherine, how are you?"

"As well as can be expected, my dear."

That voice. Helle had heard it before. Like a burbling mountain stream over shiny pebbles, it was a voice that soothed and calmed, that shushed you when you cried and cooled you when you burned with fever. Helle blinked a couple of times, trying to place it. Beside her, Jason had stilled, staring at the woman's back.

Faint scents tickled Helle's nostrils. She recognised rosemary and sage, the sweet smell of dog-roses, of wet clover, the tang of sun-warmed pine trees. Smells that reminded her of a distant childhood and endless warm summers, of laughter in the twilight and rough linen in your bed. She looked at Jason, but he was standing with his eyes closed, his Adam's apple working repeatedly. She stuck her hand into his and he squeezed down hard, his fingers hot.

"I have brought you the people I told you about," John said, his hands resting protectively on Katherine's back. She had yet to turn, and there was the slightest squaring of her shoulders, as if she was preparing for something that might be difficult. From where Helle stood, she could see her profile, a high strong forehead and an aquiline nose. She was clearly very old, her knees swollen, her hands arthritic, but her face showed little sagging under her chin or eyes. Her skin was almost translucent in its pallor. Helle got the impression she didn't want to turn, but at long last she gripped John's hand and swivelled her chair round to face them.

From Jason came a low, broken sound, the sound a small child makes when faced with unbearable heartbreak. Helle gave him a worried look, followed his gaze, and almost reeled with shock when she met eyes as golden as Jason's. Katherine gave Helle the slightest of nods, lips curving into a little smile. Helle's pulse thundered. Impossible!

Katherine's smile widened when she met Jason's eyes. She opened her arms and Jason stumbled towards her, fell to his knees, and buried his head in her lap. Helle's throat clogged when Katherine ran her hands through Jason's hair, murmuring his name over and over again.

John coughed, stared at Jason and Katherine, coughed again and turned to look at Helle, a deep crease between his brows.

"They know each other?"

"Looks that way, don't you think?" Helle was not quite sure she liked seeing her husband prostrate at the feet of another woman. Very touching, to be sure, but she wasn't entirely comfortable with it. She put a hand on John's arm. "I think we should leave them alone, at least for a while. Let's go and rustle up some tea or something, okay?"

She had to more or less shove John out of the room, his eyes never leaving the two by the window, she with her hands on his head and his shoulders, him with his face in her lap. Like a modern day pietà, except that the son wasn't dead, not any more.

"Explain," John said once they were in the kitchen. He produced a tray and loaded it with cups and saucers.

"He's her son. She's his mother."

John looked at her as if she'd lost her mind. "She's my great-aunt," he protested, confused.

"She's not his mother this time round, more like ages ago."

He raised his eyebrows in surprise, and then narrowed his eyes.

"You recognised her too."

Helle nodded. One look into those golden eyes had been enough. Nefirie had stared back at her as she did in her dreams.

"Yes, we've met."

John ran his hand through his hair and shook his head.

"Bloody unbelievable," he muttered. He threw her a look and his lips twitched. Helle nodded, a bubble of laughter tickling its way up her throat.

"Yeah, in the overall context of things, totally incredible. Up there with the idea that people can have more than one life, right?"

He laughed, a low dark sound, and she laughed with him.

Ten minutes later, Helle decided they'd given the reunited pair enough time to compose themselves and led the way back to the sitting-room, teapot in hand. To her relief, Jason was no longer kneeling, but was sitting on the sofa, close enough to hold Katherine's hand. Helle set down the pot, helped John distribute cups, and poured the tea. All the while, Jason and Katherine sat silent, as if Helle's and John's presence was a major interruption of their conversation.

"So," Katherine finally said. She tore her eyes away from Jason and looked Helle up and down. "You look remarkably the same." Unfortunately, Helle couldn't say the same. Katherine was much older than Helle remembered, and somehow heavier. But she didn't say as much, offering a smile instead. Katherine dropped her gaze to Helle's hands.

"Married already?" There was an edge to the question, and Jason fidgeted on his seat.

"Since June," he replied in Helle's stead. "At last."

"Mmm." Katherine tilted her head, pointedly studying Helle's body. "No baby on its way?" Involuntarily, Helle slid her hand over her flat stomach, pressing hard.

"No." Jason covered Helle's hand with his. "Not yet."

"What do I call you?" Helle asked to change the subject. Katherine raised her eyebrow in a gesture so like Jason's.

"Katherine will do." She smiled at her confusion. "It's all right to keep your name if it's something like Jason or John. But Nefirie would stick out, don't you think? And imagine poor Tutankhamen trying to spell his way through that at a check-in-counter."

Helle laughed. That would be kind of amusing.

"Besides, it might be to our advantage not to use my old name," Katherine continued. She didn't need to say more. Woolf would recognize her name immediately. Not that she was particularly intimidating, what with her bandaged legs and stooped frame. Somehow, Helle got the impression all Woolf had to do was fill his lungs and puff once, and Katherine would whirl away, as inconsequential as a dandelion gone to seed.

Katherine's brows rose. Her eyes widened slightly and Helle yawned. Katherine leaned forward and Helle's eyes closed.

She was not amused. Not in the slightest. Helle shook herself awake after her mini-nap courtesy of Katherine and glared at her. Katherine merely gazed back.

"It doesn't do to underestimate what you don't understand," she said.

"It's very impolite to put people to sleep." Helle glanced at Jason, but he just smiled and made as if to ruffle her hair. Helle leaned out of reach.

Katherine chuckled. "Miss Sensitivity, is it?"

Helle crossed her arms over her chest. "Let's just say I have reason to be wary of people who invade my head."

"I didn't do that." Katherine said.

"No? It sure feels as if you did." She met Katherine's eyes firmly, saw something dark in the depths of them. The hairs along her nape bristled in warning. Katherine broke eye contact first.

"I'm sorry," she said. "That was not my intention. Does he invade your head?"

"Yeah." For some reason, Helle didn't want to divulge any details.

"And can you fight him?"

"Sometimes." Helle chose not to elucidate. But she slid her hand into her pocket, closed it round the sharpened piece of wood she'd found earlier. Sink it into her palm, and the resulting burst of pain would clear her head.

She felt Katherine come probing. The lightest of tendrils sweeping through her brain. Helle punctured the skin on her thumb with her little wooden point. The tendrils evaporated. Katherine gave Helle an assessing look. Helle contrived to look confused. Something about Katherine was setting off alarms, but she couldn't put the finger on what she reacting to—beyond a swelling jealousy at the way Jason looked at his mother, as if she were some sort of angel come to earth.

Helle ducked her head. She was being pathetic. Nefirie—Katherine—would never do anything to hurt her beloved Jason, so this itchy feeling was nothing but childish resentment at being relegated to the sidelines by the reappearance of long-dead Nefirie. It didn't help that as far as Helle could remember, Nefirie had never liked her, treating her as an interloper.

She peeked at Jason. He was gazing at Katherine, a serene expression on his face. For the first time since she'd met him, he was entirely unaware of Helle's presence, and it hurt. She took his hand and it lay unresponsive in hers. She dropped it, catching the slightest of smirks on Katherine's face.

Helle spent the next half-hour trying to analyse her feelings. Jason brought Katherine up to date, all the while perched as close as possible to her. Now and then, John interjected with something, but neither Katherine nor Jason gave any sign of having heard him. At long last, Helle stood up.

"I'm tired, I'm going home." She gave Jason a bright smile. "Besides, you have things to talk about, and I guess you prefer to do it without an audience." She gave herself full points for generosity. "I'll see you later." She bent down to kiss his cheek. No reciprocal kiss, no swift caress. More or less like kissing a smooth stone.

"How will you get home?" Jason asked, as if he suddenly remembered it could be dangerous out there.

"I'll manage. Maybe John can walk me part of the way."

"Part of the way?" Jason's brow furrowed.

"All the way," John said.

Jason grunted in agreement and turned back to Katherine without as much as a smile or a goodbye. Helle seriously considered kicking him. Instead, she waved to Katherine and hurried to the door. Why was she feeling so strange? Maybe it was the mother-in-law popping out of the woodwork that did it. That, or Jason's adoring eyes on Katherine; they should be on Helle, only on her.

It was close to ten by the time they got home. Helle offered John the spare room, and after some quibbling, he accepted, dropping jacket and tie on the bed before joining Helle in the kitchen.

"Ice cream?" Helle held up the Ben & Jerry carton.

"Why not?"

They sat at opposite sides of the table, digging into the ice cream with their spoons. It was almost like having Dad here, Helle reflected, feeling a twinge of guilt. She hadn't talked to him for ages. Tomorrow, she decided—or later tonight.

"This feels so weird," Helle said, breaking the companionable silence. "For his mother suddenly to pop up, I mean."

John just raised his brows. "You're not entirely comfortable with it, are you?"

Helle tried to laugh, but it came out a bit strangled. "You mean apart from the fact that it's totally impossible to begin with?"

John shrugged. "We all are." He sucked at his spoon. "Did she like you back then?"

"I'm not sure, but I don't think so." She frowned. "Tonight, it was like being relegated from centre stage to the wings. He has never, since I've known him, been so oblivious to my presence." Helle dug out yet another chunk of ice cream. "Well, except for when he spent all his time with Juliet."

John nodded, looking very sad. "Poor Juliet."

"Yeah." What could she say? Being jealous of a dead woman made her feel extremely petty.

"I blamed him for the whole mess." John sighed. "It was so much easier to say it was Jason's fault, try to forgive Juliet and get on with our lives." He laughed softly. "Except, of course, that I never forgave her either."

"She was just as much to blame as he was," Helle said.

"He was my cousin!"

"She was your wife."

"She was." John's voice softened. "I should never have married her. She deserved someone better than me."

"How better than you?" Helle asked. "You had your own little manor, you were reliable and trustworthy, you—"

"I was a plodder. She, on the other hand, was like a butterfly. So gaudy, so gorgeous—how could I ever think she found me attractive?"

"Why wouldn't she?" John was good-looking in an ordinary way, his rather square face dominated by his brows and strong chin. A nice mouth, intelligent eyes—all in all, a well put-together man.

John gave her a little smile. "Different league, Helle. Juliet belongs with men such as Ja…" he coughed, face going bright red.

"Tough." She shoved aside the sensation of inadequacy the thought of Juliet filled her with. "He belongs with me."

"Whatever. Anyway, back then, in that other life, Juliet was in dire straits. Her father had been executed for his Royalist convictions, her mother had gone God knows where, and Juliet was left very much on her own. I think she married me out of fear—not the best foundation for a marriage."

"Probably not."

"I loved her so much," he said softly, "She was everything I ever wanted. I was the luckiest man on earth until I rode back that night. I opened the door to our bedroom and the first thing I saw was her, naked in bed. I had never even seen her naked before; she would always keep her shift on." He dug out some more ice cream. "Her eyes opened in shock, and then I saw she wasn't alone. He had seen her naked before I had, and I swear I almost ran him through with my sword there and then. I would have, if she hadn't covered his body with hers." John gave her a wry smile. "He wasn't much of a man that night. He threw himself out of the room, apologising as he went. And when I returned to our bed after physically booting him out of my house, Juliet was sitting just as she had when he left, stark naked and crying her eyes out.

"She loved him, probably still loves him wherever she is now, so much more than he does her. And I loved her so much more than she loved me. I always knew that. It didn't matter before that night, because she was mine. She was never mine again." John sighed and twirled his spoon. "I still despise him for what he did to Juliet and to me. He had no right to take her to bed. She was married, to me, his cousin! But most of all, he had no heart to give her. It already belonged to you."

Helle almost felt sorry for Juliet, definitely for John. In one rash act of passion, two lives had been blighted.

"Do you love her still? I mean like she loves him or he loves me?"

John smiled. "No, not like that. I think of her at times, and whenever I hear the name Juliet I see her face. But I have been lucky in my loves since then. Not as passionate perhaps, but so much more content. Passion burns, Helle. Exclusive love makes you very vulnerable."

Helle nodded. She already knew that.

Dad spent most of their Skype conversation talking about Woolf—or rather what he'd do to the bastard should he hurt Helle. "And how the fuck can he still be alive?" he asked. "What is he? Some sort of fish?" "More of a shark," Helle muttered, which only made Dad bluster even more. He calmed down a bit when Janine joined them, and by the time they rang off they were back to talking about normal things like Janine's upcoming birthday party.

After crossing off Dad on her to-do list, Helle worked her way through her e-mails. By the time she decided she was done it was close to midnight and her eyes ached. Jason had still not returned home and Helle turned in on her own. Well, she tried to, but whenever she closed her eyes, she relived the events in the park.

The third time she went downstairs to fetch something to drink, John appeared in the door of the guest room, hair tousled, eyes sleepy.

"He's not back yet?"

"No." He looked sort of vulnerable in only his boxers and one of Jason's old t-shirts.

"Can I help?"

Helle shook her head. What she needed was physical proximity, arms holding her as she drifted off to sleep.

The last time she looked at her phone, it was close to two a.m. Where was he? She rolled over on her side, debating whether to call him. Sleep dragged her under, and with sleep came dreams, dreams in which Jason's hand slipped out of hers and she saw him falling, falling, gone for ever. Black eyes everywhere, sandalled feet slapping against the rocky path, horses thundering after. Once again, she stood on the precipice in Dorset, once again, that red-haired angel child came to her rescue, a small sticky hand guiding her home.

Helle woke with a start. Jason still wasn't back. She found her phone. Almost four in the morning. No text. Not at all like him. She dialled his number. He picked up immediately.

"Helle?" he sounded confused more than anything.

"Where are you?" she asked.

"With Nefirie, of course." He sounded tired but happy, "I'll stay the night here."

"I was worried," she told him. Not entirely true. She couldn't sleep without him, but that sounded pathetically needy.

"I'm okay. I'll be back for breakfast." With that he hung up. Not one single question about her. She rubbed at her temple. That familiar throbbing was back. Helle got up, dragged her pillows downstairs to the Howard and put on the TV.

Some minutes later, John padded into the room. "Does it help to talk about them?" he asked, joining her on the sofa. "The dreams and all that?"

"Not much." But she told him some of it. He didn't say much; he was simply there. She fell asleep halfway through a re-run of NCIS, with John's arm round her shoulders.

Chapter 17

Jason came home just after seven next morning, bursting with energy. An entire night with Nefirie had left him buoyant with hope, and he grinned widely at Daniel, standing silent by the door.

"Any incidents?"

"None, sir." Daniel hesitated. "But we have a guest."

"A guest? At this hour?"

"He stayed the night, sir."

John. Damn, he should have guessed. Jason slipped in through the front door. Someone was showering in the downstairs bathroom, from the living room came the muted sound of the TV, and that's where he found Helle, fast asleep on the Howard. That someone had shared the sofa with her was obvious—there were indents in the cushions resting against the opposite armrest.

John appeared in the doorway. "Oh, so you're back."

"What's Helle doing here?" Jason followed John out into the hall.

"Sleeping. At last." John tucked his shirt in. "Took her some time, though."

Jason's cheeks grew hot. "And what's that supposed to mean?"

"It was a statement of fact. Your wife suffers from nightmares and crippling headaches. She also, apparently, has Woolf invading her head, a most terrifying experience to hear her describe it. So maybe it's not surprising she has problems sleeping on her own."

"So she came to you for help?" To judge from what he'd seen, that was precisely what she'd done.

"You weren't around, were you?"

"I was talking to Nefir…Katherine!" Jason glowered. "I haven't seen her for ages, so excuse me if I got carried away."

"It doesn't affect me." John jerked his thumb in the direction of Helle. "But she felt abandoned."

"Oh, and she told you this, did she?"

"No. She didn't have to." John straightened his tie and pulled on his jacket. "Please thank Helle for her hospitality, will you?"

Jason saw John to the door, managing a grudging 'Thank you'—after all, he'd ensured Helle got home safe and sound.

He stood for some time leaning against the doorpost, watching her sleep. A lock of hair was plastered to her brow, and dark lashes shaded her cheeks. In sleep, her mouth was soft and wet, and the worn material of her t-shirt clung to her breasts, outlining their roundness. He shifted on his feet. She looked vulnerable and delectable, and he didn't like it that John had seen her like this, all well-defined curves and rosy skin.

Jason sat down beside her and turned off the TV. A bare foot peeked out from under the blanket, its sole an unblemished pink. Not like her feet back then, disfigured after Samion's whipping. He took hold of her foot, massaging it gently. He'd never done this to her damaged feet, never tried to soothe the pain away. No, he'd been too busy hating—her and Samion both—and by the time he realised she didn't deserve his hatred, it was too late. Far too late.

He closed his eyes. This thing with Nefirie was doing his head in, his brain buzzing with memories and impressions he didn't know he still had. Many of them were of Helle, far too many were of Samion, explicit images that left him lily-livered and shivering. He smiled ruefully: lily-livered, did anyone even use that expression any more?

Jason slipped a cushion under his head. Seeing Nefirie—Katherine—had been quite a shock. Understatement, really: he'd given up hope on ever encountering her again, and here she suddenly was, as palpably powerful as ever, still so very much Nefirie, and yet so changed. A sharper tone to her voice, a cautious look in her eyes, the way she folded her hands together in her lap, so at odds with how he remembered her, hands always resting relaxed and open on her thighs. Subtle changes, no more—well, except for the wheelchair and all that, but Jason wasn't entirely sure she needed a wheelchair. There'd been some canes in the hall, and she'd used her foot to move the wheelchair back and forth rather than her hands on its wheels.

She'd relaxed visibly once John and Helle had left. Truth be told, so had Jason, relieved now he could concentrate his full attention on Katherine. His first mother. His mouth quivered into a smile. Nefirie. With her at his side, he could take on anything—anything at all.

Helle stretched. She rolled over on her back, and her t-shirt rode up, revealing her flat stomach.

"Hi," he said.

"Hello." She scooted up to sit, reclaiming her foot from his grip. "Where's John?"

"Gone." He tugged at one of her wayward curls. "He said to tell you thank you."

"Other way around," she said, her voice hoarse. "I had a bad night."

"More dreams?"

Helle nodded and licked her lips. "I need the bathroom."

When she came back, her face was damp.

"I didn't think you'd be staying over," she said. "I waited up for you."

"I called you," he said defensively.

"No you didn't." She plumped up cushions and folded throws, eyes on anything but him. "I did. At four in the morning."

"You sure?" Jason frowned. He distinctly recalled telling Katherine he had to call Helle around midnight, but something must have distracted him.

"Yup. I woke up and you weren't there. So I called." An ocean of unspoken recriminations in those few words.

"I'm sorry." He held out his hand to her. "I wasn't myself. Seeing Nefirie again, it was—"

"A shock?" she said drily but allowed him to pull her close.

"A miracle," he corrected. "I still can't believe she's here!"

"And do you think she'll be able to help?"

He laughed. "With Nef—Katherine—on our side, Woolf is toast." He gripped her by the waist and swung her round. "And talking of toast, how about some breakfast?"

"You're kidding me." Alison pressed her nose to the webcam. "Tell me you're making this up."

"Nope." Helle propped up her chin and sighed. "Like having the Mummy mummy come to life."

Alison laughed so hard she almost fell off the chair at her end.

Helle grinned. She'd debated long and hard with herself before she'd called Alison, but she needed someone to talk to, and over the last few weeks she and Alison had found their way back to something akin to their old friendship. It probably helped that Alison had kicked that quack Paul Davies out of her life—interestingly enough, the day after seeing Sam Woolf on TV. Maybe she'd realised Paul wouldn't be much to hold onto should the going get tough. Alison without Paul was a much nicer person, and from what Helle gathered there was a new dude on the block.

"Younger than me," Alison had confided. "Toy-boy material."

"How much younger?" Helle peered at the photo on the phone Alison held up. Young and blond was all she could make out.

"A year."

"Yeah, that really makes you sound like a cougar," Helle said.

"So what's she like," Alison asked. "His long-lost mother?"

"Not sure." Helle rubbed her forehead. Damned headache! "Let's just say I don't see us taking off for a nice spa weekend, just her and me."

"Like that, huh?"

"She …I don't know. She's intimidating, I guess. And excluding." So far, Helle had met Katherine twice. The second time, Katherine had nodded a greeting, taken Jason's hands, and just like that, mother and son were involved in a conversation that left Helle very much on the outside. "They remember, I don't."

"Oh. So Jason is weirder than ever, right?"

Helle bristled. "He isn't weird." But Alison had a point. Since Katherine's appearance in their lives a week ago, Jason was all about exploring his previous lives, returning from lengthy visits to his mother with a distant look on his face.

"We talk about our various lives and try to see if there's a pattern," he'd said only yesterday. "A reason why we've ended up the way we are."

"Oh, like her being crippled in this life because of something bad she did last time round?" Helle had asked. Jason raised his brows, no more.

"It's age related."

"Could still be retribution, couldn't it?" she'd bit back.

Helle finished her conversation with Alison and settled down to do some work. She'd been up in Leeds the previous day with Tim to visit a prospective acquisition target and had to finish her report by five—not that Jason would be in any hurry to review it, not at present. Steve and Helle had been tasked with finding alternative investments once the Samsung money came through, and the set-up in Leeds had potential. Five blokes holed up in one of the old industrial buildings, an oasis of high-end software development surrounded by silent machine halls and brick walls that were slowly succumbing to years of decay.

Once she was done, she sent off the report to Jason, Steve and Jim and suggested they discuss over a meeting at five. She was first in the meeting-room and busied herself sorting the various reports into neat stacks—one for each prospective target. First to join her was Jim, bringing with him an assortment of print-outs covered in numbers.

"What did Tim think of the Leeds prospect?" Steve asked with a wink when he entered the room.

"Crappy tea, no biscuits." Helle sat down. "It's a nice set-up. Good products, smart guys. Plus they've even got some patents to motivate the purchase price. And a building."

"They own the place?" Jim asked, looking up from his papers.

"They do. Bought it for nothing some years ago to house their future expansion. You know, for when they've become bigger than Google."

Steve laughed. "So you think it's interesting?"

"I do. That software they've just launched—it fits nicely with the cyber-security offer, and it is easy to customise." She crossed her legs. "Is Jason joining us?"

Steve looked at her over the rim of his glasses. "No idea. Wouldn't you know?" There was an edge to his tone. Steve still resented how Jason had brought Helle on board, making her a director more or less immediately.

"He left," Jim said. "Had a private meeting." He frowned at the reports spread out on the table. "We can't afford all of these."

"Nope. Which is why we have to cut them down from six to three." Helle suppressed the irritation she felt at hearing that Jason had left without telling her to concentrate on the task before her.

It was past six when she left the office.

"Do we have to do this?" she asked Tim when he drove off. "I'd much rather go home."

"There's no point in owning a gun if you can't use it," her bodyguard said.

"I never asked for a gun," she said. It had been Jason's idea to buy her a small semiautomatic, as a precautionary measure. Huh. Wasn't that why you had bodyguards? "Besides, I know how to shoot."

To judge from Tim's smile he didn't believe her.

He was very surprised.

"I told you," Helle said, relaxing her hold on the gun.

"Not bad," Tim said. "Can get better, though."

True. Helle was a decent enough shot, seeing as Janine, whose entire family were card-holding members of the NRA, had taken her out on the shooting range a number of times. Decent, yes, but she wouldn't exactly call herself proficient.

It was close to eight when Tim parked outside their black iron wrought gate, identical to all the gates on their street. Four- or five-storey houses in yellow brick or stuccoed in white were all separated from the pavement by black iron railings, some of which had huge roses growing over them. This time of the year, the shrubs and trees were mostly denuded, but here and there a tenacious white rose still flowered, lighting up the dark.

In difference to the neighbouring houses on their street, theirs was dark and silent.

"When's Jason coming home?" she asked Tim, following him up the short path to the door.

"Don't know, ma'am. Daniel is with him." Tim did a quick tour of the house, reset the alarm panels and excused himself. Helle bolted the door and made her way downstairs to the kitchen.

Some minutes later, she returned upstairs, balancing a stack of peanut-butter sandwiches and a glass of milk.

Jason came home just as she'd finished the last of her milk.

"No food?" he asked.

"You were going to cook, remember?" She focused on the TV.

"Right: I forgot." He sounded flustered.

"What's the matter?" Helle turned down the volume.

"Katherine is going away." He undid his tie, draped his jacket over a chair. "To France."

"And this upsets you because?"

He gave her a rueful look. "I'm being silly, aren't I? It's just that I have so much to talk to her about, so much to share."

No kidding. Helle went back to her TV series.

"You find that strange?"

"No. But I don't like how absorbed you've become. Suddenly it's all Katherine this, Katherine that, and—"

"Feeling ignored?" he asked

"A bit." She studied the remote control. "Wouldn't you?"

With a groan he threw himself down beside her. "I guess. I'm sorry, lioness." He took her hand, kissed each of her fingers in turn. "She's going to Lourdes for a week or so. Alone."

"Lourdes? Isn't that where people go to pray to the Virgin?"

"It is." Jason nabbed her last sandwich, bit into it, and grimaced. "Awful."

"So she goes there to pray?"

"Every year, she says." Jason stood. "Praying to be healed of her arthritis."

"But…" Helle broke off. Shouldn't a healer with Nefirie's powers be able to heal herself?

"I know: this late in the year…It's usually a summer thing, as I understand it." Jason shook his head. "She insists she has to go."

"Oh." It was strange. But it was none of her business, and frankly, Helle was mostly relieved at the thought of Katherine being gone for a fortnight or so. Unbidden, the thought that Woolf was in France popped up in her head: ridiculous, and besides, what would Woolf be doing in Lourdes? Praying for redemption? Good luck with that one.

Jason disappeared down to the gym, Helle went back to watching her show, in between catching up on her emails. A quick note to Mum telling her things were okay, an even shorter message to Dad, a couple of work mails and she was done, closing down her laptop.

On the TV, the bad guy was being roughed up by one of the cops, and Helle's breath caught in her throat when the cop raised his face to the camera. Woolf—staring right at her, black eyes glittering. She blinked. No Woolf. She blinked again, and there was Woolf, except now he was in her head, voice like molten chocolate smothering her brain.

Helle pressed the heels of her hands against her eyes. Didn't help. Sam Woolf laughed, and she didn't want to see, couldn't stop herself from seeing what he was showing her. Jason, brought down by a spear through his back—like a hunted stag. Helle herself, screaming as Woolf dragged her away by the hair. Jason's head, landing in her lap.

"No!" Helle fell off the sofa.

Jason came barging up the stairs. "What?" he demanded, throwing himself on his knees beside her. "Are you hurt?"

"Woolf," she moaned. "He…" No, she couldn't put words to the images, overwhelmed by the superstitious sensation that to speak of them was to make them real. Instead, she crawled into his arms, pressing herself as close to him as he could. He overbalanced, they ended up on the carpet, and she didn't care that he smelled of sweat, because she needed him close, had to hear the reassuring sound of his heart.

"Hey," he said softly, but Helle was all hands and mouth, tugging at her clothes, his clothes. He was here, he wasn't dead, and his head hadn't bounced off her knees to land on the dusty ground, his eyes still wide with amazement at his own death.

There. She found his mouth, kissed him until she had to tear her mouth away and breathe. His naked chest under her cheek, the steady thump of his heart. She hiccupped with relief. Jason rolled them over. He didn't ask, he just fitted his hips to hers and took her.

"My Jason," she whispered, "my fire-man, my only love." He cradled her face, crushed his lips to hers in a rough kiss.

"Mine," he said hoarsely, "only mine." Absolutely, she agreed, hooking her legs round his. Only his. Only, only his.

It was an effort to get off the floor. Helle's hips felt disjointed somehow, and they steadied each other to the shower. She'd left scratch marks on his back, he'd left blisters on her wrists, but it didn't matter, and when he kissed her under the showerhead she realised she wanted more—needed more. So did he, and by the time they made it out of the bathroom, it was filled with steam, tendrils of fog following them out into the hallway.

"I'm starving," Jason said.

"Pancakes?" Helle offered. It was the one thing she did better than he did. Jason lit up, which was how they ended up sitting in the kitchen close to midnight, each with a sizeable stack in front of them. Not, Helle decided, a bad end to the day.

Korine had another fit when she was ten. Kantor tried to hold her, his face contorting when her hands seared him. Nefirie placed her hands on Korine's forehead, whispering nothings until the child stopped shaking.

"He scares me," she said simply.

"Who?" Kantor asked, lifting Korine into his arms. Nefirie ignored him.

"Yes, he scares me too."

"My father's fires didn't help," Korine said, looking at her own small hands, where little flickers still danced from finger to finger.

"They will. He will be there for her."

"And so will you." Korine smiled.

"Yes, so will I." But not for her—not really. Nefirie would be there for him, for her son. Korine nodded and fell asleep.

"Dearest Mother, she sees them," Kantor said. Nefirie nodded and turned away. So did she, watching from a distance as her son and that golden haired girl ran and loved again. She saw the other one too, she saw his black eyes narrow with hate. She shivered and closed her eyes. Her fault. No, she protested, not her fault—she had only tried to save her son.

Chapter 18

In the last week of November, Katherine left a message that she was back. Jason arranged then and there to pop by for a visit, insisting Helle come along.

"She doesn't want to see me," Helle said.

"Of course she does." He pecked her on the cheek. "You're her daughter-in-law."

"Yeah, and that really thrills her," Helle muttered—but too low for Jason to hear.

This time, Helle did not find the monotone colour palette comforting. She followed Jason down the long passage to the living room. Afternoon sun streamed in through the uncovered windows, and the flat felt cold and forbidding, devoid of anything resembling a personal touch. Katherine was waiting for them in her wheelchair, face turned to the light. To judge from the yellow tinge to her skin and the darker shadows under her eyes, her recent visit to Lourdes had not been a success, but when she caught sight of Jason, Katherine's face was transformed, the brilliant smile shaving decades off her features. Quite remarkable, actually.

She greeted Helle with a markedly cooler smile but invited them both to sit.

"I made tea," she said, indicating a silver pot standing on the table. It didn't smell of tea: it was some sort of infusion. "It's good for you. Helps calm the nerves." She sharpened her gaze. "You need that, don't you, Helle? You were always high-strung."

"Really? That's something no one has ever called me before." Helle gave Jason a pointed look, but he was stirring honey into his tea.

If Helle felt the flat was less than welcoming, sterile almost, Katherine was the reverse, an intense personality dominating the large room. It was like being submerged in a sea of warm cotton wool, comforting but asphyxiating. Helle pressed the palms of her hands together and took a couple of deep breaths to clear her head.

Jason, on the other hand, was drowning in his mother's presence, all that was adult male and quietly self-confident replaced by a starry-eyed boy. Helle was tempted to kick him, irritated by his open adoration of the woman who poured him more tea, smiled at him, touched his hand, his cheek, all the while seeming to pretend Helle wasn't there.

One hour became two, became three. At long last, Helle cleared her throat. "We have to get going," she said. "Dinner date," she added, directing herself to Katherine.

"Dinner?" Katherine's eyes flew to Jason. Her hand shook as she set down her cup. "Oh. I was hoping…" She bit her lip.

"Yes?" Helle asked.

"My son." Katherine gave Jason a tremulous smile, holding out her hand to him. "I just can't get enough of him." Her golden eyes glittered with tears. "So many years without him." She looked at Helle. "You understand, don't you?"

"Not really," Helle said, and there was an irritated flash in Katherine's eyes. Manipulative bitch, Helle thought, one moment all teary-eyed, the other pissed off.

"I think Katherine is trying to tell you she wants some time alone with me," Jason said. Duh. Helle was tempted to roll her eyes. Instead, she smiled sweetly.

"So you come back tomorrow. We have plans, remember?" Pizza and a movie with Nigel and Miranda might not sound much, but Helle was looking forward to it.

Katherine's shoulders slumped. "Well, if you have plans…" She sighed. "I'll just pop the food I've bought into the freezer." She patted Jason's hand. "Another time, perhaps?" She sounded utterly dejected. "It's just…"

"I'll stay." Jason turned to Helle. "You go. I don't want Katherine to eat alone, not when she's gone to the trouble of buying dinner."

"But," Helle began, and Jason frowned. Without a word, she made for the door. Jason caught up with her as she was putting on her boots.

"She needs me. She's old and tired, and—"

Helle held up her hand. "Fine." She locked eyes with him. "She's coped perfectly well without you for seventy years—remember that."

"And what's that supposed to mean?"

"Just saying." She ducked under his arm. "Have a nice evening. Oh, seeing as you're not going, I'll give your ticket to John. He's up here for the weekend anyway." The last thing she saw as she skipped down the stairs was Jason's scowl. Serve him right.

"Did you have a good time?" Jason was sitting in the dark, waiting for her when she finally got home. John had been delighted to come along, and after a couple of initial tense minutes, Nigel and Miranda had made him welcome, even if Nigel's pierced brow rose at the sight of the policeman. Pizza and the movie had been followed by some drinks at a nearby pub, until Helle took pity on poor Tim and decided to call it a night.

"I did." She hung up her scarf and jacket, pulled off her boots.

"And did you miss me?" He sauntered out of the living room, whisky glass in hand.

"No." She sidled past him, making for the bathroom. "You chose to be elsewhere, remember?"

"She's my mother."

"We had plans," she retorted. She nudged the door closed. Too much beer came at a price.

"You're being unfair," he protested. "How can you be mad at me for staying with her?"

Because she's manipulating you, she wanted to say. But she didn't. "I'm not mad," she said, flushing the toilet. "Just a bit disappointed."

"Did John come?"

"He did." She grinned. "He's quite funny when he's off duty." She made for the kitchen, with Jason trailing her.

"Surprise, surprise," Jason muttered. "And Miranda?"

"Oh, her." Helle found an apple in the fridge and poured herself a glass of juice. "I'm still in two minds about her." She took a bite out of the apple. "She gets this avid look in her face, and twice Nigel had to shut her up, telling her to back off when she started asking questions about Woolf. Plus, apparently, she thinks Woolf is hot. Well, I guess he is, objectively speaking, but seriously, the most beautiful man she's ever seen?" Helle snorted. "Nigel didn't like that, let me tell you. Anyway, I think she really does want to help, she just doesn't get it, that she can't. She seems to think Woolf is possessed—she goes on and on about evil taking people over. So her solution is to perform an exorcism."

Jason didn't even smile. "Idiot. She tries something like that with Samion, she's dead meat."

"Which was what John and Nigel told her." Helle finished her juice. Miranda had looked insulted, and there'd been a very heated debate about archaic gender roles making men believe women were weak and defenceless.

"Women have never been weak," Jason said with a little smile when she shared this. "Defenceless, yes—especially in times when physical strength decided who was on top, but weak?" He shook his head and held out his hand. "Bed?"

He spooned himself around her, one arm draped over her hips.

"It didn't help much," he said.

"Hmm?" Helle was half-asleep.

"The Lourdes thing. If anything, she looked weaker than before she left."

Helle yawned. Frankly, she didn't give a shit. "Long trip. And maybe there's a waiting time for miracles."

Jason tugged at her hair. "Ha ha." His finger circled her ear. "She doesn't mean to push you away, it's just that we were always so close."

Helle didn't reply. Sometimes men were very, very stupid.

That night was hell. Nightmare after nightmare, horrible dreams in which Samion chased her, Sam Woolf caught her. Terrible sequences of images that made her sit up in bed, not quite daring to check if Jason was still there, so convinced was she that this time it had happened for real, that Woolf had finally extinguished Jason's life.

Jason woke and held her, shushed her back to sleep, but no sooner did she drift off than it all began again. The sheets were damp with sweat, her pillow wet with tears, and Jason cradled her to his chest, but it didn't help. Not until the child appeared, the girl in a shapeless linen garment reaching midway down her calves. The girl with the dark red curls and her father's golden eyes. Their daughter, the child who took Helle's hand and smiled, thereby dissipating the dark dreams that thronged her subconscious.

"How are you feeling?" Jason set down a tray on the bed, pummelled pillows into shape, and helped Helle sit up.

"Tired." She gave him a wan look. Her head was sore inside out, a steady throb behind her eyes making it difficult to keep them open. But whenever she closed them, she saw re-runs of her dreams, and that was even worse.

She made a face at the eggs. Shook her head at the yoghurt.

"You have to eat." He stroked her face.

"Not sure I can." Her stomach did a somersault. No, she definitely couldn't.

She dozed most of the day, Jason sitting beside her in bed with his laptop. At some point, she heard him talking on the phone, a hushed conversation in which he told someone that he couldn't leave her, not today.

"Who was that?" she asked groggily.

"Katherine." He pulled up the covers around her. "I cancelled our tea session."

"Tea?" Helle laughed softly. "That wasn't tea, that was some sort of witch's brew."

The next night was just as bad. Come Sunday morning, both Jason and Helle were exhausted.

"Is it him doing this to me?" Helle asked.

"Who else?" Jason reclined against the headboard. "It's Samion you dream of, isn't it?"

She just nodded. She wasn't about to tell him he featured as well, mostly as a dismembered corpse.

"Maybe sleeping pills would help," she said.

"Maybe. But they could also make it worse, lowering what little defences you have."

"Right: no sleeping pills." She scrubbed at her eyes. "I'll go crazy if this doesn't stop."

In response, he brushed his fingers through her hair, long soothing strokes that made her close her eyes. His movement stopped.

"Katherine!" he said.

"Eh?"

"She can help." He was out of the bed, rooting through his wardrobe. Seconds later, he was dressed. "Come on."

"Jason," Helle groaned. "I'm not sure—"

"Trust me on this," he said. "Katherine's hands will smooth away your headaches and banish your dreams."

"You think?"

"I don't think. I know."

Helle rolled out of bed. With Jason's help, she got dressed, trying to ignore the relentless clanging in her head. Ten minutes later, Tim was driving them to Katherine's house, Jason overruling Helle's weak insistence that she was fully capable of walking. In actual fact, she wasn't, legs shaking with every step she took.

Katherine seemed unsurprised to see them. Nor did she make any fuss, ringing off from whomever she was talking to before directing Jason to help Helle into the sitting room.

"On the sofa, I think," she said, slipping her mobile phone into her pocket. Helle was soon stretched out, her head in Jason's lap. Katherine placed her hands on Helle's head. "Hmm," she said, letting go for an instant. She looked at Helle. "Rather gruesome." She'd paled, her right eye twitching almost imperceptibly.

"Tell me about it."

Once again, Katherine took hold of Helle's head. This time, concentric rings of white light filled Helle's head. Warmth, so much warmth, a soft voice telling her she was safe, and just like that Helle plunged into a deep sleep.

She had no idea how long she'd slept. She woke covered in a blanket, its fringe tickling her nose. Jason's fingers were combing rhythmically through her hair, but she could sense he was doing it without looking at her, his body twisted away from her, facing the spot where Katherine's wheelchair would stand.

"It's only dinner," Katherine was saying. "Surely she can manage an evening without you?" Her voice fell. "I've missed you so much, son."

"As I've missed you." Jason's thighs shifted beneath Helle's head. "She wasn't too happy about me staying the other night."

Katherine made a soft sound, like a suppressed chuckle. "I noticed." The wheelchair creaked. "She resents me. One could almost say she is jealous."

"Jealous?" Jason sounded hesitant. His hand stroked her hair. "She has no reason to be jealous."

"No?" Katherine laughed. "And what about this Juliet you told me about?" What? Helle was hard put to remain where she was. He'd told her about Juliet?

"What about her?" His hand stilled.

"Oh, come off it. Juliet obviously means a whole lot to you, and as you described it, Helle goes quite green whenever Juliet's name crops up." Katherine laughed, a musical little sound that grated on Helle's ears. "But maybe she's just insecure. From what you tell me, Juliet is a woman of incredible poise and beauty, a pearl among women. How can Helle possibly compete with that? If we're going to be blunt, your Helle is quite ordinary, she's not even gifted, not like you and I are."

A special little club, Helle thought snidely, consisting of Nefirie—oops, Katherine—and Jason. And Woolf, she added as an afterthought, and for some reason this made red warning lights go off in her head. To hear it, Nefirie had been spectacularly powerful in their first life, and yet she hadn't done anything to save them from Samion. Why, Helle wondered, pretending to shift in her sleep so that most of her face ended up covered by the blanket. And why wasn't Jason telling his mother to go to hell for bad-mouthing his wife?

"She has gifts," Jason protested.

"She does?" Katherine uttered a sound midway between a snort and a giggle. "Don't be ridiculous, Jason. She is entirely unworthy of you, as ungifted now as she was then—well, apart from her nice round breasts and the fact that she must be extremely talented—and experienced—in bed. How else to account for both you and Samion drooling over her?"

Helle waited. And waited. From Jason came nothing. Right: that did it. Helle sat up, and Jason went tense. Katherine raised a brow, no more.

"Eavesdropping can burn your ears off," she commented drily.

Helle ignored her. "Well?" she demanded of Jason. "Are you going to let her talk about me like that?"

"Helle," Jason said, scrubbing a hand through his hair, "she—"

"…meant it. Every word of it." Helle whipped round to glare at Katherine. "You did, didn't you?"

"I did." Katherine looked mildly bored.

"Including the insinuation that I'm some sort of slut." Helle had the satisfaction of seeing Katherine fidget somewhat.

"Calm down. She didn't—" If anything, Jason sounded patronising.

"Shut up!" Helle jumped to her feet. "I would never let my mother make such derogatory comments about you."

Jason went a bright red. "You're overreacting."

She just looked at him. "Fine. Have it your way." She spun on her toes and made for the door. "To paraphrase what you said to me a year ago, I thought that ring you're wearing was supposed to mean something," she flung over her shoulder. "Like standing up for each other, you jerk." Grabbing her coat and her scarf, she was out of the door, rushing down the stairs so fast she nearly lost her footing.

She heaved the front door open, scowled at Tim who was standing by the car, and set off at a run.

"Helle! Damn it, Helle, don't—"

If anything, Jason's voice made her increase her speed. He caught up with her just as she reached the corner of Craven Road and pulled her to a halt.

"What's the matter with you?" he asked.

"With me? What's the matter with her? And how can you let her say stuff like that?" She tore herself free. "How would you like it, if Mum sort of chuckled and told me the only reason she could see for me being with the oh, so ordinary you is because you're great in the sack?" Angry tears ran down her face.

Jason tried out a smile. "Am I?"

She was seriously tempted to kick him in the balls. "How would I know? It's not me who remembers hundreds of lovers." She shoved at him. "And you didn't answer my question. Don't touch me!" she barked, backing away from his open arms.

"This is silly," Jason said.

"This is humiliating." She crossed her arms over her chest, sinking her nails into her palms to stop herself from crying. Some feet away, Tim was waiting in the idling car.

Jason sighed. "Let's go home," he said, gesturing towards the car.

"I want an apology. From her, but mostly from you."

"She didn't mean it that way," he began, and Helle held up her hand.

"She insulted me. You let her."

They studied each other in silence. At long last, Jason exhaled. "You're right, I did." He held out his hand. "I'm sorry, lioness."

She ignored his hand, marching towards the car. Too little, too late.

"I've said I'm sorry," Jason said from the doorway.

"And what about her? Will you demand she apologise as well?" She shoved her laptop to the side and sat back, massaging her neck.

He looked uncomfortable. "One doesn't tell Nefirie to do things."

"Oh, so it's okay then, for her to be a bitch."

He frowned. "No, of course not. But she didn't mean for you to hear."

"As if that makes things better." She looked at him from under her lashes. "And yes, I am jealous of Juliet—I've never pretended not to be."

Jason groaned. "Oh, for Christ's sake, not that again!"

Maybe it was Katherine's comment about how beautiful and poised Juliet was—so obviously a more suitable partner for her precious son. Maybe it was the fact that Jason had once admitted to living for several years with Juliet in one of his past lives, even fathering her children. Or maybe it was because she'd seen how Juliet looked at Jason, seen the familiar way he'd touch her arm.

No. Mostly it was because of those hellish months back in early spring, when Jason had sat by Juliet's bed, holding her hand and talking his way through their common memories. Months in which he'd been so focused on Juliet there had been no room for Helle in his life. That still hurt: yes, she'd forgiven him, but the scab was newly formed, and the wound beneath was nowhere close to healed—as she noticed whenever Juliet's name cropped up.

"Have you ever run into her without ending up in bed with her?" she blurted. Now where had that come from?

"Helle, please stop. You're being ridiculous. How can you be jealous of things that happened long before this life?" He made a disgusted face.

"Because you still remember. You know what she feels like, you know what she wants. You've held her and touched her like you do with me, you've kissed her like you kiss me—heck, everything you've done with me you've done with her as well, haven't you?"

He sighed. A very exasperated sound.

"And it's not all in past lives is it? It happened this time too."

He didn't reply.

"Why won't you answer my question?" she insisted.

"Because you don't want to know."

"Great." She turned her back on him and pretended concentration on her laptop. Not that she saw anything beyond visions of Jason and Juliet, her long dark hair spilled over his bare chest, his mouth curved in that special little smile she only ever saw after they'd made love.

He came over to join her on the sofa, sitting quietly beside her for some moments. His hand brushed her back.

"Why is it so important to you?"

"Because I don't like it that she knows you better than I do, or that you know her at least as well as you know me," Helle replied, still with her eyes on the laptop. "Because nothing is ever a first for you with me, and because she's had years and years with you, time unclouded by fear. I haven't—I might never have it."

His hand rested on her nape, fingers twisting and untwisting in her hair. "Oh, Helle," he said, his voice hoarser than usual. "Of course, you will."

Helle lifted her shoulders. Less of a certainty now that Sam Woolf was back from the dead. It made her stomach cramp. His hold on her nape tightened, turning her to face him.

"You will," he vowed, dipping his head so that his brow touched hers. "And if it's so important to you, I'll tell you everything about Juliet—but I want something in return."

"What? That I forgive your obnoxious mother?"

"She's not obnoxious!" He sat back a bit.

"No? You could have fooled me. What she said today, that really hurt. What hurt even more is that you didn't utter one word in my defence."

"I've already apologised for that."

"Yeah. But that doesn't mean it stops hurting." She shrugged. "But hey, at least we no longer need to pretend: she sure as hell doesn't like me, just like she didn't like me much the first time round either."

"That's not—"

"Uh-uh." She held up her hand. "Don't lie, okay? And I get it that it's a big deal to meet her after all these years, so I can understand that you have tons and tons to talk about but I feel very unwelcome at your get-togethers so I'll just skip them." If anything, he looked relieved. "And as to Juliet, I'll hold you to it but not tonight." She was too tired for that. "Besides, I have to call Dad, and we both know that means I'll end up talking for ages with Janine first." Helle rolled her eyes, making Jason laugh.

"I like Janine," he said.

"That's because you've only met her on Skype, where her double attributes are clearly visible." Helle mimed a pair of big tits. In response, Jason cupped her breast.

"These aren't too bad either."

She shrugged off his hand. "One of my few assets according to your mother."

"Don't be like that."

"Like what? Unworthy and ungifted?" She closed her laptop. "I'm going to bed."

He groaned. "You're making too much of this."

"Easy for you to say—you're not the one labelled as some sort of promiscuous bimbo. And just so you know, unless she apologises, I'm not seeing her again. Ever."

"Why are some men evil?" Korine asked, tugging at Nefirie's hand.

"No one is evil from the start," Nefirie replied, smiling at the girl. She could see herself reflected in the child's irises. "Some lose their way. They pander their soul and suddenly they have none left." She gripped the girl's chin. "Never sell your soul. Not for anything, Korine. The price is too high, but you will not know until it is too late."

The girl did not understand, Nefirie could see it in her eyes. But she nodded obediently.

"So evil men have lost their souls," she stated, looking at Nefirie for confirmation. Nefirie nodded and tweaked the child's cheek.

"Yes. And they need help to find them again."

As did evil women.

Chapter 19

"I think she did it on purpose." It surprised even Helle to hear herself say it, but now that she had, Helle nodded at the reflection in the mirror, one eye bare of make-up, the other still wearing mascara. "You there?" she asked, finding a new wipe.

"Why would she do that?" Alison's voice echoed down the line. "She some sort of mother-in-law from hell? And anyway, what kind of jerk allows his mother to say stuff like that?"

Helle winced. She knew Alison would blame it all on Jason. This time, she was right, but Helle wasn't about to tell her that. "He didn't actually—he insisted she apologise to me." Too little, too late in Helle's opinion and as she hadn't been present at the afternoon tea which had ended with Katherine calling her and saying she had been out of line, she had no idea just what Jason had said to his mother. It hadn't been much of an apology, little sincerity in that cool, precise voice, but for Jason's sake, Helle had pretended to be mollified.

"So maybe she just wants to monopolise him," Alison suggested. There was a sucking noise, and Helle had to smile, knowing that Alison was doing that thing with her chewing-gum she always did when deep in thought, pulling out a strand or two and twirling it round her finger. Quite gross, actually.

"Maybe." Helle rooted about for the dental floss. "I guess she feels entitled after three thousand years without him." She giggled. On the other side of the line, Alison giggled too, and moments later they were laughing hysterically.

"Are you sure it's her?" Alison asked once she'd got her breath back.

"Me? Not really. I mean, she looks like Nefirie, but who's to say she is? Jason seems convinced."

"But he would be, right? For her to show up in his life must be pretty amazing."

"And?"

"I don't know…" Alison's voice drifted off. "I'm just saying that he's vulnerable enough to see what he wants to see, not what there is to see."

"I don't follow."

Alison sighed deeply. "Okay, so I'm no expert on this—heck, I don't think there are experts when it comes to this—but I'd guess reincarnated souls change through their lives. And maybe that change isn't always for the better."

Helle nodded—useless, really, while on the phone. A prime example of what Alison just had said was Sam Woolf.

"Like Woolf," Alison voiced, as if reading Helle's mind. Her voice shrank, losing its confident timbre. "Any news on him?"

"Nope." Helle picked at a small scab on her hand, watching a fat drop of dark blood form before it burst to ooze down her skin. "But as far as we know, he's still abroad. The bail has yet to be set."

"What will you do once it is?"

"I don't know." Helle wiped the blood off. "Hope Nefirie will zap him?"

"Yeah, because she really likes you," Alison said.

"No." Helle sighed. "But because she loves Jason, and the person Woolf really wants to kill is Jason, not me." Just saying that out loud made her stomach flip.

"Well, let's hope your wheelchair witch is great at zapping—but just in case, get a stun gun."

A day or two later, Helle wished she'd acted on Alison's advice, mostly to zap the wheelchair witch herself. Katherine had become an invasive presence in their lives, like a damned kudzu vine she spread across their schedules, with Jason always in a hurry, always so eager to rush off and visit his mother—extended sessions, which generally meant he didn't come back until close to midnight if it was a weekday, or was gone most of the day if it was a Saturday or Sunday.

On this particular day, Helle had come with him—Jason had insisted, saying it was important to him that his mother and his wife got along. So here she was, sitting in one of the white armchairs and balancing a cup of chamomile infusion on her lap, while Jason and Katherine were involved in a marathon do-you-remember session. Today, the subject was herbal remedies, with Katherine quizzing Jason on everything from the potential benefits and dangers of foxglove, to how best to use yarrow.

Helle threw a longing look out of the window. She'd have preferred a jog in the park to sitting cooped up inside. Jason had promised they'd go later, but at this time of the year, daylight faded fast.

"If we're going to run, I think we should go now," she said, interrupting Katherine midway through a little sermon regarding hyssop. As if anyone cared: these days, medicine came in pills, not in dried herbs.

"Already?" Katherine said, looking crestfallen. She turned sad eyes on Jason, brows in an inverted 'v' that gave her the look of a depressed bloodhound.

"We've been here for two hours," Helle said, standing up. She bounced lightly on the balls of her feet. "Jason has promised me a run."

"Oh, well, in that case," Katherine muttered. "I used to love running but that was before this, of course." She gestured at the wheelchair. "I don't get out much, these days," she added. "Not for me the brisk wind of a winter day—not unless someone takes pity on me and takes me outside."

Helle was torn between admiration and irritation: Katherine played Jason as if he were some sort of violin and she its master. Already, she could see his brain churning, and any moment now he'd open his mouth and say…

"Why don't you join us?" Jason clasped Katherine's hand. "You and I can walk while Helle runs."

"We were going to run together," Helle reminded him.

"Yes, yes," Katherine said, patting Jason's hand. "Helle is right, you've promised her a run. Never mind me." Like driving the final nails into a coffin, that was, with Jason throwing Helle a beseeching look.

"I'm going for a run." She avoided Jason's eyes. "You do whatever you want." She gave Katherine a cheery wave and left. Damn the manipulative bitch! And where the hell had her man disappeared to? This Jason was about as sexy as a day-old puppy.

Fortunately, Tim was more than willing to come along to the park. Helle worked off the edge of her anger, challenged Tim to a race down the last stretch towards Kensington Palace, and did a couple of celebratory jumps when she won. Tim just grinned and shook his head.

"Why did you leave like that?" Jason demanded once he got home.

"I told you: I was going for a run. You decided not to."

"I said we'd go with you!"

"Seriously? What, you expect me to run in circles around you while you push Katherine's chair?" Helle shook her head.

"Can't you see how much she needs me?" he asked. "How she brightens in my presence?"

"Well, she sure doesn't brighten in mine." Helle dug out a pair of panties and a clean bra. These days, there was very little sex, what with Jason either working his butt off in the office or dancing attendance on Katherine. Accordingly, Helle had reverted to plain cotton underwear, to jeans and hoodies. Wearing lace and short dresses without garnering a response was humiliating.

"I'm her son," Jason said stiffly.

"Yup. And my husband, in case you've forgotten."

"Jesus," he muttered. Not the right answer, Mr Morris. Helle grabbed her laptop and retired to the study.

She was overreacting. Jason flew back and forth on the rowing machine, one eye on the wall-mounted TV, the other on the display, counting off yards instead of strokes. He'd already done twenty minutes on the treadmill, and once he was done with his rowing session, he was planning on doing some weights, and then…He caught himself with a crooked smile. He was holed up in the gym so as to avoid seeing Helle—or rather the distant and slightly disappointed expression on her face, a constant of late.

He had the impression she was closing him out, punishing him for his frequent absences. Did she think he didn't notice that her frilly underwear was nowhere in sight lately? That she lived in her worn sweatshirts and button-fly jeans? Damn! Jason stopped rowing and kicked his feet free. According to Katherine, this was a consequence of Helle no longer getting all of Jason's attention.

"You've spoiled her," Katherine told him. "You've made her think she's the sun and moon of your existence." Jason had chosen not to reply, not quite sure how Katherine would react if he were to tell her Helle was just that: his sun, his moon, his everything. At present, a very dark moon and a sun that hid itself behind a bank of clouds, but still.

He studied his weight rack, considering whether to do biceps or triceps. Biceps he decided, grabbing a dumbbell. It had been an intense week, the Samsung deal concluded, a new acquisition project kicking off, long hours with Nefirie—Katherine—and then the inquest in Smith's death. Jason tightened his hold on the dumbbell. The man arrested at the time had been sent down on a charge of GBH, and as for Smith's death, it was ruled manslaughter rather than murder, an attempt to frighten the police gone bad.

At no point had the name Sam Woolf been mentioned, and this despite Jason knowing Stapleton had prepared a heavy-weight testimony in which he'd pointed out that some coincidences were simply too coincidental to be coincidences. Not good enough, claimed the prosecutor, and Curtis had agreed, saying that there was no formal proof—especially not when the arrested lowlife had gone as mute as a rock.

"You realise what this means, don't you?" Curtis said when he came by the previous day. "Woolf's new brief is up in arms about the bail issue, and with the coroner's verdict on Smith, he'll move for a speedy decision."

"Let's just hope they stick him a huge amount," Jason muttered.

"Oh, they will." Curtis studied one of his cufflinks, frowned, and polished it against his trousers. "But if he can pay it, then he's free to come back—to fight this 'perversion of justice', as he so quaintly phrases it." He picked up Jason's letter-opener, the one he'd inherited from his father, shaped like a scimitar. "Maybe you need a real one like this."

"Or a gun." Jason glanced at the bottom drawer of his desk. Under lock and key, he kept a Heckler & Koch, yet another little memento from his father. Clive Morris had been an excellent shot, had even qualified for the Olympics back in the '70s. His son was not bad with a gun either, but Jason was averse to using them and disliked having felt obliged to install a gunsafe at home.

Jason returned the dumbbell to its rack and went back to considering his wife. He should have run with her today. He'd promised her, and he could see in her eyes how hurt she'd been when he fell for Katherine's manipulation. He was no fool, was fully aware how elegantly Katherine played him at times, but somehow he felt he owed her—he couldn't quite erase the image of her face as he'd seen her last in their original life, grief-stricken and horrified. Yet she'd helped him, held him as he chose to die away from her. For Helle's sake, which probably went a long way to explain why Katherine regarded Helle with such ambivalence.

"Did you see this?" Helle asked as he passed the study on his way to the shower. She turned her laptop round. An article about Smith and the Woolf case, written in a disparaging tone that insinuated Smith had been pursuing a personal vendetta against Woolf.

"Bastards," Helle said. "I bet he's paid someone good money for that." There was a photo of Woolf, all suave businessman, his powerful body encased in a bespoke black suit, the excellent cut of his jacket emphasising the width of his shoulders. He still looked underweight, but his protruding cheekbones highlighted his dark eyes, and the scarred cheek added rather than detracted from his appearance. Bad boy made good—except that this bad boy would never become good.

"He's coming back, isn't he?" she asked once he'd finished reading.

"Probably." There was no point in lying. Besides, since Nefirie had reappeared, Jason was less worried about Samion. Nefirie had gifts that would send most people he knew running away in panic. Fortunately, Nefirie never deployed her gifts unless all other options failed. Even better, she was firmly on the side of good—on his side, he qualified.

"That doesn't worry you?" Helle asked.

"Not as much as it used to." He kissed her brow. "Now that Katherine's here, she'll—"

"Yeah, yeah: she'll fry him alive." She sucked in her lip. "Is she really that powerful?"

"Strong enough to match Woolf, at any rate." And if the price for Katherine's protection was that he spend hours at her side, so be it.

Just because Jason wasn't too worried about Woolf, didn't mean Helle wasn't. Over the coming week, her nightmares returned with a vengeance, and after a particularly bad night she even accompanied him to Katherine, sinking into blissful sleep the moment those gnarled fingers stroked her brow. Damned creepy, really, but she woke up refreshed, sufficiently grateful to spend the evening sitting quietly beside Jason as he and his mother talked and talked.

"Are they all nightmares?" Katherine asked suddenly, causing Helle to start.

"Yes." Not all of them. Some were sun-drenched dreams in which a gentle and loving Woolf adored her, she basking in his loving gaze and willingly allowing him to do whatever he wanted with her. Beautiful dreams that midway through converted into the more familiar darkly erotic dreams, disjointed images combining pain and pleasure.

"Really?" Katherine gave her a mild look. Jason studied her with pursed lips.

"They're all nightmares." Which was true. Waking up to humiliating arousal was pretty awful.

"Ah." Katherine looked amused but went on to discuss other subjects instead, leaving Helle to sit ignored on the sofa.

When Jason next asked if she wanted to come along with him, she said no—they obviously had so much to talk about she was just a nuisance. Jason lifted his brows.

"I just asked you if you wanted to join us."

"But we both know it will be you talking to her, her talking to you, and I'll be the odd one out." She managed a smile. "I'll be fine." Not entirely true: evening after evening on her own was getting to her.

She said as much when Nigel called her late one afternoon. Half an hour later, he appeared at her door, in a leather jacket that was too small and left him exposed to the cold December wind.

"Can't you afford a new coat?" she teased. Nigel was independently wealthy, as he was fond of reminding her, having made a mint on designing a couple of computer games.

"I like this one." He shrugged out of it. His bright red t-shirt was adorned with a peace dove and there was a new piercing in his ear.

"What happens when you go through the security control at Heathrow?" she asked, fingering the heavy metal links of one of his necklaces.

"I beep. A lot." He shook his bracelets at her before saying he was freezing. When she offered to make him hot chocolate, Nigel brightened. "With marshmallows?"

"And cream." With Jason gone so often, she'd taken over the fridge, roping in Tim to take her shopping.

"So," Nigel said a few minutes later, wiping at the whisker of cream decorating his upper lip. "How's your new mother-in-law? Or should that be your ancient mother-in-law?"

"Neither. She's not Jason's mum this time round, and we never got married in that first life. So she's some sort of surrogate, I guess."

"Not to Jason, she isn't." Nigel helped himself to more cream, several dollops landing in his mug.

"No, I guess not. I don't like her," Helle admitted, throwing Nigel a guilty look. "And she sure as hell doesn't like me."

"And what does Jason say?"

"Jason?" Helle laughed lightly. "He says I'm being ridiculous."

"Hmm." Nigel eyed her over his mug.

"Yeah, hmm." Helle broke off a piece of muffin. "I can understand it's a big deal for him to meet her again—"

"Big deal?" Nigel's spoon clattered against his plate. "Mind-boggling is a better description. It must totally mess with his head."

"Obviously." Yet another piece of muffin. "So I'm giving them space and all that, but I wasn't counting on him disappearing entirely. Only time I see him is at work."

"And here." Nigel made a sweeping gesture, encompassing the house.

"Here? Not so I notice. He doesn't get back until midnight."

Nigel leaned forward and clasped her hand. "It'll pass," he said gently, and she smiled at him through her tears.

"Of course, it will."

Jason was in a foul mood when Nigel called. At their recent management meeting, Helle had called him out on every single decision, making it patently obvious to everyone present he'd only scanned through the prepared material.

"Never do that to me again," he'd told her once they were alone. "Besides, I'm following your recommendations." He shoved his papers together, not caring in what order they ended up. "I assume you've made the necessary assessments."

"Of course I have. But it's your company, not mine."

"It's ours, Helle. Ours." Jason closed his laptop. "We go with whatever you think best."

"A meth factory in Moldova?" she threw back. "Great ROI, Mr Morris."

"Don't be an idiot," he hissed, stalking out of the meeting room.

His mood didn't exactly improve once he realised why Nigel was calling.

"So she ran to you and complained, did she?" he said coldly. On the other side of his glass wall, he could see Helle, still sitting in the meeting room. She was staring at her screen, its bluish light doing little for her complexion.

"No. I dropped by, we talked." Nigel cleared his throat. "Must you spend so much time with Katherine?"

"That is none of your business." Jason scowled at nothing in particular. "Besides, she's welcome to come along."

"Maybe she doesn't want to spend evening after evening with a woman she doesn't know," Nigel said.

"Maybe if she made an effort, she'd get to know her." Jason threw another look at his wife. She did not seem to have moved since last he looked, still with her eyes stuck on the screen. She was fiddling with her rings. Round and round they went; now and then she tugged at them, a sure sign she was upset. Shit. Jason dragged a hand through his hair, returned his attention to Nigel, who was now bringing him up to date on his latest conversation with the prosecutor in the Woolf case,

"He's moving ahead with the case," Nigel told him. "The material is considered good enough to lead to a conviction."

"That's great news," Jason said.

"Perhaps. He isn't holding out much hope for a long conviction based on his criminal activities—the documentation is too circumstantial at times. But from a tax perspective, Woolf is toast."

Which would mean a longish sentence in a comfy medium security jail. "But those pictures of him with those young girls, the underage boys…"

"I know, they don't exactly paint him as a saint. And yes, in one of them he's obviously engaging in sexual activities with one of the girls. But from there to prove he's brought them into the country…" Nigel sighed. "The prosecutor said a man called Williams had come forward, confessing he's the mastermind behind the trafficking."

"And they believe him?" Jason closed his hand round a burst of heat.

"No. But his name appears in some of the emails and he's given a description of the activities—what can they do but accept his confession at face value?"

"So Woolf gets away."

"I get the feeling he always gets away. Always has, always will." Nigel laughed darkly. "Well, with the exception of the time you killed him for what he'd done to you."

"Once over the span of fifty-odd lives. Lucky bastard." Jason unclenched his hand, snapped his fingers and watched a solitary flame dance from fingertip to fingertip. "Maybe it's time for a repeat performance."

"I didn't hear that," Nigel said. "Look, I have to rush. Talk to Helle, Jason. Better yet, do something with her for a change."

Jason made a face at the phone before cradling his head in his hands. Woolf must have paid this unknown Williams a fortune to take the rap on the trafficking case, but the bastard could probably afford it. A series of successful lives must have left Samion with hidden funds all over the world, just like Jason himself.

He shifted his gaze to the meeting room. Helle was on the phone, and she was laughing, eyes bright as she gestured with her free arm. He smiled, despite his mood. Animation suited her, it brought roses to her cheeks, decisiveness to her movements. Do something with her, Nigel had said…well, he could think of a number of things he wanted to do with her, but a good starting point was probably to take her out to a long leisurely lunch.

Said and done; he was at the door of the meeting room in seconds.

"Don't be silly, John," Helle said, laughing out loud. "You can't seriously believe in stuff like that." She had her back to Jason, tilting her head to the side as she listened to whatever John was saying.

"Well, she's too old to believe in nonsense like that. Besides, she's been at Lourdes once a year the last forty years or so, apparently. If the Virgin planned to heal her, she'd have done so by now, don't you think?"

She cocked her head. "What? You didn't know? She never told you about her visits to Lourdes?"

Jason did a double take. Why were they discussing Katherine?

"You think?" Helle punched some keys on her laptop. She burst out laughing again. "Levitate? Her?"

Jason cleared his throat, incensed by the fact that she was laughing at Katherine. Helle whirled. He glared at her. She glared back, before demonstratively turning away.

"I know," she said to John, listening intently. "Sure, lunch tomorrow sounds great. Call me, okay?" She laughed again. "Uh-uh. Fish or salads, your choice." She rang off.

Jason folded his arms and waited. Helle busied herself at her laptop. Will sauntered past, throwing them a curious look. Helle continued with what she was doing. Jason leaned back against the wall. Jim popped his head in.

"Lunch?" he asked. "Steve and Angela are coming too."

"Sure," Helle said. "I'll just get my coat." She gave Jason a bland smile. "Coming?" Like a slippery trout, she evaded his hands.

"No, I have work to do." He caught her eyes. "We'll talk when you're back."

Chapter 20

The moment she got back from her lunch, Jason cornered Helle and marched her into his office.

"I don't like it when you discuss Katherine with John," he said, without any preamble whatsoever.

"Why not?" She seated herself in one of the armchairs by the window.

"Because she's my mother!"

"She's his great-aunt and discussing her with you is not exactly an option, is it?" She gave him a challenging look.

"I'd hoped we'd eat lunch together, just the two of us," he grumbled. The change in subject surprised her.

"You didn't ask, did you?" He looked tired, she noted, the dark shadow on his cheeks indicating he'd not shaved this morning. In between his mother and Helle's restless nights, he wasn't catching enough sleep or eating as he should.

Jason shrugged, no more. "Nigel called."

"Oh." She traced the intricate red pattern that decorated the blue background of the Turkish carpet with her foot.

"He said you were feeling abandoned."

"He did?" Helle crossed her legs. "I'm not sure I phrased it quite like that, more along the lines that I'd really like to spend time with you outside of the office."

His cheeks darkened. "We do. I sleep beside you every night, don't I?"

"And that's a point in your favour? That you sleep at home? Where else would you sleep?" She took a breath or two to calm herself. "We're married, remember? As far as I know, that means more than just sleeping beside each other."

"We do more than that."

"Not much." She tugged at her rings. "You spend all your free time with Katherine."

"And is that so strange?"

"Frankly? Yes, I think it is. When was the last time you played a padel tennis game with Curtis and Nigel? The last time you took me out? Sheesh, sometimes I almost think she's cast a spell on you, tying you to that wheelchair of hers."

Jason rocked back in his chair, placed his feet on his desk and crossed them. "Well, excuse me for being somewhat derailed by all this. Besides, I've always made it clear you're welcome to come with me."

"Yeah, right. Such fun for me, to hear you talk about things I don't know anything about. And it's not as if Katherine wants me to be there."

"Don't be silly," he said.

"Silly?" Helle raised her brows. "So from now on it's okay if I come along to all your marathon one-on-one sessions? Hey, I know: I can dress all in white and blend with the décor, so as not to cramp your style. That way you can continue treating me as if I'm invisible, like you've done the few times I've tagged along."

"Sometimes, I suspect she's right," he snapped. "You can't stand not being the centre of my attention."

"Fuck you." Helle stomped out of his office, heels ringing on the hardwood floor.

"Bloody hell," she heard him mutter as she went. "I don't have time for this."

Great. Moments later, she was in the Bentley with Tim, deciding she'd prefer to work from home for the rest of the day. Jason called, of course.

"Where are you going?"

"Home." Helle nibbled at one of her nails.

"Oh." He sighed. "Look, what I said, it came out wrong."

"No kidding."

"We need to talk. I'll be back as soon as I can, but I've promised Katherine that we'll have dinner together, and—"

"Sure," she cut him off. "I'll cook something for myself. Getting quite good at it by now."

He breathed deeply a couple of times. "Don't be like that."

"Like what? Alone?"

"Helle," he groaned. "She's my long-lost mother!"

"And I'm your long-lost love—or so you say."

He was silent. She hung up.

She spent most of the afternoon on her files, distracted herself by calling Mum around six and talking about everything but Katherine. Not a viable tactic with Miriam, who interrupted her midway through a little speech about the benefits of the new MS Office suite.

"So, how's the mother-in-law daughter-in-law thing progressing?"

Helle made a face. When she'd told Miriam about Katherine, her mother had been so stunned the conversation had gone seriously one-sided for the rest of that particular call, but after that first shocked reaction, Miriam had pretty much taken the appearance of Jason's long-dead mother in stride, saying that with all the odd things that were happening in Helle's life lately, one more didn't make much of a difference.

"Let's just say I have no intention of inviting her to a movie anytime soon," Helle said, trying to sound casual.

"She resents you," Miriam stated with a little sigh.

"Resents me? Maybe. She doesn't like me much, that's for sure."

"Cow," her mother said, making Helle laugh. Miriam cleared her throat. "And Sam Woolf?"

Helle tightened her hold on her phone. "So far, nothing. He's still in France." Involuntarily, she threw a look at the monitor that sat on the wall just beside Jason's desk. His study was by far the best place to work in, and it came with the benefit of also housing the control panel for the advanced home security. The feeds from all the cameras, the green lights ensuring none of the alarms were breached—they were all visible on the TV-sized monitor.

"But he won't stay there forever, will he?" Miriam's voice shook. "Why don't you do as I've said and come to visit us here? If nothing else you can work on your tan—one of the benefits of living in a desert—and maybe you'd be safer in this compound than in London." Helle rolled her eyes. As if.

"That's where Katherine comes in," she said. "She's supposed to help us put an end to Woolf, once and for all."

"And you think she can?" Mum snorted. "She's an old lady in a wheelchair."

"I think only a fool would underestimate her," Helle replied. "Jason is quite convinced she can handle Woolf."

They talked some more, Mum moaned a bit about being stuck in Saudi over Christmas, and when they rang off, Helle decided to call it a day, snapping her laptop closed. After one last look at the security monitor, she left the study, throwing a glance at the grandfather clock by the door. Already seven o'clock, so by now Jason was happily ensconced with Katherine, his long frame draped over one of her pristine white sofas while they talked about whatever it was they talked about— their gifts, maybe, she thought snidely.

An hour or so later, Helle was in clean sweats, her hair still damp from her recent shower. A long session on the treadmill had not only worked the edge off her anger, but had also made her hungry, so she balanced a plate of fried eggs in one hand, her laptop held tight under her other arm as she headed for the living room.

She lit the gas fire, waved the remote control in the general direction of the hi-fi system and selected one of her upbeat Spotify lists before folding her legs beneath her and settling down on the sofa.

There was a new email on her computer when she opened it. She clicked on it, and her screen went a dark red. White lettering marched across the screen, one word at the time; by the eighth word, Helle was on her phone, calling Jason. No reply. She stared at the words: *IF YOU EVER WANT TO SEE HIM ALIVE AGAIN, COME TO THE WOOLF & PARTNER GARAGE. NOW. ALONE. TIME IS TICKING...* A timer came up, counting backwards from forty-five minutes.

Once again, she tried Jason. And again. Still no reply. On her screen the message dissolved into an image of Jason tied to a chair, his shirt stained with blood, a dirty gag in his mouth. The same purple shirt he'd been wearing earlier, the pink and purple striped tie knocked askew. Desperate eyes met hers, and Helle's heart nosedived, her throat burning with bile.

Two more fruitless calls to Jason; Helle was about to burst. She hesitated, then called Nigel.

"You can't go!" Nigel exclaimed once she'd filled him in. "Hang on, I'll..." He put the call on loudspeaker. "John is here."

"John?"

"Stapleton. We're working on the case files."

"Oh." As if she cared—what good were the case files if Woolf already had Jason? "Look, I have to—"

"No!" Nigel and John said simultaneously. "It's a trap," John added.

"Maybe. But Jason..." She bit her lip. The timer was down to thirty minutes.

"Send me the mail," Nigel interrupted. She did, with a couple of keystrokes, no more. Her hand shook as she gripped her phone, parked Nigel's call, and redialled Jason's number. Nothing: it just went directly to voicemail.

There was a strangled sound from Nigel, a string of muttered expletives from John. "This is a hoax," Nigel said, his voice tinny over the loudspeaker function.

"Really? You know that for sure?"

"It has to be," Nigel insisted. "We'd have heard if someone grabbed him. Tim or Daniel would—"

"Daniel didn't drive him—he was taking a cab to Katherine's place." Helle frowned. Since meeting Katherine, Jason had become far more relaxed regarding his own security, saying his mother would always warn him should he be in danger. Clearly, he'd overestimated her abilities. Helle swallowed. And swallowed.

"I still say it's a hoax." Nigel's breathing whistled down the line.

"I agree," John said. "Besides, even if it isn't—"

"So you're a hundred per cent certain?" Helle broke in, not wanting to hear John conclude that sentence.

No response. A couple of heartbeats and Nigel sighed. "No."

"I can't gamble on those odds," Helle said, "I have to—"

"I'll call Katherine," John said.

"I don't have time for this." Helle was already at the door, shoving her feet into boots and tugging at her jacket.

"I'm coming with you," Nigel said.

"He said alone." Helle unlocked the gunsafe they'd installed in the hall and retrieved the small semi-automatic. She slipped two magazines of ammo into her pocket.

"She's not picking up." John came back on line. "I'll try her neighbours, and see if—"

"Bye."

"Helle, no!" Nigel's voice rose. She hung up. Time was ticking. At least Nigel knew where she was going.

She paid the cab. At this time of night, the streets round Cannon Street station were relatively empty, all the people who worked their butts off in the City during the day having long gone home. A chilly fog made her shiver, made worse by the cold sweat on her chest and back—as if she was running a temperature. She so didn't want to do this. She didn't want to set as much as a toe on Woolf's premises. Helle took a couple of steps towards the entrance, stopped and retreated. A sheer wall of glass and stainless steel rose before her, not one single light on in the entire building. Once again, she tried Jason's phone. It went directly to voice mail.

Where are u? she texted. *Please tell me you're okay. I need to know.* Maybe he was at the office, she thought, and for some seconds she considered hurrying over to Jason's offices instead. On foot, it would take too long, she calculated, drawing a mental map to Queen Street.

"Oh God," she whispered before squaring her shoulders and making for the door to the foyer. For some moments, she hoped to find it locked. The camera above the door whirred, tilted in her direction. The lock flashed green and the door swung open. She dithered, one foot on the threshold. Her pulse thumped loudly in her head. This was a bad, bad idea.

Her phone beeped, and for an instant she was giddy with relief—until she saw the sender was Nigel. Yet another text telling her to not do this, to wait for them. No news about Jason. Her stomach twisted. If Woolf had Jason, he would… A deep breath and she stepped inside. Behind her, the door closed, the lock reactivating. Trapped. For reassurance, she pulled the gun, shoved a magazine into place, racked the first round, and returned the semi-automatic to the pocket of her jacket. Didn't help much, her sweaty hand slipping on the grip.

She crouched down by the stairwell. Maybe Nigel was right, maybe she should just wait for them. She didn't know what to do. Her legs definitely didn't want to walk down the stairs, her head was telling her to wait, but her heart … she clutched at her chest, feeling a sudden burst of pain. Her phone beeped, the sound so loud in the silent building she jumped. An email. From him.

I AM WAITING, it said, accompanied by a close-up of a gun, pressed against Jason's temple. They'd hit him: one eye was swollen shut, his nose awry and bleeding. Helle had to bite her fist not to cry out. Somehow, she got to her feet, gripped the handrail and took the first step downwards.

The inside door to the garage squeaked when she pulled it open. She groped for the lightswitch. There was a laugh from somewhere in the dark, a car engine turned, and she was blinded by the headlights of the car standing some fifty feet in front of her. Her hand slipped on the light switch, fingers trembling like mad when she flipped it, causing the overhead lighting to hum into life.

"Helle—at last." The voice was soft. Every atom of air was squeezed from her lungs. He was here, and she was lost. Jason, she reminded herself, eyes flying over the darkened garage. Nowhere did she see him, nowhere was a man dangling from a noose, or sitting bloodied in a chair. She did, however, see Sam Woolf.

Accompanied by two men, he was leaning back against a black Porsche Macan, wearing black jeans and a black shirt tight on his impressively broad and tall frame. If anything, he looked younger than when she'd seen him last, his hair as dark and curly as she remembered, his face as handsome, despite the four parallel claw marks that decorated his left cheek. A memento from Helle, the result of her frenzied defence of Jason back in January.

Jason. "Where is he?" she croaked.

"Not here," Woolf replied. She gulped and retreated towards the door. It banged shut, the lock clicking in place. Helle tugged at the handle, and Woolf snickered. "I do have some tricks up my sleeve. That door won't budge." He gestured at the car. "Get in."

Her brain screeched in protest. *A trap, this is a goddamn trap, and you knew that!* Yes, of course she knew, but what choice did she have if Woolf had Jason? *If he has him*, her brain howled. *If!*

"What have you done to him?" she asked.

"You'll never know unless you come with me. And if you don't…" Woolf mimed a pulled trigger. Helle's mouth dried up completely. Once again, he motioned at the car.

Helle shook her head.

"No?" Woolf laughed and strolled towards her, waving for his two men to remain where they were. Helle was rooted to the spot by his eyes. "I don't like it when my women don't obey."

"I'm not your woman," she managed to say, and then he was standing beside her, reaching out to touch her face. Something like a tremor flew through him when his fingers connected with her skin. Such a gentle touch, and she wanted desperately to lean into it.

"No? And yet, here you are, without your man by your side. Where is Jason, one wonders?" Woolf chuckled. His breath tickled her cheek as he leaned forward. "Not here. Not with you."

Helle tightened her hold on the gun. "You don't have him?"

"Who knows: maybe he's languishing in my cellar." His lips grazed her brow. She made a futile attempt to back away, but with him this close she was sapped of any willpower, his commanding voice thudding through her blood, her head, one single word: 'Mine'.

Woolf laughed again, his fingers sending jolts through her as he ran them up and down her neck. She moaned.

"Maybe I've gone about this the wrong way," he said, nibbling at her ear. "Maybe I shouldn't threaten you with pain, maybe I should tempt you with pleasure instead." She needed to sit down. His spicy scent, his warmth, his gentle lips and equally soft fingers had her swaying on the spot. "Seduce you," he murmured, and his lips slid down her neck. "Pleasure you like in those dreams."

She tilted her head back, offering her throat to him, and he chuckled. "Ah, yes: submit to me, give yourself over to a life with me, a life in which your mind and heart is wiped free of that accursed Wanderer."

No, she didn't want that! *Oh yes, you do*, his voice mocked her, echoing through her head. *Anything to please me, remember?*

"He will forget you anyway now that his mother is here," he said. "Assuming I let him live, of course." Oh, God: he had her Jason. A loud howl echoed inside her brain, pain and panic tumbling through her veins. But she didn't protest or move away—she was incapable of doing so—and when he dipped his head and kissed her, she let him, parting her lips under his. A long kiss, sucking every last drop of resistance from her. 'Mine' his voice repeated in her head, and she was, of course she was his, she belonged with this man, had always belonged with him. He deepened the kiss, he ravaged her mouth, his hand closing painfully in her hair. For an instant, her mind cleared. What was she doing, kissing Woolf? She tried to pull free. He twisted his fingers into her hair. In her anguish, she tightened her finger round the trigger.

The resulting shots echoed round the garage. Woolf leapt back, cursing. She'd shot at the floor, a spray of bullets that left a singed hole through her pocket, a burn on her thigh. A flare of pain connected with her brain, wiping away Woolf's velvet voice. Helle was no longer paralysed; she stumbled backwards, pointing the wobbling gun at him.

"Leave me alone!"

His eyes narrowed. "Never! I'll never let that red-haired bastard keep you." He lunged, she squeezed the trigger again, and he threw himself to the floor. One of his men yelled. Woolf cursed. Helle took the opportunity and fled, making for the exit ramp. Woolf made a grab for her ankle, she went down, landing painfully on her hands and knees. The gun went off again. Helle kicked Woolf in the face and she was free, scrambling to her feet.

"Bitch!" Woolf exclaimed, and his two goons came rushing towards them. She set off at a run.

A car came hurtling down the narrow ramp. It screeched to a halt, and Jason almost fell out.

"Helle!"

"Here! I'm over here!" She rushed towards him, ignoring how her knees ached.

Something whizzed past her head and Jason spread his arms wide, a protective wall of heat causing the paint on the ceiling to blister and smoke.

"Get your arse over here!" Nigel held the back door open, Helle scrambled inside. John turned to look at her.

"All right?" he asked.

"Jason," she gasped. "How—"

"One little old lady finally answered her phone," John said drily. "He must have flown down the street to meet us." His gaze was fixed on the spectacle of Jason, backing towards the car while keeping Woolf and his two men at bay with walls of flame. "Impressive," he muttered.

"Bloody, fucking unbelievable," Nigel squeaked. "Shit, he told me about the fire thing, but this…"

This was Jason at his mightiest—and most ancient. A man silhouetted against a firestorm, flames every shade of yellow and red rising from the floor to lick the ceiling. The Porsche exploded. The garage was full of noise, wailing fire alarms echoing painfully in the enclosed space. The sprinklers came on, and steam rose from the overheated floor, the stench of burning tyres making Helle gag.

"Let's go!" John yelled, revving the car. Jason leapt inside, the car took off, negotiating the curve on its left-hand side wheels only. Up the ramp, outside, and Helle slumped back against the seat.

"Shit," she said.

"What in the world were you thinking of?" Jason turned in his seat, eyes wild, hair standing on end, hands bright red. "How could you do something that stupid?"

"Hey!" She leaned forward. "If you'd only picked up on my calls, this wouldn't have happened." With shaking hands, she ensured the safety on the gun was back on before placing it on the floor.

Jason didn't reply. John was looking straight ahead, Nigel concentrated on his phone.

"Why didn't you?" she demanded.

"I left it in my jacket," he said with a little shrug.

"On mute, right? So that my calls wouldn't disturb your endless reunion sessions with your so-called mother."

"Not now," Jason warned.

Helle crossed her arms over her chest and stared stubbornly out of the window for the rest of the ride.

John dropped them off, Nigel promising to call next morning. They were alone, locked into a silence so glacial Jason could almost touch it. Once inside, Jason reactivated the alarms and turned to look at her. She was pale, eyes red-rimmed and swollen, and he realised with a start she must have spent most of the drive back home crying.

"Are you all right?" He made as if to touch her. She backed away fast.

"Don't touch me!" She limped off in the direction of the living room.

He followed her. "How did this happen?"

"How?" She marched over to her laptop, tapped in her password, and without a word turned it towards him. He studied the e-mail, watched it disintegrate into a photoshopped picture of himself before it reformed into the original text message. Very effective—especially the detail with his clothes. He frowned. "How did he know what I was wearing?"

"No idea. But what he couldn't have known was that you wouldn't pick up." She glared at him. "What sort of an irresponsible asshole are you? I must have called you like a dozen times."

"I didn't know something like this would happen," he tried.

"No? Well guess what? That's why we have phones, so that we can tell each other when weird and scary stuff happens." She exploded out of the sofa and began pacing. "I could have been with him right this minute! With him, goddamn it and it would have been your fault!"

"I'm sorry," he began, "I—"

"Sorry? This is fucking Sam Woolf we're talking about, the man we're supposed to be fighting as a team. What sort of a team is it when one of us is always alone while the other can't get enough of his mama?" She was crying now, but when he made a grab for her, she shoved him away. "I was this close—this close!—to being abducted by him! And what were you doing? Drinking tea with your precious mother. I bet you wouldn't even have noticed I was gone until sometime tomorrow." Tears streaked her face and she wiped at her eyes with her sleeve.

"Forgive me," he said. "Please, Helle, let me—" Hold you and comfort you, he intended to add. But she was beyond cuddling, almost snarling at him when he got too close.

"You'd switched the sound off on purpose," she said, taking yet another turn round the sofa.

He fiddled with his phone. A new text, from her. His throat clogged as he read it.

"Katherine doesn't like mobile phones. She finds them stressful." He winced at the look she gave him.

"Oh, she does? She has hers sitting right beside her chair all the time." Helle pushed her hair off her face and sat down in one of the armchairs.

"That's different. She needs it in case she needs to call for help. And she never as much as looks at it while I am there."

Helle raised her brows and turned to look out the window. "Bully for her. But I assumed you would always pick up if I called—just as you've always assumed I'll do the same. After all, it's not that long ago since you yelled at me for not answering your calls, remember?"

There was nothing to do but crawl. "You're right. I shouldn't have left it in my jacket."

Which he'd done on purpose, not wanting her to call and nag if he was late. Nag? A wall of heat crawled up his throat and face. What was he thinking? Jason frowned down at his hands, studying the ring Helle had given him back in February. A heavy platinum ring, it was decorated with two infinity symbols and an engraved torch, her way of telling him she believed his story and believed in them—forever. And here he was, all knocked askew by Nefirie—Katherine—and her constant disparagement of Helle, the gossamer spells she wound round him with her voice and presence. He set his mouth, uncomfortable that he should be harbouring these thoughts about his mother.

"You're the one who decided we should never go anywhere without our phones," she reminded him.

"And I also told you never to leave the house on your own," he flashed back.

"And what would you have done, had you received that e-mail?" she asked heatedly. "Wouldn't you have done the same?"

He sighed. "Probably. But it's different, I'm—"

"Gifted. Like your mother, not like your boring wife."

"I didn't say that."

"No, but she has, remember?" Her voice was sharp with hurt. "And how come you can't tell her you need to keep your phone on you? She knows about this whole Woolf thing."

"Katherine says she'll always know if you're in real danger."

"Oh, wow. So now you trust your psychic mother more than you trust these?" She held up her phone. "Well guess what? I don't. And besides, if what she says is true, how come she didn't pick up on tonight, huh?"

"Maybe she didn't sense any real menace," he said, hearing himself just how ridiculous that sounded. Helle gave him a look so cold he winced.

"There is always menace where Sam Woolf is concerned. And clearly, she didn't pick up on Woolf being back in England, so her radar is damned deficient. Alternatively, she did, but chose not to tell you. Maybe she was hoping Woolf would carry me off and she could spend the rest of her life happily monopolising you."

"Don't be ridiculous!" he snapped.

"And don't you patronise me. Just for your information, I will not accept being relegated to second best again." She met his eyes. "Ever."

He just nodded.

After a couple of heartbeats, she stood. "I'm going to bed." She didn't invite him to join her, she just marched out of the room and up the stairs. He heard the bathroom door bang, the lock clicking into place, and he scrubbed at his face and sighed. He was in deep shit—and he deserved to be.

Much later, he sneaked up to join her in bed. Where she would normally sleep naked, now she was in a t-shirt and yoga pants, her pillows lying right at the edge of her side of the bed. He could hear she wasn't sleeping; her breathing was too irregular, but when he rolled over to kiss her cheek she didn't respond, lying as still as a corpse under his touch.

Damn. Jason flopped over on his back and threw an arm over his face. He'd screwed up big time, and Helle could at this very moment have been with Woolf. In fact, she should have been, a gun little protection against Samion's powers. She must have taken him by surprise, he thought, turning towards her. His lioness, always springing to his defence. Jason shifted as close to her as he dared, resting his arm lightly on her hip.

He dipped his nose in her hair and inhaled, trying to ignore the niggling feeling of unease regarding his mother. Helle was right: Katherine should have felt Samion's presence. If so, why hadn't she warned him? Come to think of it, she'd looked annoyed rather than worried when Jason had rushed off. He closed his eyes in a vain effort to clear his brain of these unsettling thoughts. Tomorrow, he decided, he'd have it out with Katherine tomorrow.

Korine wouldn't stop crying. Nefirie had heard her screams and come running only to find the little girl staring in fear at the wall.

"What did you see?" Nefirie said, pulling the girl into her lap. Her hands were hot, and when Nefire smoothed her hair, the heat pulsed beneath her fingers.

"Why does he hurt her?" Korine asked, hiccupping with tears, "It is so unfair, because he is so much stronger."

Nefirie shushed her.

"I only see him harming them, I only see my father dead," the child wailed, little spurts of fire leaking from her fingers. "I cannot see you, Nana," Korine turned her haunted eyes to Nefirie, "Why are you not there?"

"I am afraid, Korine," Nefirie replied, her voice catching in her throat. She buried her face in the girl's glowing curls. "I am so afraid."

Chapter 21

When Jason woke, Helle was already up. He found her in the gym, in only a sports bra and tight shorts, working through her weight routine. Jason studied her from the door, taking in the muscles on her back, the rounded curve of her buttocks, even more pronounced when she did her series of deadlifts. His wife—despite everything he smiled as he thought the word—was killing herself today, the barbell loaded well above her normal challenge.

Sweat coated her skin and darkened the fabric of her shorts and bra. He wondered how long she'd been in here and why she hadn't woken him instead. Except, of course, that he knew why: Helle was hurt and terrified and angry, and he wished he could take a damp towel and wipe her clean of all those negative emotions. He caught her eyes in the mirror. A nanosecond of communication, then her lashes lowered, breaking their contact. He sighed—loudly. She ignored him, grunting as she did the last of her reps.

"I'm seeing Katherine this afternoon," he began, intending to tell her he was going to ask his mother a number of pointed questions. She never gave him the opportunity to get that far. Without a word, she pushed past him and ran up the stairs to the bathroom. Once again, he heard the lock click.

"Will you at least listen to me?" he asked, knocking at the door. "I said, I was—"

"I heard," she cut him off, her voice muffled by the door. Moments later, the water came on.

Jason used the downstairs bathroom, dressed and cooked breakfast, and still she didn't appear. Eventually he climbed the stairs again.

"There's breakfast downstairs."

"Not hungry," she responded through the door.

213

He was tempted to tell her to grow up—adults didn't hold conversations through doors. Instead, he placed his hand on the wood, fingers splayed, and wished he was touching her.

"Are you still mad at me?" he asked, wanting to laugh at the idiotic question.

"Have a guess." She had moved closer to the door, and he imagined her spreading her palm against the wood on her side. A palmer's kiss—but with a thick layer of wood between them.

"We have a staff meeting in half an hour," he said.

"You'll have to take it without me. I have a headache."

He leaned his head against the door. "Don't be like this, lioness."

"Like what? Shit scared?"

"He'll not get to you," he said.

"He almost did last night."

"That's because you went off on your own. You know—"

"Lately, I'm always on my own," she said. He winced at the abandonment in her voice. She cleared her throat and went on in a substantially colder tone. "If you'd been here, with me, when I got that damned e-mail, none of this would have happened Or if you'd at least picked up when I called you."

"I'm sorry," he said, feeling just how inadequate those words were. "It won't happen again." He heard her breathing through the door.

"Good," was all she said. He waited for more, but she remained silent. With a sigh, he turned away.

"I'll be back around five."

No reply, just that heavy silence that made his guts twist.

"Remember, straight back home," Jason said to Tim as he stepped out of the Bentley. "And make sure she doesn't take off somewhere without you." He glanced at his watch. He'd double-checked the alarms three times as he left, but he preferred it if Tim was there as well, just in case.

"Sir," Tim nodded.

"She's in a foul mood, so if you don't want her to bite your head off, I suggest you just call to check on her once you get back."

"Let's hope she answers," Tim said lightly. Jason gave him a sour look: Nigel, Stapleton and now Tim—they'd all made it very clear just how irresponsible they'd found him. Any moment now, he expected Curtis to call and add his disapproving baritone to the rest of the chorus, and the moment Miriam found out…No, best not think about that.

Jason adjusted his suit jacket. He'd trusted his mother, assuming Katherine's gifts were as impressive now as in the past, likewise assuming Katherine would keep a protective eye on Helle for his sake. In the bleak light of the December morning, he was having second thoughts about that second assumption, assailed by far too many memories of how disapproving Nefirie had been of his love for Helle back then, reinforced by her recent disparaging comments. Yet again, something slimy and cold slithered down his spine. Later; he tugged at his shirt cuffs. He'd talk to Katherine later.

Just before noon, Tim called to report that Helle had so far not shown any indication of wanting to leave the house. He'd spoken briefly to her on the phone and been told she wanted to be left alone.

"Should I check on her?" Tim asked.

Jason chewed his lip. "No," he finally said. "She might be sleeping." He tried her phone and ended up in voice mail. It made him frown. Payback for yesterday? He sent a text instead. *Everything ok?* Seconds later, he received a brief *Yes* in reply.

At three, Nigel popped by.

"Hi," he said, hesitating at the door to Jason's office. "I just wanted to check you were okay."

Jason gestured for Steve and Angela to leave the office. "Okay? Physically, yes." He flexed his hands, still sore after the previous night.

Nigel sidled in, his gaze never leaving Jason's hands. "What you did yesterday, that was awesome. Utterly freaky, but awesome."

"Now and then it comes in useful," Jason said, snapping his fingers to produce a miniature flame. Nigel gawked, then grinned.

"Yo, brother, you one cool dude," he said in an atrocious attempt at an American accent.

Jason snorted and busied himself saving his open documents. "I don't have much time, I'm off to see Katherine."

"Again? Today?" Nigel didn't even try to sound anything but disapproving. "Shouldn't you be sucking up to Helle instead?"

Jason ran a hand through his hair and gave his best friend an exasperated look. "I'm going to tell her Helle comes first."

"About bloody time." Nigel sat down. "Why does your so-called mother dislike Helle so much?"

"She doesn't," Jason responded automatically. Nigel sniffed. "She doesn't," Jason insisted. "She just doesn't think Helle is the best partner for me."

"By now she should have given up on changing your mind." Nigel gave Jason a narrow look. "Or maybe she has succeeded."

"What the fuck is that supposed to mean?" Jason bristled.

"Recently, you haven't exactly been standing devotedly at Helle's side, have you? If my mother had spoken about Miranda like Katherine did about Helle, I'd—"

Jason held up his hand. "We've been over that. And yes, I should have behaved differently, but it's just..." He fell silent, not knowing quite how to phrase this. "For endless years, I've been wondering if Nefirie was still around. She was so devastated by my actions back then—a Wanderer was not supposed to kill, we were healers, not takers of life—and I... well, I suppose I wanted an opportunity to talk to her again, explain myself and hope she'd understand that I did it because I had to.

"My Helle was gone, and the moment she died back then, my life ceased to be, the only thing keeping me breathing was this dangerous desire for revenge." Jason shut his laptop and undocked it. Not much of a life, to live only to kill. And all those lives when he'd searched the world for Helle—they'd not been a walk in the park either.

"And did she?" Nigel asked, interrupting his thoughts.

"Hmm?"

"Katherine. Did—does—she understand?"

Jason shrugged. "I'm not sure. But seeing her, talking to her, has somehow dulled the guilt." He gave his friend a thoughtful look. "I no longer feel responsible for her distress. In fact, there are days when I wonder if it isn't the other way around. Maybe she could have stopped what happened to Helle and me." He inhaled deeply. "But I feel like a shit for even voicing that thought."

"How stopped?" Nigel wondered.

"She was always opposed to our union." He laughed at Nigel's expression. "Our marriage, then. So maybe she didn't protect us as much as she could have."

Jason zipped up the computer bag. "Would you do me a favour? Could you drop by and check on Helle? It'll be a couple of hours before I'm home, and she's been alone—and damned quiet—all day." Come to think of it, he hadn't received one single e-mail from her, which was strange given their ongoing acquisition project. Maybe she hadn't felt like working today, but on the other hand, Helle always used work to distract herself from things.

"Sure." Nigel grabbed his rucksack. "I'll pop by after I've been to the dentist. You can cook us dinner when you get home—no red meat, mind you, and I'm staying clear of carbs as well."

"You are?" If anyone needed carbs, it was Nigel.

"Yes." Nigel patted his belly. "I need to stay in shape now that I have a veritable Lilith in my bed."

"Miranda doesn't strike me as a demon," Jason commented drily.

"No? Well, you haven't battled my temptress in bed."

"Nor do I intend to." He wasn't much looking forward to ever seeing Miranda again.

"I should bloody well hope so. If you did, I'd have to kill you." Nigel gave him a little wave and sauntered out of the room.

Katherine had made tea. A delicate scent of jasmine tickled his nostrils as he entered her flat, but instead of imbuing him with a sense of peace, he found it cloying. The white walls, the white furniture, the white cups, the absence of any other sensory stimuli—for the first time since first entering this flat he felt suffocated by all this whiteness. Jason sank down on the sofa and accepted a cup of tea, studying Katherine over the rim of his cup.

He wasn't looking forward to this conversation. Either it would confirm his faith in his mother was misplaced because she no longer wielded the powers she once had, or he'd have to accept she did not care for Helle's well-being. Whatever the outcome, one thing was certain: he could never trust her as he had done.

If she picked up on his preoccupation, Katherine hid it well. As unperturbed as always, she sipped her tea, allowing the silence to lengthen.

"I gather it was all a lot of smoke and no fire yesterday," Katherine said after a while.

Jason set down his cup. "What exactly is that supposed to mean?"

"Helle. She came to no harm, did she?"

"That depends on how you define harm," he said. "Close to an hour thinking Woolf had grabbed me and was about to blow my head off probably left her in drowning in panic."

Katherine snorted. "You? If Woolf had tried to harm you, I'd—"

"Have done what?"

"Stopped him, of course."

"How?" Jason asked.

Her mouth curled into a little smile. "Do you need to ask? I'd have known the moment you'd been in danger and—"

"Like you said you'd sense if there were any threats to Helle," he interrupted.

"I said that?" Katherine studied her tea before raising those almost yellow eyes in his direction. "Maybe I was wrong. After all, she's not my flesh and blood, not like you are."

"You're never wrong," Jason said harshly. "You may lie, by intent or omission, but you're not wrong." He felt the power surge around her, her mouth setting in a firm line. "So why,

218

Mother? You told me I could safely leave my phone in my jacket, you would warn me if anything was wrong, and yet you didn't."

Katherine shifted on the seat of her wheelchair. "I'm not infallible, Jason."

"Oh, yes you are." He met her eyes. "Explain."

"She wasn't in any real danger," Katherine said at long last, dropping her gaze to her hands.

"So you did know," Jason stated, a knot of ice forming in his stomach.

Katherine shrugged, still with her eyes on her clasped hands. "No specifics, I'm not a clairvoyant. But yes, I could sense that he'd reached out to her."

"Reached out to her? He set a trap for her! A trap he baited with me, knowing full well she'd feel she had no choice but to do what she could to try and save me." His lioness, his woman, strong enough to overcome her fears for his sake, just as she'd once endured months with Samion to keep him alive.

Katherine gave him a condescending look. "Samion would never kill her."

"Not immediately, no," Jason replied, setting his teeth. "But over time, he'd destroy her, ripping her soul to shreds."

She snickered. "So dramatic, Jason. What he wants is what you want—Helle. Not, I might add, as a corpse, but as a living woman who pleasures him in bed and gives him children." Her casual tone made him want to slap her. She was talking about Helle as she would about a brood mare or a cow. He took a couple of breaths to calm himself. Losing your temper with Nefirie—Katherine—never helped.

"She doesn't want him."

"No." Katherine sighed. "She never did, did she? Fortunately, Samion can be quite seductive when he wants to. I dare say she'd enjoy the experience of being enthralled by him."

"Mother!"

"What? I am merely stating a fact. He'd seduce her—he's done so before, remember?—and soon enough she'd forget about you."

"Seduce her?" Jason wanted to throttle her. "Last time round, he broke her."

She gave him one of those unperturbed looks that reduced him to the level of a child of six. "She disobeyed him, humiliated him. Had she wed him back then, we wouldn't be here right now. We'd be up there..." She gestured vaguely at the triangle of sky visible through her window, "...at peace."

"So this is all her fault, is it?"

"Who else's?" If anything, Katherine sounded bored.

"It was his fault," Jason hissed. "It was Samion who—"

"You killed! You committed suicide because of her!" Two spots of red appeared on Katherine's cheeks. "You left me because of her! Always because of her!" The vitriol in her tone made him lean away from her. Scales fell from his eyes: before him sat a woman corroded with jealousy, bitter-green and poisonous.

"Don't make me choose between you," he warned, rising to his feet.

"Choose?" Katherine's hands gripped the armrests of the wheelchair, talon-like almost. "You came to me for help, not the other way around."

"I did. But if that help involves letting Helle go, I don't want it. I'd rather die than lose her." Jason looked down at her, at the snow-white hair, at her face, that exquisite bone structure making it as striking in old age as it had been when she was young. "If you want to blame someone for this entire mess, it should be Samion. What he did to her, to me, during those months of captivity, that's what ultimately drove me to despair and death. He alone carries the blame."

Katherine had gone quite grey, lips almost bloodless.

"Mother? Are you all right?"

"I'm fine," she croaked. "Just a touch of angina." She took a couple of deep breaths. "What do you want from me, Jason?"

"A life," he replied simply.

"You already have one. In fact, you've had several."

"All without her," he said bitterly. "And now that I've finally found her again, that accursed Samion has to show up!"

"Of course, he does," Katherine said. "Your fates are intertwined. They've been knotted together since the day you eschewed eternal peace by murdering him in revenge."

"Peace?" Jason gave her a tired look. "There is no peace for me, not without her." Katherine held his eyes for a long time. With a little sigh, she raised her gnarled hand to his face, cupping his cheek.

"Oh, Jason," Katherine's face softened into a tender smile. "For your sake, I'll do what I can to fix this."

"Including keeping Helle safe?"

Katherine's mouth flattened, but she nodded all the same. "Including that."

"Good. Because if anything happens to her…" He left the rest of the sentence unsaid, an implied threat that he'd hold her responsible.

Katherine cleared her throat. "Message received, loud and clear. And now, could we—"

She was interrupted by Jason's phone, chirping loudly. She made a face, he shrugged. After yesterday, he would never put his phone on mute again, not unless Helle was with him.

It was Nigel. "She's not here."

"What?" Jason's hand tightened on his phone. "What do you mean, she isn't there?"

"Is there anything ambiguous about the statement? The house is empty. No Helle—anywhere."

"Can you see anything on the security feeds?"

"Hang on." The sound of fingers flying over a keyboard echoed down the line. "No break-in," Nigel said, and Jason's shoulders relaxed. More tapping. "Shit." Nigel cleared his throat. "She's gone."

"Gone? How gone?"

"She left the house at 8:05 this morning."

"What?" That was just after he'd left her.

"She's in Tor Cottage," Nigel interrupted, "at least according to her phone—and the tracking device in her bangle. Should she really be there on her own?"

"No." Jason pinched the bridge of his nose. "But at present, she'd tell you she's just as alone here as she is there."

"She has a point," Nigel said, an icy edge in his voice. Jason dragged a hand through his hair. Yes, she most certainly did. Not anymore, though; he rang off and turned to Katherine.

"I have to go."

"Of course. Helle always comes first," she said in a sour tone.

"Yes, she does. And she always will."

Katherine waved her hand in the direction of the door. "Just go, Jason."

Chapter 22

The moment she'd heard the Bentley drive off, Helle was out of the bathroom, releasing a cloud of steam in her wake. All through her morning workout, all through her shower, she'd been analysing last night's events, starting with how propitious it was that Sam Woolf should have sent that damned e-mail when Jason was with Katherine. One could almost think it was planned, with Jason adequately distracted while Woolf played out his little stunt. But that would mean...no: she banished these thoughts and concentrated on pulling on some clothes instead.

Minutes later, she reactivated the alarms and locked the house, ran down to where the Tesla was parked much further up the street, and threw her bag into the back seat. Jason's house was situated on one of those typical Kensington streets with elegant detached houses and well-kept front gardens, manicured shrubs spilling over black wrought-iron fencing. A nice quiet neighbourhood, so affluent every single one of these houseowners had at least two cars, and therein lay the problem, with parking being a constant squeeze.

The car hummed into life and she programmed her destination into the large embedded screen on the centre console. According to the stats, there was sufficient power in the battery to get her to Tor Cottage without a problem, so once she'd succeeded in manoeuvring the damn car from its ridiculously tight parking spot, she drove off, keeping a careful eye out for Tim—who should not be back for another thirty minutes or so anyway—and black luxury SUVs.

Helle shivered when she caught sight of a black Porsche Cayenne. The driver was a small woman, and she relaxed. During the night, she'd decided that she couldn't stay here, in London, not after last night, and as there was only one place where she felt truly safe, that was where she was going.

There was another benefit to her little plan: let Jason come home and find the house empty, let him experience a couple of minutes of heart-stopping fright—like she'd done yesterday. Not, she admitted to herself, the most mature approach to things, but she'd had it with his tendency to take her for granted which was what he'd done back in spring when he'd put Juliet's needs before hers, was doing again with his mother. Just thinking of Katherine made her grit her teeth. Once again, she was swamped by dark thoughts: had Woolf known where Jason was? He had definitely known Katherine was around.

Tor Cottage midway through December was not quite as picturesque as during the summer. But despite the cold and the rattling branches of the denuded trees and shrubs, Helle only had to set foot inside the porch to feel safe, an index finger tracing the protective wreath that adorned the heavy wooden door. The rowan leaves crumbled under her touch.

She pushed the door open and carried in her bag, standing for a moment in the kitchen to allow the sensation of peace and quiet to settle round her shoulders. Like a spiritual comfort blanket, she mused as she put away the foodstuffs in the fridge before inspecting the kitchen and pantry for any signs of mice. Helle sat down on Anne's chair. Home.

Jason texted her around noon, a short little thing that deserved nothing more than the one word reply she sent back. Idly, she wondered how long it would take for him to discover she wasn't sitting as snug as a bug in his—their—Kensington house.

At half past five, her phone rang.

"I'll be there in two hours," was all Jason said before ringing off, and she squirmed inside. He was angry with her and even if he damned well deserved it, she was slightly ashamed of her little stunt. The phone rang again.

"You realise you've landed me in the shit, don't you?" Nigel said drily.

"You?" Helle strolled over to the sofa, sinking down among the multi-coloured little cushions that decorated the purple monstrosity Jason refused to throw out.

"I've just had my head chewed off, along the lines that your phone should be constantly monitored, the house alarms should sound if someone leaves the house as well as enters it, and why haven't I put some sort of electronic cat bell on the damn Tesla?"

Helle laughed. "So he was upset?"

"Upset?" Nigel snorted. "Mostly with himself, I think," he added in a more normal voice. "I get the feeling there were words between him and Katherine."

"He can't use her as an excuse," Helle said.

"No." Nigel sounded hesitant.

"What?"

"She sounds…umm…intimidating. And from what Jason said, she's guilt-tripping him into spending time with her."

"How subtle," Helle said. "Guilt for what?"

"For having lost the will to live once you'd died? I don't know, but to hear it, that Nefirie was a rather demanding mother."

"Maybe." She didn't know.

"Another thing," Nigel said just before ringing off. "Woolf has just given a press conference in France. They've given him bail."

"Fantastic." She clenched her teeth. "This time, there are four of us to prove he was in that damned garage—one of them a police officer."

"Ah, yes…" Nigel cleared his throat. "John is not so sure it would be a good thing to push the matter. Leaving aside the car wreck, Jason's fires caused quite some damage. The electrical wiring and the entire ventilation system has to be revamped."

Once again, Woolf was slipping through their fingers. She brushed at her neck, following the path he'd traced last night. Such a light touch, leaving a wave of dark and shameful desire in its wake. Helle pressed her thighs together and sank her nails into her palms. Desire? No, this was not desire, this was compulsion, tinged with fear.

She'd just added the coriander to the chicken soup when she heard the car come down the drive. It bumped over the cattle grid and came to a halt beside the Tesla. Jason got out, his features faintly illuminated by the lamp over the main door. He was still in his suit and tie, carrying only his Tumi bag. He must have taken off directly from Katherine's once he heard she was here.

He leaned into the Bentley, talking to someone. Tim, Helle guessed. She was just about to suggest Tim join them for dinner when the Bentley reversed and drove off.

"He could have stayed the night," she said to Jason in lieu of greeting.

"I didn't want him to." He stepped out of his shoes and undid his tie. "I wanted to be alone with you." He went directly to the blinking panel by the kitchen door, fingers flying over the touch screen. The overhead lamps blinked a couple of times when he activated the electrical perimeter control.

"Come here," he said once he was done. Helle hung back.

"Lioness, don't play games with me. Not now, not today." Three strides and he had her caged against the wall, his mouth crushed against hers—more bruising than tender. "Forgive me," he said, releasing her lips. "Forgive me for being a self-absorbed fool, for not listening to you, for…" His hands slid up the column of her neck, cradling her face. "Damn it, Helle, he could have snatched you!"

Once again, his lips covered hers; this was a kiss filled with desperation, with sufficient heat to light a small bonfire.

"But he didn't," she said when they came up to breathe. She set her hand on his chest, and his heart thundered beneath it.

"No thanks to me." He kissed her eyes, her nose. "Or Nefirie." He spat out the name. "She knew," he said, giving her a stricken look. "She admitted as much, that she felt Woolf's presence close to you."

Having her suspicions confirmed did not bring the satisfaction she'd expected. Instead, her legs folded. Katherine had known and not said? She gripped Jason's arm for support.

"How could she?"

He lifted his shoulders. "No idea." He rested his forehead against hers. "She blames you for my death all those years ago."

"Great. How fair of her."

Jason's mouth set in a firm line. "It's as if she needs a scapegoat," he mused, "and it can't be me, of course." He smiled crookedly. "Adored son can never be blamed for anything. Anyway," he continued, slipping his arms round her waist. "She's promised to do what she can to keep you safe—for my sake."

Well, excuse her for finding that less than comforting. Jason set a finger under her chin, tilting her face up. "I told her: anything happens to you, I'll hold her accountable." He laughed, a humourless sound. "She didn't like that." He released her. "I always thought..." His voice drifted off.

"What?"

"That she loved me enough to love the woman I love." He gave her a crooked smile. "I don't think she does."

"I'd say she loves you too much to share." Helle sank her fingers into his thick hair, brushing it back from his face. "But she'd better get used to having me around. I'm not going anywhere."

"Good to hear." He tightened his hold. "And I wouldn't let you if you tried."

"Neanderthal," she chided.

"A very hungry Neanderthal," he told her.

He should have changed channels—or turned off the TV. Instead, Jason was as mesmerised as Helle, watching Woolf pander to the assembled journalists. He'd gone for casual today, tight jeans hugging his hips, a deep red shirt setting off his black hair and pale skin. Like bloody Snow White, Jason thought: hair like ebony, skin like ivory and lips like blood. The blood part suited, at least, but the female journalists were oblivious to the coiled menace in the man sitting so relaxed in front of them. This was Sam Woolf at his most affable, oozing charm and sexiness in everything from how he smiled to how he sprawled in his chair.

"A first step," Woolf said, nodding at something one of the journalists had said. "And I'm convinced that my name will soon be cleared of these absurd accusations." He rested his elbows on his knees and leaned forward, staring straight at the camera. "Not that I want to sound conceited or anything, but I've never had problems finding willing sexual partners." His lip curled, the tip of his tongue visible for an instant.

One of the female journalists audibly inhaled, a little blonde thing in a tight black dress. "But the accusations are far more serious than those of paying for sex," she said. Jason mentally tipped his hat at her: not a bimbo, after all.

"The accusations are bogus. Only an incompetent moron would think otherwise." Woolf's voice was like a whiplash and the journalist quailed. Jason smirked. The wolf had just shown its fangs, and it wasn't pretty. Woolf's chest expanded, he held his breath and let it out, slowly.

"I'm sorry," he said smoothly, turning a dazzling smile on the female journalist. "I shouldn't have taken my frustration out on you." He sighed. Once again his eyes met the camera. "Someone has set out to frame me, destroy my good name. That someone will pay." He smiled sardonically. "As far as the law allows, of course."

He took some more questions and ended the conference by saying he was delighted that he'd now be able to celebrate Christmas at home.

"Anyone special you want to celebrate with?" one of the journalists asked.

"Oh, yes." Woolf's eyes glittered. "I can't wait."

Helle switched off and threw herself backwards on the sofa, covering her face with her arms.

"Shit," was all she said. She peeked at him. "Once he's back in England—"

"He'll have other matters to handle," Jason said firmly. "Just because he's been granted bail, doesn't mean his movements are entirely without restriction. And Stapleton still hopes to have the bail revoked, claiming attempted murder is too serious an accusation." He moved closer to her. "Curtis is filing a civil suit as we speak, on my behalf."

"He is? When did you discuss that with him?"

"I haven't only been dancing attendance on Katherine," he replied with a wry smile. She raised her brows.

"No? I wouldn't have guessed."

Jason chose to ignore her comment. "Between them, Curtis and Stapleton will keep him occupied, and for all that his new solicitor is some sort of human bull-terrier—or so Curtis says—he lacks the legal edge to stand any chance against Curtis." Jason grinned. Not only was Curtis the size of a professional rugby player, but he was also possessed of one of the finest intellects Jason had ever encountered.

"And what if Woolf goes after Curtis?" Helle asked. "Or John?"

He didn't like it, how her voice softened at the mention of John. "They're big boys," he answered in a light tone. And as to Curtis, Tim had been charged with the task of finding him adequate protection, Jason overriding Curtis' heated protests. Stapleton would have to take his chances—the man was a police officer and should be able to handle his own security.

"But we must call them, tell them to be careful!" She was already digging for her phone. "If Woolf does something to John—"

"Stapleton can look out for himself!"

"What's with you and John?" She shoved at him. "The least he deserves is that we warn him."

With a low curse, Jason launched himself from the sofa and stalked out to the kitchen. He was standing by the window, hands braced on the old countertop, when she entered some minutes later.

"He's a friend," she said to his back. "A good friend."

There it was: the insinuation that John had been around much more for her lately than he'd been. Jason kept his eyes on the garden, at present illuminated by the half moon.

"He likes you too much," he muttered.

"Oh, like you and Juliet?" she bit back, and he bowed his head.

"Maybe he likes you precisely because of Juliet," he retorted. "You know, his way of getting his own back."

"What a bitchy thing to say. All those hours with Katherine have really rubbed off on you!"

Jason wheeled. "And what's that supposed to mean?"

"She's not a nice person. She's disparaging and rude, condescending and mean to all but you." She folded her arms over her chest. "Just like you were mean just now."

"I don't like it that you like him!" He strode over to her, took hold of her shoulders. "It makes me feel—"

"Jealous?" she filled in.

"Insecure," he corrected. "Do you really think she's so bad?" He wound a strand of her hair around his finger.

Helle snorted. "In Nefirie's eyes, only Wanderers count. I guess that's why she never liked me in that first life. I was distracting you from your destiny."

A most correct assessment. In Nefirie's book, no one—not even a princess descended from Helios the sun god—was as good as a Wanderer. She'd been the one urging Kantor to wed Helle to Samion, she'd been the one who repeatedly told Jason to forget Helle—Wanderers did not marry royalty. Belatedly it struck him that where he had thought her comment was meant to indicate his inferior status, it had instead been the reverse: Nefirie did not want to see him wed to Helle, Kantor's daughter not good enough for her precious son.

"You are my destiny," he said. "And my mother better get used to it." He released the strand of hair, watching it revert immediately to a little corkscrew, just by her temple.

Helle nodded. "Good. And as for John, he likes me for myself." Turquoise eyes met his, a challenging gleam in them. "But that doesn't mean I intend to sleep with him or that he wants me to. Not all of us are like you and Juliet."

He tightened his hold on her shoulders. "Me and Juliet?"

"You know, incapable of staying away from each other," she said lightly, but her lashes fluttered down to hide her eyes. Jason sighed deeply. This was why he resented John's presence in their lives: as long as he was around, he kept Juliet very much alive in Helle's head.

"Look, Helle, about Juliet," he began, but was interrupted by her ringing phone.

"Hello? Hi Mum, hang on." She looked at Jason. "Hold that thought," she said before going back to her mother.

Jason watched her move over to sit in Anne's chair, laughing softly at something Miriam was saying. She pulled Anne's old shawl round her shoulders, and as she did it was as if a shimmering shadow detached itself from the wall, came to hover round her. Jason smiled. Katherine might not like Helle, but the spirits of Tor Cottage most certainly did.

"Keep her safe," he whispered. The shimmering outline seemed to nod, was joined by yet another, smaller, shadow. For an instant, he saw a mass of copper curls, eyes the colour of amber in the sun.

Chapter 23

By the time she'd finished talking to Mum, Jason had been fast asleep on the sofa, the flickering light of the fire dancing over his face. So there'd been no discussion about Juliet that night, and over the following days the subject had not cropped up again. But Helle hadn't forgotten—nor, she suspected, had Jason.

Katherine, however, was a recurring subject. Jason's absolute faith in his ancient mother had been permanently damaged but he still spoke to her every day.

"We still need her," he explained to Helle. "And no, I don't trust her as I used to do but that doesn't change the fact that she's our best hope of wiping Woolf off the face of the earth."

Hmm. Helle was finding it hard to forgive the old witch for the recent events in the garage. She'd known and had done nothing to stop Woolf. Question was how much she'd known. Helle had days when she suspected Katherine might even have been in on things, but the one time she'd voiced that to Jason he'd shut her down so fast she decided to let it go—for his sake. He was struggling as it was with reconciling those burnished memories of perfect Nefirie with the reality of bitchy Katherine, even if he never used that particular adjective when describing her.

"I guess I can't quite see her facing up to Woolf," Helle said after Jason yet again had expressed just how powerful Katherine was. "He's a man in his prime, she's an old lady in a wheelchair."

"You have no idea," Jason said with a little smile. "He doesn't stand a chance in hell." That made Katherine sound like some sort of ninja. An overage and somewhat immobile ninja, but still.

"Good description," was all Jason said.

On the day before Christmas Eve, Tor Cottage was invaded by their friends. Nigel and Miranda, Curtis and his beautiful wife Amanda, John Stapleton and his sergeant, descended on the huge buffet Jason had prepared, for all the world like starving locusts. Even Katherine was there, a regal presence in her wheelchair—quid pro quo for inviting John.

Well, Helle reasoned, she supposed it would be a tad cruel to leave Katherine all on her own over the holidays, and to give the old lady her due, she was on her best behaviour, joining in their conversation with surprising wit.

Jason had gone Turkish with his buffet. Hummus, börek, a mouth-watering lamb stew spiced with cardamom and pistachios, miniature skewers with chicken or veal, spicy sausage, dolme of several varieties and a steaming bowl of köfte. There was an aubergine dish that made Curtis roll his eyes and groan out loud, slow-cooked lamb shanks where the meat fell off the bone, bean salads, yoghurt with mint—and pitta bread.

Jason was everywhere, handing out plates and napkins, serving wine. Now and then, he'd squeeze himself past Helle, ostensibly to fetch something, while his real reason was to give her an affectionate pat, or press his hips against her backside, or kiss her on the nape.

"Jason!" she hissed when he released her after a rather long kiss. "We're not the floorshow." Self-consciously, she tugged at the short skirt of her tight blue dress.

"No?" He laughed. "I want everyone to see just how much I love you."

By everyone he meant Katherine—and perhaps John— and Helle had to admit she didn't mind treating Katherine to these open displays of affection and barely contained heat. These last few days, Jason had been making amends, loving her with an intensity and single-mindedness that left her constantly uncoordinated—and needy. Not being stupid, she was fully aware he was also using sex as a distraction technique—anything to keep her mind off Sam Woolf. It worked surprisingly well.

"More beer," Jason told her in passing, and Helle ducked into the pantry, loading her arms with assorted bottles of IPA, all from local microbreweries.

From the beam hung bunches of dried herbs, yet another wreath of rowan and ivy was situated just above the window, ensuring no evil sneaked in this way. Helle smiled. Tor Cottage was like a welcoming embrace, a safehaven. Even her dreams changed, in that here the red-haired child appeared already at the beginning, sometimes as a toddler, at others as a lanky gap-toothed girl, but always with the capacity to stop the dreams from turning into nightmares of fear and loss.

"Need any help?" Miranda popped her head in, and the beads in her multiple braids glittered in the lamplight.

"Here." Helle handed her the bottles, filled her own arms with more.

"You're going to bathe them in beer?" Miranda teased, pressing the bottles to her sequined top.

"Huh. Just you wait until Curtis gets going." Helle winked. "And the fair Amanda downs impressive amounts of ale as well." Not that it showed—Amanda was as tall as Curtis but svelte like a panther, all long limbs and pronounced cheekbones.

"Are you all right?" Miranda asked, eyes on the bottles she was carefully setting down.

"Sure." Helle smiled brightly.

"I mean with this whole Woolf stuff," Miranda clarified.

"I know you do. But I don't have any intention of discussing it—not today." Or anytime soon.

Miranda gave her hand a quick squeeze. "Understood. But I want to help, in whatever way I can."

Helle gave her a vague smile. God help them—and poor Miranda—should she attempt to help. Woolf would squash her as he'd do an irritating bug. But Miranda's intentions were good, so Helle nodded and muttered 'Thanks', before adding that she really needed to check on her desserts.

Just as Jason was pulling the veal casserole from the oven, there was a loud knock on the door. Helle froze, eyes darting over to Jason's.

"Open it," he said with a smile. "It might be Father Christmas."

So she did, and there were Mum and Phil, with a smiling Tim hovering behind them.

Helle cried. She laughed. She cried some more, and Mum did the same, arms so tight round Helle she could barely breathe.

"Surprise," Jason murmured in her ear before hugging Miriam.

Helle wiped her eyes, giving him a wobbly smile. "How…"

Jason tapped his nose. "We have our devious ways."

"What he means is that he called me and asked us to come," Miriam said. "No undercover mumbo-jumbo involved." But she smiled at Jason, embracing him as tightly as she'd just hugged Helle. Phil handed over a bottle of cognac, presented Helle with an armful of red tulips, and then they were inside, being introduced.

Miriam sized Katherine up, was sized up in return. Two alpha-females who smiled and gushed, sharp eyes assessing the competition. It made Helle drag Mum off to the table, urging her to try the veal, the börek—well, everything, essentially.

"She doesn't look all that intimidating," Mum commented *sotto voce.*

"Appearances can be deceptive." Helle nabbed a piece of bread and dipped it in the red pepper pesto Jason had made.

"Yup." Miriam flexed her arm, making Helle laugh. She took a step back: Mum did look very fit, emphasized by the figure-hugging dress she was wearing.

"Life in the desert agrees with you," Helle said. Miriam was tanned, her brown hair pulled back in an elegant knot.

"Huh. Life in the desert has little going for it except for the pool and the tennis court." Mum made a face. "Four more months to go."

"Is Phil enjoying it?"

"You know him: present him with a little tax challenge and he goes wild and crazy."

"What you see in him is a mystery," Helle teased, turning to look for Phil. "He…" Her voice trailed off. Phil was standing to the side, regarding Katherine as if she were an unreconciled tax return. "Does he know her?"

Miriam turned as well. "If he does, he doesn't like her much, does he?"

"Welcome to the club." Helle's cheeks heated with embarrassment. Katherine looked frail and pale. In contrast, Phil appeared like a matador eyeing the bull he would shortly skewer. In a flamboyant burgundy shirt—too tight, all Phil's shirts were too tight—his shaved head and black pants, all that was missing was a sword and a cape.

Helle handed Phil a plate and invited him to serve himself, watching with some admiration as he proceeded to fill up his plate.

"Do you know Katherine?" she asked.

"Know her? Me?" Phil shook his head and added one more meatball to his already tottering pile.

"You looked at her as if you did."

"Second-hand impression," he replied. "She's not been very nice to you, and that thing with Sam Woolf, well, that didn't win her any brownie points." He patted her cheek with his free hand. "No one hurts our girl." He grinned. "And just so you know, I'm speaking for Ben as well. Or, as we call him in the family, Benny-boy."

"Dad would kill you if he heard you call him that," Helle said, grinning back at him.

"Well, as far as I know, he isn't here, is he?" Paul popped a piece of crumbling goat's cheese in his mouth.

"He's back in England," Stapleton said to Jason in an undertone. No need to ask who he was, Jason thought, frowning at the interior of the dishwasher.

"Do you know where?"

"I do." Stapleton handed him yet another stack of dirty plates. "London. We're keeping tabs on him."

"As long as he lets you."

Stapleton inclined his head in agreement. "You're right. But he won't come here, will he?"

"No." Even Woolf would have problems with the electric fence.

"What are you two whispering about?" Katherine's voice startled them both. She looked from one to the other. "Ah.

236

Samion." She made a sweeping motion with her arm. "He is powerless here." She smiled faintly. "And not because of your little fence, but because the house itself will defend its inhabitants." She nodded approvingly. "Whoever set the wards knew her job and the proximity to the Tor helps."

Jason threw a look outside. An almost full moon backlit the Tor, a conical shape striving towards the heavens. A repository of ancient power, it reminded Jason of a giant sentinel, standing silent under the stars.

"So what happens next?" Katherine asked.

"We go after him," Stapleton said. "Attempted murder…"

"Murder?" Katherine interrupted. "He didn't try to murder Helle, he—"

"…tried to murder me," Jason interrupted. "I told you, didn't I?"

Katherine blinked. "You did? I don't recall you doing so."

"Back in January. Shot him twice." Helle moved over to stand beside Jason, depositing dirty glasses and plates beside the sink. "And then he tried again in May."

"Helle saved my life," Jason said. "Both times."

Katherine studied Helle. "How?"

"Back in January I sort of flew at him." Helle sounded embarrassed.

"Ah." Katherine's hand tightened on her armrest. "Imagine that, you bringing down the powerful Samion." Eyes like topazes studied Helle. "Yet another thing he'll want to punish you for."

Beside him, Helle stilled. Jason shot Katherine a look, overcome with a need to shake her until her teeth rattled.

"Not about to happen," Jason said. "We're here to protect her, aren't we? All of us."

"Yes," Katherine mumbled, averting her eyes. "Of course we are."

By now, all the guests had made their way to the kitchen, and once broached, the subject of Sam Woolf was impossible to get away from. Everyone had an opinion, an idea, voices rising as one suggestion after another was aired and discussed. Only Helle sat silent, hands jammed under her thighs, face growing increasingly pale. Jason edged towards her, caught Miriam doing the same, and shared a look with his mother-in-law.

"What do you mean, it won't hold?" Nigel's voice cut through the discussion. "Of course it will hold. It must hold! Money transfers, e-mails, pictures—we can prove the trafficking."

"But not that Woolf did it, especially not now, when that moron Williams has stepped forward to take the blame," Stapleton replied. "In fact, the only thing we can potentially prove is that he doctored the CCTV footage in France. And the only thing that proves is that yes, he was probably in the vicinity of Netley Abbey when Jason was shot, but that's it."

"So then what's the point?" Helle stood up. "Why bother, when you're all convinced he'll get away with it anyway?" She inhaled. "I…" She tried again. "I…" She waved away Jason's hand. "Is there nothing that will stop him?"

"Death," Katherine said laconically. "What?" she continued, looking round the room. "Why the shocked faces? To hear it, you all agree the man's a monster."

"We can't go about killing people," Curtis protested.

"Of course not." Katherine nodded a couple of times. "But sometimes, there's no choice."

"You can't say things like that," Jason said later. He handed Katherine a glass of whisky, held the bottle aloft to offer Helle some, but she shook her head.

"Why not?" Katherine's eyes never left him. "It's true, isn't it? To stop Woolf, we have to kill him."

"Hear, hear," Miriam said, lifting her wine glass. "He comes after my baby and I'm fully capable of blowing him to pieces."

"Mum!" Helle exclaimed, shifting to make room for Jason in the sofa.

"While I like the sentiment, I must disagree with you," Katherine said. "You'd stand no chance against Samion."

The house was quiet now that everyone but their mothers and Phil had left. Jason would have preferred it if they too had been staying at the George & Pilgrim down in Glastonbury, leaving him alone with Helle. Unfortunately, he'd suffered a moment of temporary insanity and offered them to stay at the cottage.

"And you would?" Phil asked from his corner, most of his face in shadow.

"Right time, right place, yes." Katherine sipped her single malt. "Otherwise, no." She looked at Jason. "He's singularly powerful, and very driven."

"Well, for now we leave the matter with John and Curtis," Jason said.

"Pshaw! Like flies round a bull." Katherine drank the rest of her whisky and set down the glass. "But they serve the purpose of keeping him preoccupied."

Miriam poured herself some more wine, her hand shaking. "So how do you see this ending?"

Katherine regarded her in silence. "I'm not sure," she finally said. "It depends on the sacrifice."

"Sacrifice?" Phil sounded derogatory. "What, we offer some sheep to the gods?"

Katherine swivelled to face his corner. "Oh, I don't think sheep will do." All of a sudden she sounded tired. "There is always a price to pay. Always."

"And us?" Helle asked. "What about us?" She'd taken Jason's free hand, was clinging to it.

Katherine looked at them. "The child," she said cryptically. For an instant, her mouth trembled. "A child. A promise."

"What child?" Helle asked, and the hope in her voice touched Jason to the quick.

"A promise?" Miriam asked. "What does that mean?" Precisely the question Jason had been wanting to ask.

"That," Katherine said, "is none of your business." Her jaw tensed, her mouth tightening into a thin line. Jason recognised that expression, knew it would be futile to push further.

"I don't understand." Miriam moved close enough to pat Helle on her leg. "Do you?"

"Not really." Helle squeezed Jason's hand, pressing it against her abdomen. "A child," she whispered, so low only he heard it.

He squeezed back. In her wheelchair, Katherine sat slumped, shaking hands picking at the fabric of her skirt.

"She's not that bad," Miriam said early on Boxing Day. She was whisking eggs and milk together for French toast, while supervising Helle as she fried the bacon.

"Maybe the Christmas spirit infected her or something." Truth be told, Katherine here was a totally different person from the white witch of Notting Hill. Maybe it was Tor Cottage exerting a benign influence, or maybe Katherine was truly attempting to make amends. Huh. Helle was not as yet convinced, and she still had that tendency to monopolise Jason, mostly through hinting at her general frailty.

What had truly surprised her was earlier this morning, when she'd come down to the kitchen for a glass of water only to find Katherine standing—standing!—by the sink. She'd ducked back behind the door, peeking as Katherine shuffled over to her wheelchair.

When she'd shared this with Jason, he had looked unimpressed. "I worked that out some time ago," he said. "Why else all those canes she has lying about in her flat?"

"Canes? I've never seen them."

"Well, you haven't been there as much as me, have you?"

Helle just looked at him, deriving quite some satisfaction from how he squirmed. "Shit, just hanged myself, didn't I?" he muttered.

"Yup. And I didn't even give you the rope." But she'd snuggled up to him, her hand straying down to fondle his balls, and things were really heating up when Mum banged on their door, saying she wanted to cook breakfast and would Helle help—which was why she was frying bacon and making coffee, while Jason was probably wanking off in the shower. All in all, maybe a good thing, as Helle had just discovered she'd forgotten to bring a new set of pills. She frowned: she was due to start a new cycle tomorrow, but deep inside she knew she didn't want to.

"I'd expected her to be cold and aloof," Mum continued, now soaking bread. "But she's mostly old, don't you think?"

"Hmm," Helle replied. Katherine was doing the little old lady in a wheelchair act so well even Helle had almost bought it.

"And all those lives...No wonder she's a bit fey."

"Fey?" Helle burst out laughing. "Katherine?" Someone more hard-nosed than Katherine was difficult to imagine.

"Okay, brittle then. As if she could explode into a multitude of pieces, each one representing a different life."

Helle considered this. Her mother had a point: at times Katherine seemed to be bubbling with internal pressure, no matter how cool and composed a face she turned on the world. As if she was struggling with some sort of mental burden... Maybe multiple lives could affect you like that.

"Is Jason the same?" she asked.

"Jason?" Miriam pursed her lips. "No, if anything Jason is an extremely centred person. But it's different, isn't it? He's had an objective with all his lives—to find you again—while Katherine...I don't know, I get the impression she's not had much choice, that she's been reborn out of obligation rather than desire." Mum nodded in agreement with herself. "Like a penance, you know, like—"

"Ahasverus." Helle gave Mum a fond smile.

"Or Cain—condemned to roam the world forever after killing his brother."

"She hasn't killed anyone," Helle protested. Not yet, at any rate, even if the old lady seemed determined to take on Samion should it be necessary.

"How do you know?" Mum waved the spatula at her. "That woman drags a ton of guilt around."

"She does?" An intriguing thought. But before they could discuss this further, Jason entered the kitchen, smelling of body wash. Somehow Helle did not think discussing Katherine's potential guilt would go down well with him.

"Come back here," Nefirie snapped, trying to peer into the gloom. She heard the girl giggle somewhere in the dark.

"Korine?" Nefirie took a tentative step into the blackness, suppressing the ripples of ice that ran up her spine. The soft burbling

241

of running water was to her left, from where the little underground stream channelled its way towards the light. Nefirie looked back over her shoulder to reassure herself that she could still see the opening.

"Korine?" she repeated, her voice wobbling with fear.

A small flame of light appeared at her side, and she looked over to see Korine staring at her. The child's eyes glittered in the light of her fire.

"That was not nice," Nefirie said sternly, her body slumping with relief at the sight of the burning little ball that her grandchild juggled in her hand.

"You fear the dark," Korine stated. Her voice was that of an adult, not that of a girl still hovering between childhood and puberty. Nefirie nodded, moving as quickly as she could towards the visible patch of sky. She feared it, and it crept ever closer.

Chapter 24

"At last!" Jason groaned exaggeratedly and staggered over to a chair.

"It was your idea to invite them," Helle said, joining him at the kitchen table.

"Remind me to never do it again, at least not all three of them at the same time." He rubbed at an ancient scratch on the oak table top. "But now that they're gone, we can start making up for lost time." Just like that, he lifted her up onto the table. These last few days, they'd had no privacy, and once they'd retired to their bedroom, Helle had been too tired—or so she'd said.

"Here? Now?" She laughed—a bit nervously, he thought.

"Why? You have a better idea?"

"I do actually." She pointed upwards. "A long bath would be nice now that Phil doesn't use up all the hot water."

"Bath it is."

If there was one area of his homes in which Jason did not compromise, it was his bathrooms. Tor Cottage was no exception,their private ensuite a large room in blue and white, with huge tub set in the middle. Candlesticks cluttered the floor and the window ledge, and even with daylight streaming in through the windows, he insisted on lighting them, producing a combination of light and water that made him think of old hammams.

In Jason's opinion, the invention of running water, and especially *hot* running water, had to be one of the most important in human history. Helle laughed at him when he said it, but then she had no memories of living lives in squalor, of having at most a pitcher of cold water with which to clean oneself.

Helle held her breath when she stepped into the tub. "What, you want to boil me alive?"

"I like it hot." He also liked how steam curled off the surface, how the warm, damp air resulted in a myriad of miniature curls along her hairline. After a lot of fussing about she finally sat down, reclining against his chest. He cupped her breasts and leaned back against the rim, eyes closed.

"So, Juliet," she said. He started and sat up, spilling water over the edge. "You promised."

"Hmm." He forced himself to relax, drawing her even closer. Juliet, now? One of the nearest candles hissed and spat, the flame elongating into a bright blue before it contracted.

"I told you I want something in exchange," he told her, sliding his hands down her wet arms. "I want you to tell me everything he did to you."

Helle stopped breathing. "I can't," she said in a strangled voice.

"Why not?" he asked, rubbing small circles up and down her arms. She softened under his touch.

"Because it's awful and vile. Because it will only hurt you."

"Just like me telling you about Juliet will hurt you."

Helle shook her head vehemently. "It's not the same. She didn't force you, she didn't laugh at you as she hurt you, she…" Her voice broke. "Don't ask me to do that," she continued in an unsteady voice. "Please don't. I don't want to remember, I don't…damn it! I…"

"Shh, I'm here, my love." He slipped his arms round her torso, held her to him. Under his hand, her heart was like a frantic woodpecker, picking out a rapid staccato rhythm. He moved, water sloshed, and she was in his lap, her cheek pressed to his shoulder.

"I try so hard to forget. He puts these pictures in my head, and they're devastating. Even more because they're not his horrid fantasies, they're what he actually did to me."

Jason closed his eyes, seeing a progression of images. Helle, as she'd been the day Samion captured them, when she'd been sun-kissed and beautiful, vibrant with life. Helle, the screeching, snivelling wreck that had been thrown into the cart with him months later, on the same day she'd birthed their daughter and had the babe torn out of her arms. Helle, reduced to a silent wraith, sitting under Elessa's rosebush, with her pleading eyes fixed on him. Eyes he'd ignored, and all because he'd believed she'd gone willingly into Samion's embrace.

"Oh, Helle, my beautiful Helle." His voice shook slightly. "If only I could have saved you from it." If only he'd listened to her side of the story, if only…

"Ow," she protested, and Jason released his hold. His fingers had left red marks on her skin.

"Sorry," he said, and he wasn't only apologising for scalding her.

Helle shrugged. "No big deal." She patted his cheek. "There was nothing you could do. Not then. But I don't want to talk about it, okay?"

"All right," he promised. He stuck his nose in her hair and inhaled, holding her scent in his lungs. "About Juliet, are you sure you want me to tell you?"

"I am." She sat up, meeting his eyes. "But I'll stop you if I change my mind."

That, in Jason's opinion, would not happen. For some reason, Helle was determined to hear everything about Juliet, and while he wasn't exactly leaping about with joy at the prospect of sharing these details from his past with her, he could, at some level, understand why she needed to know. Had it been Helle, meeting up with a recurring lover…The thought made his mouth fill with something acrid. Jealousy tasted of bitter almonds, he reflected.

"You already know about the first time, when she was a nun," he began, fiddling with her wedding and engagement rings. His rings, he corrected himself, marking her as his.

"Yeah, short-haired and gorgeous in the hayloft," Helle muttered. Very gorgeous, Jason thought. And young and innocent, and so unhappy in the convent. He cleared his throat.

"I ran into her again in Normandy just before the battle of Hastings. A very brief run in, a couple of weeks before she was to wed. Even she could see how impossible it would be for us to live together, she the daughter of a well-to-do merchant, me a member of a travelling troupe of acrobats."

He smiled; one of his better lives, actually. "But we stole some moments in a shaded clearing, and she went to her wedding more experienced than she should have been."

Helle made an irritated sound, splashing him with water. "Come on Jason, just say it like it was. You took her virginity. Who knows, maybe you left her pregnant as well." She moved over to sit opposite him, her feet in his lap.

He gave her a dark look. "No I didn't."

"Whatever. So, two meetings, two rolls in the hay. Go on."

"I've already told you about Kenilworth," he continued.

"You did?"

"Yes." He massaged her foot. "She died with a cross-bow bolt through her throat." A bad death, a bad life—both for him and Juliet.

"Next time I met her was just after the Black Death. It was in Italy, in the vineyards of Tuscany. Fields lay untended, slowly reverting back to nature. So many people had died." Yet another dismal life, at least initially. "There were whole areas where there was nothing left. Farms stood empty, small villages were abandoned. Sometimes I saw bands of children, feral little creatures that would surround you and steal everything you had."

"How did you survive?"

"How?" He shrugged, eyes on the sunlit floor tiles. "I was alone, I lived alone. At the time I was working as a shepherd up in the Apennines, and I had no idea what had ravaged our world until I came down after the winter and saw the gaping doors of our church."

"Oh."

"I first saw her just outside the village. She was weeping in frustration as she tried to make the mule move. She didn't recognize me, but I knew her immediately. So I followed her, keeping my distance as she led the stubborn animal back to her small property."

Thin and dirty, Juliet had still been a welcome sight, even more so in a world left eerily bare of human life.

"As gorgeous and irresistible as ever, right?"

"Gorgeous? She was starving." He paused. "Do you want me to go on?"

"Yes." She made a zipping gesture across her mouth.

"She was a young widow. Her husband and his whole family had all succumbed to the plague, leaving her to fend for herself and her young son, Luigi." He smiled fondly. "Imp," he said, shaking his head, "just like his mother in looks. Anyway, Juliet was struggling. It was hard work, and she had to do it all herself. There were simply no workers to be had and her neighbours were slowly moving in on her."

"Moving in on her?" she asked. "Like they wanted her to leave or they wanted to live with her?"

"Both, I would imagine," Jason replied. "There were not that many women left, and definitely not of childbearing age. Niccola, her closest neighbour, had buried all his sons during the plague, as well as his wife, and he had his eye very firmly set on her.

"When I walked up the lane to her house, she stood at the door. She smiled, then she raised her hand in greeting as if it was only yesterday since she had seen me last, not almost a century before." She'd taken off her veil, shaken out her hair, still as dark and lustrous as always, and then she'd picked up her skirts, flying to meet him. A very warm welcome, a welcome he'd needed.

"So, did you stay?"

He slid her a cautious look. "Yes, I did. For about five or six years."

"What about me?" She sounded petulant—and very young.

Jason swooped, took hold of her hands and towed her towards him. Water spilled every which way.

"You? I had walked through most of Europe, looking for you, but I hadn't found you that time either. I was tired. I didn't think I would ever find you again." He leaned forward to press his lips against her brow. "I thought that a lot, you know. I would wake up one morning as a young adolescent and know I was committed to finding this vague dream of a girl, and I didn't know how to.

"All my lives have been the life of a vagrant. I have been a tinker, I have sold bibles. I have been a travelling monk and a doctor. I have been a juggler and a swordsman for hire. I have never had a permanent home, never sat at rest. You have been my Holy Grail, and I have looked and looked." He raised her hand to his mouth, kissing every finger in turn.

"The world is a very big place, Helle, and with every one of my passing existences my despair grew. How would I ever find my lioness again amid so much humanity?"

"But you did," she said, and the smile she gave him almost made his heart stop. It made his stomach turn to molten lava.

"Yes, I did, lioness." He drew her closer. Breath mingled with breath, lips hovering only millimetres from each other. There: a soft pressure on his mouth, her hands in his hair, and he groaned into her mouth. A chaste kiss at first, building up to one of the longest and best kisses they had ever shared.

Juliet was forgotten. Helle was warm and wet in his arms, and he wanted to take her there and then, love her until they'd emptied the bathtub with their motion. But when he gripped her buttocks, urging her to straddle him, she slid away, and there was a look in her eyes he couldn't quite decipher.

"What?" he said.

She smiled, shaking her head.

"Don't you want to?"

"Want to? I do—I always do. How can you even ask?"

"Good," he growled. "So come here, woman, and do your work."

"I…" She hesitated.

Jason stood up, took her by the arm, and pulled her up as well. "Bed," he said. "Now."

The cool air of the bedroom made her damp skin break out in goose bumps. Or maybe it wasn't the air, maybe it was the way he was looking at her, or the fact that she hadn't told him about the pills. Helle swallowed. Everett had spoken of a child, Katherine had done so as well, and these days Helle walked about with a constant ache in her belly, a yearning for a child—his child.

"Come here," he said, and the huskiness of his tone, the gleam in his eyes, sent a shiver of anticipation through her. She took one step, she took two. She took three and she was lost, his hands roaming her body. She should tell him, she thought fuzzily. Or not, because now she most definitely didn't want him to stop.

Jason lifted her onto the bed. The sheets stuck to her skin, but she didn't care, not when his warm, warm hands travelled up and down her thighs.

"Do you have any idea how often I would imagine you like this?" he asked, his eyes eating their way across her body. She flushed under his scrutiny, squirming a bit. "Lie still," he said, "just lie still and let me look at you.

"I had such vague memories of you, making out in daytime, hasty affairs in the dark. I never really saw you fully naked in that first life. Not to really look. But now," he said in a tone of quiet satisfaction, "now you're mine. My wife. And I can ask you to expose yourself to me as much as I want."

He fell silent, eyes the colour of molten copper smiling down at her. His hand pushed a lock of hair from her face, travelled down her cheek, her throat, her shoulder.

"I feel like an object on display." She gasped when his fingers closed on one of her nipples, tweaking it.

"You are. My wife, on display for me." Yet another tweak. His lips captured hers, sucking gently on her bottom lip. The sheets rustled as he moved, a patch of sunlight warmed her lower legs, and there was his cheek, the bristles scratching the tender skin of her inner thighs.

"There are still nights when I start awake, convinced that this last year or so has been nothing but a dream, that you are not for real." Jason's warm exhalations tickled her skin. "And when I turn my head to see you sleeping beside me my heart almost stops with relief."

"That would be kind of unfortunate," she said, more than affected by the intensity in his voice. He didn't hear, or at least he pretended not to.

"I look at you and know I can put my hand on your body, feel your skin warm under my touch, your pulse thudding at your throat." Like now, when his touch was rapidly igniting her, his fingers teasing at her pubic hair, delving deeper to slide between her folds.

"I can touch you here," he said, a digit circling her clit. "Or here." He rimmed her opening, slid a finger inside of her. "I can, because you are mine, only mine." Two fingers, and Helle moaned, lifting her pelvis to meet his touch.

His fingers disappeared. Moments later they were in her mouth.

"Taste yourself. Feel how wet you are for me. Only for me, right?"

She nodded, sucking his fingers clean.

"I wake with my balls aching for you and you're here, warm and moist and all mine, there for the taking. And every time, Helle, every bloody time, it's still like a dream come true." He gave her a brief kiss and slid further down.

"Oh, God," she said when he spread her thighs. He laughed softly, rubbing his nose up and down her folds. His breath, his mouth, that skilful tongue, those teasing fingers…For a while they were silent. Well, he was. She wasn't, but she wasn't exactly talking either. He paused. She groaned. He went back to what he was doing, and she floated off on a sea of sensations—until he paused again.

"Jason!" she protested. He didn't reply. She lifted her head, met eyes aflame with lust. "I…"

"Shhh," he said, strong hands holding her still. Once again, those lips, that mouth. Helle gasped his name, he laughed against her skin, his tongue flitting out to tease her clit. So close, so very, very close, and he stopped.

"Oh, come on Jason!" she exclaimed. "You're driving me crazy!"

"I sincerely hope so," he replied, lifting himself upwards so that he hovered over her. "That's the whole point, isn't it?" He kissed her, and she could taste herself on his lips. For an instant, he rested on top of her, his erection hot and hard against her belly. Then he slid back down, and coherent thought escaped her. This time, he took her right to the edge. Her heart thundered, her insides shivered and twisted with desire. No, lust. Primitive, overwhelming lust. He sat up and she groaned, bereft of his fingers, his mouth.

"I want every drop of your blood, every cell of your skin, every molecule of your bones to echo with my name," he said hoarsely. "I want all of you to shout that you're mine." He stroked himself. "I want you to beg for this."

"I already do." She sat up, covered his hands with her own, and his penis jerked in their combined hold. "I want you. All of you. Only you. You could tattoo your name all over me and I wouldn't mind, as long as it said Jason, Jason, Jason."

"I don't really like tattoos." He smiled, guiding her down on her back. His legs between hers, the head of his penis nudging at her.

"Well thank heavens for that," she murmured, sinuously moving against him. "Because I don't either."

He slid in. He slid out.

"Jason!" Her fingers clawed at him. He laughed, sitting back on his heels. His hands on her legs and she was flipped over. His cheek rubbing across her back, his teeth marking her nape and she rose on her knees, arching her back as she offered herself to him.

"God, you're beautiful," he said, his hands caressing her butt. He slapped her: once, twice on each butt-cheek and the sting sent tingles of warmth all the way to her sex. His fingers gripped her hips. His hard, hard cock slid inside.

"Oh, God!" she gasped, pushing back to take him even deeper inside. He stilled.

For what seemed like an eternity, they were frozen, he halfway inside her.

"Please," she begged.

"Not yet, lioness." But she could hear it in his voice, how close he was.

His hands were back, stroking her butt. When she tried to move, his fingers tightened, holding her in place.

"Relax, lioness." A hand slid up her back to grip her by the nape. Gently, he pushed her downwards, until she was lying with her chest and face on the bed, her ass in the air. "Lovely," he said, and his fingers circled her anus. She groaned out loud when he pushed a finger inside her. He moved, gentle thrusting motions with his finger mirrored by his cock. Too little, she needed more, she wanted...

"Ah!"

He'd added another finger. His hips flexed and he sank his penis so deep his balls pressed against her entrance. His fingers moved: quick deep thrusts and she had forgotten how to breathe, submerged in all these tactile sensations. So close. She rocked back against him. Yes, yes, yes...

Once again, he stilled.

"No, no, no!"

"No?" He laughed and then his other hand slid over her hip and belly. Warm strong fingers circling her clit, warm, strong fingers driving into her ass while his cock surged in and out.

"Good?" he asked when she moaned his name out loud.

"You have no idea," she managed to gasp.

"Oh, I think I do, lioness."

The muscles in her thighs quivered. Sweat beaded her face, her hands were clutching at the bed clothes. All she could think of was him. All she wanted was him. All she needed was him, him, him.

"Come for me," he said. "Come now, lioness."

And she did, crying out as all that building heat exploded into fireworks.

"Wow," she muttered some moments later.

"Mmm." He was still moving inside her, still very hard. "My turn, I think."

He pulled out. She turned over. He was on his knees, his erection glistening with her juices. His fingers closed almost painfully in her hair when she took him in her mouth. His thighs clenched, he breathed her name, and his hips flexed, filling her with as much of him as she could handle. She sucked and licked, his breath came in loud rasping gulps, his penis hot and throbbing.

"No!" He pulled himself free, lifted her up to kiss her. On her back, her wrists held high above her head, his fingers at her clit. It was unbearable. It was wonderful. It went on and on.

And just when Helle thought she couldn't stand it any longer, when desire collapsed into one single point of agony, he took her, driving into her with long, hard strokes. He made her whole, he filled her senses. There were no boundaries; he was she, and she was he, and they burned and died and lived again.

"I think this is the first time I could do with a towel," she told him afterwards, her heart fluttering like a trapped bird inside her chest. "I'm wet all over."

"Yes, talk about lying in a burning bed." He traced a faint line of blisters on her wrists. "I'm afraid I got a bit carried away."

"I would never have guessed, and by the way you have a gigantic bite mark on your shoulder, so I guess it's tit for tat."

He pulled her close and inhaled. "You smell of me." He kissed her thoroughly. "You taste of me. I like it when you do, it marks you as mine."

He slid a finger between her legs and drew it out, trailing their combined moisture over her belly. "And here, it is us. Me and you, lioness." He kissed his damp finger and placed it softly on her mouth. "You and me, Helle. Forever."

She nodded, blinking furiously. "Forever, Jason."

Afterwards, Juliet was no longer an issue. Helle didn't care, not any more. Well, at least not for the moment. He is mine, she thought, pillowing her head on his chest. Juliet had only borrowed him for brief snatches of time, no more. Never again though, she added silently. Should she ever so much as pick up a whiff of Juliet close to Jason—and these days Helle considered very little to be impossible, no matter how dead Juliet was—she would personally pluck every long, beautiful dark hair off Juliet's head, leaving her as bald as an egg. Helle smiled at the thought, plastering herself to Jason.

"You're hot," he protested, "and sticky."

"Tough," she replied. "I want to hold you anyway. I like holding you close."

"I should bloody well hope so." He smiled lazily. "After that performance."

253

"Again?" she asked hopefully.

He gave her a look from under half closed eyes. "What are you? Insatiable?" He grinned. "Not that I'm complaining, lioness, but not just yet. Later."

Chapter 25

Rarely can one live only in the good moments and forget about the bad stuff, or so Helle thought when she woke far too early on New Year's Day to the sensation that something was not quite right, only to discover Jason by the open window.

His nude body was an eerie white in the pale light of dawn. His hands, however, were glowing, and that in itself had Helle sliding soundlessly across the floor to join him.

The garden below was empty. The area beyond the humming fence was also empty—or so Helle thought at first. A dark shadow moved, separated itself from the silent trees beyond. A man. He approached the fence.

Blue sparks spat in warning, the man came to a halt. Despite Helle knowing the fence carried enough electricity to kill an elephant, she shrank against Jason. An icy gust of night air made her break out in goose bumps.

"Woolf?"

"Who else?" Jason raised his hands. Fire danced between his fingers, little sparks that turned blue with heat. The man turned their way. In the waxing light, there was no doubt: it was Sam Woolf. He approached slowly, arms spread wide. A tremor shook the ground beneath him. Woolf came to a halt.

Wisps of dark smoke stood round him, his hair lifted in the wind, and for a moment he was no longer in modern clothes but was surrounded by swirling robes in bright red and gold. Golden bands adorned his arms, in each hand was a ceremonial dagger, and as Helle watched, the air filled with a blood-red mist.

"Posturing," Jason sneered. "Any good illusionist could do that." His nostrils dilated, he flung his arms wide, and a shimmering wall of heat rushed towards Woolf. The winter grass spat and hissed, fire rose towards the skies, but Woolf held his ground, a sweeping movement of his hand causing the flames to shrink and die. He took yet another step towards the fence, and the ground pitched and heaved below him.

"Yes!" Jason hissed. "Come closer, you bastard, and I'll fry you with electricity."

As if he'd heard him, Woolf stopped. He raised his face in their direction, staring at their window. Endless seconds, and then he turned, directing his attention to the cattle grid instead. He crouched beside it, tilting his head as if listening to the humming of the current in the metal bars. Woolf stood, and black smoke rose from beneath his feet. He lifted his fingers, and the smoke thickened, creeping across the cattle grid to span it.

"Damn," Jason muttered. Below them, Woolf set a foot on his ephemeral bridge. Jason widened his stance, his fingers shimmering with contained fire. Woolf took a careful step. The ground shook. Another step, and the ground on their side of the grid rumbled in warning. Woolf balanced on his smoky bridge, hands held out as he muttered some sort of incantation. In response, the ground cracked open, and Woolf's little bridge tilted this way and that. Jason spread his arms, and fire roared into life beneath Woolf's feet. The ground heaved and pitched, the rumble became a roar, and Woolf's bridge began to disintegrate. The bars of the cattle-grid glowed red-hot and sweat broke out along Jason's spine and arms.

With a curse, Woolf leapt back to firm ground on the other side of the grid. He had problems remaining upright, and for an instant or two it seemed as if he'd be pitched head-first onto the glowing cattle grid, but then he regained his balance and staggered backwards. He looked straight at them before disappearing in a swirl of black smoke. In her head, Helle heard him curse, and a thundering headache flared into life.

She slid down to sit on the floor. By the window, Jason set his glowing hands on the sill, breathing hard.

"The wards held," he said after a while, closing the window.

They had. Woolf had been here. Woolf was now gone, the ground itself rising in warning when he got too close. More than Helle could properly take in at six o'clock on a winter morning—to be honest, more than she could take in at any time. Around her, the old house seemed to settle down again, floorboards creaking. Jason sat down beside her.

Helle rested her head on his shoulder. The headache was gone, as quickly as it had come, and already the entire experience was acquiring a dreamlike quality, as if Woolf had not just now stood outside, staring at the house.

"He came, he saw…"

"But didn't conquer," Jason filled in. "Not that Sam Woolf has much in common with Caesar."

"You think? Ruthless and power-hungry the both of them."

"Caesar served his country. Woolf serves himself." Jason shivered and got to his feet. "It's nice to know he can't reach us here."

"Yeah. Maybe we should never leave here." She took his offered hand and stood up. "Live happily ever after in our moated castle."

"Happily ever after?" Jason shook his head. "We'd go crazy."

Too right. Besides, it wasn't them that should be imprisoned, it was Woolf.

Three days later, they returned to London, to a state of being constantly on their guard. Sam Woolf, it seemed, was everywhere. The man was running a PR campaign, newspapers and TV drowning in images of his handsome face and black hair, that mouth of his curling into smiles that rarely reached his eyes.

"He's very photogenic," Miranda commented, folding up the paper—second Sunday in a row with Woolf's face on the front page.

"If you're into dark and dangerous," Helle muttered, ensuring Woolf's picture wasn't visible. Whenever she saw his face, no matter in what medium, she had the distinct feeling he was looking directly at her, eyes digging into her brain.

"Aren't all women?"

"Only the ones stupid enough to think they can control the darkness."

Miranda went bright red but was smart enough not to say anything. Apparently, Nigel had managed to talk some sense into his girlfriend or maybe he'd just shown her some of the explicit photos from the case files.

Helle's phone beeped.

"Shit." The daily text—always from an unknown sender, always undeniably from Woolf. Today, all he'd sent was a picture of silver manacles. *For you.* Yesterday, it had been a studded collar. *For the wolf bitch.* The day before it had been an armful of red roses. *To the soon-to-be widow.*

"He's using burn phones," Nigel had told Helle some days ago, with an apologetic shrug. "I can't stop them."

The texts were bad enough. Never going anywhere without Tim was driving her crazy. But worst of all were the dreams, the recurring nightly invasions of her subconscious, nightmares that resulted in her waking up drenched in sweat. Always with Woolf chasing her, always with Jason's decapitated head bouncing on the ground, recently with the novelty of trying to put the head back on Jason's twitching body…Ugh!

"No wonder you look like a zombie," Alison said after listening to Helle's descriptions.

"Hey, thanks." Helle scowled at the webcam. But Alison was right: three weeks of interrupted sleep were beginning to tell.

"A nice zombie," Alison qualified. "One that hasn't been dead too long."

"Ha ha."

"Except that you have been," Alison went on. "Like for thousands of years."

"Zombies hang on to their original bodies. I upgrade between lives." She laughed, Alison joined in. It was nice to indulge in this rather morbid humour, making the weird reality she presently inhabited less threatening and more… well, weird.

"Weird? Is that better?" Jason asked, smoothing long warm fingers over her brow.

"Sometimes. Not always." She turned. "Zip me up?"

They were going to some sort of function at the Turkish Embassy, where Jason had been invited to give a speech on innovation technologies. A formal occasion, so Jason was in a three-piece suit, a crisp white shirt and a lavender-coloured tie that matched the sheer silk wrap Helle covered her shoulders with.

It was mostly men attending, Helle concluded, gripping Jason's arm as he escorted her further into the building. Belgrave Square had been chockfull of cars offloading guests, there were policemen everywhere, and several waiters walked about with trays offering Turkish lemonade and sparkling water.

"That's the ambassador," Jason said, nodding in the direction of a middle-aged man with glasses.

"Oh."

"And there's Selim Bey," Jason added, lengthening his stride.

Helle shook hands with Selim, the founder of Jason's Turkish company, but as their discussions became increasingly technical, she wandered off, smiling vaguely at the other guests in between studying the amazing carpets that decorated not only the floor but also the walls. Now and then, she ran into women, some of them covered, some of them not. All, however, were modestly dressed, and Helle congratulated herself on her choice of dress—tight and black, it sported long sleeves and fell to well below her knees in a swirling skirt that billowed when she moved.

She was admiring the beautifully decorated border of a wall-hung nineteenth century carpet from somewhere called Usuk, when someone approached her from behind.

"More mint lemonade?"

The voice had Helle's thighs bunching, preparing for flight. Her eyes sought the nearest exit. Woolf chuckled, standing close enough that she could smell that distinctive cologne of his, sandalwood and myrrh, overlaid with notes of citrus.

"Aren't you going to turn around and say hello?"

"No." She made as if to walk away, was arrested by his hand round her wrist.

"Of course you are." He twirled her round, and there were his eyes, there was that beautiful if cruel mouth, only inches away from her. "You look very nice," he continued. "Soon enough, you'll be wearing substantially less in my presence." He grinned, she yanked at her hand. His fingers tensed ever so slightly, and she restrained a yelp.

"Let me go." She tried to avert her face, a futile attempt to break eye-contact. Where was Jason? Woolf laughed.

"Why?" His eyes trapped hers. All she could hear was his voice, all she could see were his eyes, all she could feel was his hand. His brows rose, his fingers sliding up her arm in a caress. Helle wanted to scream, but her vocal chords were rendered useless, her body submitting to his presence.

He leaned forward. His lips were at her ear, and he was telling her just what he wanted her to do—now. It was humiliating, but she could no more disobey him than she could eviscerate him, so she stumbled and began to fiddle with her dress. He wanted it off, he wanted her naked and kneeling before him.

"Helle!" Jason's voice. Hot—far too hot—hands on her shoulders, clearing her head. He helped her to stand, tugged her dress into place, and when next she looked Woolf was gone.

"What…" Helle licked her lips, touched her head. Had it all been a figment of her imagination?

"Woolf." Jason drew her close. "What did he say?"

"I…" she stuttered. "I…" She inhaled, clearing her head of the last vestiges of Woolf's presence. "He…" She hung her head, feeling soiled and cheap.

"Nothing happened, lioness."

"Take me home," she said. "I can't be here, close to him." Only Jason's timely arrival had stopped her from complying with Woolf's instructions, and at the thought bile rushed up her throat. "I have to…" she croaked, and then she was running for the restroom, Jason at her side.

He held her as she threw up, he helped her wash her hands and face, then he whisked her off, talking to Tim as he hastened them towards the entrance.

"Your speech," she protested.

"Selim will manage without me."

"It's not right!" Jason's hand tightened round the tumbler. "That fucking bastard has murdered and raped, he's sold drugs and children at his clubs, and he just swans into a diplomatic reception?" He scowled at the webcam.

"He was invited by the Economic Counsellor," John said, his voice tinny through the loudspeakers. His bushy brows pulled together into one very hairy ginger caterpillar. "Apparently, they go a long way back. Is she all right?"

"Helle?" Jason downed the Armagnac. "No." Neither was he, shivering at the thought of what he potentially had interrupted. To see Helle fall to her knees, eyes blank—damn it, he'd told her to always avoid Woolf's hypnotic eyes!

"I tried!" She'd yelled, tears and snot on her face. "But he was too close, and I…"

"…ruined his evening, I hope," John said, recalling Jason to his ongoing Skype session.

"Eh?" Jason shook himself free of images of his distraught wife. At present she was safe, asleep in their bed. These mental bouts with Samion always left her exhausted.

"I said, I took the opportunity to inform Woolf that we consider ourselves to have sufficient proof on hand to charge him for your attempted murder." John gave Jason a mirthless grin. "He didn't like that."

"And do you?" Jason asked, pouring himself some more Armagnac.

"Not really. But there's enough to keep him sweating for a while. And once he's sweated that one out, I plan to charge him with Juliet's death."

"He didn't kill her—Duncan did." Jason made a face. Blond, cheerful Duncan had not been himself the last few months of his life, his mind and soul taken over by Woolf's powerful presence.

"But it was Woolf who set fire to her car with the intent to kill."

"You can't prove that."

"I know. But it's Sam Woolf on the bike tailing Juliet's car just before it goes up in flames, and it's…"

"Circumstantial," Jason said.

"Absolutely. But the more I throw at him, the more I rock his boat."

Jason nodded. The tax authorities had come down like a ton of bricks on Woolf, and Nigel, who kept a discreet—and utterly illegal—eye on the happenings in Woolf's office, said Woolf was under severe pressure regarding unpaid taxes. "Every little bit helps, I suppose," he said.

When Jason went to see Katherine next day, he insisted Helle come along, ignoring her protests.

"I'm not leaving you alone," he said. "Not after last night." She'd tossed and turned, she'd wept and gasped, and all in all it had been an awful night for both of them.

"I'll be fine!"

"But I won't." He gripped her chin. "I need you close." Those green-flecked eyes of hers widened.

"You do?"

"Always." He released her.

To Jason's irritation, John was seated on Katherine's sofa when they arrived. He leapt up at the sight of Helle, teacup in hand.

"Are you all right?" he asked, looking as if he wanted to hug her.

"Sort of." Helle pressed herself closer to Jason. She'd been like a plaster all day, always touching or holding on to him.

"Son." Katherine held out her hands in greeting, lifted her face for a kiss on her cheek. "John was just telling me about his conversation with Samion last night." She smiled at John. "You're keeping him busy."

"Irritating him, at any rate." John set down his tea-cup. "I have to go."

"Like a fly," Katherine laughed. "But more like a horse-fly than a blowfly."

"Thanks a lot," John said.

"It was meant as a compliment." Katherine patted him on the leg, John stooped to kiss her cheek, and left. She turned her attention to Helle. "You look wan."

"Tired." She offered Katherine a little smile, but it did little to erase the pinched look on her face.

"I can see that." Katherine beckoned her forward. Helle hung back. "Bad dreams?" Katherine asked.

"Very." Helle sounded curt. She hated discussing her dreams. No matter how Jason tried to pry, she just shook her head, saying she couldn't quite remember. But she did remember, he could see it in how she held herself, in how her hand came up to rub at her neck, her wrists.

"And yet mostly they end with her, don't they?"

Her? Jason looked at his mother. Whatever else she might not tell him, Helle had admitted the dreams were about him, Samion.

Helle sat down on the sofa, a wary look on her face. "How do you mean?"

"Your child saves you, doesn't she?" Katherine said. "She always said she did."

What? Jason placed a hand on her arm. "What child?" Katherine ignored him, her attention on Helle.

"My child?" Helle's hand slid down her stomach, eyes hidden by the sweep of her lashes. "How do you mean?" There was a tone to her voice Jason couldn't quite place, hopeful and hesitant at the same time.

"What I said: your child. Yours and Jason's."

Helle sat back, glad for the support of the sofa. She willed herself not to rest her hand on her belly, not look at Jason. Shit, she didn't like the assessing look in Katherine's eyes, and at present Jason's hand on her shoulder mostly made her want to cringe. She should have told him—if nothing else when she decided not to continue with her interrupted pill-cycle. Instead, she'd opted for leaving everything to her favourite new word: fate.

"Her name was Korine," Katherine continued, and Helle was jolted out of her guilt-ridden musings.

"Who?" she asked, but now she knew: the girl in her dreams, the little child with billowing red curls and eyes the colour of amber, that was Korine. In her head, the child hopped and twirled, sandaled feet splashing through puddles that spattered her light linen tunic with mud.

"Mother? What are you talking about?"

"I'm talking about your daughter," Katherine said. "The child Samion stole."

"Our baby?" Jason sagged down to sit beside Helle, groping for her hand. Their fingers braided together. "The one I spent months looking for?"

"Yes." Katherine sighed loudly. "But she was no baby when they brought her to me. She was a wild and disturbed little girl, not much more than skin and bones—and hair, of course." She smiled. "So much hair, like a fiery mane atop a matchstick."

"My baby." Helle half-smiled. "My little girl." She'd had a bad start to life and Helle's heart went out to her unknown daughter, so small and so alone.

"Korine," Jason said slowly as if tasting the name. "And she ended up with you?"

Katherine nodded but looked away, pulling the shawl tight round her shoulders. "I didn't want her. I didn't know who she was, only that she was a difficult child, gifted and out of control. But they pleaded with me, begged me to at least see her, and in came a ragamuffin with a head of bright curls and my son's eyes." A smile tugged at her mouth. "My Korine, our little fire-girl."

"The fire-girl?" Helle's head filled with images of a little girl, fingers spouting fires. "Like her father?"

"Much more powerful than her father." Katherine straightened up, and she was Nefirie more than Katherine. "She was my grandchild—my power ran through her veins, coupled to that of her father's."

"And her mother's," Jason put in sharply.

Katherine's gaze flitted over to Helle. For a couple of heartbeats, their eyes met and held. "Yes," Katherine finally said. "The child had the heart of a lion."

Wow. Her first ever compliment from Katherine, however indirect. Helle felt Jason's fingers tighten round hers and knew he was smiling.

"My lioness," he murmured. Whatever. At present, this was a very pissed off lioness.

"But why haven't you told us this before?" she asked. "We had a right to know."

Katherine raised her brows. "A right? You were dead. I was the one who raised her."

"She was mine!" Helle exclaimed.

"And mine," Jason said. "You knew I looked everywhere for her."

"But you didn't find her, did you? And then you chose to end your life, leaving me behind to cope alone."

"You knew why! You knew I had to—"

"Had to?" Katherine snorted. "You made a choice. You went after Helle, and so you weren't there when they came with your daughter." Katherine's hands tightened on the armrests of her wheelchair. "I wanted her to be only mine, love only me." She laughed, eyes brimming with tears. "But she never was. Korine always knew just who she was—she was yours, and she loved you both so much."

"How could she?" Jason asked. "She never knew us."

"Oh yes, she did." She nodded at Helle. "She saw you in her dreams as you see her in yours." Katherine leaned forward and brushed her fingers over Helle's cheek. A loud gasp and Katherine sat back, staring at Helle.

"What?" Jason asked. "Mother, what is it?"

Katherine blinked. "Hmm? Oh, nothing, son, nothing." She reached over to pat his hand. "A glimpse of the future, no more." She cleared her throat. "Could you get me some water?"

"I'll do it." Helle was already half-way to the kitchen. She had to get away from Katherine's far too discerning eyes. When she got back, she sat down beside Jason and took his hand.

"Tell us," she said. "About Korine."

Katherine's mouth tightened, and for a moment Helle thought she might refuse.

"We deserve to know," Jason told her, and Katherine's features softened.

"Yes, I suppose you do." She stroked the fabric of her shawl; up and down her hand went, eyes lost in the distance.

"When I first met her, she was a thin ghost of a child who spouted fire when she was angry or upset. She understood everything, but she refused to speak." She smiled sadly. "Mute, they thought her—and possibly a demon, what with her fires."

"A toddler with fire hands?" Helle asked.

"You can imagine—impossible to control. At least at first." Katherine touched Jason's hand, lying open and relaxed on his leg. "You were old enough to handle it. She wasn't.

"The first few days she was like a stray cat. She padded after me and froze when I turned towards her. When I served her food she took it and retreated to a corner, bolting it down. Not so surprising, the Wanderers who brought her found her scavenging among the offal in one of the various villages that dotted the coast. No one seemed to know where she came from, or with whom she had come, and she was dirty and unkempt, her belly swollen with hunger."

Helle's throat tightened. Her child, left to fend for herself like a wild animal. She sneaked her hand into Jason's, biting back an oath at the responding surge of heat.

"But where had she been?" Helle asked. "She was only a baby when she was stolen from Samion's nursery."

Katherine sighed. "I don't know. She never said anything."

"She wouldn't have known," Jason protested, "she was too young."

Katherine looked at him and shook her head slightly. "She knew. She just chose not to tell. After a week I took her to see Kantor," Katherine looked away and sighed. "He was crushed by both your deaths and it didn't help when Elessa died within a year."

"Nana?" Helle's mind filled with images of an old wrinkled face framed by thick grey braids. "My grandmother, she died?"

"People do," Katherine said drily. "Especially old people. Anyway, when Korine saw him, she walked straight up to him and kissed him, telling him that this kiss was from Helle. Those words were the first she uttered." Her's lips twitched. "The little minx. He was putty in her hands after that, of course. She wasn't above utilizing her gifts for her own benefit at times."

"Gifts? More than one?" Jason asked.

"Yes." Katherine sighed. "She was burdened with the Sight, a terrible gift to have. It drives you crazy to see the past, the present and the future simultaneously. She'd wake up screaming in the night, her fingers flaring with fire, unable to express what she had seen." Katherine turned her face towards the window.

"I always kept a bucket of water by her bed to cool her hands in. With time she learnt to control her gift of fire, but every now and then it would burst from her, wild and untameable, often when she saw things to come."

How awful. Helle wondered how she would have coped with a child so afflicted. To judge from Katherine's slumped shoulders, she'd found it a trial as well.

"In everything but colouring she was very much like her mother. But as she grew, I could see more of my son in her. She was tall and willowy, half a head taller than you, Helle, and she moved like Jason does. Fluidly. And once she began to talk, she spoke like her father, carefully rather than impetuously. In general, she preferred her own company to that of others, and she'd spend whole days up by the little waterfall, your special place, playing complicated games with her straw dolls."

Alone, always alone. It made Helle's heart shrink.

"Didn't she have friends?" Jason asked. Katherine didn't reply, sinking into a very long silence.

"She scared people," she finally said. "It took time before they trusted their children to be close to her. But she did, in time, make friends. She swam like an otter, and she and the boys would dive for crabs and shells and pretty stones."

Like her father, a fire child in love with the sea.

Katherine threw Helle a sidelong glance. "She was as stubborn as a mule at times. She refused to eat her cabbage, telling us her mother didn't like it, and she wrinkled her little nose in disgust at beans and chickpeas."

Jason muffled a laugh. "I guess she would have thrived on peanut butter and chocolate."

"She thrived anyway," Katherine said with an edge. "We loved her, we taught her to cope with her gifts, and she became a beautiful but reserved young woman. Boys gawked but kept their distance, intimidated by her composure and dignity. All except one. He never gave up." She smiled. "That Laon...He was a good husband to her. They had three sons, and I helped all of them into the world."

"Sons," Jason said softly, and he brushed his lips over Helle's forehead.

"When Kantor died, she became queen to Laon's king. Not everyone was comfortable with that, because she induced more fear than love. Yet her gifts served her people well, and she kept them safe. But all the years I knew her, she would now and then wake and scream, her eyes flooding with tears as she saw things that would happen long after she was dead."

"What was it she saw in the future that scared her so?" Jason asked.

Helle shared a look with Katherine; she already knew. Katherine nodded infinitesimally.

"She saw you. She saw Samion. That's why I'm here."

Jason bit his lip and looked away.

Katherine cleared her throat. "She reburied you together."

"Reburied?" Jason frowned. "But you knew I wanted to—"

"Well I didn't," she cut him off. "I felt I deserved to keep some part of you for me, only for me." She lifted her chin. "Helle took everything else, didn't she? Your love, your life..."

Helle's cheeks flamed, and beside her Jason ground his teeth, looking at his mother as if he'd gladly set her alight and leave her to burn.

"How," he began, but Katherine waved him silent.

"Korine was angry with me, accusing me of loving my son too much, her mother too little." Katherine met Helle's eyes and shrugged. "She said it was the least she could do, to let you share in death what you had never shared in life, a peaceful sleep." A shiver travelled up Helle's spine. Dead bones sharing a tomb, yet here they were. Jason seemed just as perturbed, tightening his hold on Helle's shoulders.

Katherine manoeuvred her wheelchair so that she was facing the window, presenting them with her back. "And then one day she rode off," Katherine said bleakly. "No one ever saw her again. No one ever heard of her again." She lifted a hand towards the winter sunlight, streaming in through the window. "That loss I did not survive. That time my heart did not heal."

"You don't love her as much as you love him."

Nefirie turned to face the girl, currently staring at her from under dark brows.

"What do you mean?" she hedged.

"You love him best. My father," Korine repeated.

"Jason is my son, of course I love him best." She didn't love Helle at all and she had never forgiven her for stealing him away.

"She is my mother," Korine replied. "You must help them both."

Nefirie sighed, yet again cursing herself for that moment of weakness when she'd promised she'd help those future incarnations of her son and his woman.

"I will never forgive you if you fail her. Never." The quiet conviction in Korine's voice shook Nefirie to her core.

"I will do my best, child."

"That will not be enough. Not if you fail her to save him."

Korine's eyes were cold, the eyes of a much older person. She stared at Nefirie until she nodded reluctantly.

"I will save them both," she vowed. But if she had to choose, she'd save her son.

Chapter 26

After Katherine's revelations, Helle and Jason walked about in an emotional daze for days. Helle wanted to hear more—much more—Katherine refused, and Jason was caught somewhere in between: on the one hand curious about this unknown child of his, on the other worried that whatever Katherine would tell them would be difficult to handle. A child—his child—burdened with two such terrible gifts.

But he couldn't help speculating, trying to envision Korine, and now and then it seemed to him he caught a glimpse of her especially at times like these, when he lay wide awake in a house submerged in darkness.

Jason adjusted his pillow, careful not to jolt Helle, fast asleep with her head on his chest. Only the slight tang of sweat that clung to her was any indication of her recent nightmare, this time so violent she'd fallen out of bed before waking, disoriented and afraid. As always, she'd refused to talk about her dreams, but tonight she'd wept, crawling into his arms to hide. Jason stroked her bare arm and stared up at the ceiling, wishing he could do something more to help her than just hold her.

In her sleep, Helle turned, sliding off his shoulder to bury her face in her pillows. He smiled at the picture she presented, a mass of curls, a bare back disappearing into the folds of the duvet. He rolled over on his side, played with a strand of her hair. It was still a miracle that she was here, with him, and he just had to set his lips to her throat and the reassuring throbbing of her pulse.

Helle made an irritated sound. Jason moved that much closer, enveloping her with his larger body. She muttered something before relaxing against him. Jason slid in his hand to cup her breast —warm, soft and heavy. She squirmed.

"Ow," she mumbled.

"Ow?" He kissed her nape.

"I'm sleeping."

"I'm not." He moved closer, and in her drowsy state she reciprocated, her round arse pressed against his groin.

"Sleep," she muttered. "So tired."

"Too tired for this?" His hands followed the contours of her body, stroked her skin, and with a humming sound Helle turned towards him. "Or this?" He lifted himself on top, she parted her legs, a soft exhalation escaping her when he came inside.

"Nice," she murmured, flexing her hips in time with his. A slow sensuous rhythm, that didn't quite succeed in waking her fully. But her body responded to his, her arms and legs tethered him to her, and when he came, she clung to him, wet mouth pressed to his cheek. He fell asleep in her arms, his last conscious thought being that he really should move—but he didn't want to.

When next he woke, it was well past nine. Rain pattered the windows, and beside him Helle was curled up on her side, watching him.

"Hi," she said.

"Morning." He stretched, turning to look at her. "All right?" He rubbed at the imprint of the pillow that decorated her cheek.

"Hungry." She snuggled up to him. "I could eat a horse."

"Sorry, don't have any." He sat up. "Omelette okay?"

She tagged him down to the kitchen, set the table and managed to eat several slices of toast before he had the omelettes done. Jason smiled at how she threw herself at the food.

"We did eat last night, didn't we?" he teased, and Helle reddened, setting down her fork.

"I'm just hungry. I guess all that nightly exercise takes its toll."

"Exercise?" Jason laughed, leaned over to tweak her cheek. "You, Mrs Morris, barely woke up."

"Maybe Mr Morris needs to up his game," she replied tartly. She stuck her tongue out, looking quite the picture in her dark blue silk kimono and all that messy hair.

"Now?" he asked, capturing her hand just as she'd forked a piece of omelette.

"Now? I'm eating!" She grinned. "And then we're going to Katherine, right?"

"She can wait, lioness."

It was well past noon before they made it to Katherine's. Jason had been insistent and attentive, and Helle had chased away her little niggles of guilt to give herself up to the moment, promising herself that she would tell him about the pill issue—she had to tell him—but not right now.

"Mother?" Jason called as he ushered Helle into the white hall.

"In here," Katherine replied, and when they entered the sitting room she was standing by the window, tending her plants.

"You can walk?" Helle asked, although she already knew she could.

"When I want to," she replied, her eyes meeting Helle's briefly.

"Oh, and you don't always feel like it." Helle said sarcastically. Katherine moved over to the sofa and sat down carefully.

"Decrepitude is a good disguise," she said, busying herself with unwinding the bandage round one of her knees. "And there's some truth to it," she added, exposing a very swollen joint. "Arthritis."

"Can't you heal it?" Helle asked. Reasonably, the best healer around should be able to cure herself, right? Katherine just looked at her before pointedly turning to Jason and asking if there were any news about Woolf.

Helle listened with half an ear. She'd reached a point where she couldn't quite find the energy required to walk about constantly frightened, so instead she avoided thinking about Woolf as much as possible. His daily texts were deleted unread, she no longer opened her e-mails unless she knew the sender or they'd been vetted by Jason, and she'd stopped reading papers or watching TV. As a consequence, her life had shrunk into a monitored existence where she only felt truly safe at home and, somewhat ironically, here, at Katherine's.

The incident at the Turkish Embassy had resulted in a sharply worded protest, Curtis demanding Woolf's bail be revoked. After hours of acrimonious discussions, the prosecutor had decided that for now, the bail would stand. For now, he'd added, telling Woolf's solicitor in no uncertain terms that unless Woolf stayed well away from both Jason and Helle, he'd end up in a cell.

"Better than nothing," Katherine commented. "Besides, it's not as if a cell can contain him anyway."

No, Helle sighed. Woolf was quite capable of tormenting her from a distance.

Jason disappeared into the kitchen to fix tea and scones, and Katherine asked Helle to fetch her a cane.

"In the hall," she said. "In that bamboo cylinder."

There were three canes, one of them a very distinctive thing in black wood adorned by silver serpents. She recognised that particular cane. Helle gripped it, lifted it and studied it closely. An autumn day in the park, those joggers converging on her, and on a bench an old lady gripping a cane. This cane. Helle stormed back to the sitting room.

"It was you," she said. "You were there—it was you who made my feet burn!"

Katherine neither pretended not to understand nor denied it. She merely shrugged.

"How could you?" Helle demanded. "You were helping them—him!" She backed away. "How can I ever trust you?"

"You don't trust me," Katherine said drily. "You never have." She sniffed. "You were always ruled by your instincts rather than your intellect." Katherine peered at Helle over the rim of her glasses. "Somewhat primitive, but effective."

"Bitch!" Helle snarled.

"Maybe." Katherine shrugged. "And as to whether you can trust me, let's just say my agenda has changed." She placed a hand on Helle's belly. "This changes everything."

Helle shrank away from her touch. "What does?" She didn't know—not for sure.

"Don't be obtuse. The child." She raised her brows. "Have you told Jason yet?" She leaned closer. "Does he even know you've stopped taking your pills?" Katherine smirked. "Tell you what: you don't tell him about the incident in the park, I don't tell him about the baby."

"Of course I'll tell him!" Helle threw the cane at Katherine.

"And what exactly will you achieve?" Katherine hissed. "We both know that if you do, he'll cut me out of your lives, insist he can defeat Samion on his own." Her voice dropped further. "But he can't, you hear? None of you can!" Before Helle's astounded eyes she grew in size, the old crippled lady replaced by an apparition in white, dark red hair swirling round her. This woman held life and death in her hands, a giant sword lifted towards the skies. "Without me, everything you see in those dreams of yours will come true. Without me, it will all be blood and gore and it will be your fault that he dies."

Helle backed away, hit her calves against the coffee table and almost fell.

"Helle?" Jason called from the kitchen. "I need your help."

Just like that, Nefirie was gone, replaced by infirm Katherine. But her eyes still glowed with determination, a claw-like hand closing over Helle's wrist. "So, what is it to be?"

Helle pulled her hand free. "You already know the answer." She glared at her mother-in-law. "But I will be watching you, you hear?"

Katherine snickered. "You do that, my dear."

"What do you want to do tomorrow?" Jason asked as they walked back home, shadowed by Tim.

"Tomorrow?"

"Valentine's Day." He smiled. "And don't try to tell me you didn't know."

She threw a nervous look over her shoulder. "Couldn't we just stay at home?"

Jason's face darkened. "Because you want to, or because you don't dare to go out?"

"Both." She took his hand. "I like being at home, just the two of us." She slid closer. "You, me—the possibilities are endless."

His mouth twitched. "You're right. We could re-caulk the bathroom."

"Idiot."

Once home, Jason disappeared into the study, already talking to Arthur, his man in New York. Helle went to call Mum.

Her conversation with Katherine had left her jittery, not only because of the incident in the park, but also because of what Katherine had said about a baby. A baby…Helle smoothed a hand over her cable-knitted sweater, incapable of suppressing the smile that burst across her face, while butterflies swarmed in her stomach. She took a deep breath and dialled.

The first few minutes were spent reassuring Miriam that Helle had recovered from her latest interaction with Woolf. After that, Helle told her the whole thing about forgetting her pills, not telling Jason, and now potentially being pregnant—or so Katherine said. A long silence met all this.

"You disapprove, don't you?"

"Disapprove? Of course I do!" Mum made an exasperated sound. "You've gone behind his back."

"I know." Helle pressed a hand to her forehead in a futile effort to contain the blooming headache. "It's just…" And it all came out, how she dreamed of a little girl, how scared she was of never having the time to have a family with him this time round either. By the time she was done, she was crying, loud noisy sobs that she couldn't quite contain.

"Oh darling, don't cry," Mum said.

"I…" She hiccupped. "He'll be so mad at me, won't he?"

"I don't know. But I do know that you have to tell him, as soon as possible." Her mother cleared her throat. "First you do a pregnancy test, then you tell him."

"But Katherine—"

"…is not a gynaecologist, is she? So don't take her word for it, take the test, darling—today."

275

"Great Valentine's gift," Helle muttered, experiencing a sinking feeling in her stomach.

"Better than some I could think of," Miriam said, and there was a smile in her voice. "He loves you. Things will be fine."

As things turned out, it wasn't until next morning that Helle found the opportunity to do the test. Jason was off to do his padel tennis thing, and Helle had Tim take her to a nearby Boots, saying she needed, well, women's things. Tim went a bright red, standing with his back to her while she completed her purchase.

Thirty minutes later, she was staring down at the little line that indicated she was very pregnant—four tests, all of them showing the same result.

"Things will be fine," she croaked. "Fine," she added firmly, placing her hands over her belly. "Very fine." A fizzy feeling rushed through her. A baby—Jason's baby!

"Ma'am?" Tim called from below. "Delivery for you."

"For me?" On a Sunday? She hastily swept together tests and packaging and dumped them in the wastebasket.

Tim was smiling when she came downstairs. In the doorway was a small man holding a huge bouquet of roses.

"Wow." Helle reached for the flowers. Jason really had a flair for romantic gestures.

"Sorry miss, I need you to sign for them first," the delivery man said.

"Sign for them?"

"New rules." The man shrugged. "I've..." He pulled a crumpled piece of paper out of a pocket. "If you could just..."

"Sure." She beckoned him inside, found a pen and scribbled her signature.

"Thank you." The man handed her the flowers, and there had to be about fifty of them, so many Helle couldn't see much beyond the dark green leaves and perfect red roses. There was a scuffle, a loud shout that ended in a gurgle, and moments later Helle was shoved backwards, spilling roses all around her.

"What the fuck!" she exclaimed, and then her windpipe shrivelled. There, on the threshold stood Woolf.

"Alone at last," he said, taking a step towards her.

Helle fled, making for the living room and the door to the garden. He came after her.

"No running," he said. "You know what I do to women who run."

God, yes she knew! Her feet burned with remembered pain. He stalked her, she scrambled away from him, keeping first the sofa, then the central circular fireplace between them.

Woolf smiled. "Do you truly think you can flee?" He held out his hand, closed his fist, and Helle's brain howled. Black eyes bored into hers, a velvety voice told her it was over. She was lost. She hung her head in shame. She was lost, and he, the man standing in front of her, had the right to demand her submission. Woolf chuckled, sat down on the sofa, and crossed his legs, eyes never leaving Helle. She tried to swallow, but her mouth was as arid as a desert.

"Nice room," he said. "So much light." He smiled "Not much light where you're going, little Helle. In fact, I don't think you'll ever see the sun again." He snapped his fingers and she jumped. "Darkness and me, little Helle. That's all you'll get, for the rest of your life."

No. She managed to shake her head, and he laughed, his voice as loud on the inside of her skull as on the outside. Her phone rang, and the sound distracted him sufficiently for him to look away from her. The blackness in her head lifted, and Helle took the opportunity to shuffle away, create further distance between them. Her hand closed on a glass paperweight. A weapon.

His eyes were back, but this time Helle refused to meet them, eyelashes swooping down protectively. It irritated him, and the voice in her head snarled at her to obey. No. Pain exploded through her brain, causing her to stumble. Again, and she shrieked, throwing the paperweight at him. It struck Woolf full in the chest, but other than making him scowl it had no effect.

"Bitch," he said coldly. "That will cost you." He stood, undid his belt, and pulled it free. His voice was everywhere. It echoed in her head, it rang in her ears. Helle swayed and

277

shook, incapable of coherent thought. When he folded the belt together, she flinched. When he beckoned her towards her, she cringed. But she moved in his direction, that invasive presence in her mind making it impossible not to obey.

"Look at me."

No, no no! Her brain went into red alert, her knees buckled.

"I said, look at me." Such a beautiful voice, soft like silk and as dangerous as crushed glass. It caressed her ears, shredded her soul, leaving her empty inside. She lifted her eyes, met his blazing gaze. She could see herself in his eyes, a disobedient woman who deserved everything she had coming. *No*, her brain protested weakly.

"Undress."

Her fingers fumbled over buttons and zippers. Jeans, hoodie, bra and panties—all of them neatly folded together. He walked around her, slapping the belt into the palm of his hand.

"Kneel."

Helle fell to her knees. He laughed, dragging the belt over her shoulders.

"I'm going to enjoy this." He leaned forward. "First, I'll belt you. Then, I'll fuck you—right here, in the Wanderer's living room." His hand gripped Helle's hair, forcing her head back. "And then, I'll take you, and he will never, ever find you again."

Tears formed in Helle's eyes, slid silently down her cheeks. Her toes dug into the carpet, her brain shrieked at her to run, and for an instant she considered it, tried even, but he snarled her name and she couldn't move, not with his voice in her head.

"Prostrate yourself."

She did.

The first blow had her gasping. The second set fire to her skin. The third cleared her head, and Helle screamed and sprang to her feet. Behind her, Woolf cursed. Helle sprinted for the front door, yelling for Tim. Strange: the door was ajar, an arm caught between the doorblade and the jamb.

"Tim?" Helle trod on the roses, felt thorns sink into her soles and heels. "Tim?"

A hand on her shoulder wrenched her backwards. Another hand in her hair, and she was dragged over the slate tiles, over the trampled flowers. It hurt, but pain was good, it helped her fight his hypnotic presence. She grabbed hold of a thorny rose-stem.

Woolf released his hold. She collapsed to the floor. They were back in the living room, the hardwood floors cool to her overheated cheek.

"I told you not to run." He crouched beside her, his eyes seeking hers. "Now I'll just have to punish you even harder." His fingers caressed her cheek, slid into her hair. His voice whispered its way into her head, but this time she dug the thorns into her palm. Think, she urged herself, but came up with a blank. His hand was on her back, and she shuddered, even more so when he flipped her over, one hand tightening in her hair to hold her still.

He smirked when she whimpered. He lowered his head, his lips hovering over hers. A soft kiss, and she gagged. Those fingers sliding down her front…they made her skin crawl. She caught sight of his belt, lying discarded on the floor. If only… Oh, God, his hand on her breasts, on her belly, moving slowly towards her pubic mound. It froze, a heavy weight just below her navel. He pressed, hard, fingers sinking like claws into her skin.

"What is this?" he hissed. "What is this?" he roared, and the pain when he dug his fingers into her made her jerk upright, her knees slamming into him.

"Let me go!"

"A child?" He appeared stunned. "His child?" His hold on her hair loosened. Helle tore free, was up on her knees, on her feet. His hand on her ankle, one determined tug, and she fell. He was on top of her.

"Well, we can't have that, can we?" he said, and the tone of his voice made her blood turn to ice. "Not again. So," he continued, "change of plans. I fuck you and then…" He pressed her to the floor. "We kill it."

"No!" She bucked. He laughed, she heard the sound of his zipper, and...God, no, not this! She reached back, got hold of something, and yanked. He howled, his weight no longer squashing her flat. This was the best opportunity she'd get. Helle elbowed him in the face.

"Fucking hell!" He clapped a hand over his bleeding nose. Helle managed to regain her feet, leaping away from him.

She panted with fear. Woolf snarled and shook his head before turning towards her. His nose was miraculously whole, but his normally so controlled façade had crumbled, and what faced her was a growling beast, eyes narrowed, hands like talons.

"I'm going to tear it out of you," he said. "And then I'm going to..." He mimed a hand swiping over his throat. Helle backed away, glad of the sofa between them. His voice was back in her head, an angry toothy thing that had her vision blurring. With the grace of a panther, Woolf threw himself over the sofa.

She screamed and clawed at his face with both hands. He staggered backwards. Helle darted round to the other side. His voice. It commanded her to give up. *No, no, no!* Her head thudded with the familiar headache that sprang from somewhere just behind her eyes. The light from the windows made her squint, his voice rose and fell, and when he leapt towards her again, she barely managed to evade him, this time putting the fireplace between them. At least he couldn't jump that.

"Get over here!" he told her. He picked up his belt, whirled it over his head before bringing it down on one of the scattered cushions.

Helle shook her head, biting her lip in an effort to clear her head of his voice. He laughed, and the noise made her bend over, covering her ears. She couldn't move, not even when his shoes appeared in her field of vision. There was a whooshing sound. The belt-buckle connected with her shoulder. She fell to her knees.

"Unfaithful bitch! I'm going to kill you for this!" Over and over, the belt-buckle dug into her skin. A wave of vomit rushed up her throat, and she retched, vomit spattering her arm, the floor.

Helle curled up, arms protecting her head, her stomach. His foot drove into her ribs, into her legs. The belt came down repeatedly, and all the time she heard him howling in her head, screaming that this was not how it was supposed to be, because she was supposed to be his, his!

He was going to kill her. She tried to drag herself away from him, but it was futile. A ferocious kick to her buttocks had her skidding across the floor. Blood. She could smell it, taste it. Her blood. She was going to die. Die. In her head, the red-haired child was crying, but Helle didn't want to think about her, not now. Jason. Her Jason. If only she could hold his hand as she died, see his eyes, hear his heart. Jason.

Kantor found her under the junipers. She crouched, her tear-streaked face a pale blob in the surrounding gloom.

"Korine," he said softly, "come, little heart."

She sobbed and moved further away. He grunted as he crawled in after her, his knees creaking with the effort.

"What is it?" he asked, his index finger tracing the outline of her nose. She shied away.

Kantor wheedled and cajoled, until she finally let him take her by the arms and back out, dragging her with him. Nefirie was waiting in the sun, and she swept Korine into her arms, ignoring the overly warm hands.

"It was awful, Nana," the child sobbed. "I couldn't help her. I couldn't make her see me. She saw only his blackness." Her voice broke and she hid her face. "He hurt her and I couldn't stop it. But I was made to watch." She opened her mouth and wailed.

Chapter 27

Jason had just scored another point for his side, when his phone rang. Simultaneously, Nigel's did the same, a loud wailing tone. Jason hurtled towards his bag, numb fingers digging for his phone.

"Security breach," Nigel gasped from beside him. He was out of breath and bright red, sweat coating his face and assorted piercings.

Jason wheeled, sprinting for the entrance with Nigel at his heels.

"Hey, wait up!" Curtis came thundering after.

"Helle," was all Jason could say.

"My car." Curtis set off at speed, long sleek legs outpacing them both as he rushed towards his car, a silver BMW.

They took off with a roar. Up to Whitechapel, a sharp left, and Curtis honked and blinked his lights as he wove through what traffic there was. Jason dialled Helle's number.

"Tell me," Curtis said.

"The alarm's gone off—front door wide open," Nigel replied from the back, fingers dancing over the touch screen of his phone. "She isn't picking up?"

Jason's hand shook. "No."

"Shit." Curtis increased his speed. "Tim?"

"No answer." Nigel sounded grim. He clasped Jason's shoulder. "Call Stapleton."

Before Jason could do so, his phone rang. Katherine.

"Hurry!" she said. "He's there, with her, I can feel it. He's going to hurt her, Jason, and if he finds out…" she broke off.

"Finds out about what?"

"He's there! With her. Hurry, son, she needs you." The line went dead. Jason clenched his jaw in an effort not to scream at Curtis to drive faster. There was a band of pressure over his chest, a loud thumping in his ears, and his hands were beginning to sizzle. He stuck them in his pockets, trying to bring the heat under control.

"Hey." Nigel's hand on his shoulder again. "We'll get there in time."

How do you know? Jason wanted to yell. Instead he swallowed and looked straight ahead, noting distractedly how people and cars veered every which way as Curtis guided his car at breakneck speed along Fleet Street.

"Jesus!" Nigel exclaimed, after Curtis squeezed between two cars. "Watch out!" he yelled when Curtis drove up on the pavement, honking madly to clear the way.

"Stapleton," was all Curtis said. Jason pulled out his phone, but his hands were too hot, his fingers swelling with heat. Curtis threw him a sidelong look. "What the fuck?"

"Allergy," Nigel responded. "Bad reaction to adrenaline." He leaned forward, lifted Jason's phone out of his hands. "I'll call."

"Adrenaline?" Curtis asked, revving the engine. They barrelled down the road, doing close to eighty miles per hour. Big black hands rested confidently on the wheel, on the gear stick.

Jason nodded, not trusting himself to speak. Helle— with him. From behind came Nigel's voice, briefly bringing Stapleton up to speed. Jason closed his eyes.

"Mother," he mumbled, "keep her safe, Mother—in this life as you didn't do in that first one." Mother? He couldn't remember the last time he'd prayed to his first deity, the powerful Mother Goddess that ruled Nefirie's and his world all those years ago. Please, he added silently, please keep her safe.

"Where did you learn to drive like this?" Nigel asked from the back seat, just as Curtis decided to shortcut straight across the oncoming traffic.

"I haven't always been a bloke in a suit," Curtis replied, turning abruptly into a smaller street.

"No, you've obviously been standing in for Lewis," Nigel muttered.

"Lewis Hamilton?" Curtis snorted. "He drives on a racetrack. What fun is there in that?" He zigzagged his way through Belgravia, ignored a one-way sign and then they were on the Cromwell Road, Curtis blaring his horn. Jason kept his eyes on the road, knotting his hands to stop the fire from leaking through.

They ran a red light at Kensington High Street, and Curtis gunned the engine up the last incline. No sooner had the car screeched to a halt, than Jason was running for the door.

Tim was lying on the doorstep, white shirt dark with blood. "Take care of him," Jason ordered, already pushing the door wide open. Someone was screaming invectives and Jason flew towards the sound.

Sam Woolf was standing over Helle, trousers undone, belt in his hand. He hit her, screaming in anger. Her body jerked, but she uttered no sound, lying like a broken puppet on the floor. So focused was Woolf on what he was doing that he didn't react until Jason jumped him, searing hands grabbing hold of Woolf's arms. This time, Jason allowed his fires to explode, uncontrolled, and Woolf's eyes widened, the belt falling to the floor. There was a stench of roasting meat, and Woolf fell to his knees, trying to protect himself from Jason's glowing fists.

The wood below Jason's feet began to smoke. He flung his arm wide, spraying fire over Woolf's head, and the man yowled, beating at the flames that sprang from his hair. Kill him. Jason's breathing deepened, his pulse slowed. Kill him. He raised his hands, wanting nothing more than to strangle the kneeling bastard to death.

Helle moaned. Jason's single-minded concentration on Woolf wavered. With a growl, Woolf regained his feet—a Woolf reduced to a wild-eyed, incoherent beast, cornered and lethal. Jason threw himself at him, planting red-hot hands on Woolf's chest. Woolf howled, swinging blindly at Jason's head. Jason ducked. Woolf shoved, sending Jason flying backwards. By the time Jason regained his balance, Woolf was gone, escaping through the garden.

Jason sucked in air, did it again. There, by his feet, was his wife. Stark naked and covered in welts and bruises, here and there streaked with blood, she was moving weakly in the direction of a burning patch of carpet. Jason stamped the fire out, pulled a wrap from the sofa and kneeled beside her.

"Helle?" He cleared his throat. She looked at him, and there was blood on her lips, blood on her face, on her hands. She smelled: of vomit and fear, of sweat and of Woolf. What had he done to her? Woolf's trousers, gaping open, his wife, stark naked...Jason swallowed painfully. He tried to hold her, but she gasped when his overheated hands touched her, and then her head lolled back and she went limp.

Hours later, Jason was sitting in the waiting room of St Mary's Hospital, still in his sweaty t-shirt and scorched shorts. Nigel had at long last gone home, Tim was still in surgery—the knife wound had been deep, damaging a number of internal organs—and so far he had not been allowed in to see Helle.

Jason rested his head back against the wall. What an effing mess! Tim, almost dead. Helle...his breath caught. From what Nigel and Stapleton had been able to deduce, it had all been very well-planned. A flower delivery—an extravagant delivery—and Woolf had used the distraction to attack Tim and get in.

"Mr Morris?" A young female doctor stood in the doorway.

"Yes?" He rose, suddenly feeling very tired. The doctor gave him a brief catalogue of Helle's injuries: two cracked ribs, multiple lesions and cuts, some inexplicable burn marks on her upper arms, a badly bitten lip...

"She is resting," the doctor finished, giving Jason a reassuring smile. "She will be fine—and so will the baby."

"The baby?" Jason stuttered.

"Ah." The doctor blushed prettily. "You didn't know? Oh dear, and here am I stealing her surprise."

Jason was mute. A baby? Their baby?

"It's still very early days," the doctor prattled on, "she's in her eighth week or so."

Jason counted back in his head. A baby. The thought was like wildfire through his veins. His baby, probably conceived during that spectacular lovemaking session just before New Year's Eve.

"Can I see her?"

"Of course."

Helle wasn't asleep, but looked frail and pale. Thick curly lashes were sticky with tears, the fingers of her left hand fretting with the thin blanket. She was on her side, and from what the doctor had told him this was on account of the multiple gashes on her back, some of them so deep they'd required stitches.

"Hi," he said, pulling up a chair. She nodded a greeting, her eyes on anything but him.

"Lioness?" He brushed at her bruised cheek, and she flinched.

"I'm…I'm…oh, God!" She began to weep, her right hand curling protectively over the rings on her left. "He…"

"Shh." He covered her hands with his. "It'll be fine, Helle." And he didn't want to hear. As long as he hadn't heard it, it hadn't happened. He chuckled mirthlessly at his own irrational logic. Whatever had happened, had happened, and here was his wife, bruised and beaten, and he didn't have the courage to listen? He stiffened his spine and tightened his hold on her hands, running a finger over the rings he had given her. For better and for worse, he reminded himself.

"Tell me," he said softly.

"I…" She gulped. "He…the belt…his voice, in my head, his…"

"Helle." He set a finger to her lips. "Tell me, from the beginning."

So she did, and Jason died a thousand deaths as she described just what Sam Woolf had put her through.

"He didn't," she said, avoiding his eyes. "He just…"

Beat her to an inch of her life. If only he had burned the bastard to death!

"He was going to kill me." Her voice was no more than a whisper. "If you hadn't come…"

"But I did." He smiled at her, tucked a lock of hair behind her ear. "I did, lioness."

286

"Yes, you did." She peeked at him. "Are you very mad?"

"Mad?" He gave her a confused look.

"About the baby." Her mouth curved into the softest of smiles. "Our baby."

How could he be? Frightened out of his wits, yes, but angry? "No. But you should have told me."

"I know. I was going to—today." She sighed. "I had hoped to do it under different circumstances."

Helle was discharged next morning. After detouring to visit Tim—a futile endeavour, seeing as the poor man was still out cold, connected to so many beeping monitors it made Jason feel uncomfortable—Jason took her home.

He watched her halt just inside the door, shoulders hunching. Her eyes flew to the floor, to the wall. He'd spent most of last night cleaning every surface, sweeping up each and every petal. Never was he going to give her red roses again.

"Come." He took her hand, she hung back. Jason insisted, however gently, leading her into the living room. He'd turned the Turkish carpet so that the singed area was hidden under the sofa, he'd scrubbed the floor, wiped the walls clean of soot and other spatters. Stapleton had been livid, talking about forensic evidence, but when Jason had handed him the security tape, he'd shut up.

Helle took a hesitant step towards the fireplace, did a slow turn. "It looks just the same," she said in a low voice, but her hands twisted together, knuckles standing stark against her skin.

"We'll redecorate." Anything to wipe whatever vestiges remained of Woolf from his home. Helle nodded, sitting down on the edge of the closest chair.

"Have they found him?"

"No." He turned on the gas fire and stood staring at the flames for a while. "They think he's left the country."

He heard her exhale. When he turned, she was crying, hiding her face in her hands.

"He's gone?" she said through her sobs. "For real?"

For the time being, he thought, but that wasn't what she needed to hear, not right now.

"It seems so," he said, giving her a reassuring smile.

The prosecutor had taken one look at the tape, said something very colourful along the lines that some men should be hung up by their balls and left to rot, and had called Woolf's solicitor to inform him the bail had been revoked and his client had an hour to turn himself in.

By then, Stapleton's men had already been at Woolf's home, but there'd been neither hide nor hair of him there, or at any of the other locations they'd tried. The stuttering solicitor insisted he had no idea where Woolf might be, and by the time airports and harbours had been contacted it had been too late. In Jason's opinion, it had been too late long before that. Whatever else he was, Woolf wasn't stupid, and he'd have made for the Continent already last night.

The painkillers made Helle tired, which was why she was fast asleep on the little sofa in his study when Katherine came by.

"She says he came to abduct her," Jason told his mother, adjusting the soft blanket over Helle. Katherine rolled her chair closer, smoothed a long finger over Helle's creased brow. As if by magic, the little frown disappeared, Helle's face softening into a peaceful expression.

"She's probably right. But then he realised she was with child. The ultimate betrayal, in his world, especially as she tricked him into believing the baby she carried in your first lives was his. He has never forgiven her for that."

Katherine placed her hands on Helle's body. Helle twitched and muttered something in her sleep, but didn't wake, not even when Katherine put a finger to each and every one of her lesions.

"How would he know she was pregnant?" Jason asked, fascinated by his mother's hands, by how those fingers smoothed away the welts and bruises.

Katherine raised her brows. "Same way I did. He touched her and felt it."

"It?"

"The new life." Katherine made a dismissive gesture. "No major skills required." She returned to her ministrations, muttering something that sounded like a prayer.

"Thanks a lot." He moved over to his desk, saved some of his files, and once Katherine was done, suggested they leave Helle to sleep. Now that Katherine was here, he felt more comfortable about leaving her alone—and she had sunk into a sleep too deep to object.

Katherine manoeuvred her wheelchair into the living-room, all the way to the ceiling to floor windows that gave on the garden.

"Just because he's gone, doesn't mean he's given up."

"And you think I don't know?" He gave her a black look. For once, there was proof. For once, they could have had him locked up, and instead that accursed devil of a man went up in smoke.

"He'll try to kill her." Katherine looked up at him. "And you."

"So what else is new?" he said bitterly.

"The baby." Katherine adjusted her cardigan. "That's my grandson in there. He will not come to harm, not while I draw breath."

"A son?" Jason sank down on the sofa.

"Of course a son." Katherine smiled at her reflection in the window. "Your daughter was mine to raise. There will be no more girls."

"But more sons?" He could hear it himself, how pathetically hopeful he sounded. Katherine sighed.

"It's in the hands of the Mother, Jason," she said. "But this little one, I will keep safe."

"And his mother? His father?"

Katherine looked away. "It all comes at a price, son. But I will do my best."

"You do that—and remember that if Helle dies, then I am dead as well."

Katherine gave him a sour look. "We've already had this conversation. As far as I'm aware, I do not suffer from dementia, so yes, I will remember."

"Good," he said lightly. There were still moments when Katherine gave off far too many conflicting vibrations. At present, he could sense she was worried for him, even for that unformed foetus, but there was little concern for Helle beyond her role as the mother of the coming child. He studied Katherine, wondering just what she meant when she said it all came at a price.

The next day, Miriam showed up. Helle fell into her arms, and for the three days Miriam was in town, Jason was relieved of nursing duty, something he felt very ambivalent about, no matter that it gave him an opportunity to catch up with work, with the police, with poor Tim, with… At times, he felt exhausted, and it was a treat to come home to Miriam's excellent cooking, to see Helle flash him the occasional smile.

"If I ever get the opportunity, I'll relieve him of his balls with a pair of nail scissors," Miriam said one evening. They were sharing a bottle of wine in the living room, him on the sofa with Helle's head pillowed in his lap, Miriam curled up in one of the modern armchairs.

"Nail scissors?" He stroked Helle's back. She made a contented sound and burrowed closer, fast asleep.

"So that it takes a long, long time." She drank deeply. "He was going to kill her, wasn't he?"

"Yes." What else could he say? His fingers curled.

"But he didn't." She poured herself some more wine, topped up his glass as well.

"No, he didn't."

"This time." Miriam emptied her glass and fixed bleary eyes on him. "If you don't keep her safe, I'll…," she swallowed, "kill you."

"You won't have to," he said bitterly.

In the week following Miriam's departure, Jason worked from home, reluctant to leave his wife alone. She seemed to feel the same way, keeping him always in her sight. She healed rapidly—no doubt thanks to Katherine's skills—and by the time it was Friday, she moved about quite unhindered.

The better she got, the more affectionate she became, craving, so it seemed, physical proximity. She'd brush his hair in passing, squeeze herself down on his lap while he was working, hug him from behind when he was cooking, and every time she did, he could hear the subtext: love me, touch me. Except that he couldn't, because whenever he looked at her, he saw her as she'd been that Sunday, naked and bloodied, and standing over her Sam Woolf, his trousers undone.

He tried to banish these images and the even cruder ones that now and then presented themselves for his inspection. Of Helle, undressing and folding her clothes before kneeling before Woolf. Of Woolf, holding her down as he prepared to take her. Shit! The thought of Woolf forcing her down before him, wrenching her up on her knees, was driving him crazy. He hadn't raped her, he reminded himself. But still… He was plagued by images of Woolf unzipping himself and looming over her. He had no idea how to hold her, how to touch her, not sure if this was because he worried about her reactions or his own.

Hesitantly, he broached the subject with Nigel. They were in the study, reviewing the security set-up, while Miranda and Helle were watching a movie Miranda insisted was "girls only". Nigel listened, sucking at his lip in a way that made his piercing wobble.

"She needs you," he said once Jason had finished.

"But I—"

"Don't want to touch her—not like that." Nigel drank his whisky and held out his glass for a refill.

"Is that so strange?" Jason sloshed a generous measure into his own glass as well. "What if I hurt her?"

"No. But…" Nigel frowned. "You're not exactly helping her, are you?"

"And what is that supposed to mean?" He'd been a constant, attentive presence the entire week, drawing the line only at sex.

"Exorcism, Jason. That's what she needs."

"Fucking great," Jason muttered.

A fortnight after her ordeal Helle insisted on returning to work. Now that Stapleton had been able to confirm Sam

Woolf had left the country, she was more relaxed than she'd been in months, or so it seemed to Jason, who watched her as she smiled and laughed with Jim and Will, shared a hug with Angela. They had lunch, retired as they usually did for a work session in his office, and halfway through he felt her foot come exploring his leg. Jason moved just out of reach, ostensibly to get a file. Moments later, she closed her laptop and left, saying she had a meeting with Steve. Not true, he knew, seeing as Steve had just left for the day, but he nodded and pretended absorption in his documents.

After work, they visited Tim and he held her as she cried at the sight of the bodyguard, still in a coma, still hovering between life and death. She was quiet afterwards, retreating into a silence he found most unnerving, and once they got home she escaped to the gym.

"Be careful," he said, "you shouldn't exert yourself too much yet."

"I'm fine," she said curtly. "Tim isn't, but I am—at least physically." She stuck her earpieces into place and upped the speed on the treadmill.

He heard her later, talking to Miriam, and she sounded sad and scared, crying as she told Miriam just how close to death Tim was.

"Hey," he said once she'd hung up. "We'll be there for him." He hugged her, buried his nose in her hair, and inhaled her scent. Her arms slid round his waist, she rose on her toes and kissed him. A kiss that wanted much more than he could give—at least for the moment—so he kissed her back gently before asking if she wanted chicken or fish for dinner. Helle shrank in his arms.

"Whatever," she said, stepping out of reach. To his shame, Jason felt relieved.

On the Friday, she took her time getting ready for work, appearing in the kitchen wearing that clinging Dianne von Furstenberg dress he so loved, with black stockings to match. He smiled approvingly, but when she pressed herself against him, he disengaged himself, saying they were already running late for the staff meeting. A flare of hurt in her eyes made him feel like a veritable cad, which was why he tried to take her hand. She snatched it back, and without a word marched out of the kitchen, ignoring his carefully prepared breakfast.

Jason sighed: he should probably talk to her about how he felt, explain it had nothing to do with her. Except that it did, of course, because it was her he saw on her knees, with Woolf panting like an animal above her.

In the event, she was the one who brought the subject up. They'd just returned home after work, it was dark and wet outside, and when he suggested they go to a nearby Italian for dinner, she shook her head.

"We need to talk," she said, leading the way to his study. These days, she never entered the living room unless Jason was already there.

"About what?" he asked, although he already knew. She squared her shoulders.

"I can't do this," she said. "You're treating me like glass, and it's getting to me." She gave him a dark look. "You know it does—you know how insecure I feel when you retreat into some sort of exaggerated caring mode, avoiding any real intimacy." She leaned against the wall, arms folded protectively over her chest. The neckline of her dress stretched, revealing the lacy border of her bra.

Jason dragged a hand through his hair. "You've just lived through a harrowing experience."

"Yeah, and from the way you're acting, it has permanently killed your desire, hasn't it?"

"Don't be silly, of course it hasn't. It's just—"

"That you can't stand the idea of touching me."

"Touch you? I touch you all the time, don't I?" To exemplify, he reached out to caress her cheek, but she slapped his hand away.

"I don't need pats on the back, Jason! I need you to want me, to fuck me silly, not this…this…polite, suffocating attention." She drew in an unsteady breath. "I need you to wipe away the memory of his hands, the way he…" She shuddered. "But the

293

way you're behaving, it's as if you can't stand the idea of being close to me, as if he's permanently marked me."

"I don't..." He fell silent. What could he say? Yes, he avoided intimacy, yes he couldn't quite look at her without seeing Woolf holding her down, preparing to... Rage burnt through his lungs, his throat. He met her eyes.

"I don't need to be coddled, okay?" She wiped at her eyes. "Damn it, Jason, you're making me feel unloved and dirty."

"Unloved? Shit, how can you even say that?"

"How?" She shrugged. "Have a guess. He put me through hell, Jason. But this..." She gestured at the distance between them. "This hurts much, much more."

He closed the gap in two strides, pressed her back against the wall. "I don't want to hurt you," he said, "but—"

"You're overthinking things," she interrupted. "Just go with it, okay?" She grabbed hold of his hair and kissed him. After a couple of heartbeats, he responded, his tongue thrusting into her mouth.

Her hands had hold of his belt, yanking him that much closer. Deftly she undid him, and he let her, even if at present he was more soft than hard, still not entirely sure he could go through with this. But then her hands found his balls, his cock, and she fondled him before squeezing hard enough to make him draw a sharp breath. It sent a flare of angered lust through his loins, and he gripped her wrists, freeing himself from her fingers.

"Jason," she half-moaned when he pinned her against the wall. She was back to tugging at his trousers, his boxers, while kissing his neck, his jaw. He lifted her, and it was groin against groin, the heat in her spreading to him. His hands slid up her stockings, to her hips, all the way to her garter belt, and there were no lacy knickers, nothing to impede his access.

"You've walked about like this all day?" he groaned.

"Yup. But so far, no action."

"No action?" He flexed his hips. "Well, we can't have that, lioness." And just like that he was inside of her. It reminded him of the first time he'd made love to her—no, fucked her, because there was nothing gentle about this, and from the way she was pulling at his shirt, digging her nails into his skin, she didn't want gentle.

Jason drove into her. Hard, unrelenting. In and out, in and out, because this woman was his, damn it, his to fuck, his to pleasure, his to claim.

"Yes!" she cried.

Yes, he thought, yes, yes, yes. He pushed as deep as he could, did it again and again, and all the while she was clinging to him, hot air tickling his ear. She was wet and hot, he was burning up from the inside out. He slammed into her, eased out, picking up pace as he went. There, at last, came his release. Yes! Jason grunted her name as his hips jerked over and over again.

"About that Italian," Helle murmured some time later, now sitting on the floor between his sprawled legs.

"No." He kissed her head. "I'm not done with you yet."

"But I'm hungry," she protested.

"Really?" His nails scraped over her bare thighs. "Well, you'll just have to wait, lioness."

Chapter 28

For a couple of weeks, it was as if Sam Woolf had gone up in smoke. The press had a field day, and thanks to Nigel's obscure connections, a lot of sensitive stuff made it to the front page. It had Stapleton hopping with rage, and from the bollocking he gave Jason over Skype, John knew exactly who was leaking material—and why.

"You're compromising the investigation," he yelled, face florid, eyes sharp.

"Me?" Jason sounded insulted. "Me? If anyone wants Woolf behind bars, it's me."

"Fantastic. We have a common objective—don't blow it, you moron."

Helle decided it was time to intervene. "Hi John," she said, turning Jason's laptop towards her and smiling at the webcam.

"Helle." John's face lit up, his voice softening. "Are you all right?"

"Getting there." No longer having nightmares helped, as did the absence of texts or e-mails. She felt Jason's hand sliding down her back, parking itself on her butt. An active love-life most definitely contributed, and recently they'd been ravenous for each other, in Helle's case partly fuelled by a need to wipe out all memories of what Woolf had done.

"Have you found him yet?" she asked, and John's mouth turned down.

"No. Wherever he is, Woolf is keeping well below the radar."

"Of course he is," Jason muttered. "Doesn't take a genius to work that one out."

"Sooner or later, he'll pop up," Stapleton said. "Unfortunately."

"Yeah." Helle shivered. To hope Woolf was gone for good was futile.

She said as much to Tim when she visited him next day. He nodded, no more, still finding it painful to speak. That he'd survived the blood loss was nothing short of a miracle, the doctors said, but now that he had they were relatively hopeful—a man could live without his spleen, and even the loss of a portion of intestine was, apparently, no big deal. But besides stabbing Tim in his midriff, Woolf had also slashed at his throat, which was why Tim's voice was a reedy thing he preferred not to use.

These days, Helle was always accompanied by Deb, a new addition to the keep-Helle-safe team. Well, at least it made Tim happy, Helle reflected, smiling at how Tim and Deb sneaked looks at each other.

The day Woolf reappeared in their lives was a bright March day. They were at Tor Cottage, busy in the garden, when Nigel called, and moments later Helle was seated in Jason's lap, his arms round her waist as they watched the short video sequence Nigel had just sent them.

Sam Woolf was sitting in the sun, eyes intent on the camera. He'd lost weight, a dark shadow covered his cheeks, and his mouth was set in a grim line. A black shirt, black jeans—the only thing that alleviated all this black was the red notebook lying on the table beside him.

Of course he denied everything. His voice was as cultured, as smooth, as always, but there was a tension to it, mirrored by the tightness round his eyes, by the way his left leg kept jumping up and down. He spoke of conspiracies, of planted evidence, and his hands clenched automatically. Right at the end, he leaned forward, and Helle reared back when his black eyes bored into her.

"I will have what's mine," he said softly. "That's all I want— what's mine. The Mother promised. The Mother will deliver." The screen went black.

"Well," Helle managed to say. Jason tightened his grip on her.

"He sounds insane," he said.

"Not exactly news, is it?" Helle slid off his lap. She needed a drink.

"Insane?" Katherine laughed. "Samion? I don't think so. Obsessive, yes, insane, no." They were sitting in Katherine's white living room, as pristine as always. Not a spot on the carpets, not a stain on the white upholstery—whoever did Katherine's cleaning must be going through tons of textile shampoo. "And one could argue he has a point," Katherine continued. "You were promised to him, not Jason."

"What can I say? Love won," Helle said—mostly to antagonise her. Beside her, Jason muffled a chuckle.

"Love won?" Katherine snorted. "You died, Helle. Samion died, Jason died—so how did love win?"

"We're here, aren't we?"

"Yes, and it's all so happily ever after, isn't it?" Katherine rolled her eyes. "It would have been best for everyone if Kantor had honoured the contracts and handed you over to Samion."

"Not for me," Helle protested. "He'd have hurt me."

"Perhaps." Katherine sounded indifferent. "No more than what men did in those days to curb their disobedient wives. You'd have come to terms with it."

"Mother!" Jason snapped.

"Oh, don't mother me!" Katherine said. "I'm just telling you the truth. In time, Helle would have accepted her life as it was. In time he would have made sure she forgot you, Jason, or at least pretended to forget."

"But that's not how it happened, is it?" Helle said, moving closer to Jason. God, at times she was tempted to rake her nails down Katherine's face.

"No." Katherine looked away. "The Mother had other plans."

"She always refers to God as the Mother," Helle said as she and Jason walked back home.

"How else? To Katherine, the Creator by definition is female—she's never bought into all that patriarchal stuff."

"Wonder why," Helle muttered.

"To me," Jason went on, ignoring her comment, "God just is. Both male and female, God encompasses everything."

"And when Woolf talks about the Mother, is he talking about the same deity as Katherine?"

"Yes." Jason smiled at her. "There's only one Mother."

"And she must be really pleased with how Woolf turned out, right?"

"He worships other gods as well—old, strong powers like Malok and Baal." To Helle's surprise, Jason crossed himself, looking very self-conscious. "Old habit," he muttered.

"So they're like the devil or something?" Helle asked, sneaking a hand into his.

"Not quite as black. The devil is evil through and through. He was once good. Even his name indicated that he was a bringer of light rather than a prince of darkness."

"Lucifer" Helle said, shoving at him. "I'm not totally uneducated. I do read. A lot."

"Good for you. Anyway, Lucifer chose to turn himself away from God so he is altogether damned." Jason's brows creased into a little frown. "Today we have priests who will tell you God exists, but that the devil probably doesn't. I think that might be a mistake. Good and evil go hand in hand, unfortunately. The devil is the antithesis of God but that does not by definition make him an impossibility."

Helle chose not to comment. Raised in a home where God had rarely been discussed, she found all this religious stuff borderline strange. Of course, given the turn her life had taken over the last eighteen months or so, she rarely ruled out anything as impossible any more.

"So, Baal and what's-his-name," Helle prompted.

Jason's face clouded. "Dangerous powers to serve. Baal gives as he receives. You sacrifice to Baal, and you get powers in return."

Helle laughed. "It sounds as if you believe in this guy."

Jason wasn't amused. "People have bowed to him for thousands of years. They probably still do, under new names."

The way he said it made Helle shiver.

"Baal gives what you ask for. He will not discern, not tell you this is bad or good. You do that yourself. He just asks for something in return," Jason continued.

"Like what?" Helle asked, intrigued. Maybe she should do some little prancing around an altar of her own and ask for

Samion to be turned into a tree. Then Jason could burn him down.

"Sacrifices. Animals and even people in the old days. Or a piece of your soul."

"Your soul?" Helle coughed in a weak attempt to disguise her laughter. Jason drew her to a halt.

"I'm not being funny," he said. "The more you worship Baal, the more you lose yourself. And one day, there's nothing left—nothing but permanent darkness."

"So Samion is stuck there?" Serve him bloody right.

"Yes." He started walking again. "Forever."

"And you? What do you think lies waiting down the line?"

"What is this? Existentialism-lite?" he teased.

She ignored him. "Tell me."

Jason slid her a look. "The peace of resting in God's presence." He sounded yearning.

"And that is something you really want," Helle stated.

"Yes, I do. You know that. I want this one shot at a life with you, and then I would like to finally rest."

For some odd reason, this made her feel abandoned—and scared. "Will I be there as well?" she asked in a small voice. He stopped and turned to face her, taking both her hands in his.

"I think so. I hope so." Jason stooped, pressing his lips to her brow. "But first we have a life to enjoy, children to raise, places to go…"

"Yeah," she said, but all of a sudden the fear was back: how long would they get this time round? She placed a protective hand on her belly. Jason covered her hand with his own.

"No one is going to hurt our son." He met her eyes. "No one." Waves of warmth emanated from his hand. "And talking about babies, it's time for tea."

Helle grimaced. These days, tea was no longer code for scones and cream and cakes. Nope, ever since Jason had realised he was to be a father, he'd gone into health mode, which, Helle suspected, meant tea would once again be something full of nuts and spinach and chicken and whatever else Jason deemed good for his baby.

She wasn't wrong. Once they got home, he busied himself in the kitchen, and soon enough a plate appeared before her, and there was spinach and walnuts and roasted chicken and cranberries.

"Seriously?" She eyed the plate and sighed.

"Absolutely. It's good for…"

"The baby," she filled in. "Personally, I don't think some chocolate would do any harm."

"No?" He pointed at her plate. "Once you've finished that, we'll see." He winked, picked up his fork and dug in.

Helle hid a little smile. If all else failed, she had a secret stash of her own.

She'd made her way through half of the spinach when Jason's phone beeped. He pulled it out, swiped, and froze, his fork halfway to his mouth.

"What?" she asked. Jason shook his head, eyes glued to the screen.

"I just…" He shoved his chair back. "Nigel. I have to call Nigel."

Helle's fork clattered on the plate. "Sam?"

"Who else?" He was still staring at his screen.

"Let me see."

"No."

"Jason!" Helle reached across the table and grabbed hold of his hand. "Let me see."

"It's—"

"Awful. It always is with him." She had hold of his phone. A picture of a wolf—a dog?—lying in a pool of blood. The animal had been disembowelled and lying on the ground beside it were three pups, one of them still in its amniotic sack. *Your bitch will pay*, was all it said.

Somehow, she managed to let go of the phone. Somehow, she succeeded in keeping the spinach down. She was even able to nod in response to Jason's question if she was all right. And then the trembling began.

Jason steadied Helle up the stairs, helped her undress and proceeded to bathe her, sliding in to sit behind her in a tub of water so hot wisps of steam floated up towards the dark beams above. Slowly, the shivering subsided, her head resting against his shoulder as he soaped her skin and rinsed her free of suds. He didn't talk, neither did she, and they lay in the water, surrounded by burning candles of all shapes and sizes, both of them lost in their own thoughts.

He stroked her arm, slid his hand down to braid his fingers with hers. He shouldn't have let her see the picture, should have deleted it as soon as he received it. He rested his head against the tub and closed his eyes.

"Son of a bitch," she muttered, breaking the silence. She turned in his arms, slippery and warm. "Who the fuck does he think he is?" She straddled him as well as she could in the confined place. "I won't let him—"

He cradled her head, kissed her silent. "Neither will I."

"Good." She kissed him again, he kissed her back, but it was more anger and fear than passion that had him pushing his tongue into her mouth, that had his fingers gripping her hips. She was as rough as he was. Not lovemaking, this—no this was a confirmation that they were welded to each other, for better or worse, until death.

Her fingers closed on his penis, her mouth devoured his lips, his ear, his neck.

"Now," she breathed against his skin.

"Now," he agreed, groaning when she mounted him. Water sloshed. The shampoo bottle hit the floor. Her breasts bobbing up and down, her hot breath coming in short gasps, her thighs clenched round his. She rode him, moving up and down with her head thrown back, an expression of intense concentration on her face. He took hold of her waist and pushed her downwards, all of him buried in her, his hot, throbbing cock trapped inside of her.

"Leave it," he said some time later, lying diagonally across the bed. Helle was making a half-hearted attempt to dry up the water on the floor. "Come here instead."

The bed dipped under her weight. He gathered her close, one hand sliding round her waist to rest on her belly, as yet as flat as ever. Fourteen weeks, he calculated, wondering vaguely just how big that little cluster of cells had become by now. The size of his thumb? So small, so vulnerable, and yet already all-powerful, firmly entrenched in his parents' hearts.

She nestled closer, he pulled their combined duvets over them both. Other than the flickering candles, the room was sunk in darkness. He toyed with her hair, hearing how her breathing deepened as she drifted off into sleep. Only once she was fast asleep did he call Nigel.

As always, Woolf had ensured the e-mail was impossible to trace. As always, that first e-mail was followed by several, but in contrast to before, all of them were addressed to Jason. One gruesome picture after another showed up—none of them with quite the same impact as the first one—and in general the accompanying messages were very short. *The Mother has promised, now she must deliver*, was a frequently repeated message, as was *The Wanderer belongs with the Mother, the bitch is mine.*

"What's with all these references to the Mother?" Nigel asked, nudging Miranda so he could squeeze by her chair and slide into his own. The four of them were out for dinner at an Italian restaurant close to Miranda's tattoo parlour. Food to die for according to Miranda.

"His way of saying Jason will soon be with God," Miranda said, miming a sliced throat. "It is, isn't it?" she asked, looking at Jason. She reached for another slice of garlic bread. "Very progressive, this Sam Woolf. All for gender equality on the God front."

"Unfortunately, he doesn't advocate it anywhere else." Helle gave Miranda a cool look. "Look at how he treats those poor girls he's smuggled into the country."

"He doesn't treat the boys any better," Miranda objected. "Or those men he sells as slave labour."

"Right: so he treats them all equally badly—how big of him."

"Woolf has no sense of morality. He feels entitled, and other people only exist to cater to his needs." Jason shrugged. Woolf's repeated invocations of the Mother disturbed him.

"Not something the Mother can approve of." Nigel said.

"What god would?" Helle asked, pushing her food back and forth on her plate. She wasn't eating much lately, wasn't sleeping much either—but neither was he. Jason scrubbed at his face, feeling exhausted. After a hiatus of several weeks, the dreams were back with a vengeance, leaving Helle a wide-eyed wreck.

"Lioness," he admonished in an undertone, nodding at the food. "Please," he added, and she sighed softly but speared a shrimp and popped it in her mouth.

"Still having those dreams?" Miranda asked. She studied Helle intently. "Bad ones?"

"Nothing I want to talk about," Helle replied.

"That bad, huh?" Miranda dug about in her purse. "This may help." She produced a little paper bag that smelled faintly of lavender. "Vervain, lavender and comfrey. Soothes a troubled mind." She sat back.

"Nigel told you, didn't he?" Helle accepted the little packet of herbal tea. She smiled at Nigel, who smiled back.

"He did. And from what he told me, those nightmares of yours are very graphic," Miranda said.

Jason's brows rose. No matter how he wheedled, Helle refused to tell him anything about her dreams. He tried to catch her eyes, but she pretended not to see. Jason swirled his wine around. Once they got home, it was time to talk.

"I can't tell you!" Helle's fingers tightened on the mug of herbal infusion—not that Jason held out much hope that it would help, but there was no harm in trying.

"I die, right?" he interrupted calmly. She gave him an anguished look but nodded. "And it's all rather bloody and messy," he continued. She nodded again. Jason sat down beside her. "But it won't happen." He kissed her cheek. "Dreams don't come true." He draped an arm round her shoulder. "And I don't like it, that you share stuff with Nigel but not with me."

"I haven't exactly given him much detail either," she said. "After all, I try to forget them as soon as I wake up."

"Not working, apparently."

"Nope. But I try." She set down the cup. "What does help is when Korine shows up."

"Ah." He smoothed her hair off her brow. "What does she do?"

"She takes my hand. And when she does, Woolf disappears." She took his hand. "She's just a child, mostly barefoot and in some sort of oversized nightshirt, but it's as if she radiates some sort of power—well, at least she does in my dreams."

"From what Katherine tells us, she did so in real life as well." Bits and pieces only, was what Katherine was willing to share. Little anecdotes around Korine's childhood, the odd smile as Katherine recounted some incident or other involving one of Korine's sons, but whenever Helle pushed for more, Katherine clammed up, muttering that she didn't remember.

To Jason, Katherine had been somewhat more forthcoming, describing the terror of living with a firechild who woke up in flames after nightmares in which her mother and father were killed, or who could sit for hours staring out at the ocean, insisting she could see Helle—and Jason—in this their present life.

"It made her cry," Katherine had confided in him some days ago. "She made me promise to—" Katherine broke off.

"To do what?"

"Well, I'm here, aren't I?"

"And Korine? Is she here as well do you think?"

"Korine?" Katherine had smiled sadly. "No, the Mother loved her too much. She is safely at peace—or so I believe."

"Do you think she was unhappy?" Helle asked, interrupting his musings.

"I think she was conflicted," he answered truthfully. "But from what Katherine tells us, she had a good life. A man who loved her, sons she adored..."

"And yet something drove her to ride off and never return."

"Yes." His unknown daughter had buried them together and then ridden off into the sunset, never to be seen again—and from the way Katherine refused to talk about it, Jason deduced it had something to do with her.

Some days later, Jason grabbed his briefcase and made for the door. Yet another awful night, yet another morning when he suppressed yawn after yawn. Things hadn't exactly been enlivened by the e-mail he received just as he was eating breakfast. A picture of Michelangelo's Pietà, but with the white marble decorated with garish red streaks, the dead Jesus reduced to a bloodied mess cradled by his grieving mother. As always, the accompanying text was brief. *Who will keep her safe when you are dead?*

"Daniel?" he asked Deb as he stepped outside. These days, not even he went anywhere without a bodyguard.

"He's just parking the Bentley."

"I'll be in the Tesla." He nodded in the direction of his car, for once parked almost in front of his own house. It was a nice April day, he reflected, with daffodils bobbing along the borders while the magnolia Anne had planted was covered in white flowers, faintly pink around the edges.

"Yes, sir."

He had passed through the little wrought iron gate when his phone rang. Katherine. Jason checked his watch. Now? Katherine was rarely up and about before ten or so.

"Mother?"

"Get away from the car!" Katherine shrieked. "Get away from it now!"

Jason vaulted over the iron fence just as the Tesla exploded. Glass rained from the heavens, flames shot out every which way, and on the opposite side of the street a car alarm began to wail. He was bleeding, there was a singed sensation to his face, and the large magnolia was gone, replaced by a splintered stump.

The Tesla was reduced to a pile of smoking, twisted metal. Jason staggered to his feet. There was something sticking out of his arm, a loud ringing in his ears. He blinked, trying to clear his eyes.

People were converging, Deb had the front door wide open, her phone at her ear. Helle was running towards him. Jason's head spun.

With a little grunt, he collapsed by the gate, noting that he was holding the handle of his briefcase, but there was no briefcase attached to it, not any more. His mouth was full of the distinctive taste of blood, metallic and salty, and he tried to spit, but that only resulted in more blood.

Helle. Her lips were moving but he had no idea what she was saying. Her hands on his face, and he tried to smile, tell her he was fine.

An arm round his shoulders. His head fell back.

Helle's eyes, as turquoise as the Aegean Sea. Helle.

Chapter 29

It was all too familiar. Jason on a gurney, loaded into the ambulance. Jason, unconscious, his hand warm and sticky in hers. So much blood, his dark suit and shirt reduced to rags that smelled of smoke and heat. There was a metal shard protruding from his right biceps, a myriad of minor cuts on his face and exposed chest. But by the time they reached the hospital, he was conscious again, his eyes fixed on hers. Major difference from last time round, after the shooting at Netley Abbey—and a very good difference.

Five hours later, they were back home. Jason had been cleaned up, had some of the deeper cuts stitched, and sported a huge bandage on his arm. According to the doctor, both eardrums had burst, but the ringing in his head would abate over the day, and the bitten tongue would heal itself, no matter that it continued to bleed.

The wreck was gone, a dark patch on the street indicating where it had stood. Someone was already at work sawing down what was left of the magnolia, and Deb had cleared up the broken glass. Jason insisted on walking on his own, steadying himself for an instant against the doorpost, before proceeding to walk slowly to the living room, where he sank down on the Howard, so pale Helle could count every single cut that adorned him.

"Whisky," he said.

"You're not supposed to, not with—"

"Get me a damned whisky!"

So she did. His hand shook when she handed him the crystal tumbler. He tossed it down in one go and then sent the glass flying. Helle flinched when it crashed against the wall.

"Bastard!" His chest heaved. "No matter where he is, he can still reach out and destroy us."

"But he didn't," she tried, sending up yet another grateful prayer to whatever power it was that had alerted Katherine.

"Not this time, no." He dragged a hand through his messy hair, the mahogany tone highlighted by the afternoon sun that streamed in from the uncovered windows. Such a beautiful day, Helle reflected, one of those spring days where even in a city like London one could feel the crispness of fresh winds. She sidled away from him, leaned her cheek against the cool glass of the window.

"Helle?"

At present, she couldn't face him, not when in his voice she'd heard the fear that next time Woolf would succeed, leave her to face a world without him. God, she was so tired of this melodrama! She pressed a hand to her belly, and anger rose hot and thorny within her—at Woolf, for being the bastard he was, at Jason for sounding so despondent. Well, she wasn't giving up. Ever.

"Helle?" His hands closed on her shoulders, but she shook herself free.

"You said you were never going to let him win," she said, backing out of range.

"Of course I'm not!"

"Not what it sounded like, just now."

"You think I'm giving up? Why, because I just had my car blow up in my face?" His nostrils flared, eyes darkening to a deep copper. "I'm going to kill the fucking maniac."

This sentiment was echoed by Katherine when she arrived a few moments later, accompanied by John Stapleton. From John's high colour, Helle gathered there'd been a lot of heated discussion between him and Katherine on the way over, probably along the lines of what the police were doing to keep mommy's boy safe and sound.

"Just shoot him!" Katherine said. "How difficult can it be?"

"First of all, it would be illegal," Stapleton pointed out. "Secondly, we have no idea where Sam Woolf might be."

"No," Katherine muttered. "He's hiding and getting ready to strike." She gave Stapleton a withering look. "What are you doing about it?"

309

"What would you suggest?" he snapped back. "Seeing as you're so patently dissatisfied with how we've handled things so far."

Katherine's brows shot up, her chin rose, and somehow she managed to look down her nose at him, despite John being on his feet while she was in her wheelchair.

"And you find that surprising?" she asked. "My son almost died today! My son!"

"Fortunately, he didn't," Helle put in.

"No thanks to his lot," Katherine grumbled, glaring at John.

"Stop it," Jason said. "And please sit down, John. Watching you bounce up and down on your toes is not precisely relaxing. Now," he continued, once John had complied, "what are your suggestions, Mother?"

John shot him a venomous look. "Her suggestions? Why would…" He subsided into silence when Jason lifted his hand. For a man whose day had started with an exploding car, he was remarkably in control of things. The long-sleeved t-shirt he was wearing not only hid the bandage but also strained over his set shoulders and defined muscles, the tension in his arms reflected in his tight features.

"It's easy," Katherine said. "We have to lure him into the open."

"Ah." Jason nodded a couple of times. "And we do this by…"

"Baiting a trap." Katherine waved a hand in the direction of Helle. "And there's your bait."

"My wife?" Jason said, in a voice so cold Helle could almost see the ice crystals forming.

"What other choice is there? It's not as if he'll find you sufficiently tempting." Katherine's chair creaked when she shifted her weight. "He wants her to play with—she's the mouse to his cat."

"Play with?" Helle croaked.

Katherine regarded her calmly. "Yes." She turned to Jason. "And we do it in Turkey."

"In Turkey?" John and Jason said simultaneously. "Are you out of your mind?" Jason demanded. "Take Helle to Turkey and risk facing Samion?" He gripped Helle's hand. "No."

"Absolutely not," John agreed. "You stay here and we protect you."

"Protect them?" Katherine hissed. "And what about today? Jason could have died!" She coughed a couple of times, took a deep breath and directed herself to Helle. "You can't live an entire life looking over your shoulder. Not now, not when there's a child to consider." No, Helle agreed, she couldn't.

"But…" Jason said, only to be silenced by an imperial wave of his mother's hand.

"He'll never risk coming to England," Katherine went on, "so we have to choose another venue."

"Another venue?" Jason laughed harshly. "It's not an effing football game."

"No, it's a game of life and death," Katherine replied. "A game started all those years ago when you killed him."

"Wrong." Jason leaned forward. "It started the day he found us on that hillside and took us captive. It started with months of humiliating captivity—months in which I believed I was to die like a rat in a hole." He looked away. "And not once during those long months did anyone from Kantor's court come looking."

How strange, Helle thought. Reasonably, they should all have suspected their abduction had been orchestrated by Samion. She glanced at Katherine, whose hitherto calm countenance had blanched, her mouth wobbling for an instant.

"Some things were meant to be." Katherine's unperturbed voice stood in contrast to her grey face.

"Like me and Jason," Helle said.

Katherine regained control over her features and gave her an irritated look. "Or like the tribulations you lived through. Maybe the Mother was trying to tell you something." Katherine cleared her throat. "All of that is history. But if you want a future, going to Turkey is your only option."

"Why?" Helle asked.

"Because Sam Woolf will know the moment you set foot on Turkish soil, and he will not be able to resist the temptation of coming after you to destroy you where it all began."

"Nice," Helle mumbled, glad of the weight of Jason's arm around her shoulders.

"But that is not what will happen," Katherine continued. "I will see you safe." She smiled at her son. "I will always see you safe, son."

"Against Samion? On his home turf?" Jason sounded doubtful.

"You're forgetting something." Katherine stood, remarkably steady on her feet. "It's my home turf as well. He will overreach, confident in his own abilities. And when he does..." She looked away, a distant expression on her face. "Penance," she muttered darkly, but refused to explain what she meant.

"What do you think?" John said, directing himself to Helle.

"Helle has no idea what she is up against," Katherine said dismissively.

"You think?" Helle was tempted to spit in the complacent old hag's face. "I've been on the receiving end of Woolf's anger more often than you have."

"I merely meant that—"

"I'm not gifted enough to either understand or be of any use. Well, beyond being the happy bait."

There was a hoarse sound from Jason Helle interpreted as suppressed laughter.

"I apologise," Katherine said. "That came out wrong."

"Yes, it did, didn't it? Especially as it is my life—mine and Jason's—on the line." She cupped Jason's cheek gently so as not to hurt him, what with all those little cuts. "Today, you could have died. If going to Turkey can put a stop to all this, then I'm all for it."

It took days of discussions, but finally Jason gave way, fixing Katherine with a fiery look as he told her he would never forgive her if anything happened to Helle or the baby.

"If they don't return unscathed, I will curse you to hell and beyond," he said, pacing back and forth in Katherine's living room.

Katherine looked mildly amused. "Is that supposed to be a threat?" She shook her head. "What makes you think I haven't already been there?"

"Mother!" Jason recoiled as if struck.

"I'm joking," Katherine said. "And yes, I will see you safe." She found a tissue and wiped her runny nose. "Assuming this cold doesn't kill me first."

"Are you truly okay with going?" Jason asked as they drove back home.

"Not much choice, is there?" Helle lived in a constant state of sleep-deprivation, Jason's inbox was bursting at the seams with one explicit picture after the other from Woolf, and as far as Helle could see, the police could do nothing. Sam Woolf had dropped off the face of the earth, impossible to trace, even for such an accomplished internet traveller as Nigel.

"Stapleton has offered to contact his colleagues in Istanbul," Jason said.

"And will it help?" Helle asked.

"Probably not. After all, having the police around may cramp our style." He flexed his fingers.

"Do you..." She broke off, tried again. "Would you be capable of killing him?"

"Sam Woolf?" Jason kept his eyes on the traffic. "Yes, lioness. However terrible this may sound, it would give me the greatest joy to wipe him out of existence." He sighed. "Except, of course, that I can't. The moment I've killed him, he'll pop up again in another life."

"And Katherine?"

"I don't know." His brow furrowed. "I can't see her killing someone—she isn't allowed to. But contain him, somehow strip him of his powers, yes, that she could do."

"She sounds as if she wants to kill him."

Jason laughed. "She wants to keep me safe. She has always wanted that."

"And has she?" Ever since Jason had mentioned it, she'd been wondering how Nefirie, the most powerful healer of her time, renowned in every kingdom that bordered the Black Sea, had not been able to work out just who had abducted her precious son and come to claim him.

"What is that supposed to mean?"

"Nothing." Katherine was still a prickly subject. Speculation would only make him irritated. Besides, what did she know? Maybe Nefirie had not been quite as impressive as Jason remembered—or maybe she'd been duped by Samion, which did not exactly inspire confidence regarding the upcoming Turkish adventure. She rested her forehead against the window, suppressing a little sigh: going to Turkey scared the living daylights out of her as did placing her life in Katherine's not-so-loving hands.

Jason cooked as she watched, smiling at how effortless it all seemed when he created a mixed warm salad topped with a perfectly grilled fillet of beef. To please her, he'd made dessert, and she made happy sounds at his raspberry panna cotta topped with roasted almonds.

In the soft light of candles his face was a collection of planes and shadows, but even in the dimness she could see the various scabs that still decorated him. The stitches were gone, everything was healing, but both of them now carried multiple scars, courtesy of Sam Woolf.

"What?" he asked, pouring himself some more wine. She, of course, was strictly on water, the future father being adamant that alcohol was bad for the baby.

"I was thinking about scars," she said. "Those that show, and those that don't."

"Ah." He touched her face. "Does it bother you that much?"

"To carry his marks on my back? Yeah, it does, actually." She couldn't quite explain why. It wasn't as if there was a huge *Sam Woolf* engraved on her skin.

"His marks?" Jason's dark voice dropped to a husky growl. "On my woman?" He shook his head slowly from side to side. "Can't have that, can we?" He held out his hand. She took it, shivering when his fingers tightened round her wrist. He held her eyes. A flash of heat no more, and she knew he'd given her a bracelet of minute blisters. "Come."

He undressed her. One button at a time, and it all took far too long, but he smiled and wagged an admonishing finger when she tried to speed things up. Her shirt was discarded. A

314

finger traced her bra straps; up and down it went, and she tilted her head to the side, offering him her neck, but he just chuckled. Inch by inch, the straps were nudged off, one at the time. His mouth left a trail of kisses over her now bare shoulders, his tongue slid slowly along the lace that edged the cups.

The bra was gone. His tongue was not, and her nipples hardened and swelled. He turned his attention to her back. She didn't want him to, but she quickly realised that she did, because his lips travelling wetly up and down her spine, the slight sting when his mouth covered some of the scars and he sucked, hard, had her groaning and trying to reach for him.

"Stand still." His voice was a hot rush of air tickling her ear. "You may not move, my lioness." Warm strong hands disappeared under the waistband of her jeans. The top button popped open, he tugged at the zipper, and she swayed drunkenly on her feet when his finger slid over the sheer lace of her panties. One swift move, and he was on his knees in front of her, her jeans and panties pulled halfway down her thighs.

His hair tickled her stomach. His thumbs travelled up the inside of her thighs, meeting at her clit. She pushed her pelvis forward. It made him laugh against her skin.

At last she was naked, and he prowled round her, a sizzling finger now and then touching her flank, her breast, her belly. With a little smile, he held up one of his ties. She didn't understand, not at first. But she nodded and he covered her eyes with the heavy silk fabric, tying it in place. Helle licked her lips. Her pulse was loud in her head, her skin buzzed under his touch. She shifted, trying to compensate for the tilting sensation induced by the blindfold. His hands steadied her.

No hands, no mouth. She could hear him moving about. Sounds she recognised—cuff links landing on a flat surface, a belt eased out of the belt loops. She clenched her buttocks. He wouldn't, would he? The belt landed on the floor, and she relaxed. He was back, strong hands sliding up her front to cup her breast, lean her backwards as he kissed her neck. A whiff of cologne, and her nostrils flared, recognising the familiar scents of patchouli, of cedar and lime.

His cheeks were bristly, leaving a tingling abrasion behind when he dragged his face down her arm. He sucked her fingers, one by one, and then he guided her hand to his penis, hard and silky at the same time. She explored with her fingers, and he flexed into her hold, the sticky head of his glans nudging her hip.

One moment she was standing, the next she was on her back in their bed, and his head was buried between her legs, his hands holding her still. He rubbed his nose over her clit, kissed and sucked gently. Too gentle. She bucked her hips demandingly. He laughed and complied; Helle thrashed and sank her hands into his hair.

The bed swayed. He straddled her, his thighs strong on either side of her. He moved upwards. She knew what was coming, and she wanted to taste him. Jason's breathing was still too controlled for her liking—she wanted him to pant and groan and call her name.

He shoved a couple of pillows behind her head. His glans brushed her lips. She opened her mouth, he laughed and pulled just out of reach. His penis was back, and this time she managed to close her lips over its head, using her tongue to trace that sensitive slit. It made him groan her name, his hips jerking as he thrust into her mouth.

The bed dipped. The blindfold came off, and she blinked, had time for a smile before his mouth crushed hers. His thigh slid in between hers. She felt his buttocks tense as he entered her. She hooked her legs round his, he lifted himself up on his elbows. They moved together, rocking back and forth. No haste, no urgency—not at first. Jason brushed his nose against hers.

"Helle," he whispered. "My Helle."

"Yours." She traced the outline of his mouth. It made him smile. He flexed his hips forcefully. Again. He rose on his arms, gyrated his hips, and smiled down at her as he pushed, harder.

"Ah!" She raked her nails over his lower back. In response, he slammed into her, and the bed groaned and shivered. "Yes!"

"Yes," he echoed, picking up pace. She gripped his hard biceps. His breath came in short, shallow gasps, his head thrown back. She met his thrusts, grinding her pubic bone into his. In, out, in, out…she fixed her eyes on the ceiling, felt the bed shake, felt him, all of him—his skin, searing into hers, his muscled thighs wedged between hers, his penis, pounding into her. Him. All of him—only him.

"Do you think," he said much later, lying so close their noses touched, "that the baby knows?"

"Knows?" She yawned. "Knows what?"

"When we make love—does he know what we're doing?"

Helle turned her face into the pillow to muffle her laughter.

"Helle!" He poked her, making her squeal and laugh all the harder.

"No," she managed to say, still laughing, "I don't think he knows." She moved closer, captured his mouth in a tender kiss. "And guess what? Even if he does, tough; I'm not giving up on this. You're far too addictive, Mr Morris."

That had him breaking out in a huge grin. "Addictive? I don't think anyone's called me that before."

"Were they ever happy?" Korine's voice was low, her fingers pushing the needle through the white linen in precise, small stitches. Nefirie flattened the cloth on the table, smoothing it out with her strong hands.

"Of course they were. They did not live with a feeling of doom hanging over them. They were more happy than unhappy, in the total balance of things."

Nefirie was seeing Jason, that long-ago afternoon; his flushed skin, his dazed eyes. She had cornered him as he walked through the courtyard.

"What have you done?" she had asked, even though she already knew. She could see it in how he turned to watch Helle as she mounted the stairs, in the small smile that lit up his face.

"We'll be wed by the new moon," he said, evading her eyes and her question.

"You have bedded her," Nefirie stated. Jason blushed and nodded

"Yes" he admitted, his face suffused with joy. "I have made her mine."

Chapter 30

Katherine shed years on the plane to Turkey. Okay, her hair didn't suddenly grow longer and turn fiery red, but otherwise the transformation was eerily disturbing. Her eyes became clearer and the skin of her face tightened around her bones. The wrinkles around her eyes and mouth smoothed out, the slight sag to her chin disappearing as if she'd performed a magical face-lift.

The knuckles on her hand diminished in size and the papery skin of her arms plumped out, acquiring a pinkish healthy hue. Fortunately, the business class cabin was full of people who showed no interest in their travelling companions, most of them immersed in their laptops and work. Only the flight attendants seemed to notice something was going on, stopping with quizzical expressions as they passed her seat.

"Amazing," Helle said to Jason in an undertone. "She should sell whatever it is she's doing. Package it in a bottle and she'll be a millionaire before she can blink."

Jason made a noncommittal sound, his attention on his laptop. Since they had boarded, his face had grown increasingly darker, and by now he was a bundle of nerves, in turns scowling at his mother and gripping Helle's hand to squeeze it.

"Hey," Helle said, elbowing him. "Look at her. If she can do that…" Jason glanced at his mother, did it again, eyes widening. He blinked, looking slightly dazed.

"Bloody impossible," he muttered, but his hold on Helle's hand relaxed, his fingers sliding to interlace with hers rather than to crush them.

The closer they got to Turkey, the more jittery Helle became. If Katherine was right, it would not take Woolf long to catch on to where they were and come after them. The thought made sweat break out in her elbow creases, on the insides of her thighs. What if Katherine was wrong? What if…No, she admonished herself, don't go there. All the same, she leaned her head against Jason's shoulder.

"Jason?"

"Mmm?" There was a slight furrow on his brow, eyes lost in whatever document he was reading. She took his hand and placed it over her heart.

"This is yours, forever."

That made him smile, one of those smiles that glowed more in his eyes than on his mouth. He took her hand and kissed it before he placed it over his heart.

"And this is yours. For just as long." They held hands as the plane closed in on Istanbul. They held hands all through the descent. Only when the seatbelt sign flashed off, did they let each other go.

As they stood in the aisle, waiting to disembark, Helle tugged at Jason's sleeve, cocking her head in the direction of Katherine. Straight as a birch sapling, she stood in front of them. Gone were the swollen joints and the iffy knee, gone was the need for cane and wheelchair. A seventy-plus British citizen got on the plane in London, a woman with aches and pains, slightly bowed with age. An ageless woman stood waiting to get off. Katherine was gone and Nefirie stood in her place, tall and willowy, her eyes wide and clear. She was as just as Helle remembered her from that first childhood, the mightiest Wanderer alive.

Nefirie must have felt their eyes on her, because she swivelled gracefully on the spot. Her eyes went to her son, and she smiled blindingly.

"Home," she said. "At last!"

Jason nodded and took Helle's hand again. He didn't look quite as thrilled.

"Let's hope she makes it through the passport control," Helle said, mostly to make him smile. "It's sort of unusual to look younger than your picture."

His mouth twitched. "Knowing her, she's got that covered."

They breezed through Customs, Nefirie reverting for some minutes to Katherine Healey, albeit an extremely healthy and glowing version of this supposedly infirm old lady. All the way to the hotel, Nefirie sat with her eyes glued to the window. Soft exclamations of surprise burst from her as they navigated the chaotic midday traffic, and when they drove onto the suspension bridge over the Bosporus her eyes lit up with joy.

"Look" she said pointing to the eastern bank, "our shore."

Helle rolled her eyes. Their shore, three millennia ago, when it was all forest and coastline, not like now, the vibrant Asian side of Istanbul. Beside her, Jason smiled at Katherine's enthusiasm, but the smile didn't reach his eyes. He was ill at ease, his head turning in all directions as if he expected Woolf to materialize out of the blue. Helle was mostly struck by the heat. Only April, and already it was hot enough for the red vinyl of the car seats to stick to her skin, her shirt damp with sweat. The waters below glared in the sunlight, shards of light making the surface look white rather than blue.

It was afternoon by the time they arrived at the hotel, a small bijou place down on the eastern shore of the Bosporus, set into an old distillery building.

"We could have stayed on the other side," Helle said as she drifted towards the railing on the large terrace. The view before her was magnificent: the blue of the water, hugged on both sides by the shores of the Bosporus, a checkerboard of green vegetation and buildings in light shades. Straight ahead, was one of the bridges crossing the strait, and further beyond Helle could just make out the silhouette of ancient Constantinople.

"Kath…Nefirie didn't want to." Jason gave her a crooked smile. Katherine was gone, or so Nefirie had said during their long drive from the airport. From now on, she was Nefirie.

"Maybe I did." She could have done with a stay at one of the more renowned luxury hotels, especially the one just by the Hagia Sofia with that very enticing roof terrace—if nothing else to celebrate her upcoming birthday.

"Next time," Jason promised. He leaned closer. "When we don't have Ms Xenophobia with us."

Helle burst out laughing. Katherine—right, Nefirie—had made it very clear that staying in the oldest parts of Istanbul was out of the question.

"That's the Greek side!" she'd said, looking as if someone had just offered her a drink laced with arsenic. "I can't stay on the Greek side."

"It's Turkish," Helle objected. "Nothing Greek about it."

"Hmph!" Nefirie had shot her a sharp look. "Well, you wouldn't understand, but for me, who was persecuted by those damned Hellenic idiots—"

"Three thousand years ago!" Helle had exclaimed.

"Feels like yesterday to me." Nefirie sniffed. "But you wouldn't know, would you? After all, you don't remember—not like me and Jason." She'd held out her hand to Jason, but luckily for him, he'd chosen to wrap an arm round Helle's waist instead.

"It's all in the past, Mother," he'd said. "Who cares about those old Greek colonists?"

"I do."

Which was why they were here, staying in a building that had once housed one of the Ottoman Empire's best raki producers.

In spite of Nefirie's refusal to stay in the Sultanahmet district, she was very eager to go there. Once they'd installed themselves in their rooms, they made for the pier and the hotel launch that was to carry them across. The sun was warm, the wind was not, and it was with very chilled hands Helle watched the contours of central Istanbul rise before her. She recognised the Galata Tower and the adjoining bridge that bristled with fishing poles. Straight ahead was the skyline of the old heart of the city, minarets jostling for space with remnants of old Byzantine walls, with the odd modern building.

"Beautiful, isn't it, *birtanem*?" Jason murmured in her ear, slipping his hands round her waist. Helle smiled at the endearment. She supposed it was being in Istanbul that had him reverting to calling her 'my only one' in Turkish.

"Yeah." She slipped her ice-cold fingers into his, and in a matter of seconds they were nice and warm again. "How will we know?"

"Know what?" He kissed her earlobe.

"When Woolf shows." She shivered—the wind, she tried to tell herself. "It would be sort of unfortunate if he sneaks up on us."

"Oh, that won't happen," Nefirie said, materialising at their side.

"Why? You'll know he's here?" Helle asked.

"Me?" Nefirie shook her head. "But you will. The moment he sets foot on Turkish soil, he'll make sure you know he's here, close enough to snatch you away."

Helle's stomach muscles contracted. Jason's hands tightened on hers.

"Well, try to," Nefirie amended distractedly, busy snapping photos with her phone.

Nefirie did not want to visit Hagia Sofia. She definitely did not want to see the inside of the Blue Mosque or the Topkapi Palace. But she was happy to walk up and down the little streets of Sultanahmet, and she disappeared for an hour or so when they visited the bazaar, reappearing with multiple bags.

"Fantastic place!" she said, throwing herself into a chair. She beckoned a waiter over and ordered wine before helping herself to an olive. "A gorgeous blend of cultures," she continued, waving at their surroundings. "Those Ottomans were good at cherry-picking."

"They were also a bunch of despots," Jason said. "And some of the sultans were quite insane. It wasn't pretty, the last years of the Ottoman Empire."

"Revolutions tend to be bloody." Nefirie popped another olive in her mouth. "Everything comes at a price, remember?"

"Tell that to all those who died," Jason said.

"For the greater good, Jason." Nefirie downed her wine. "Progress costs. No revolution, no Atatürk, no modern Turkey." She glanced at a couple of covered women, hurrying down the street. "Mind you, it doesn't look that modern. Women in this region have been covered since the birth of time."

"You as well?" Helle asked.

"Me?" Nefirie stretched. "No, not me. Wanderers did not believe in veils and such. You on the other hand…" She gave Helle a condescending look. "…you'd have lived out most of your life

322

under veils. Such was the lot of a woman destined for marriage and motherhood. Right," she stood. "I'm off. I have to buy some new clothes, and I want to walk around and get a feel for the place." She gave them a little wave and hastened up the street.

"Incredible," Jason muttered, his eyes glued to his mother's back.

"Totally impossible," Helle agreed. "She must have lost like thirty years on a five-hour plane ride. That's a good sign, right?"

Jason smiled. "Yes. I think it is."

"I just hope she buys clothes appropriate for her age," Helle continued. "I don't want to be in the company of an old lady in cut-offs."

Jason chuckled softly. "I've never seen her anything but adequately dressed. I don't think she plans to flash her flesh at her very advanced age."

"Stranger things have happened." Helle sipped her tea. "What did she mean about me being a covered woman?"

"Well, you were veiled at thirteen and would have remained that way." Jason helped himself to the last of the olives.

"Really? Even as your wife?"

"Most certainly as my wife." He grinned. "I'd have kept you well and truly out of sight."

"How misogynist."

"Possessive, lioness." His face fell. "But things didn't happen that way, did they? I never got to swathe you in veils, never had the pleasure of knowing only I knew just what you looked like under all that fabric." He sighed.

"Hey, I'm here, right?" She took his hand.

"Yes, so you are." He brushed a finger down her cheek. "And I'm still just as possessive."

"Really? Show me."

He laughed softly. "Here? I don't think so." His fingers slipped round her wrist. "But just so that you know what you have coming…"

"Ow," she protested, but with little true heat. He let go, and she studied the reddened skin that encircled her wrist. "Kinky."

"Me or you?" He kissed her fingers, one by one.

Helle needn't have worried about her mother-in-law's shopping. When she saw Nefirie later that evening she was elegance personified, in wide black linen pants and a cream blouson with long sleeves and a series of miniature buttons down the front.

"Wow," Helle said.

Nefirie blushed. "You look quite nice too." Fantastic, a compliment from her cranky mother-in-law! Helle congratulated herself on her choice, a simple dark blue dress with matching high-heeled sandals. "Did you have time for a nap?" Nefirie asked, her gaze on the beautiful Rolex set with rubies now on Helle's wrist.

"Yeah," Helle lied. What Jason and she had been doing did not exactly fall into the sleep category, but it had been very relaxing and… fulfilling. A perfect birthday celebration, complete with champagne and the watch. She met Jason's eyes. He winked and asked the waiter for the wine list.

"So, it is all very different, right?" Helle asked Nefirie as she tore off a piece of the warm bread and dipped it in one of the many little dishes surrounding the breadbasket. Nefirie did her best are-you-for-real look.

"Of course it is. Last time I was here was around the ninth century BC, with Jason. None of this existed. One little hamlet on this side and a small port on the other. It was full of Greeks." She made a disgusted face. "We didn't exactly get along, the Greeks and I."

Jason nodded in agreement. They were extraordinarily alike as they sat side by side in the soft candlelight. Same brows, same nose and same long mobile mouth. Except that his was somewhat fuller. Fantastic lips, Helle thought, smiling to herself.

"Those ancient Greeks were greedy bastards with a misogynist take on life," Nefirie went on, frowning. "They didn't appreciate strong women, and I was very self-sufficient. Not a shrinking violet, if you know what I mean."

Jason snorted with laughter at this flagrant understatement. "You scared the daylights out of them, Mother. You healed where they could not. You could see things soon to come and beyond."

Nefirie studied the piece of bread she was tearing apart. "Yes, you're right. But had I been a man they would not have been so quick to call me a witch."

"None of the Wanderers fared well with the Greeks—they killed off most of us." Jason's voice was grim. "Man or woman, it didn't make much of a difference."

"And yet we're still around," Nefirie said. "Most of us still walk the Earth in some form or other. Those ancient Greeks are gone, dust in the wind for the last thousands of years. But we remain." She took Jason's hand. "We remain."

Helle hadn't thought her dreams could get any worse. She was wrong. That night, she dreamt of sunlit seas, and by the shore was Jason, white linen pants flaring in the breeze. She hurried towards him, carrying the precious bundle that contained their child, and she supposed she called out, because he turned towards her. His eyes, golden in the sun. And then they were gone, plopping wetly to the ground, and Jason screamed and fell to his knees, blood oozing from his mouth and the cavity that used to be his chest.

Helle turned to flee. A hand in her hair brought her up short. Another hand tore the baby out of her arms. A red-haired baby, Jason's baby. Woolf laughed as he crushed its skull against the wall. He handed her another child. Black-haired, black-eyed, it latched onto her breast and suckled greedily. At her feet, Jason crawled, dying in a pool of blood. And her baby, her baby...

"No!" She sat up. Her throat hurt, her heart hurt, her eyes hurt. She covered her belly with her hands. Oh, God. She stumbled to the bathroom and splashed her face with cold water, wiping away the tears and snot.

"Here." Jason handed her a damp towel. "That bad?" he asked, supporting her back to bed. Helle nodded. She just had to touch his face, his brows, his eyes. They were still there, he was still there.

"Worse than before?" Jason pulled the sheets up round them both, spooning himself around her. She nodded again. He kissed her sweaty nape, held her even closer.

"Better now?" he asked some minutes later, and Helle nodded for the third time. Not that it was. She stared at the wall opposite, determined not to fall asleep again.

At some point she did drift off, waking to the distant sound of a muezzin calling the faithful to prayer. The room was sunk in half-light; beside her Jason was fast asleep, long legs tangled with hers. Such a sad sound, she reflected, as if the devout had given up on the rest of the world, but still made a determined effort to remind them to say their prayers, worship their God. Without conscious thought, she clasped her hands, and lying in her husband's warm embrace she prayed: for Jason and their baby, for a future and a life.

In the hotel dining-room, Nefirie took one look at Helle and her cup halted midway to her mouth. "Bad dream?"

"Yeah."

"They will get worse," she said, and looked out across the water.

"Thanks. What a cheering thought," Helle muttered.

"They are only dreams, fantasies, not reality."

Helle cradled her head in her arms. "It always ends with him dying," she said, indicating Jason who was standing over at the buffet table, by the vast selection of cheese, plate in hand.

"He won't die. Not by Samion's hand. I will not allow it," Nefirie stated.

Helle couldn't help but notice Nefirie didn't extend the same protection to her.

Chapter 31

"How long will we stay here?" Helle asked, hanging over the railing of the boat taking them back from their excursion into the Marmara Sea.

"Until he has found us," Nefirie said, adjusting her sunglasses. "It's important he does. Even more important that he follows us when we go east."

"East?"

"Home." Nefirie smiled.

"And he will follow us there because..." Helle left the rest hanging in the air.

"It's home for him as well. It's also where all of this started. He, I think, will appreciate the symmetry."

"The symmetry." Helle shook her head. "Who gives a shit about the symmetry?"

"I do. He does." Nefirie lifted her face toward the sun, just as Jason joined them with several bottles of water.

"Drink," he said, uncapping one of them before handing it to Helle. "You look pale."

"I feel pale." She felt drained, actually. Three nights here, and every night the same dream replayed over and over again. All she wanted to do was sleep, yet the one thing she didn't dare to do was sleep, apart from a quick nap during the day. Well, she reflected as she drank, at least there were no headaches.

"I'm meeting Selim this afternoon, want to come?" Jason asked as they negotiated one of the steeper inclines behind Hagia Sofia.

"What's the alternative?" Helle cast a discreet look in the direction of Nefirie, more or less bouncing on the cobblestones. "She's sort of exhausting to be around."

Jason chuckled. "So you come with me."

"Or I go back to the hotel. Catch up on my sleep."

"Alone?" He frowned.

"He's not here, is he?" Helle suppressed a yawn. "Our resident wizard says I will know the moment he is, and so far nada."

"Wizard?" From his tone, she deduced he didn't like her calling his mother that.

"Sounds better than witch." She frankly couldn't care less. She wanted to talk to Mum, she wanted someone to wrap her in cool sheets and somehow wipe her brain free of dreams, gifting her one whole night of uninterrupted sleep. She'd even asked Nefirie if she could do something, but Nefirie had pursed her lips and said that when it came to matters of the subconscious she couldn't help—not beyond offering an hour or two of recuperative sleep. Helle wasn't sure she believed her.

"Look," she said, "I'll be fine. You go and drink Turkish coffee with Selim, go all wild and crazy over your little charger, and I'll go down to the spa, have a pedicure or something."

"No, I won't leave you alone."

"I'll stay with her," Nefirie said, having rejoined them. "So, off you go."

Reluctantly, he agreed, but insisted on accompanying them back to the hotel first.

The bar in the hotel was manned by a very nice young man called Mustafa. Tall and thin, he had huge brown eyes and a timid smile—plus he spoke excellent English. Helle felt somewhat refreshed after her spa session, and her toenails glittered in red and gold—a tad over the top, but it wasn't as if all that many people studied her feet closely.

"More Coke?" Mustafa asked, wiping at a stain on the bar. "Or maybe something stronger?"

"No thanks." She studied the displayed bottles of whisky. "Do you drink?"

"Drink?" Mustafa laughed. "Sometimes. Beer mostly, with my friends."

"Ah. The future engineers." Mustafa was an engineering student, majoring in something that sounded utterly incomprehensible to Helle but had Mustafa's eyes glittering with enthusiasm. When she'd promised to introduce him to Jason, his smile had grown so wide she'd been worried he'd tear a facial muscle, and then he'd gone on to explain that he had some distant relative who worked in the R&D department of Jason's Turkish company, and from what he'd heard, Mr Morris was not only an investor but also a keen proponent of innovative technologies—such as the ones Mustafa intended to develop.

"Small world," Helle commented.

"My chosen field is not so big," he explained with a shrug. "Few people see the beauty in genetic algorithms."

"I wonder why," Helle teased, thinking that Jason would probably hit it off big time with Mustafa.

She was right. Once Jason came back, she introduced them, and over a number of beers, Jason and Mustafa bonded while Helle took the opportunity to call her mother.

"Istanbul." Miriam sounded as if she'd been force-fed castor oil.

"Yup. It's nice this time of the year."

"And what exactly are you doing there?"

"Oh, you know: Jason is visiting his company here, and I decided to come along."

"With Katherine."

"Yeah."

Mum snorted. "As if you'd voluntarily spend any time with that old bat." Not so old anymore, Helle thought, watching Nefirie glide over the polished floor to join Jason at the bar.

"It's about him, isn't it?" Lately, her mother never said Sam Woolf's name out loud if she could help it.

"Yes." No point in lying, Miriam was like a truffle-hound when it came to untruths. "We're hoping to flush him."

There was a very long silence. "Flush him? How?"

"Oh, you know. Somehow you entice him into the open and then bang, bang he's dead."

"Except that this is not the Wild West," Miriam snapped.

"No. More like the Wild East." Helle studied her sandals. "I've had my toenails done."

"You've what?" There was a choked sound. "You're in Istanbul on some hair-brained scheme to get rid of *him*, and you tell me you've had a pedicure?"

"They look very nice. Gold flowers on a dark red background."

"Helle!"

"I can't think about all this weird stuff all the time, okay? So now and then I pretend the only thing I need to worry about is how to paint my toenails." She gnawed her lip.

"Oh, darling." Mum sounded close to tears. For some moments, they listened to each other's breathing, then Mum cleared her throat. "How are you feeling? You know, with the baby and all that?"

Helle leapt at the change in subject. "Great. We're great." She rubbed her belly and smiled. "I bet he'll have red hair."

"He?" Miriam asked. "You've checked?"

"Not as such." Helle watched Nefirie laugh with Jason. "Let's say it's a hunch."

It was a bit of a shock to see Nefirie next morning. Her hair was red again. Helle gawked.

"It comes out of a bottle," Nefirie said drily, patting her head self-consciously. "Where's Jason?"

"He's still in the shower." Helle popped a dried apricot in her mouth, chewing slowly. She was feeling somewhat queasy today and had only managed half a bread roll so far. "Are you sure you can defeat Samion?"

"Can one ever be sure?" Nefirie spent some time peeling her boiled egg. "Let's say I think the odds are in my favour."

"You sounded more convincing back in England." Helle smiled her thanks at the waiter and added some sugar to her tea. "If you're not sure, why are we here?" She made a point of looking Nefirie up and down. "Maybe you're just here for the rejuvenation experience."

"What, gloves off?" Nefire said, putting down her spoon.

"About time, don't you think? So why are we here?"

"I'm here because I promised Korine," Nefirie said, her voice breaking over the name. "I made her a promise almost three thousand years ago, and I intend to keep it. Otherwise, she will never forgive me, and I can't bear that thought."

"What did you promise her?"

Nefirie took a sip of her coffee before she answered. "To keep you safe. Both of you." Her eyebrows rose. "Korine always knew I never loved you."

"I wouldn't have guessed." Helle tried to sound unperturbed.

"Well, what do you expect? You stole his heart and you indirectly caused his death."

"As he caused mine, you mean?" Helle asked.

"Your death? Samion killed you!"

"And Jason killed himself—with your help." Helle took a deep breath, took two. "If only Samion hadn't found us that day, none of that would have happened." She ran her palm over the tablecloth in front of her, smoothing it. "As they say here in Turkey, maybe it was *Kismet*."

"*Kismet*," Nefirie echoed, setting down her cup with a shaking hand.

She excused herself when Jason came down, muttering something about her sunglasses. Jason watched her leave the room with a quizzical expression on his face.

"Have you quarrelled?" he asked

"No more than usual. I think she was miffed because you didn't notice her hair."

"What?" he asked, digging into the breadbasket.

Helle gave him an exasperated look. "She's a redhead today."

Jason dropped his cutlery. "How?" he stuttered

"Courtesy L'Oreal, I imagine," Helle replied, smiling at his confusion. "She's dyed it. It hasn't suddenly shifted back to red because of magic."

"Well, you never know with her," he muttered.

In actual fact, one never knew anything about Nefirie, Helle thought, but decided not to voice this out loud.

When Selim called an hour later to ask if Jason would be interested in participating in the upcoming R&D presentations, Helle laughed and told him to go.

"You look like an eager four-year-old," she said with a laugh. "Go and knock yourself out."

"But you—"

"Will be fine. Nefirie's here, isn't she?" Besides, she didn't feel like going anywhere: that initial queasiness had developed into a stronger sense of nausea.

"Right. I'll be back for a late lunch." He kissed her, snatched up his laptop bag and was off.

Helle retrieved her laptop and decided to spend the morning on the terrace catching up on work. She detoured by Nefirie's room to tell her where she'd be, and almost crashed into her, sporting a beige linen jacket over a white shirt and dark pants.

"I'm going out," Nefirie said, smiling down at something on her phone before slipping it into a pocket.

"You are? But what if—"

"Woolf makes an appearance?" Nefirie produced a shawl from her handbag, draping it elegantly round her neck. "I told you, had he been anywhere close you'd have felt it." She peered at Helle. "No headaches, right?"

"No." But she didn't precisely like it, to be left on her own.

"Good. Well, I have other things to do but babysitting. I'll be back when I'm back." Nefirie breezed off, without as much as a backward look.

She considered calling Jason, even pulled out her phone to do so, but decided not to—he needed some time pretending everything was normal. Besides, had Nefirie suspected Woolf was anywhere close she'd have stayed. Of course she would.

The terrace was sunk in shade and, apart from a couple of ladies playing cards some tables away, empty. Helle waved a greeting to Mustafa before settling down to do some serious work. She checked her e-mails, spent a long time writing one to Dad, sent off a substantially shorter one to Alison, and even managed a short Skype session with Jim and Steve—an intense discussion about "the lads in Leeds" as Jim had dubbed their latest venture.

"I'm sending down the final version of the SPA tomorrow," Steve said, "and Jim here has drafted some sort of retainer bonus that will ensure they stay on for at least three more years."

"Seeing as the only real asset is their brains, that's good." Helle rubbed a finger over her brow. For the first time in several weeks, there was a dull throbbing in her head. She smiled her thanks when Mustafa set down a glass of water on the table.

"And the buildings," Jim put in. "Don't forget those deliciously derelict old buildings."

Helle laughed. Jim had fallen in love with all that red brick, proposing one more preposterous scheme after the other to utilise its "raw industrial charm".

She rang off, fiddled some more with her files, added a few calendar entries and decided she was done for the day. In front of her, the Bosporus glittered in the sun, boats all over the place. It was really quite an amazing place, Istanbul, even more so when one considered just how old it was. Repeatedly, the city reinvented itself on the ruins of its previous manifestations, and the end result was a breathing, living organism, its ancient heart still beating to the rhythm of centuries. A bit like me, Helle thought, suppressing a little titter. Except that she was older…

Helle stretched, froze halfway through the movement. Abruptly, her head exploded with jagged pain. She gritted her teeth. That didn't help, as the mother of all headaches sank its claws into her tender brain and squeezed. Mother of God! She tried to stand, but her legs folded beneath her. One moment, her brain was being seared by fire, the next it was being torn apart by sharp slivers of ice-cold glass. Helle pressed the heels of her hands against her brows in a feeble attempt to push back the throbbing that made her hair bristle, her skin itch.

Woolf was here. Oh, God, he was very, very close, and she could hear his voice, hear him whisper her name. Flee, she thought Once again, she tried to gain her feet. Once again, she fell back in her chair. Then his shadow fell over her, and she quailed. Woolf had found her—just as Nefirie had said he would. Unfortunately, Nefirie had been wrong about the forewarning. Even more unfortunately, she was nowhere around to help.

"Helle." As always, his voice was dark and soft, like syrup oozing from a bottle. Helle tried to lift herself out of the chair, but the voice in her head, the weight of his presence kept her immobilised. It was all she could do not to look at him, keeping her eyes stubbornly on her laptop.

There was a scraping sound as he pulled out the chair beside her, sitting down far too close. Her skin shrivelled in panic when he placed a hand on her bare forearm. His scent invaded her: sandalwood and myrrh, scents that reminded her of pain—and pleasure. Helle pressed her thighs together. He chuckled, running his hand up and down her arm.

"I won't hurt you. Not this time." He lied, because his fingers were already exerting sufficient pressure to make her wince. Helle attempted to yank her arm free, an uncoordinated movement that had no effect whatsoever, beyond making him tighten his hold. She gasped.

"Well, I might if you don't behave," he said, releasing her arm sufficiently for her to be able to breathe again. Her legs trembled. She opened her mouth to scream for help, but there was no air in her lungs, no capacity for forming any sounds beyond a soft bleating.

"Scared?" He had her by the chin, forcing her face up. "Of course, you are. And you should be." Gently, his thumb swept over her cheek. "So much unfinished business, little Helle." She swallowed, wanting to spit him in the face. His eyes. Black and bottomless, they bored themselves into her poor aching head. She shivered all over, and here came his mouth, and this was a bruising kiss, his tongue invading her, claiming her. From somewhere came a spark of anger. She bit him. Blood in her mouth, her forearm screeched in protest, but at least his mouth was gone.

"Like that, hey?" Woolf wiped at the blood that stained his beautiful mouth. Helle took the opportunity to turn her gaze, fixing it on his legs instead. Ripped jeans over thigh muscles that shifted with his movements. Thighs that would soon... No. She managed to shove her chair back, giving her a hand's breadth or so of more space between them. Not that it helped when he had her arm in a vice, when his voice was in her aching head.

"Look at me when I'm talking to you." He increased the pain in her head, but she continued to stare at the faded denim. "I said look at me." His voice slithered like tentacles through her brain. Soft and sibilant it urged her to obey. Obey and he will be kinder. Disobey and you will pay. A little cackle accompanied this last statement, and her stomach tightened. But she lifted her eyes to his.

She was trapped like a mouse in the hypnotic stare of a snake. Rational thought escaped her. Her mind went blank. This man was her master, he held her fate in his hands, and she could not as much as blink without his permission. Sam Woolf laughed, leaning forward to run a finger over her mouth. It made her want to cringe, but she wasn't allowed to move.

"You cheated me. All those years ago, when you made me believe the Wanderer's bastard was mine." He tapped her on the nose. "Now, that was not a nice thing to do, was it?"

She shook her head in agreement.

"So of course you agree when I say I'm entitled to be angry, don't you?"

Helle nodded. She had done him wrong. She deserved his anger, his voice told her. Of course she deserved his anger. He stroked her trapped arm, and she was mesmerised by his manicured nails, by his fingers travelling up and down her skin.

"And you know just what that means, don't you?"

Punishment. She deserved it. She licked her lips and nodded.

"It will hurt—a lot." His black eyes swam before her. "But you won't fight it, will you?"

No. How could she? She had cheated him. He was entitled.

He kissed her again, and she let him. He demanded that she kiss him back, and she did, not doing anything to stop him as his hand slid in beneath her skirt to cup her sex. A gentle touch, sending shivers through her while her head was populated with images of herself, naked, of him just as naked and aroused. Such a beautiful, beautiful man, and soon he would claim her and make her soar. As long as she obeyed. As long as she never forgot who was the master and who was the slave. Her master. His tongue explored her mouth. She let him. He released her with a chuckle.

"So obedient. I like that." He leaned closer. "First, we must rid you of that vermin you're carrying." His mouth was at her ear, his eyes no longer burning into hers. "You understand, don't you?" His hand hovered over her belly, fingers flexing. Her baby? Something jolted through her, and there in her head was Korine, screaming at her to not let him touch her there, because if he did...Images of blood and gore flew through her head.

"You owe me a child. We must make room for it."

No. Never. Warmth suffused her belly, white light blazed through her head and for an instant the fog in her brain lifted. Helle's free hand groped for her glass. She crashed it against the table, and he cursed and sat back. She found a shard, closing her fingers round it. Stinging pain rushed up her arm, up her spine, clearing her brain.

He made an amused sound. "Pain, is it? Is that how you've fought my presence in your brain? How apt, given what I will do to you—starting now." He yanked her to her feet, dragging her towards the door. His voice was back in her head, and the shard was slippery with blood, making it hard to create the pain she needed.

"Mrs Morris?" Mustafa appeared before her. "Are you bleeding? What—"

"Get out of the way," Woolf said, shoving at the waiter.

"Mrs Morris is our guest," Mustafa said. "I must—"

"Move!" Woolf hollered, just as Helle managed to sink the glass into her palm again.

"Let me go!" She yanked at her arm, hard enough to put Woolf off balance. "Mustafa, help me! Help me!"

To Mustafa's credit, he didn't hesitate, swinging the tray he was carrying at Woolf's head. Sam Woolf stumbled, his grip loosened, and Helle fell, landing on the terrace floor.

"What's happening here?" One of the card-playing ladies was coming towards them, as were the concierge and two of the guards, one of them already fumbling with his gun. Woolf hissed, shoved Mustafa out of the way, and fled.

She could breathe again. Helle's head was still throbbing, but there was no voice, no Woolf. She picked herself up, allowed the ladies to fuss while Mustafa found a napkin to wrap round her hand. The ladies insisted she had to sit, had Mustafa bring hot, sweetened tea, and kept on asking just who that man was, and what had happened?

Helle opted for blankness, saying she had no idea, the man had asked to join her, and then...She lifted her shoulders, while clamping her legs together to stop them from trembling. After some minutes, her newfound friends returned to their card game. Mustafa remained where he was, hovering like a protective angel.

"We must call the police," he said. "I'll have the guards do so."

"No!" She shook her head. "No police, Mustafa, please. It would be too embarrassing, too..." Useless, actually. Mustafa gave her a long look.

"You knew him," he stated, shivering despite the sun. "And I felt his presence, and it was evil."

Evil—yes, that sort of summed him up. Helle studied the blood staining the napkin. After some moments, she heard Mustafa sigh and leave.

"Sometimes I almost feel sorry for him," Korine said, unwinding her veil. Nefirie studied her carefully.

"Sorry for who?"

"For him," Korine said simply, "for all that blackness that rots him from the inside and out." She caressed the belly that housed yet another son and stared out across the sea. Her unbound hair lifted in the evening breeze. Nefirie nodded and looked away.

"Yes," she agreed, "his is not an easy life. Full of all that rage and hate."

"But why Nana? Why can he not let it go?"

Nefirie shrugged and turned to meet her grandchild's gaze.

"He has no choice, not any more. He has gone beyond the tipping point, and all that exists in his head is this one single driving force; to reclaim her and punish him for stealing her."

"But he didn't," Korine protested. "You can't steal a heart. She gave it to my father." With a soft grunt she bent over to undo her sandals before lifting her skirts to wade out into the water.

337

Nefirie sighed. "He never saw it like that." Neither had she, resenting Helle for her hold over her son. "So Samion destroyed them. That is when it all began. That is when the light began to seep away from him." And from her. The Mother help her, but also from her, the constant guilt spreading like a stain of soot over her soul.

Korine mulled this over, eyes lost in the distance. "And now he wanders, lost in all that dark. Poor him."

Nefirie didn't reply.

Chapter 32

Jason found her in the shower. She must have been in there for quite some time to judge from the steam and the foggy glass.

"Helle?" He almost slipped on the damp tiles.

She was scrubbing herself, harsh, jerky movements that rubbed the washcloth over skin that looked red and abraded.

"No." He kicked off his shoes and joined her in the scalding water, fully dressed. She screamed at him, cowering in the far corner, and it killed him to have her looking at him without any sign of recognition. "Lioness." He had to clear his throat a couple of times. "It's me."

She huddled on the floor, staring up at him. He crouched beside her, wiping at the hair that was plastered to her face. "It's me, Jason."

There was a loud gulp. She hid her face in the washcloth and rocked back and forth. There was only one thing to do. He sat down beside her and took her in his arms, and she clambered onto his lap, hiding her face against his shoulder.

Jason had no idea how long they sat like that, but at long last her sobs quieted. He turned off the water, found a towel and wrapped her in it, depositing her gently on the bed before proceeding to strip off his wet clothes.

"What happened?" He sat down beside her. All Mustafa had said was that Jason had to hurry back, because his wife had had a visitor, and she was bleeding.

"Woolf."

Yes, he'd gathered as much, if nothing else from her reaction.

"I was on the terrace, working, and he just walked in."

"But I thought Nefirie was with you."

Helle shook her head. "Other things to do, other places to see."

Anger at his mother was an unfamiliar emotion, but right now, Jason was drowning in it. She'd promised she'd keep Helle safe! How could she just abandon her for some sightseeing whim or other? And as for himself, what had he been thinking of?

"It's not your fault," Helle said, reading him correctly. "Besides, Nefirie said I'd know when he was close." Her face fell. "She didn't say I wouldn't know until he was practically standing in front of me."

"Maybe she didn't know." Even now, the instinct to defend his mother went deep, he reflected.

"Seems to me there's a lot she doesn't know." Helle touched her head. "It still hurts. Like having a gong going off all the time." She gave him a tremulous smile. "Well, at least we know the first part of the plan worked. He's here." She flexed the fingers of her injured hand, placing it on her slightly rounded belly. "He wants it gone."

"Of course he does. It's mine." He placed his hand over hers, pressed hard. "He will not harm him." Given recent events, he could only imagine how unconvincing that sounded. Helle plucked at her towel, not saying anything. "I just wish…" He gave her a bleak look. "If only I could stop him from invading your head—but I can't, damn it, I can't!" Jason wrapped his arms around her.

There was a knock at their door. "Jason?" Nefirie's voice was muffled by the thick wood.

"Shit," Helle mumbled, sitting up and wiping her eyes.

"Jason? Helle? Are you all right?" Nefirie pounded at the door.

"Give us a moment," Jason called out, already rifling through their bags in search of clothes, which they pulled on quickly. Jason opened the door. Nefirie started towards him, arms held out, but he shook his head. Instead, he pulled Helle close.

"We're going for lunch," was all he said.

"I came as soon as I could," Nefirie said, striding along beside them. "I—"

"You left her!" Jason glared at her.

"So did you." Nefirie's chin rose. "She's your wife, not mine."

340

"But we're only here because you thought it was a good idea," Jason reminded her.

"It's the only way." Nefirie was back to sounding as calm as she usually did. "Anyway, nothing happened, did it? But now at least we know he's here. Time for the next step."

"Fantastic. Can't wait," Helle said in a dull voice.

Mustafa appeared the moment they entered the restaurant. Helle hung back, clearly uncomfortable with the young man's concern. Jason met the younger man's eyes and shrugged, trying to express it had nothing to do with him.

Once seated, Jason fixed his mother with a steely look. "I told you I didn't want to bring Helle here."

"And I keep on telling you there is no choice." Nefirie went back to studying the menu. "Not unless you want to live out the rest of your life in constant fear." She glanced at Helle. "You don't want that, do you?"

"No." Helle had regained some of her normal colour but seemed disinclined to eat. She did, however, drain her glass of water, thanking Mustafa with a brief smile when he immediately replenished it. "I don't want to die either. Or end up with Woolf."

"Die?" Nefirie gave her an exasperated look. "Well, sorry to break it to you, but someday you will die—we all do. More to the point, you've already died—several times."

"That's not what she meant," Jason said.

"No." Nefirie pinched the bridge of her nose, a gesture Jason recognised as one of frustration—he did it himself. "How many times must I tell you?" She sounded tired. "I can end it here. I will never have the strength to end it anywhere else."

With an oath, Jason left the table.

Nefirie waited until Jason had left the room to turn on Helle, eyes as cold as ice.

"Did you enjoy his kisses? His intimate caresses?"

"His what?" Helle couldn't help it: she scrubbed at her lips with the back of her hands.

"Don't lie to me! I saw it, all of it." She tapped at her head. "There you were, as transfixed as a rabbit, and you did nothing—nothing!—to fight him."

"What, you think I want him in my head? Do you have any idea what that feels like? How helpless it makes me?" Helle knotted her hands round the need to slap the old bitch.

"You'd best learn to fight it," Nefirie said.

"I do!" Helle held up her bandaged hand. "I try as well as I can!"

"Not good enough." Nefirie's elegant fingers tore a bread roll in two. "Not that I'm surprised. You're too ambivalent when it comes to Samion."

"Ambivalent? How dare you? I hate him!"

"Oh, you do, do you? He almost dragged you away with him, and you did damn little to stop him." She looked away. "Too bad he didn't succeed in doing that in that first life."

"He did, actually." Helle traced circles on the table. "Not the best months in my life, as I recall."

Nefirie snorted. "What? Waited on hand and foot, living the life of a preferred concubine? There are worse existences. As I recall, Samion was convinced you were enjoying it."

Helle just looked at her. Nefirie reddened, all the way from her cleavage to her cheeks.

"You knew?" Helle asked.

Nefirie averted her eyes. "It didn't exactly require a genius to work that one out."

"Oh." Helle leaned over the table. "Look at me!" When Nefirie refused to do so, Helle got hold of her arm and shook her. "I said, look at me!"

Nefire did, adopting her most regal look.

"So let's see if I've got it right: you knew Samion had us—you even spoke to him—and you just left us to rot?"

"Rot? You weren't exactly rotting, were you?"

"He abused me! Every single night. And as to Jason…" Helle had to take a deep breath. "Your son, locked away in the dark. How could you?"

Nefirie shrugged, no more.

"Did Kantor know?" Helle asked. "Did you tell him where I was?"

"No. That would only have started a war that he would have lost—that could have cost him his life." Nefirie's face softened.

"Not your decision, was it?" She no longer wanted to slap the woman sitting in front of her. Helle wanted to throttle her, kick her black and blue. "After all, he might have considered my life—my life, goddamn you—more important."

"Don't be so melodramatic," Nefirie said. "Women have been abused for centuries. Your life wasn't that important. Besides, you didn't die, did you?"

"Inside I did, and more importantly, so did Jason." Helle sat back, staring at the incomprehensible person in front of her. "Your son, the son you purportedly love so much, and you let him hang in chains for months. Months!"

"He didn't die. I knew he wouldn't," Nefirie retorted. "And he needed to be taught a lesson. Wanderers don't wed royalty. And as to you..." Nefirie lifted one shoulder.

"You're crazy." Helle said. "What do you think Jason will feel when I tell him this?"

Nefirie laughed. "He won't believe you. He'll just assume you're being irrationally jealous again."

"Wow." Helle shook her head. "You really don't like me much, do you?"

"Not much, no. He loves you too much and I had other plans for him."

"Plans?" Jason's voice made Nefirie jump. Where had he come from, Helle wondered, realising he must have been standing just behind the nearby pillar for some time. He was drained of any colour, eyes a burning copper hue that reflected the heat in his hands. She could see them smoulder, saw how he struggled to keep the fires under control. "And what were they?"

"Jason, you don't understand—" Nefirie began.

"Oh, but I do, Mother. You took it upon yourself to play the goddess and punish me for my sin of pride."

Nefirie nodded, looking relieved. "I knew you'd—"

Jason banged his hand down on the table. "Shut up! I'm your son. Your son! And you just left me to…" He choked. "And for the record, you're not a deity. In fact, I'm not quite sure what you might be; a demon?"

"Jason," Nefirie's eyes filled with tears. "Son, please—"

"No." He held up his hand. "I don't want to hear your excuses, I don't want you to spin me some story—not now." He lowered his head, staring her straight in the eyes. "What I want is to hear you promise—on the Mother and on all other gods—that you will do everything in your power to safeguard Helle and the child she is carrying."

Nefirie opened her mouth, closed it again.

"Say it!" Jason hissed. "Say it, or so help me God, I'll…" All of him quivered, smoke rose from the tablecloth. Helle knocked over her glass, and the water hissed and spat. Neither Jason nor Nefirie noticed, locked in a silent battle of wills.

"I promise," Nefirie finally said. "I will do everything I can to keep you and the child safe."

Jason shook his head. "Oh no. Let us be more specific."

Nefirie threw Helle a look loaded with antipathy. She cleared her throat. "I swear, on everything holy, on the Mother that gives us life, that I will keep both of you and the child safe or die doing so." She sagged. "Happy now?" She looked devastated. Not that Helle cared.

"Happy?" Jason gave a short bark of laughter. "Not really. But whatever I feel right now, doesn't matter. For now, I need your help to destroy Samion. After that, we'll see." He held out his hand to Helle. When she took it, he closed his fingers round her, so hard it felt as if he was crushing her bones. Heat surged, but she didn't say a word, following him as he left the dining room at a half-run.

He didn't have to explain. She knew him so well, understood him so well, which was why Jason wasn't surprised at her response when he pushed her back against the wall, slamming the door to their room closed with his foot. He needed her—now. She opened her arms to him, offered him her mouth, and there she was, pressing her denim-clad crotch against his. Jason groaned as she tightened her arms around his neck.

She could have been gone. He could have been left alone—without her. But it hadn't happened, and she was here, still here with him. He staggered backwards to the bed, fell into it with her on top. He kissed her, rubbed his two-day beard against her cheek. His whole body pulsed with heat, his hands burned from within, and she didn't flinch under his touch, she attacked him as hungrily as he gripped her.

No time for foreplay. He rolled them over, tore at the buttons on her jeans, at the waistband, and slid them down her hips together with her panties. All of him twitched with need, with an overwhelming desire to have her, possess her. A tug at his zipper, her hands on his jeans—demanding hands, hands that struggled to push the fabric down over his arse—and just like that he entered her.

Jason stilled. Just what he needed, a tangible reassurance that she was still here. This had nothing to do with love, this was anger and fear—anger at the accursed Samion, at his mother, fear that it would end too soon, fear that the resulting pain would tear him apart. If he lost her once again he'd not survive. He'd just roll over and welcome the final death, knowing he had failed. Failed! He moved. Hard, thrusting movements, sinking deeper and deeper into her, impaling her, over and over again, as he panted and grunted his way towards some seconds of release, moments in which nothing else mattered.

"Fuck!" He threw himself to the side, breathing heavily. His cock still thudded, still burned, still stood like an effing ramrod.

"Hey," Helle said, propping herself up on an elbow. "You're trying too hard."

That almost made him laugh. Almost. She sat up and pulled off her t-shirt. It landed on the floor. The bra went the same way. Holding his eyes, she freed her legs from her jeans. Then she began with him. Her hands slid up his ankles to pull his socks off. Her mouth kissing his toes and he groaned. Soft hands on his hips, his thighs, and ever so slowly she tugged off his jeans and boxers. Her mouth on his calves, on the inside of his knee. A series of soft kisses up his thigh, a teasing tongue that swirled round his sac.

One button at the time and his shirt fell open. She licked his nipples, trailed her fingers over his belly and downwards. There: her hands on his cock and he steadied her as she straddled him. His arms were full of her, his naked wife, moving sinuously up and down his body. She kissed his neck, sucked ever so gently on his earlobe. Warm, soft breasts were pressed against his chest in slow, languid movements as she rubbed them up and down.

She rose, he fitted his cock to her entrance before pulling her back down on him. Skin against skin, she a collection of curves that fitted so perfectly with him. Her hands danced over his body, her voice murmured his name, soft lips pressing burning kisses on his chest, his neck, his face.

He was still hot and hard, but the urgency was gone. Now he wanted to make things last, leave his imprints all over her. She was his. Only his. She groaned his name when he sat up, burying himself all that much deeper inside of her. Her skin reddened when he scraped his bristling cheeks over it, her breathing changed, her thighs quivered. He found her mouth. A long, long kiss and she bucked in his lap.

Jason lifted her off and flipped her over. She scrambled to her knees, presenting him with her round arse and wet sex. His. He eased in, his hands sliding down her back to close on her shoulders. His. He withdrew, inhaled, and pumped into her. He tightened his hold on her shoulders, did it all again. His. He eased out, slammed back in, out, in, out, in.

"Mine," he said through gritted teeth. "Mine!"

Slowly, he returned to himself. They'd fallen to the side, still joined, and his mouth was pressed to the point in her neck where her pulse leaped. He slipped his hand in under her arm to cup her breast, she covered his hand with hers, toying with his wedding band.

"All right?" he murmured. She turned in his arms, leaving his shrinking cock feeling bereft and cold when separated from her moist warmth.

"Never better." She kissed his nose. "You're quite possessive, at times, Mr Morris." But he could hear that she didn't mind.

All in all, a good thing, he reflected sleepily. After all, she was his, wasn't she?

"You're going to have to talk to her." Helle pulled up her legs and reclined against the headboard. She was in one of his t-shirts, insisting she had to wear something while they ate their room service dinner.

Jason moved the tray off the bed before replying. "I know." He sat down beside her. "But I don't want to." He threw his phone a look. So far, ten unanswered calls from Nefirie.

Helle didn't say anything, a neutral expression on her face.

"How could she?" he asked, his gaze on the window and the glorious sunset beyond. "What sort of a mother leaves her son in the clutches of a man like Samion?"

"Or her future daughter-in-law."

"Yes, that too."

"Just goes to prove I was right: she never liked me."

"Or me, apparently." It left him with a hollow ache to say that.

"You? Don't be silly. She was counting on your Wanderer blood protecting you from any serious damage," Helle said.

"Didn't work, did it?"

"No." She snuggled up to him, and he kissed her head distractedly, his thoughts still on Nefirie. If there'd been one certainty in his life, it was that his mother stood firmly on the side of the good, so much so that she could always rise above her own personal desires to do what was right. And now…Everything he thought he knew about Nefire had to be re-examined, starting with her love for him. After all, a loving mother did not knowingly leave her son to hang in the dark for months, did she? And as for her feelings for Helle…Jason shifted on the bed. He needed Nefirie to vanquish Samion but he sure as hell didn't trust her, not anymore.

"Maybe we should go back home," he said.

"And then what? I can't do this anymore, Jason. Somehow, we have to end it before he drives me insane."

He ran a light finger over her forehead. "I'm afraid."

"So am I." She took his hand. "But if you believe Nefirie is right when she says this is the only place we can stake that bastard to the ground, then we have no choice but to try. For our sake—and for his." She placed his hand on her stomach. Warmth rushed up his arm, bright light filled his vision. Dear Mother: a gifted child! His child. She was right: they had no choice, no matter that it coated his guts with ice.

His phone vibrated. Yet another call from Nefirie. With a sigh, he rejected it, weighing his phone in his hands for some moments. A short text, he decided. *Tomorrow, 8:00* was all he wrote. She didn't reply.

Helle refused to come along. "This is between you and her. I'll have breakfast later." With that, she burrowed back under the covers, complaining that she hadn't slept too well. Jason patted the bump that was her arse. As far as he could make out, she'd been ridden by one nightmare after the other. It made him feel so helpless, to only be able to wake her and hold her.

He wasn't sure the word 'contrite' could ever be applied to Nefirie. She was too aloof, had always measured herself against other standards than those which applied to the people around her. Once, he'd found this logical: Nefirie was a law unto herself, too gifted, too wise, to have to comply with rules set by narrow-minded societies. Now he wasn't so sure, and he took quite some pleasure in seeing her puffy eyes and abject face. She looked as if she'd spent the whole night awake, her recent rejuvenation somewhat dimmed around the edges. Contrite? No. Apprehensive? Yes.

"I think you owe me an explanation," he said, sitting down opposite her. Understatement, really. Life after life, he'd been plagued by guilt for having coerced her into helping him commit suicide in that sorry mess that went for his first life. Now it seemed she was partly to blame for what had happened to him—or at least could have done something to stop it.

"And how would that help?" Uncharacteristically, she added spoonful after spoonful of sugar to her coffee. "I failed you."

"Putting it mildly." He felt sick.

"Oh, for God's sake! Do you think he gave me a tour of the dungeons? I happened to come by, on healing business, and I asked for you." She was lying—he could sense that, even if he couldn't quite isolate the lie. Healing business to Samion's court? As he recalled it, she'd been a frequent guest at the Kolchis royal palace—come to think of it, extremely frequent—so maybe that part was true. He tried to gauge her expression, but she concentrated on her coffee, eyes on anything but him. She cleared her throat.

"He didn't deny he had you but promised you wouldn't come to any harm—he was only teaching you a lesson."

"One you felt I deserved."

"Yes! She wasn't meant for you, she—"

"But I had made my choice, Mother and so had she."

"She?" Nefirie snorted. "What was she but a young infatuated girl, spoiled rotten by her grandmother and father? She was nothing, Jason, nothing! She didn't deserve you and once he'd filled her womb a couple of times, she'd have forgotten you. That's what I saw, her, sitting in the sun with her swelling belly. She didn't look unhappy to me—she looked well-cared for, in clean robes and with a servant at her beck and call."

"Servant? Jailer more like it."

"In retrospect, yes. Then, that wasn't what it looked like." She gave him a sly look. "She was pregnant, and I suppose I drew the same conclusions you did."

That hurt. Once free, he'd treated Helle with utter contempt, accusing her of being false, of being Samion's willing whore. And all she'd done, she'd done for him, anything Samion asked she'd done to keep him whole.

"But that is all bygones," Nefirie said. "What I did then, I did and there's nothing I can do to change it. Yes, I should probably—"

"Probably? He abducted us!" Jason hissed.

Nefirie shifted on her seat and averted her eyes. "It happened." The cup shook as she lifted it to her mouth. She drank, set it down carefully. "What can I say to make you forgive me?"

"Nothing."

"No, I gathered as much." Nefirie's face fell. "But this time I am here to help. Atonement, if you will."

"And you think that will mean I forgive you?"

"I don't know. I hope so." She looked away. "It was all my fault, wasn't it? If only I had never brought you to Kantor's village, if only you'd never met Helle."

"How can you say that?"

"Because it's the truth." She sighed. "Not that it serves as an excuse."

"No, rather the reverse." He poured himself some coffee. "I don't trust you." The words left a sour taste in his mouth. If there'd been one certainty in his life—all of his lives—other than his love for Helle, it had been that his mother always had his back.

Nefirie arched a brow. "I know." She leaned forward and clasped his hand. He had to make an effort not to tear free. Her touch no longer soothed, it made his skin shrink. She noticed, taking back her hand. "I will do whatever it takes to regain your trust, no matter over how many lives."

"Lives?" He shook his head. "There are no lives, mother. There is this life. This one single life with Helle, and then I'm done."

"And do you think that is up to you?"

He met her eyes. "Yes."

"Lucky you," she said bitterly.

Nefirie had not wanted to come, but Korine had insisted she had to. And now here they were, while at their feet yawned a newly-dug grave. Korine herself lifted the shrouded remains into place, fragile bones that were all that remained of Jason and Helle. Her son. Nefirie closed her eyes, and in her head he was still alive, still that young beautiful man he had been before. Before she, his own mother, had…No, Nefirie could not bring herself to conclude the thought.

Two bundles laid to rest, as close now in death as they had been in life. Angry tears clogged Nefirie's throat, blurred her eyes.

The stone slab was moved into place, sealing them in, together in the peaceful dark.

"The lioness is with her mate," Korine said. "The fire-boy is now at rest. They lie together—as they should." She turned to look at Nefirie, and in those burning eyes, Nefirie saw contempt and despair. Dearest Mother, she knew: somehow, Korine had found out.

Chapter 33

Well, this was cosy, Helle reflected, sitting in one corner of the back seat of the taxi, with Nefirie sitting as far away from her as possible. Jason was in front, talking to the driver. Not that Helle understood anything, and besides, it was too early in the morning for her to nudge her intellect awake. The plane to Trabzon was leaving just before eight, which was why they were on their way to Atatürk airport at this ungodly hour. Traffic in Istanbul was never cooperative, the receptionist had told them with a little smile.

She hadn't spoken to Nefirie all day yesterday—truth be told, she hadn't even seen her, and the atmosphere in the car crackled with tension. Helle glanced at Nefirie, at present busy with her phone, and went back to looking out of her window, attempting to banish the lingering nightmare.

Woolf was upping the stakes in his nightly visitations. Jason was still fatally mutilated, but as a new little quirk the dream now had Woolf obliging her to sink the knife into Jason's eyes to save her child. Except, of course, that the red-haired child always died as well, and there she was surrounded by a sea of blood in which golden eyes floated, while at her breast nursed an entire litter of black-haired infants—Woolf's children.

If the dreams drove her crazy, her reaction to them was getting to Jason big time and her refusal to tell him about them—how could she?—had sparked an acrimonious argument earlier this morning which ended just as quickly as it began when Jason swept her into his arms, kissed her and whispered an anguished apology. Since finding out about Nefirie's betrayal, Jason walked about like a wounded bear, over-sensitive to anything that might sound like an 'I told you so', just as sensitive to anything he defined as mollycoddling—into which category he felt Helle's refusal not to share her dreams fell.

All yesterday, Jason had paced the grounds of their hotel, a frown on his face as he scanned any male within hailing distance. It had been downright embarrassing to have him scrutinise every waiter, every hotel guest, as if expecting them to suddenly morph into Sam Woolf. When he'd subjected an elderly gentleman to an intimidating stare, Helle had snapped at him, telling him not to be such an idiot. That had not gone down well. Jason had glared and reminded her that Woolf, just like Nefirie, was fully capable of advanced disguises.

And now they were off to Trabzon, from there to take a car and drive towards Georgia—or Kolchis, as Nefirie preferred to call it. A mythical kingdom come to life, Helle reflected, wondering whether the grove that held the Golden Fleece had been on Turkish ground or Georgian. Both her travelling companions had looked disapproving when she'd ventured that maybe the fleece as such had not existed, with Nefirie snorting mildly before saying that without the fleece there'd not have been a Kolchis—or Medea, and Nefirie could personally vouch for Medea's existence.

The airport was as big and crowded as she'd expected. By the time they'd made it through security, Helle was battling a raging headache and Jason more or less carried her to a nearby café, ordering Nefirie to keep an eye on Helle while he went to find them some water.

"It's a headache," Nefirie said. "Surely you can handle that?"

"I'm trying." Helle pressed a hand to her throbbing brow. "And how about you help me?"

Nefire sat back. "Me? No, I think not. Pain has to be borne."

"We both know you can take it away if you want to."

Nefirie eyed her calmly. "Maybe, maybe not. But it's not my fight—it's yours."

Thanks a million. Maybe she should practice handling pain, starting by slicing off a finger or two. Nefirie's hand gripped hers.

"You have to do this. For you, for Jason, for the baby. Find that lioness inside of you, the one Jason always goes on about. Lionesses always defend their own. Always."

Oddly enough, that helped—for a while.

Helle didn't see much of Trabzon beyond the airport, situated just by the Black Sea.

"The older parts of the city are to the west," Jason explained as he guided them through the airport. "We're going east."

"Older? How old?" Helle had to jog to keep up, irritated by just how swiftly Nefirie and Jason moved, long legs striding in synchronisation across the ground.

"Not as old as us, but old enough." Jason pointed in the direction of the car hire service. "Set up as a Greek colony in the eighth century BC."

"And you know this because…"

"I've lived here," he replied shortly.

"You have?" Nefirie sounded curious. "When?"

"In the eighteenth century."

"Ah, in the Ottoman days," Nefirie said.

"Yes." Jason looked relieved when they reached the counter and threw himself directly into a discussion with the agent. Clearly, this Trabzon life of his was something he didn't want to discuss. Nefirie seemed to have reached the same conclusion, light eyes regarding him with mild amusement.

"When you were here, was Juliet around as well?" Nefirie asked once they were at the car. If looks could kill, she'd have been reduced to something slimy and smelly, given how Jason looked at her.

"Yes."

"Ah." Nefirie slid Helle a look, a little satisfied smile on her lips.

"Was it a good life?" Helle asked, applauding herself for sounding so calm. Jason busied himself loading the luggage.

"It was," he said. "One of the better ones."

Helle slid her arms round him from behind and pressed her face to his back. "I'm glad. You deserved some of those." There; that shot Nefirie down mid-flight. But even more important was how pleased Jason looked when he turned to face her, his fingers sweeping tenderly over her cheek.

"Do you think he swallowed the bait?" Jason asked his mother as he drove out of Trabzon.

"We'll know soon enough." Nefirie was studying the landscape with a wistful smile. "It's still as beautiful, isn't it?"

It most certainly was. To their left, the Black Sea was an endless expanse of sunlit water, to their right the ground sloped upwards, hills becoming mountains. Rugged ground, and if Helle closed her eyes she could see forests of stately spruce trees, valleys dotted with lakes and springs. Her legs twitched. She knew this terrain, had lain on her back and watched eagles soar above her, bathed in rivers so cold you came out bright red.

"The Pontic Mountains," Jason said.

"Did we—"

"No lioness, not here. We were further east."

"Oh." But she couldn't tear her eyes away from the mountains. It was as if they were welcoming her home.

They stopped for lunch, and the moment they left the car, Helle knew he was here. Somewhere. It was as if someone was driving nails into her head, sharp spikes of pain that made it impossible to walk or talk, that had her vision blurring. Her stomach did somersaults in protest, acid bile flooded her mouth, and everything was spinning, the mountains dancing round her to the tune of Woolf's echoing laughter.

"Helle?" Jason's hand was at her back, steadying her.

"He's here," she managed to say before doubling over.

This was becoming a humiliating pattern. Helle washed her face, her hands, washed her face some more, and couldn't quite stop herself from crying. She hated it that Jason had to see her like that, spewing her guts out. And the headache…it had abated somewhat after her bout of vomiting, but it was still there, a steady throbbing in the background.

No matter how much Jason cajoled, Helle refused lunch, sticking only to water. They were sitting on a terrace overlooking the sea, and even if the wind was nippy, the view more than made up for it, the hills below falling in soft green folds towards the shoreline.

"Tea," Jason said, gesturing at the hills. "Green gold."

Helle nodded, no more, listening with half an ear as Jason and Nefirie reminisced, pointing this way and that. Jason even laughed at something Nefirie said, but when she touched his hand he pointedly moved out of reach, draping an arm round Helle instead.

On they went. The further east, the more the headache grew, from a minor irritant to a roaring monster. The light hurt her eyes, the motion of the car made her sick, and it even hurt to breathe. Pressure built behind her eyes, it dug into her brain, and all the time she heard his voice, unctuous and soft, whispering her name.

She inhaled, and to her surprise her mouth filled with the taste of blood. She coughed, and there seemed to be blood everywhere.

"Jason?" she croaked, only vaguely registering how the car veered when he looked at her. She had her hands to her face, there was blood seeping through her fingers, dripping onto her top.

"For God's sake, Mother, help her! She's bleeding!" Jason's voice came from a distance, scarcely penetrating the red fog in Helle's head.

"I can see that." Nefirie's voice was as cool, as detached as ever. "No one dies from a nosebleed. She just has to learn how to fight it—or bear it."

There was a long astounded silence. The car screeched to a halt, there was a door slamming, and Helle was aware of her door opening, strong arms lifting her.

"What are you doing?" Nefirie asked.

"None of your business," Jason snapped. "But unlike you, I can't stand by and watch the woman I love suffer like this."

He was walking through undergrowth that snapped underfoot, releasing scents of herbs and fresh grass. She opened her eyes and gazed up at the sky, and there hung an eagle, straight overhead.

"I can't help her," Nefirie's said, her head blocking the view of the sky. "Not without revealing to him just how strong I am."

Jason groaned. "Look at her!" He must have knelt down, because everything tilted, and then Helle was lying on the ground, the long grass tickling her skin.

"I know, son, I know." Nefirie leaned forward, wiping at Helle's face with her shawl. Her cool fingers offered some relief, moments of welcome numbness. Nefirie frowned. "I told you, find the strength within. Fight him, don't just let him walk all over your brain."

"How?" Helle croaked.

"Think of something you will never let him have."

That was easy. Helle closed her eyes. Jason, fast asleep in the garden at Tor Cottage. Jason, smiling at her over his laptop. Jason, juggling with his fires. Jason, lying bloody and…Her eyes flew open.

"No." Nefirie shivered. "That image is his. Hold onto your own."

Jason. Helle breathed deep. Think of Jason, Jason, Jason. She thought his name in time with her pulse, and the headache growled in protest but faded to something manageable. Helle sat up. His voice was gone. In its stead she heard the sound of a child laughing, warmth spreading in waves from her belly.

"Better?" Jason asked, helping her up. Nefirie was already walking back towards the Audi.

"Much." She took his hand and followed him to the car.

Just after Rize, they turned off from the highway and drove up into the mountains. The road narrowed as it twisted its way up through dense stands of trees, or mountain meadows in full flower.

"Makes me think of *Heidi*," Helle commented as they passed one wooden chalet after the other. "All you need is a herd of goats or something." As if on cue, Jason brought the car to an abrupt stop as three dark-haired boys in oversized woollen sweaters and armed with staffs and slingshots shepherded a collection of goats and sheep across the road.

357

They arrived at a small hotel boasting a huge glass veranda, a steeply gabled roof and windows with wooden shutters. This far up, the air was cool, the view an uninterrupted sequence of hills and forests.

"Why here?" Helle asked.

"Why not?" Jason parked the car behind the hotel, out of sight from the road.

"Too far from the sea?" She missed the eerily familiar sight of mountains plunging to meet the glittering waters of the Black Sea.

He just shrugged. "Nice and remote."

Yeah. Plus the building was impossible to approach undiscovered.

The moment they entered their room, Jason moved over to the window and opened the curtains—left over from the happy seventies, judging by the combination of orange and brown. In fact, the entire room followed the same colour scheme, complementing varnished wainscoting and a worn wall-to-wall carpet. Twin beds, a clean if small bathroom and a small boxy TV—not exactly in line with Jason Morris' normal preferences. Come to think of it, way below Helle's standards as well, if nothing else because there was no wifi.

Helle glanced at Jason, standing by the window.

"You think he's close?" Even she could hear how strangled her voice sounded.

"One never knows." Jason's eyes never left the outside. "But he'll not catch us unaware."

But unarmed, Helle thought. Jason must have seen what she was thinking, dark brows swooping into a heavy frown.

"Not entirely," he said, snapping his fingers. Five little flames sprang into life, twirling like miniature dervishes until he closed his hand around them. Helle sank down on one of the beds and massaged her forehead. The headache was back, and it didn't exactly help to see Jason taking up guard duty.

"I want to go home," she said, looking down at her worn Converses.

"So do I." He joined her, taking her hand in his. "But we have to finish this first."

"Do you think we can?"

"I…" Jason caressed her wrist.

"Don't lie to me, okay?" she said, pressing herself closer to him.

"I won't." He inhaled. "I hope we can. Mostly I think we can, but now and then…" His voice trailed off.

"Yeah, me too." They sat silent and close together, his thigh pressed against hers. She pressed back, half-turning so that her breasts brushed his arm. "Let's not waste any time," she whispered, kissing his neck. "Let's make more memories. Make me burn, Jason. Engrave your being in my soul so that I will never, ever forget you again."

His hands shook when they reached for her. Golden eyes spoke volumes when they met hers, and that mouth of his stole her air away, leaving her breathless and hungry for more.

Memories. A bed that creaked in protest, the way his legs felt as they tangled with hers. The sweetness of his kiss, the salty taste of tears—all of them memories, as was the sensation of being filled to the brim when he entered her, so very, very slowly, his hoarse voice whispering just how much he loved her—all of their yesterdays, today and all of their tomorrows, he would love her, only her.

Afterwards, they lay close together. Helle stroked his back, traced the supple play of muscles along his spine. She closed her eyes, and in her head swam an image of a red-haired little girl, her arms clasped round a baby. Their baby. Korine nodded and danced out of sight.

A sharp knock on the door had Jason leaping out of bed, groping for his clothes.

"Jason?" Nefirie said, and then she just opened the door and came in. Jason threw the sheet over Helle and turned his back on his mother as he pulled up his jeans. The room smelled of sex, he smelled of it, and Helle most definitely smelled of it—of him, to be more precise.

Nefirie's nostrils flared and she smiled faintly. Not, Jason suspected because she was amused by them having sex, but more due to their consternation.

"Do you mind?" Helle said, scowling at her.

"Mmm? Oh, well, excuse me. Dinner in ten?" Nefire departed, leaving a faint trace of perfume behind.

"Sheesh," Helle muttered. "She's worse than Mum." She heaved herself out of bed and padded over to the bathroom, as naked as the day she was born.

Fifteen minutes later, they made their way down the stairs. They still smelled of sex—albeit somewhat overlaid by soap.

They were the only guests. The food was good if simple, the wine was atrocious, and the raki was strong enough to make Jason's eyes water. The proprietor insisted on plying him with it, slapping him repeatedly on the back as he urged Jason to tip yet another shot down his throat. Fortunately, now and then the man was called away by his wife. Jason took every such opportunity to tip the raki into a nearby flowerpot.

Nefirie ordered them all coffee and baklava, and sat back. "How's your headache?"

"Manageable." Helle was curt—had been curt throughout dinner.

"I can't help you," Nefirie said. "You understand, right? He'd feel my presence immediately."

"Really? You've helped me before." Helle bit into the baklava.

"It's different now. We must make him believe he is strong and we are weak." Nefirie drank her coffee and gestured for more.

"If you worry that he'd feel your presence, does that mean you can sense him?" Jason asked.

"When he's close enough." Nefire smiled. "He can't sneak up on me."

"Impressive. Like you're attuned to each other? You know, two old souls that like to hang out together." Helle set the rest of the baklava to the side.

Nefirie looked her up and down. "Hang out together?" There was an edge to her voice that was not only anger. Jason pursed his lips together, studying his mother.

"Well, you did that the first time round, didn't you? You know, sat and had tea or whatever in his garden while your son was sitting in some sort of hellhole and I was forced into the role of his concubine."

Nefirie's eyes spat fire. "Tea? I was merely passing by." She sounded defensive, her left hand curling into a fist before she forcibly relaxed it. Passing by? Jason snorted softly.

"So you say." Helle shifted closer to Jason, a not so subtle message that it was them against Nefirie. "But Samion's palace wasn't exactly an afternoon's walk from our home, was it?"

"Not exactly." Jason regarded Nefirie intently. "I'd say it was at least two days away."

"You know me," Nefirie said, her voice calm. "I was an itinerant healer. Two days was nothing."

"If my son had disappeared I'd be looking for him everywhere." Helle caressed her belly. "And once I'd found him, I wouldn't leave him to rot. But hey, that might just be me."

Nefirie set down her cup. "How long will you keep harping on about this?"

"I don't know. A few years?" Helle shrugged. "Seems reasonable, don't you think?"

Nefirie gave her an exasperated look. "I made a mistake. I took Samion at his word."

"And that's the real mystery here." Jason put in. "You knew what Samion was. No one alive at the time was unaware of what he was."

"Oh, really?" Nefirie crossed her arms over her chest. "So what was he?"

"Evil. Abusive. Had a tendency to crush any opposition by the use of brutal force." And he enjoyed it, the bastard. Men, cut down as they fled from Samion's chariots, children trampled underfoot, women carried off to slavery.

"Like most of the rulers of his time," Nefirie said, with a shrug. "And as to evil, well, he always treated me and my fellow Wanderers with courtesy."

"Not me," Jason reminded her.

"No," Nefirie conceded. "Not you. And had I known what you were going through, I'd have done my best to free you. But I thought—"

"That I was merely held in genteel confinement, kicking my heels while Samion had his way with my woman."

"Yes, exactly," Nefirie said.

"And what could possibly be worse than that?" Even in the weak light, he could see her blanch.

"Nothing," she said after a while. "I realise that now."

"You okay?" Helle asked once they were back in their room.

"Not really." These discussions with Nefirie frayed his temper—and brought to life far too many vivid memories of those long months he'd spent as Samion's prisoner. Besides, he was feeling the consequences of all that raki.

"Friendly guy," Helle said with a laugh. "Here," she added, handing him a bottle of water.

"Thanks."

She took her time in the bathroom, emerging in only her panties and with her hair damp.

"I don't like it that the beds are apart," she said. "I want you to hold me."

"I can do that anyway." Jason patted the bed he was sitting on.

"You're not getting undressed?" She yawned, sliding in under the sheets.

"No. You sleep. I'll just—"

"...keep guard." Helle half sat up. "You need to sleep, Jason."

"I'll be fine." There was no need to tell her he believed Woolf to be very close. If nothing else, the way she'd been massaging her temples the last hour or so had made him suppose that was the case. The closer Woolf got, the more acute Helle's headaches, and even if she seemed to be coping better now, she looked drained, her mouth compressed.

It took Heller some time to fall asleep. He waited until her breathing deepened before moving over from the bed to the

362

chair he'd placed by the window. This deep in the country, the night was truly dark. No street lamps; the nearby houses were as sunk in darkness as the hotel was, and the proprietor had even turned off the neon hotel sign. Once his eyes got used to the dark, Jason could make out the ribbon of lighter grey that was the road, the surrounding mountains silhouetted against a night sky that was full of stars.

He rested his head on his arms and studied the stars, amusing himself by picking out the constellations he knew. Beyond the visible stars were the hazy smudges of the Milky Way, light so ancient it had been travelling through space since well before the foundation of ancient Ur. Such deep thoughts made his head ache—or maybe that was the raki. A shadow detached itself from the porch to his left. Even in the dark, he recognised Nefirie, watching as she paced back and forth, something glowing in her left hand. A cigarette? Yes, a small dot of glowing embers she repeatedly raised to her mouth. Once the first cigarette was gone, she lit another, then a third, a nervous chain-smoker walking back and forth beneath his window. She trod the third butt into the ground and fished something from her pocket. Her phone, to judge from its bluish light.

On the bed, Helle began to toss. "No," she moaned softly. "Not Jason, no." More tossing, her head whipping back and forth on the pillow. He tried to wake her, but the nightmare had her in its grip. She cried and lashed out, screaming his name as she sat straight up.

"No!" Her voice changed, no longer pleading but forceful. "I said no, you bastard!" She fell back on the pillow. "No more," she mumbled, turned on her side and tumbled back into undisturbed sleep.

Jason returned to his vigil, just in time to see Nefirie slip inside. Nothing else moved. His eyelids drooped. A snatched moment of sleep no more, his brain begged him. With an oath, he shook himself awake, found another bottle of water and drank it. The window glass was cool on his forehead, there was a draught from just under the windowsill, icy air that brought home just how cold it still could be up here in late April. Jason shivered and closed his eyes. Just a few moments, he thought, just…

"I will leave on the morrow." Korine's voice caused Nefirie to flinch.

"And go where?"

"Beyond the mountains." Korine watched Nefirie in silence. "I can't stay here. Not now."

"Korine…"

"No." Korine shook her head. "There is nothing you can say, Nefirie."

Nefirie's heart cracked. Korine had never used her given name before.

"I can leave," she said. "You must stay—this is your home, those are your boys."

"Too late." Korine smiled sadly at her sons. "Years of fighting this accursed Sight, years of battling to control the fires that live inside of me, but this…" She cleared her throat. "I saw what you did. You, his mother!" Korine clenched her hands, but to no avail, sparks flying through the air in every direction. "It broke something inside of me, and I dare no longer stay—not when I am afflicted with so much anger. I see the conflagration that will kill them everyone I love unless I leave."

"Korine," Nefirie repeated. She extended her arms in a beseeching gesture. "Give me the opportunity to make things right."

"How? They are dead—have been dead for years. Because of you and your jealous heart."

"It wasn't meant to end like that. I only wanted—"

"To punish them. Him for loving her more than you, her for stealing his heart."

"He was my son!"

"And she was my mother, he was my father. Dead because of you." Korine spat at Nefirie's feet. "I cannot bear the sight of you." She turned away. "But I will hold you to your vow."

Chapter 34

The sky was shifting into that pinkish grey that presages the sun's rising when Helle woke, feeling surprisingly refreshed. She stretched, rolled out of bed and made for the bathroom. By the window, Jason was fast asleep, his head cradled on his arms. She paused beside him, wishing there was something she could do to smooth away the worry lines that marred his brow. She opted for a soft kiss instead. Jason woke immediately, his amber-coloured eyes going from befuddled to vigilant in a matter of seconds.

"Hi," she said, brushing his hair off his brow. She gestured at the bed. "Sleep, honey. I'll keep watch."

He didn't even protest. He was fast asleep when she returned from the bathroom, still fully dressed, still with his shoes on.

As they drove back down to the coast, Helle kept her eyes glued to the window, looking for black SUVs. So far she'd seen nothing resembling the sleek vehicles Sam Woolf preferred. No one spoke for the first few miles.

"Today we're going home," Jason said, breaking the silence. "At last, one might add, although I wish we were returning to the place where we first met under different circumstances."

"Home?" Helle smiled as the sea came into view. "Won't he expect us to?"

"That's what we're counting on," Nefirie said, turning slightly in the front seat to look at Helle.

"We are?" Helle wasn't sure she wanted to do this anymore.

"Too late to turn back." Nefirie shrugged. "It all has to end."

"And what if things don't end the way we want them to?"

Nefirie gave her an inscrutable look. "At least it'll all be over."

"Wow." Helle leaned forward and touched Jason's shoulder. "Let's go back home to England instead."

"This is your one opportunity to rid yourself of Samion. If you don't do it now, you'll never succeed." A dry statement of fact, delivered with no emotions whatsoever. Nefirie looked away. "Of course, if you prefer taking your chances with Samion always at your heels..." A delicate shrug, no more.

Jason's hands tightened on the steering wheel. Briefly, he met Helle's eyes in the rear mirror. He was leaving it up to her.

"East or west, Helle?" Jason asked, slowing the car as they approached the highway.

West to the airport, to England—to a life of constantly looking over her shoulder. East to God knew what, but maybe to some sort of closure.

"East," Helle decided, even if it left her feeling uncomfortably short of breath.

"You sure?" Jason asked. She realised then that he was just as torn as she was. But the red-haired imp in her head was pointing to the east, and even if she was never going to admit to her trust in this figment of her imagination, Helle nodded. Nefirie looked pleased, relaxing in her seat.

The road continued to hug the mountains, while to their left the waves crashed against the shore. What little traffic there was, was mostly lorries, now and then a car. No SUVs.

"Headaches better?" Nefirie asked.

"Yes." Surprisingly, today the headache was nothing but a low hum, uncomfortable rather than painful.

"And the dreams? Any change in them?"

Helle frowned, trying to remember last night's dream. Only one, to start with, and... "Yes," she said hesitantly. "Something changed."

"Really?" Nefirie turned in her seat to look at her. "Do you remember what?"

Helle stroked the slight bump that contained her child. "Nothing more than a brightness, a light in the tunnel." And she'd had Jason by the hand, running to that light, while behind her Samion roared in anger.

"It's the child." Nefirie turned back to face the front. "An old soul, wise enough to know you need him."

Helle stifled a laugh. Seriously? "So why now?"

"Because it is no longer dormant. Your baby has become cognisant of everything that surrounds it, including your subconscious."

"Eeuw."

Nefirie laughed. "I dare say he can handle it."

"So, home," Helle said, not entirely comfortable discussing her baby's spiritual status. "Will there be anything left of Tarokyie?" She pronounced the name slowly.

"After all this time?" Jason shook his head. "Our people built in clay, Helle."

"Your people didn't build at all," Nefirie corrected. "We slept under the stars."

"In tents," Jason said drily. "And I was just as much a part of Helle's people as I was of yours. That's what you didn't like, remember?"

Nice put down. Nefirie flushed and for some minutes silence ruled.

"So no houses, no sun-baked courtyards," Helle said, trying to alleviate the tension. Too bad. She had looked forward to seeing the courtyards and the roses, to touch the smooth whitewashed walls of her father's house. She stifled a nervous chuckle. Her father lived in a modern brick house on Lake Michigan, for cripes' sake!

"All gone." Jason sounded wistful.

For the next half-hour, Nefirie was oppressively silent. "Here," she said when the road turned abruptly towards a little bay.

Jason nodded in agreement. "Yes, here."

Helle looked around and was so disappointed she didn't know whether to laugh or cry. Two ramshackle buildings stood by the side of the road, the mountains behind them. On the other side of the motorway, a narrow tongue of land ran out into the sea, creating a natural breakwater. She squinted and for a moment the placid pool of water was dotted with shadowy boats and the faint outlines of men in long tunics and women in veils.

"Kantor's port," Jason explained. He waved a hand up the nearby slope. "The village was up there." He turned off the motorway and guided the car up a road, slowing as the tarmac disappeared to be replaced by a dirt track.

When he finally stopped, Helle did some reassessing. The view was stunning, the green-clad slopes falling in undulating pleats to the bright blue sea. Jason opened her door and held her hand as she stepped outside. She inhaled; the scent of pine trees mingled with that of sun-warmed grasses, of moist earth. Without needing him to guide her, she walked straight into the undergrowth, making for where she knew the cluster of houses had been. A sheer drop to her right, and she remembered a palisade of sorts on top of it, while a giant cliff offered protection to the east.

"The well was over there," she said, pointing towards a tangle of green bushes halfway down the slope. Far enough that she was sent to fetch water by her Nana at least twice a day. She turned towards the sea. "It's much further to the sea than I thought." It looked like quite a hike, and the hill would be killing in the heat but in her memories they had run down to the sea on a daily basis.

"You got used to it," he replied, sinking down onto a patch of grass, his eyes never leaving the sea. Helle sat down beside him.

"I always won," she said triumphantly. He'd hated it, that this scrap of a girl bested him up the hill, just as she hated it that he was always the better swimmer.

"You did." He took her hand, braiding his fingers with hers. "Until we started running like this."

"We were older then," she said with a laugh. "Old enough to do other stuff than run."

"But we were still children." He sighed. "You died an adolescent that time round."

They shared a simple meal in the sun. Some bread and cheese they'd taken from the hotel, some water and a jar of olives. Nefirie did some fiddling with her phone before sitting down somewhat to the side, hugging herself as if she was cold. She waved away Jason's polite concern by reminding him she was old—and tired.

They all were, and a little nap here sounded like just the thing. Helle stretched out, wondering if the sky then had been as blue as the one she was presently staring at.

"Let's explore further." Nefirie pointed upwards.

"Up there?" Helle slid Jason a look. She vaguely recalled a glade almost at the top of the mountain—their place. Jason smiled at her.

"Do you want to?"

She nodded.

Nefirie wasn't up to walking, but fortunately the road was passable if bumpy. Jason negotiated one steep incline after the other, before parking beneath an ancient oak. They walked hand in hand up a narrow path bordered by boulders, Nefirie some steps behind them. The path widened, and they were in an area the size of a basketball court, covered with high grasses. To one side, the mountain continued to rise, the slope covered by trees. To the other, the ground just disappeared, and Helle walked tentatively towards the edge. The view was magnificent. An eagle soared upwards on a thermal, in front of her the Pontic Mountains dipped and rose, dark forested areas contrasting with the lighter colours of the cultivated fields in the valleys far below.

She turned, trying to locate where the spring might be. She could hear the sound of water and she took a step in the direction of the stand of poplars, rustling softly in the breeze. Midway between her and the trees was a huge rock. Something crawled up Helle's spine. That rock…Her vision fragmented, and she was being dragged towards it, held down on it as Samion whipped her feet to shreds. She shivered and moved closer to Jason.

The moment they stepped into the glade, Jason regretted coming here. This was where…Damn! He'd been so caught up in the other memories, those of him and Helle spending endless hours together here, she so young and trusting, he not so much older and so in love, that he'd forgotten what had happened the last time they'd been here. Three thousand years ago, yet he recalled that afternoon in far too much detail—a couple of minutes in which all his hopes and dreams had been permanently destroyed.

He watched Helle study the view, saw her cock her head and turn towards the poplars, come to a halt at the sight of the rock.

She shifted closer. "This is where—"

"Most perceptive of you." The dark voice had Jason closing his eyes. How the fuck had he known where they would be? Sam Woolf emerged from under the the shade of the poplars and came sauntering towards them. "I wasn't sure you'd remember," he continued, pausing to run a hand over the uneven surface of the rock. "But I see that you do." He slashed through the air with the switch he was carrying before snapping it in two.

"No back-up?" Jason asked, moving so that he stood in front of Helle.

"Here? No need." Woolf bowed to Nefirie. "The mother herself has promised to deliver."

The mother? Suddenly all those references in Woolf's e-mails made sense. He wasn't referring to the goddess, he was referring to her, to the woman who was standing some feet away, looking as if she wanted the ground to swallow her whole.

Jason cleared his throat. "No." He tried in vain to catch Nefirie's eyes. "My mother wouldn't—"

"Wrong verb," Woolf sneered. "Shouldn't, not wouldn't. She was there in the park when those morons I'd hired to grab Helle failed." Woolf gave Helle a cold look. "The little bitch saved herself that time. I wonder if she'll be able to do the same today."

"Mother?" Jason said. "Is this true?" But it was, he could see it in how she avoided his eyes.

"Of course it's true. Who do you think she met when she went to France? Our Lady of Lourdes?" Woolf laughed. "She met me. Me! She helped me when I lured Helle to the garage— she provided the visuals we needed with her little phone—and as icing on the cake she's led you here as I ordered her to."

Nefirie licked her lips. "Jason, I—"

"Silence!" Woolf thundered. Nefirie recoiled as if he'd slapped her. She opened her mouth as if to say something. Woolf snapped his fingers and Nefire's features contorted, fingers tearing at her hair, her cheeks. "What?" Woolf laughed. "You think you can withstand my powers? Here?" He laughed. "You think you can somehow save your precious son?" When he swept out his hand Nefirie fell to her knees, clutching at her stomach.

"No," she gasped. "Not my son. Not my..." Yet another sweeping gesture and she was sent sprawling.

"Fool! Nothing can save your son. Not today." Woolf turned. Jason tried to back away, but his feet seemed soldered to the ground.

"Run," Jason said to Helle. "Run for your life, lioness." He sent a bolt of fire at Samion, and the grass hissed and smoked but Woolf just laughed and continued his progress towards them.

"Not without you." She was trembling all over.

"Save yourself, Helle. You and the baby—"

"No!" Just like that, Helle exploded into action. She dragged Jason with her, and they were flying over the ground, her legs moving so fast they blurred. Almost at the pathway, and he was beginning to hope they would make it when Helle slammed into something. The ground beneath their feet was heaving, and in the middle of the clearing Woolf was standing with his arms spread wide, summoning invisible barriers to pen them in.

"Mother!" Jason yelled.

"Don't waste your breath." Woolf sneered. "She can't help. And even if she could, she probably wouldn't. She has never forgiven Helle for stealing you away from her, which was why she did what she did in that first life."

Jason heard Helle's loud gasp.

"After all, how was I to know just where to find you?" Woolf gestured at their surroundings. "Such a secluded little place, far away from any paths I would normally travel."

Jason's head whirled.

"Why you fucking bitch!" Helle's voice soared upwards. "You told him where we'd be! You!"

"I—" Nefire staggered to her feet, looking more fragile than Jason had ever seen her in her torn and dirty dark blouse.

"Shut up! You were a fucking treacherous witch then, and you're just the same now." Helle spat.

"I did what I had to do!" Nefirie screeched.

"Yes," Woolf said, "she couldn't have her precious son wedding some inconsequential princess, could she? Oh no, for Jason she wanted a gifted Wanderer girl."

"How could you?" Jason had problems talking. "What are you, some sort of monster?"

"Me? She enthralled you!"

"I loved her! Just as I love her now!"

"It was wrong."

"Wrong?" His fires burst from him, a wall of flame roaring towards Nefirie who leapt to the side. "It was love. But you couldn't stand it that I loved someone more than you, could you?"

"She was meant for him, not for you." Nefirie held out her hands towards Jason.

"No," Helle said, "I was always meant for Jason, but you were too jealous to see that."

"Jealous?" Nefirie straightened up, her gaze sweeping Helle from head to foot. "Of you?"

"May you burn in hell," Jason said. "I, Jason, repudiate you."

"No!" Nefirie fell to her knees.

"I have no mother, no father. You are nothing to me, you're faithless and unloving, tainted with darkness. I curse you, I beg the Mother to throw you into the abyss and leave you in darkness. May you never again see the light, may you wander through eternity and know that you are alone—utterly alone."

"No," Nefirie begged, "you don't understand, Jason. Please."

Jason turned his back on her.

"Jason!" Nefirie screamed.

Jason didn't reply. He threw himself at Woolf.

They were for once evenly matched. Jason was terrible in his wrath, an avenging angel spouting fire from his hands and, surprisingly, from his head. A crown of flames surrounded him and his hands glowed red hot in the sun. But Samion was shrouded in a heaving cloud of black, and where fire met smoke, the air hissed and spat. The ground shook beneath them. Jason crashed into Woolf, was shoved aside, crashed into him again. Kicks, punches—blood flew through the air. Woolf began to chant. His deep voice rose and fell, a melodious sound that made the ground bow to his will, pitching Jason back and forth, incapable of holding his balance.

Helle crouched, getting ready to spring. Let Woolf turn his back and she'd be on him, throw him to the ground. Something grabbed hold of her. Helle shook free, gaping at Nefirie. No longer looking as if Woolf had used her as a doormat, her mother-in-law from hell was now swathed in linen garments of pristine white, her dark red hair floating like a veil around her. Yet again she made a grab for Helle, sinking talon-like fingers into her arm.

"Let me go!" Helle yanked, just as Woolf swiped Jason's legs from underneath him. "No!" A flail of punches, fire rushing up Woolf's arm and causing him to howl, but now Woolf was definitely on top, and there was a knife in his hand. Helle swung at Nefirie. "Let me go, you fucking bitch!"

Golden eyes bored into her. "Stay," Nefirie commanded, and Helle was incapable of moving. She didn't understand. Did Nefirie want Samion to harm Jason? Kill him? Helle moaned. Of course she did. That's why she'd brought them here. For some inexplicable reason, she wanted them both to die.

Jason was back up on his feet, and Helle heard him grunt as Samion drove a knee into his stomach. He stumbled backwards and brought Samion down with him, managing to twist so that he was suddenly on top, his bright, fiery hands pounding into Samion, time and time again. There was a sickening crunch as Jason broke Samion's nose and blood spurted from his face. Jason didn't stop: he punched Samion again and again.

Nefirie muttered under her breath and moved closer, dragging Helle with her.

Samion roared, the ground growled in response. Jason lost his balance. That was all Samion needed; he threw Jason to the ground, grinding his knee into his back. He brandished his knife.

"No," Nefirie pleaded, wrenching Helle forward with such force she landed on her knees. "Him for her, Samion. Take her but spare my son."

What?

"No." Jason twisted to look at her with eyes that burned with hatred. Nefirie flinched.

"Now, Samion," Nefirie said, lifting Helle back onto her feet.

Samion nodded, pulling Jason up to stand, bleeding, in front of him. Jason put his hands against Samion's thighs, and Samion cursed.

"You can't do this," Jason slurred, his eyes never leaving his mother. "You can't do this to me."

She didn't reply. She just nodded at Samion and pushed Helle towards him, opening her arms to grab at the tumbling body of her unwilling son.

Helle landed at Samion's feet, but she was up on her toes, retreating from him so fast his hand missed. Jason was screaming with rage, fighting the iron hold of his mother. She didn't give an inch, holding him as firmly as if she had bolted him to the ground with iron chains.

"So this is why Korine left," Helle called out, maintaining a careful distance from Woolf. "She found out, didn't she?"

Nefirie was silent.

"She must have found you despicable," Helle continued. "A traitor—even worse, a mother who gladly leaves her child to suffer."

"I did not—"

"Shut up!" Helle yelled, leaping to the side to avoid Woolf's hands. "Couldn't stand the sight of you, could she? That's why she left."

"No!" Nefirie said.

"Our daughter will hate you forever," Jason said, breathing heavily. "As will I." He roared, struggling against her hold. Nefirie's linen skirts were on fire, the grass around them crackled with heat. "Cursed!" Jason shrieked. "May you die a thousand deaths, may you drown in pitch!" Not only his hands, but his arms glowed with heat, a sickening stench of burning flesh filling the air. Nefirie staggered, mouth shaped round a soundless scream—but she didn't let go.

Helle darted to the side, evading Woolf, and ran flat out towards Jason. Together, they'd be able to free him. She would gladly break Nefirie's fingers if that was what it took.

"Helle, watch out!" The ground rose before her. One moment she was running, the next she as flat on her face, Woolf's long body on top of her. Her chin hit the ground, her mouth filling with blood. His weight nailed her down, his breath hot and moist in her ear.

"How convenient: me on top, as it should be," he said, making Helle's hair stand on end.

She was flipped over onto her back. His voice. It roared and demanded entry to her brain, but this time the red-haired little girl stood in its way, just as much on fire as her father was. Where Woolf demanded her acquiescence, Helle fought. She clawed and punched and spat. It didn't help. She was pressed to the ground, her legs wrenched apart to accommodate him. No. Never that.

"Look," Woolf snarled. He grabbed and twisted her head so that she was forced to look at Jason, a trembling mass of fury, muscles on his forearms knotted with tension as he fought Nefirie's hold. "He is helpless, your Wanderer, but maybe he will like to watch."

Oh, God, this was going to be just like one of her dreams. He was going to make Jason watch as he took everything he wanted and then he would tear Jason apart in front of her eyes, handing her the bloodied head to hold.

Helle bucked. She scratched his face, his neck. Woolf slapped her, hard. That made her gasp, for a moment knocked into submission. But when he began to grope her, she found the strength to rise off the ground and bite his ear, hanging on like a terrier when he attempted to dislodge her.

One moment she was on the ground, the next she was on her feet, his left hand clawed into her hair.

"Enough," Woolf hissed, wiping at the blood flowing down his neck with the back of his free hand. "For the last time, little Helle: me or him?"

"You? You can go to hell! I'd rather die than live with you."

"Ah." A knife glinted in the sun. "So be it, then. Are you ready to die?" he asked, running the flat of the blade down her face. She shook her head. She didn't want her last vision to be that of Woolf's black eyes, she wanted it to be of Jason.

"No? So will you come with me? Leave him for me?" In response, Helle spat in his face. His features hardened. "Very well." A twist of his hand and she was standing in front of him, helpless when he set the tip of his knife to her throat. She was going to die. Now. Her eyes found Jason and she tried to smile, tried to tell him just how much she loved him.

"Don't." Jason's voice came as if from a distance. "Let her go and kill me instead."

"How chivalric of you. But I'll kill you anyway." Woolf's hand slid down her front, stopped to squeeze one of her breasts, slid further. The child in her belly seemed to wail in pain when his fingers grazed her skin, the red-haired girl was screaming at her to flee, to do something. Do what, when his knife nudged at her neck?

The child inside her howled. Heat emanated in concentric circles from her belly, bright light danced before her eyes. No. She'd never let anyone hurt her child. Never. Helle knotted her hands. Heat rushed down her arms. Her baby's fire, burning through her veins. God, it hurt! And the heat—like having your hand held over an open flame. She inhaled. This would hurt too. She set her overheated hands on Woolf's thighs just as she jerked her head backwards. Pain burst through her skull when her head connected with his chin. Woolf exclaimed and staggered backwards. She felt the pressure of the blade waver and slumped, collapsing downwards. Her neck stung as the blade sliced into her skin.

"You promised!" Korine shrieked. "You promised you would help her!"

"Calm down child," Nefirie said, reaching for the warm little body.

"Don't touch me," the girl spat, "don't put your horrid hands on me again."

Nefirie tried to hug her and hold her but the child squirmed, screaming as if her heart was breaking. The flames from her hands seared Nefirie, and she had to let go, forcing Korine's overheated hands into the bucket by the bed.

"It's a dream, Korine," Nefirie said. "Not necessarily the truth."

"You failed her." The girl turned herself away from her and hugged herself into a tight little ball.

"It's only a dream," Nefirie repeated.

"It is?" The child threw her a long look over her shoulder. "I don't believe you."

"Korine," Nefirie said, "I have given you my word: I will be there."

"You are there!" Korine dragged her sleeve over her face. "But you're doing nothing to help her."

"Trust me," Nefirie said. "Just trust me, child." She ignored the blistering heat in those little hands and picked Korine up, crooning softly as she rocked back and forth. At long last, the child slept. Nefirie wept. What was she to do?

Chapter 35

Jason's heart stopped. Blood ran down Helle's neck, as she hung, a deadweight in Woolf's arms.

"Damn!" Woolf released his hold and she spilled to the ground, a lifeless heap of arms and legs.

Behind Jason, Nefirie cried 'No!' over and over, her grip slipping. He tore free, a wordless howl burning up his throat as he leapt towards Woolf.

This time, Jason was going to fry him out of existence. He tackled Woolf to the ground, and he was everywhere, fire leaking from his hands and arms, dripping from his head. He burnt holes in Woolf's clothes, blackening the skin beneath. When Woolf went for him with the knife, Jason closed his hands round Woolf's wrist, channelling so much heat the red-hot blade fell to the ground, leaving Woolf's hand charred and smoking.

"She's alive!" Nefirie's voice cut through his rage. "She will live, Jason."

Live? Not as long as Samion remained alive. With Woolf prowling in the background, she would never live, never breathe freely. Jason's hands closed round Samion's throat, he stared down at eyes as black as the night, and increased the pressure. Woolf put up no resistance. All he did was look straight back at Jason, and in the depth of that black gaze Jason saw himself, a man converted to a destroying demon, all of him alight. Woolf's smile was derisive. Triumphant.

"Stop!" Nefirie's voice was like a whiplash. "I told you, she's alive. If he dies at your hands again, it never ends. Release him. Now!" Jason had no intention of obeying. He tried to tighten his fingers, but his body refused to cooperate. "I said now." Nefirie set a hand to his arm and he was propelled backwards. He wanted to yell at her, tell her she'd done enough meddling, but Nefirie shook her head, and Jason stood mute, incapable of moving. His heart rushed, his limbs trembled. What did she intend to do?

"Jason?" Helle's voice was hoarse, but surprisingly steady. She was pressing her hand to her neck, blood streaking her fingers and throat. Jason tried to move in her direction, but whatever invisible fetters Nefirie had put in place made that impossible. He wetted his lips, wanted to tell her that he loved her, but could produce no sound. But he could look at her, meet her turquoise eyes with his own in a silent attempt to convey just what he felt. To his horror, she got to her feet and came limping towards him. No, he tried to yell, stay away, run! But of course there were no words.

Woolf groaned, sitting up carefully. He inspected the damage Jason had done him, ran a hand over lesions and burns, and just like that the bastard healed himself, even patting his clothes back into shape.

"You really do hate her, don't you?" he said to Nefirie. "So fine, let's go back to our original agreement. I take her, you take him."

Jason shook with futile rage. Woolf made as if to grab Helle.

"No." Nefirie placed herself in front of Helle. "This has to stop."

"Stop?" Woolf broke out in harsh laughter. "This stops when I say it stops. Get out of my way, you old fool, and be grateful I'm leaving you and your precious whelp alive."

Nefirie stood her ground. "No." She straightened up and spread her arms. Power rippled through the air like miniature heatwaves. Woolf sneered, but eyed her warily.

"What, you're hoping to work yourself back into your son's good books? Too late for that, don't you think?"

"Maybe." Nefirie sighed softly. "But I'm not doing any of this for him. I'm doing it for her."

"For me?" Helle sounded astounded, retreating to stand behind Jason.

Nefirie glanced at her. "For you? Why would I do anything for you?" She returned her attention to Woolf. "No more killing. You take one more innocent life and the darkness swallows you. Forever."

"What do I care?" Woolf said. But Jason could see how his jaw tightened, a sudden sheen of sweat on his forehead. "Besides, it's all his fault." He snarled at Jason, showing his teeth. "She should have been mine but he stole her and then he murdered me and mine. That's what started all this. Why should it be only me wandering in the halls of darkness? Why not him?"

Jason was tempted to yell at him that these recurring lives had been nothing but one long tramp through darkness. Something touched his hand. Helle, gripping his unresponsive fingers.

"What Jason did, he did for love." Nefirie looked at Jason. "And he's paid for that rash act of vengeance."

"Love? He was wrong to love her to begin with! She was promised to me, not him, not an upstart Wanderer whelp!"

"Yes," Nefirie agreed, "she should have been yours. It would have been better for all. But the Mother had other plans."

"That's not what you believed back then," Woolf said. "Back then, you were more than eager to help me rectify the wrong done to me. You even betrayed them to me on the eve of their wedding. Tell me, was that done out of love?"

Nefirie fiddled with her garments, her gaze locked on the distant mountains. A soft breeze soughed through the trees, rustled through the knee-high grass. The eagle Jason had seen when they first arrived had been joined by one more, circling lazily above them. Beside him, Helle shivered. In front of him, an immobile Woolf was staring at Nefirie, sunk in thought so deep one could almost believe she'd stopped breathing.

At long last, Nefirie turned to face them. "No. It was done out of hubris, a refusal to acknowledge that maybe my plans were not the right plans." She bowed formally to Jason, then to Helle. "I was wrong."

"And is this where you expect us to give you a group hug and tell you we forgive you?" Helle asked.

"Forgiving is more important to the forgiver than the forgiven," Nefirie said with a shrug. "And frankly, what you may think of me doesn't bother me—I never liked you. But my son I loved, I've always loved him, and as for Korine..." She paused, closing her eyes briefly. "It has to end. Here, where this vicious circle of betrayal and revenge once started."

"How?" Woolf asked bitterly. "And more importantly, why? What is there for me but eternal darkness anyway?"

"The Mother shows compassion to those who show contrition." Nefirie breathed in deeply. "What you need is someone to guide you back towards the light."

"There's no going back for someone like as me," Woolf replied. "Not anymore." No, Jason agreed silently, not for bastards such as Woolf. He deserved to rot in the dark.

"There is always forgiveness. Always redemption." Nefirie took a step towards Woolf. "For you and for me." This last she said while looking straight at Jason. He averted his eyes.

"Seriously?" Helle threw Woolf a black look. "He just apologises and that is that?"

"Just apologises?" Nefirie's brows rose. "God, you are a shallow, uneducated creature, aren't you?"

"At least I'm not the back-stabbing mother from hell," Helle retorted.

Nefirie ignored her, turning back to Woolf. "I will go with you. I will be your hand in the dark."

What? His mother, tied for eternity to Samion? Yes, she'd betrayed them, but compared to Woolf's, Nefirie's soul was as white as driven snow. Jason groaned out loud, realising with a start that Nefirie had released him from whatever spell she'd cast on him.

"You can't do this," he said. "Not for him."

"I must." Nefirie turned to face Samion. "So what will it be?"

"What are the choices?" Woolf asked, shifting his powerful shoulders in a way that made Jason's muscles tense, heat leaping down his arms.

"The choices?" Nefirie turned slightly, her gaze on the soaring eagles. "I can stand aside as my son attacks you, and we both know that will end with his death. I will do my best to save him, but here it is likely I lose—your roots run too deep here, are too powerful. So I'll die as well." She glanced at Helle. "And she is no match for you. You could snap her like a twig, should you want to."

"So I win," Woolf said, crossing his arms. Win? Never! Jason took a step forward.

"Yes. Here, today, you win." Nefirie looked at Jason. "He's too powerful, son. He'd tear you into pieces before our eyes." From Helle came a stifled moan. "But if he does, he sinks forever into the sea of darkness." Nefirie visibly shuddered, her hands tightening into fists, before turning to face Woolf. "Or you take me up on my offer," she continued after a moment. "But it is your choice. It has to be your choice." She met Jason's eyes. "All I've done, I've done to lead us to this moment. It has to be like this, son. A free choice. It cannot end otherwise."

Jason didn't reply. A free choice? And what if the bastard chose to obliterate them here—all three of them? As if she'd heard him, Nefirie shook her head. *It will not happen*, she whispered in his head. Jason looked away, no longer sure what he felt or believed about his mother. Instead, he shifted closer to Helle, his leg pressing against hers, and Nefirie's hesitant smile turned into wry grimace.

The sun blazed down from above, the eagles continued to soar, and Woolf stood silent, head bowed. A long, long silence. Helle shifted on her feet, her hand tightening round Jason's. He squeezed back, all the while keeping a careful eye on Woolf.

At long last, Woolf lifted his face. "I could have loved you," he said, looking at Helle. "Once, I had it in me to love. Now…" His face contorted. "I hate him," he hissed, lunging at Jason.

"Samion!" Nefirie grabbed hold of him. Jason rushed over to help contain the bastard, but was met by Nefirie's arresting hand. Below them, the ground pitched and heaved, growling with Woolf's anger and anguish. There was a crash as one of the poplars went down. The air rang with a high-pitched keening that seemed to come from the mountain side above them. Helle was on her knees, hands pressed to her ears. With a loud crack the large rock in the centre of the clearing split apart, raining fragments of stone everywhere. A sliver penetrated Jason's arm, he heard Helle cry out as a block of rock the size of a frying pan came flying towards her. Jason threw out his arm, creating a wave of heat that reduced the rock to gravel.

Things quieted. Nefirie was standing with her arms round Woolf.

"How long?" he asked, leaning into Nefirie's embrace.

"Thousands of years," Nefirie replied, and Woolf's shoulders bowed. "We have to put your soul back together. Every sliver you have carved off we have to find and reclaim with your penance. But the alternative is worse."

Woolf straightened up. "Extinction, but no oblivion," he muttered. "Fucking awful."

"So, will you do it?" Nefirie asked, releasing him.

Woolf lifted his face to the sky. "No sun."

"No." Nefirie's voice quavered. "No sun, no moon, no stars."

They looked at each other. Woolf cleared his throat and held out his hand. Nefirie took it. Jason suppressed a shiver of revulsion at seeing them standing like that, hand in hand like lovers. His mother, Nefirie the Wanderer, and Samion, Prince of Kolchis, yoked together for eternity. Nefirie looked at Jason and smiled, disengaging herself from Woolf's hold.

"Time is all we have, son." She held out her hand to him, and after some moments of hesitation he took it. He could feel the thrumming of her pulse, the cold sweat that covered her skin.

"We're talking endless centuries of darkness," he said. "He doesn't deserve your help."

"Everyone deserves help." She bowed her head. "Besides, it has to end." Her free hand fluttered over his face, not really touching. "Light a candle for me when you can." She lifted his hand to her mouth and kissed it.

Helle braced her hands against her knees and took a couple of deep breaths. Out of the corner of her eye, she registered the intense conversation between Jason and Nefirie, but it was to Woolf her gaze returned, over and over again. His beautiful mouth softened into a smile, black eyes met hers, and her heart double-thudded. Those dark eyes narrowed, and she had the sensation of being touched, gentle fingers brushing at her hair, her cheek. She straightened up, trapped by his eyes, by the need she saw in them.

Sandalwood and myrrh—the distinctive scents floated towards her. In her head she saw that huge canopied bed, the silk sheets crumpled beneath her. A looming shadow, eyes the colour of jet that smiled down at her, and those large hands were gentle and careful as they lifted her up to meet him. Sweat broke out along Helle's spine, she felt blood heat her chest and her cheeks.

It could have been good, his voice whispered in her head, *it could have been us, little Helle.* And the sadness in that lovely velvet voice almost made her want to cry. But then she remembered what he had done, how often he had hurt her and humiliated her. She raised her chin and shook her head. It would never have been good, not when he expected her total submission.

Nefirie was still clutching her son's hand, Jason's eyes fixed on her. It made Helle itch, somehow. Whatever game Nefirie had been playing, it had come close to backfiring and had involved far too much danger and pain for Helle to be capable of forgiving her. She studied her man, at present a colourful collection of bruises and dents, one of his sleeves dark with blood. As to herself…Helle's fingers trembled when she inspected the gash along her neck. It stung, long and deep enough to still be oozing blood.

"So now what?" she asked, moving closer to the trio. Not close enough to come within reach of Woolf, though.

"Now we die," Nefirie said calmly. Woolf shifted on his feet, something dark moving over his handsome features.

"Here?" Helle asked.

"Yes." Nefire inclined her head in the direction of Jason. "You know what to do."

"Me?" Jason's normally deep voice squeaked.

"You."

Woolf smiled—more a showing of teeth than anything else. "Admit it: you've been longing to do this for ages."

"I can't." Jason's face twisted together. "Please, Mother, don't ask this of me."

Helle looked from one to the other. "What, you want Jason to..." She couldn't bring herself to finish the sentence.

"How else?" Nefirie asked.

"Jump?" Helle suggested, pointing at the edge.

"Not high enough to guarantee death," Nefirie said. "Besides, there'd be remains to identify, police to pacify—it could all get very messy."

"But it will hurt!"

"It always hurts to die—more or less." Woolf sounded bored. "But I don't think the Wanderer has the balls to do this." In contrast to his tone, he looked apprehensive. Perspiration coated his face, and the sour tang of fear rolled off him in waves.

"Immolating one's mother is not something anyone would feel comfortable doing," Helle shot back.

"Depends on the mother," Woolf replied, and the way he smiled at her made her realise he knew exactly what she thought of Nefirie. Probably Nefirie did too. Tough: the bitch deserved it.

"Jason, do as I ask," Nefirie said.

"Mother, no, please..." Jason bent over as if in pain.

"Do it," Nefirie ordered. Jason staggered backwards, shaking his head. "Jason! Trust me. Just do it." She gripped Woolf's hand. "Don't keep us waiting."

Jason gave her a resigned look. "Dearest God, give me strength."

"Wrong deity." Nefirie gave him a brilliant smile. "The Mother will guide you."

Jason's arms shook. His fists clenched and unclenched, sparks flying every which way.

"Concentrate," Nefirie said. "Build up the heat."

"I can't," he said lowering his arms.

"You must. Just like I must go with Samion." She raised her arm and pointed at Jason. "Now!"

Fire exploded from his hands. It roared towards the skies, an uncontrolled wall of heat and flames. It leapt over the ground, sucking oxygen from the surrounding air. Helle coughed, covering her nose and mouth with her arm. Jason was standing with his arms raised, attempting to control this raging inferno, but this fire was not his to tame. It grew and twisted, it snarled and spat. It was unbearable to breathe, and Helle hopped from foot to foot, the heat of the ground burning her feet through the soles of her shoes. There was a loud whoosh, an instant of white light, and just like that it was over. Where Nefirie and Samion had been, was a patch of blackened ground, ashes floating upwards towards the distant skies.

Jason fell to his knees and covered his face with his shaking hands. "What did I just do? I killed her!"

Helle sat down beside him. "No you didn't. She only needed you to light the fire. The rest she did herself."

"You think?"

Helle just had to lie down. "Yeah. That's what it looked like to me." Not a lie, not the truth. She had no idea, frankly, beyond knowing that Jason needed to believe he hadn't incinerated his mother. She found his hand, braided her fingers with his. "It's over. He's gone."

"She's scared of the dark, and now she's condemned herself to years and years of it—with him."

Seeing as Nefirie had been happy enough to conspire with Woolf while alive, Helle was not exactly overwhelmed with compassion.

"I thought she'd betrayed us," Jason went on.

Not to put too fine a point on it, she had, but Helle chose not to say that. Instead, she turned her attention to his arm.

"Does it hurt?" The deep gash would need stitches.

"No." He lifted her chin, rubbed gently at the cut. "Does this?"

"A bit." She closed her eyes. The grass beside her rustled as Jason lay down beside her. Nothing but the sound of trees and wind, the distant call of a bird—so quiet. Helle rubbed at her temple. No headache—in fact, she felt strangely empty, the black cloud she'd lived with for so long gone, leaving echoing, uncluttered space. It made her feel sick, in a relieved way.

It took them ages to pull themselves together. Helle just couldn't find the energy to do anything more than stare at the sky. The shadows lengthened, the previously so warm day shifted into chilly evening, and still she didn't want to move. Finally, Jason staggered to his feet.

"Let's go."

Neither of them looked back.

Oh Mother, it was dark, an inky blackness with no shape or substance to it; dark with an absolute absence of light. And there was no ground, no sky, only a suspended existence in all that black.

"I hate the dark," she whispered weakly and heard the sound echo eerily as it bounced off eternity.

He laughed hollowly. "You'll get used to it," he promised. "After all, there's plenty of time."

She drew close to him and was glad of his presence, of the comforting warmth of his hand.

Chapter 36

Every morning, there was a moment just as Jason woke when he didn't quite remember it was over. And then, every morning, there was a rush of relief as he recalled Sam Woolf was gone—for good.

Eight weeks after that momentous day in Turkey, Jason woke to the cheerful warbling of blackbirds, June sun dancing through the large east-facing windows of their bedroom at Tor Cottage. Beside him, Helle was sunk in sleep, dark lashes brushing cheeks that showed the beginning of a tan. As usual, her duvet was bunched around her middle, naked legs protruding from below, arms and shoulders bare. She said this was due to sharing a bed with her own personal heater, he teased her that she mostly did it to drive him crazy with the sight of her heart-shaped arse.

He snuggled up to her, so close that his nose was almost touching hers. Her lashes quivered, her mouth twitched. One eye opened sleepily, shooting him a turquoise look. Helle stretched and rolled over on her back, exposing her breasts and her visibly rounded belly. Their belly, he amended, placing his hand on the taut skin. Their child, now an unambiguous source of wonderment and joy, no longer tainted by fear or premonitions.

"Hi, baby," he said, sliding down to kiss her just below the navel.

"Are you talking to me or the kid?" she mumbled, running her fingers through his hair. At present it was too long and shaggy for the City look, but Helle liked it this way, seemed to never get enough of finger-combing it, so for now it remained uncut.

"Both." He rested his cheek against her belly.

"So I no longer come first?" She slid her hand down to toy with his diamond ear-stud.

"Before my son and heir?" He brushed a finger over her pubic mound. "I'll have to think about it."

"Jason!" She shoved at him, making him laugh as he easily pinned her to the bed before sliding further down. He tugged gently at her pubic hair.

"Stupid questions deserve stupid answers." He tugged a bit harder. "You always come first." He rested his chin on her hipbone and looked at her, one hand tracing the contour of her belly, up to circle her breast, her nipple. "You're beautiful." He tweaked her nipple. "Like a golden cat, stretched out in my bed. My cat, my lioness." He clambered over her, straddling her legs. "Question is, can I make her purr?"

Her eyes darkened, the tip of her tongue flickered over her lips. Nipples tautened under his gaze, her back arching so as to lift her breasts towards him. Beautiful breasts, somewhat heavier and rounder now. He liked it, how they were always on the verge of spilling out of her lacy bras, and although she grumbled a bit, she did not seem to mind overmuch, at least not to judge from how she showcased her cleavage in tight tops with interesting necklines.

Jason flicked his finger over one of her nipples, watching with interest as it hardened further. When he bent forward to kiss her, he ran his fingers down her flank, and all of her shivered in response.

She tasted of sleep. A slight tang of morning breath, but a couple of deep and wet kisses later, who cared? He was already hard and hot, she was soft and warm, her arms coming round his neck as he thoroughly explored her mouth. She scraped her nails lightly along his back, down his sides and all the way to his groin. Fortunately, his lioness sheathed her claws when she gripped his cock, her hands moving up and down.

He kept on kissing her. A leisurely dance of tongues, lips that moved together. Distractedly, he wondered if he could kiss her to climax. The way she was writhing beneath him made him think he probably could—but he had other plans.

It was strange, he reflected, how their lovemaking had been affected by the recent events. Gone was that undercurrent of urgency, those instances of fear that had now and then flashed through Helle's eyes. But the fire remained, her touch searing his skin, her eyes burning holes in his heart. He kissed her tenderly, and she smiled under his mouth, her fingers fondling his balls and cock. He rocked back and forth, thrusting into her hands. So good. But not yet.

Jason took hold of her wrists, lifting her hands above her head. She wet her lips, an expectant look on her face. He just had to kiss her again.

"Stay," he said as he got off the bed. In seconds, he'd found what he was looking for, returning with a short silk scarf. He threaded it through the headboard. "Hold on, don't let go."

"What, no knots?" she teased, gripping the ends.

"No." He blew on her nipple. "If you let go, I'll simply stop what I'm doing." He grinned. "I can assure you that would be a major loss."

"For me or you?"

"For both." Enough of this. Jason moved down her body, pausing to drop a series of kisses over her belly before positioning himself between her legs. She lifted her head and looked at him. Jason licked his mouth, and she giggled.

She was already wet. He slid in his finger, pulled it out, and circled her clit. Did it again and she shifted restlessly. Two fingers entering her, and she tilted her hips. Jason gripped her by the hips. He ate her, he used lips and tongue until her hips gyrated. She placed her hand on his head; Jason stopped, raising his face enough to give her a quelling look.

"You let go, I stop."

"Jason," she protested. "I…" But she returned to gripping the scarf. Jason sat back on his heels and stroked himself. Hard, heavy strokes, that had him closing his eyes and throwing his head back. She kicked at him.

"Hey," she said. "If you're allowed to touch yourself, then I will too." But she was still holding on to the scarf.

"You like it better when I do the touching, don't you, lioness?" A combination of fingers and tongue had her thrashing, all of her straining upwards, her voice hoarse as she begged him to…

"What do you want?" he asked, bracing himself on his arms as he moved over her to kiss her mouth.

390

"You. Only you," she replied, and the look in her eyes scalded him. With a soft grunt he entered her, his hips flexing as he buried himself in her. She clenched in response, he cupped her arse, lifting her that much closer. She came, in wave after wave. And still she held on to the scarf.

"Hold me," he said, increasing his pace.

"Always." With legs and arms she clung to him, her eyes never leaving his as he drove himself to a finish.

When he flopped over on his back, she rolled with him, pressing her mouth to his neck before resting her head on his chest. They must have dozed off, because when he woke the sun was no longer in his eyes, it was patterning the foot of the bed. There was a loud knock on their door.

"You planning on sleeping all day?" Nigel asked. "I'm starving out here."

"There's cereal and milk," Jason called back.

"I have that every day at home. Here I expect omelettes and stuff."

"Help yourself." But Jason was already up, not so sure he wanted Nigel cooking anything in his kitchen. Last time he'd done so, the damned stains had taken days to fade.

"What can he do? Explode the Aga?" Helle teased.

Jason gave her a dark look. "You have no idea."

He left her laughing.

"Good start to the day?" Nigel enquired when Jason entered the kitchen.

"Very. Until you interrupted."

"I've said it before, I'll say it again: all that horizontal activity may have a detrimental effect on your brain."

"Oh, so you don't have sex with Miranda?"

"Only standing up," Nigel replied, laughing when Jason told him to spare him the details. He fetched eggs and milk for Jason before sitting down on the old table to look at him.

"What?" Jason asked.

"Everything's okay now, isn't it?" Nigel said.

"It is." Jason whisked the eggs, frowning as he considered poor Tim. His voice would never recover from the damage to his larynx, nor would he ever return to working as a bodyguard. Together with his spleen and whatever other parts they'd taken out to save him, Tim had lost his nerve.

"And Helle, is she okay?"

Jason turned to face his friend. "Why do you ask?" Nigel studied his bangles, shaking his arm experimentally to make them all rattle.

"She's quite the little toughie." Nigel gave Jason a thoughtful look. "But I'm not so sure she's comfortable in your Kensington house anymore."

Jason sighed. Ever since Woolf had invaded their London home, Helle avoided the living room. This had not changed after their return from Turkey, and although he'd suggested they should totally redecorate, he knew it wouldn't help. For Helle, that room was forever tainted, it reeked of fear and humiliation.

"So why not move here?" Nigel suggested.

"Here? It's a bit of a commute, don't you think?" But Jason liked the idea, seeing this kitchen full of Helle and their children, protected by the benign presences that still, it seemed to him, tended to hover round Helle whenever she entered here.

"Welcome to the age of internet, Mr Dinosaur." Nigel rolled his eyes. "Ever heard of video links? Of stuff like Teams and Skype?"

In response, Jason threw an egg at him. It made a very pleasing stain on Nigel's black t-shirt.

"Move here?" Mum settled back in the sun lounger. "Sounds like a great idea."

"I think he's only doing it for me," Helle said, extending her bare legs to the sun.

"So?" her mother shoved her sunglasses down her nose to look at her.

"His work—our work—is in London."

Miriam snorted. "Your work is on the cloud."

"In the cloud," Helle corrected. "And the cloud is just a storage functionality, it's not as if it replaces an office."

"You have that nice young man Jim to handle the day to day." Mum grinned. "Scared him half to death when I handed him my little accounting test, don't you think?"

Little? Miriam had presented Jim with what looked like a minor novel. "But he passed it."

"Yup. You didn't."

"I'm not an accountant. I'm an analyst." Helle tossed her head, making Mum laugh. "Anyway, so you don't think he'll be unhappy if we leave London?"

Miriam smiled at her. "My darling girl, if you're happy, he's happy."

Helle snorted. "Very clichéd."

"But true." Miriam yawned. "Besides, the two of you could do with some peace and quiet, don't you think?"

"Yeah." Helle patted her stomach. "As long as it lasts." Ever since the events in Turkey she'd been trying to get her head round the fact that their baby shared his father's gift.

"That's not what I was referring to." Mum did her sunglasses thing again, fixing Helle with a penetrating blue look. "Your life hasn't exactly been normal lately."

"No." Helle studied the nearby rose bush, at present an explosion of perfumed pink flowers. Almost two months ago, they'd watched Sam Woolf and Nefirie literally go up in smoke and since then there'd been no nightmares, no headaches, no red-haired little girl. But it happened, at times, that Helle woke in the middle of the night, to the disconcerting sensation that Woolf had just been there, watching her.

"Was it bad?" Miriam asked.

"Pretty much." They'd worked up the nerve to return to the glade some days later because Jason wanted to place a wreath of flowers on the spot where Nefirie had disappeared. There'd been nothing to see. The blackened patch was gone, birds hopped and chirped in the bushes.

"She did it to punish herself," Jason had said, propping the wreath up against a little stone. "Her way of atoning for what she did to us in that first life."

Helle had held her tongue. She remained ambivalent about Nefirie, and there were far too many times when she wondered how things would have played out if Woolf had been successful in his attempts to grab her. Somehow, she suspected Nefirie would have spent her time consoling Jason rather than helping him reclaim his wife.

"Your face is very easy to read at times," Jason had said. He smiled ruefully at her. "I prefer to believe she had a plan all along."

"Maybe she did." But they would never know.

Mum's voice recalled her to the sunny garden. "You're not going to tell me, are you?"

"Nope." The anguish in Jason's face when they talked about it, the way he occasionally looked at his hands—as if he wanted to cut them off—made it a very easy decision not to share this with anyone, not even her mother.

"I'm here if you need to talk." Miriam gripped Helle's shoulder.

"I know." She smiled when Jason whooped, leaping straight up after scoring yet another point against Nigel and Phil. In shorts that hung off his hips and a badminton racquet in his hand, he looked carefree and young, even more so when he high-fived Miranda. As if he felt her gaze on him, he turned her way, those startling eyes of his a rich amber in the sun. He blew her a kiss. Miriam snorted loudly.

"Sheesh," she muttered. "It's almost nauseating."

"Tough." Helle blew him a kiss back.

When Jason interrupted his game to start dinner, Helle automatically rose to follow him inside. Since Turkey, they'd been inseparable, each of them restless unless the other was in sight. It could have been over—something neither of them could forget. Those first few days after the events in the glade had been spent in a daze, clinging to each other. On the plane from Trabzon, something had eased, and several days spent exploring Istanbul at their leisure had allowed them to revert to some sort of normality. Assuming they could ever be considered normal, of course.

The last morning in Istanbul Helle had woken Jason by trailing kisses down his back. He had turned, his arms reaching for her while still half asleep, and gathered her to his chest.

"What might you want?"

"One soft boiled egg and a pot of tea please," Helle had replied, biting his shoulder. "I'm starving here."

"Well. Mrs Morris, you'll just have to wait." He aligned his hips with hers. "Besides," he'd added in a sultry voice, "I don't do soft." But he did. Helle smiled at the memory of his fingers tracing her spine, his lips nibbling at her earlobe. Most definitely soft: unbearably soft.

"What are you thinking about?" Jason demanded, fast forwarding Helle back to the present. He indicated that she should chop the shallots he'd laid out in front of her and went back to his garlic.

"Us. You," she replied, making him smile.

"Apart from that," he teased, "even though I've grown to accept you're a bit obsessive when it comes to me."

"Lucky you. I mean, more than one year married, it's all a bit same old, same old."

"Old? I haven't noticed. I still think about you. A lot." The innuendo in his voice made her toes curl. He crooked his finger at her. Helle danced over to him, pecked him on the mouth and darted away.

"Later," he growled.

It was warm enough to eat outside, or so Miriam decided, going on and on about the refreshing temperature of an English summer evening. There were tea-lights everywhere, little twinkling earthbound stars, all of them lit by Jason—using matches. Helle gave him a long look: his gift had become an albatross, a constant burden of guilt. Time to change that, she thought, making room for him beside her.

Wine, good food and an entire day in the sun took its toll. First Phil and Mum, then Nigel and Miranda excused themselves, leaving Helle to snake her arms round Jason's waist in an effort to steal some of his body heat.

"Cold?"

"A bit." She looked at the stars above. "But not enough to want to go inside yet." She nestled closer. "Good conversation with John today?"

"Better than the previous one." Jason twirled a strand of her hair round his finger. Explaining to John what had happened to his great-aunt had been a challenge, with John alternating between utter disbelief and angry accusations, saying it was all Jason's fault that Katherine was now officially missing—which, apparently, was a major pain in the ass for Stapleton who had relatives crawling out of the woodworks demanding to know what had happened to dear, sweet auntie. As if: Helle suspected John enjoyed guilt-tripping Jason and had said as much when she spoke to John some days back.

"You spoke to him, didn't you?" Jason tugged at her hair.

"I did. Told him to lay off or I'd kick his ass."

"Kick his ass?" She could hear the smile in his voice.

"Yup." She took his hand, running a light finger over his palm. "How about you light some fires for me tonight?"

"No." His tone was curt, his hand closing into a fist. Helle wiggled her fingers into his fist, working insistently until his hand uncurled.

"This has to stop," she said. "You're treating your gift as a curse."

"It is a curse." He gritted his teeth.

In reply, Helle took his hand and placed it on her belly. "Is that what you will tell your son the day his fingers spout fire?"

"That's different," he muttered. "But I…" He flexed his free hand, and for an instant, his fingers glowed. "I set them alight."

"She asked you to."

"I burnt them to death! My own mother…" His lower lip trembled. Helle climbed onto his lap and gripped his head between her hands. When he tried to wrench free, she sank her hands into his hair, holding him still.

"Look at me, honey. Look at me," she repeated, when he didn't comply. With a sigh, he did. "Very many years ago, when I was still a child in braids, I met the fire-boy. My fire-boy." She kissed his eyes, the corner of his mouth. "Then a boatload of shit happened, and for years and years I didn't see my fire-boy. Until that day almost two years ago when you walked back into my life, no longer a fire-boy but a fire-man." She released his face, took hold of his hands and raised them to her mouth, placing a soft kiss on each palm. "My flame juggler, my torch-bearing lover, the man who'd carried a flame through eternity and beyond for me. The man I can't live without, the man who lights up the dark. For me."

"Helle, I…"

"You did as she asked. Won't you do the same for me?"

There were some moments of heavy silence before he tapped her on the nose. "You're being transparently manipulative."

"Any way that works, Mr Morris."

He lifted her to sit beside him and stood, looking down at her. "And what do I get out of this?"

"A sizzling bed," she replied, making him laugh.

He backed away a couple of steps and held out his arms. A snap of his fingers, and his hands began to glow; another snap, and miniature flames forming fiery patterns snaked across the sky.

He decorated the dark with strands of glittering sparks, he drew burning hearts and scattered firework stars above their heads. For a little while, he set the heavens on fire for her, and when he clapped the fires into non-existence, she was already moving towards him.

He lifted her in a high arc, spun slowly on his toes and set her down on the ground, hugging her hard.

"I love you." He buried his nose in her hair. "With every beat of my heart, with every breath of my lungs, I love you."

"Like I love you," Helle replied, "today, and all our coming tomorrows." Mushy, mushy, as Nigel would say, Helle thought with a smile.

But true.

About the Author

Had Anna been allowed to choose, she'd have become a time-traveller. As this was impossible, she became a financial professional with three absorbing interests: history and writing.

Anna has authored the acclaimed time travelling series The Graham Saga, set in 17th century Scotland and Maryland, as well as the equally acclaimed medieval series The King's Greatest Enemy which is set in 14th century England. (Medieval knight was also high on Anna's list of potential professions. Yet another disappointment…)

With Jason and Helle, Anna has stepped out of her historical comfort zone and has loved doing so – so much, in fact, that she already has a new story brewing, replete with magic, love and suspense.

Find out more about Anna by visiting her website,
www.annabelfrage.com

or her Amazon page,
http://Author.to/ABG